WILD CONQUEST

HANNAH HOWELL

ZEBRA BOOKS
Kensington Publishing Corp.
http://www.kensingtonbooks.com

ZEBRA BOOKS are published by

Kensington Publishing Corp.
119 West 40th Street
New York, NY 10018

All Kensington titles, imprints, and distributed lines are available at special quantity discounts for bulk purchases for sales promotion, premiums, fund-raising, educational, or institutional use.

Special book excerpts or customized printings can also be created to fit specific needs. For details, write or phone the office of the Kensington Special Sales Manager: Attn. Special Sales Department. Kensington Publishing Corp., 119 West 40th Street, New York, NY 10018. Phone: 1-800-221-2647.

Zebra and the Z logo Reg. U.S. Pat. & TM Off.

ISBN-13: 978-1-4201-0464-6
ISBN-10: 1-4201-0464-0

First Zebra Books Mass-Market Paperback Printing: November 2009
Previously published by Avon Books.

10 9 8 7 6 5 4 3 2 1

Printed in the United States of America

KISSING THE SCOTSMAN

"I best get back to my work." She attempted to move away from him, but his hand on her hair held her in place. "I am really quite busy. I am making bread."

"I hadnae expected ye to be so domesticated, Pleasance Dunstan."

There was the hint of insult in his words, but she ignored it as she had so many other times. That was not important at the moment. What was important was the fact that she was letting him tug her into his arms. In fact, she thought with additional self-disgust, she was positively melting in his embrace. She did not need the way she trembled as his hand traced her spine, then came to rest at the small of her back to tell her that in his arms was a dangerous place to be. It was dangerous to her heart, to her morals, and, she mused as she stared into his darkening gray eyes, to her very sanity.

Tearlach kissed her forehead, then each cheek, and felt her sigh. She was soft and pliable in his arms. As her eyes turned a rich warm blue and grew heavy lidded, he read desire in them. Her full lips were moist and slightly parted. No man should be expected to resist such temptation . . .

Books by Hannah Howell

Published by Zebra Books

Chapter One

Worcester, Massachusetts Bay Colony—1769

"I do not wish to marry John Martin," Letitia whined.

Pleasance watched her pouting younger sister closely, inwardly grimacing at her childish tone. From the moment Pleasance, Letitia, and their parents had sat down at the huge, heavily laden table to eat breakfast, her sister had kept up a steady stream of complaint. Although Pleasance continued to calmly eat her eggs and ham, she felt a tight knot of uneasiness begin to steal her appetite. She did not like the direction the conversation was taking. Whenever Letitia expressed displeasure, it cost someone dearly. And that someone was usually her.

She covertly watched her parents. Thomas Dunstan's face was flushed, and Pleasance knew he was failing to control his anger with Letitia. He wanted a marriage with the wealthy Martins as a means to increase his own prestige. His wife, Sarah, was fiddling with her heavy lace fichu, a clear indication of her agitation. No doubt she had already been secretly planning an elaborate, ostentatious wedding. Pleasance's elder brother, Lawrence, was studying with his tutor, and she was glad of it. Lawrence was exactly like their father, and there was already quite enough bombast at the table. Her younger brother, Nathan, was off on some mysterious business— probably eluding customs agents trying to collect unpaid duty on shipments he had made to the other colonies.

"John Martin is a fine young man," Thomas Dunstan said, tugging his elaborately embroidered waistcoat over his rounding stomach before filling his plate with a second serving of smoked ham and scrambled eggs from the ornate pewter serving dishes. "He has a residence and a profession. He also comes from a family of prominence in the colony. The Martins are well respected in Worcester."

"I am not concerned with that," Letitia replied. "You said I could choose my own husband, Father. You promised."

"And just whom do you think you want if not John Martin?"

"I want the Scotsman."

A sharp pang ripped through Pleasance. She could feel the blood drain from her cheeks and tried to calm herself before anyone noticed. Her sister's preference should not have come as such a shock to her, yet it had. She did not want to believe that her sister could be so cruel. The Scotsman, as her family insisted on calling him, was wooing *her*.

"The Scotsman?" bellowed Thomas. "That backwoods trash? He is not good enough for you. 'Tis bad enough that he is not of reputable English stock, but he is a common trapper besides."

"You let him court Pleasance," argued Letitia, carefully arranging her thick blond curls to drape artfully over her right shoulder.

"Pleasance is nearly a spinster. She cannot be as selective."

"How kind," Pleasance muttered, hiding her sarcasm by quickly taking a sip of tea.

"Well, you told me that I can be as selective as I want."

Letitia's usually sweet voice had a distinctive edge. "And I have selected the Scotsman." She turned to fix her steady gaze on Pleasance, her usually soft blue eyes hard and cold. "After all, if my dear sister finds the Scotsman entertaining, he cannot be so very bad a choice, can he?"

"You might call this man you claim to want so badly by his name," Pleasance said, praying that for once Letitia's demand would not be granted.

"Such a heathen name. I find it difficult to train my tongue to it."

"If you listened to the man say it, Letitia, you might find it easier. It is 'Tear'—as in *rip*—and 'lach'—as in *lack,* or something wanting—then 'O'Doone.' Tearlach O'Duine. Simple enough, although I am sure I do not say it as correctly as he does. *Tearlach* is but the Gaelic word for *Charles."*

"Then why not say 'Charles'?" snapped Letitia.

"Because he is not an Englishman?" Pleasance replied sarcastically. Absently tucking a stray lock of hair back in place, she caught herself wishing her chestnut hair was the same much admired gold as Letitia's, and silently cursed.

"Do not speak so pertly to your sister," scolded Thomas, before turning to his youngest daughter. "Letitia, the Scotsman is rough, probably unschooled, and, as I have said, he is no more than a fur trader. They are a restless, undependable breed of men."

"I do not care. I cannot dictate to my heart, Papa. It aches for Master O'Duine. I tried to summon up some feeling for John Martin to please you, but I cannot help myself." Letitia's full bottom lip trembled, and she dabbed at her eyes with her fine monogrammed linen napkin. "For Pleasance's sake, I also tried to direct my affections elsewhere, but it was impossible. I fear I am sick with love for Master O'Duine."

Pleasance felt close to gagging as Letitia tugged fretfully at one of her fat blond curls and put on her most forlorn expression, tears brimming artfully in her big eyes. It was a well-used ploy and it had never failed, and Pleasance felt a deep, almost irresistible urge to scream. She could see the beginnings of acquiescence on her parents' round faces. Letitia was the jewel in the Dunstan family crown. Whatever she wanted, she got.

Pleasance wished her younger brother, Nathan, was here, for he had always supported her. But she was on her own. For once, she decided, she would fight for what she wanted. Tearlach O'Duine was worth the effort.

"I fear you are too late in making your desire known, Letitia," she said. "Master O'Duine has chosen me."

"Has he offered you marriage?" asked Sarah Cordell Dunstan, primly patting her mouth with a napkin as she watched Pleasance closely.

"Well, nay, not as yet, but he courts me assiduously."

"But does not ask for your hand. It would appear, then, that he has *not* made his choice." Sarah turned to Letitia on her left and patted her attractively plump hand. "Pleasance will step aside, dear, and you may have the Scotsman."

"You make him sound like some bundle of pelts being tossed back and forth," Pleasance said.

"Do not be so crude, Pleasance," scolded Sarah, frowning. "The man is Letitia's choice."

"How nice. Mayhaps *she* is not *his* choice." Pleasance could see from everyone's expressions that they found that idea absurd. "He did come courting *me,* with barely a glance toward Letitia."

"He undoubtedly felt that Letitia was far above his touch."

Pleasance wondered how her mother could be so casually cruel. "I simply cannot tell the man to go away and start courting my sister."

"What you can and will do is turn aside his attentions."

"But that would be unkind and a lie of sorts, for I do not really wish to do it."

Sarah Dunstan regarded Pleasance with cool disdain. "You would rather break your sister's heart *and* defy your own parents than bruise the vanity of this Scotsman? Or is it your own vanity which persuades you to be so disobedient?"

Her mother's anger sent a chill down Pleasance's spine, but she stiffened and pressed on. "But you just said that the man is too common for Letitia. She would be marrying beneath her." Such words tasted bitter in her mouth, but Pleasance knew that her family considered such differences important.

"Of course he is beneath her, but we must abide by our promise."

"And I believe that the man has some potential," Letitia added. "Why, using a little education, I am certain I can make him more presentable."

"John Martin is already very presentable," Pleasance argued.

"I want the Scotsman."

"He lives in the wilderness, or did you forget that?"

"Nay, I did not forget. I am sure I can convince him to remain here and give up that wild land he owns."

"But—"

"Enough!" Sarah snapped. "You are becoming tedious, Pleasance. The matter is settled. You shall turn Master O'Duine away."

For a long moment Pleasance considered arguing further, but the rigid expressions on her parents' faces told her that their minds were firmly set. Anything she said now would be treated as gross impertinence or unkindness toward Letitia. Both were considered great sins by her parents. Pleasance knew that continuing to argue would only result in them locking her in the attic for impudence, and she dreaded that.

Even as part of her cursed her own weakness and scorned h deep need to please her stern mother and father, Pleasan resigned herself to losing the one man who had shown a re interest in her.

She tried not to think that she might be giving up her on chance at marriage . . . and happiness.

Pleasance sat on the hard marble bench in her mother tidy garden, the scent of roses heavy in the air, and watch Tearlach O'Duine approach. He wore the same courtir clothes he had worn for the last two weeks. He always look and smelled clean, but he must be low on funds or he wou have had at least one other set of clothes.

She twisted her lace handkerchief in her hands and tri to match his smile of greeting. She was perspiring and kne it was not from the heat of the late July afternoon. It ha been four hours since her parents had ordered her to s Master Tearlach O'Duine aside, and she had spent eve minute trying to think of a way to please both her family ar herself. There did not seem to be one.

Tall, lean, and dark, Tearlach O'Duine was a fine figu of a man. His snug black breeches and hose revealed lon smoothly muscled, and well-shaped legs. His black coat ar silver-and-black waistcoat fit tightly over broad shoulde and a flat stomach. She liked the way the white lace at h cuffs and throat enhanced his sun-bronzed complexion. B when he stopped before her, lifted her hand to his lips; ar brushed a kiss over her knuckles, she was torn betwee wanting to weep and the urge to run away. As she met h smoky gray eyes, she wondered how she could bear to reje him for herself, let alone send him into Letitia's arms.

"Please sit down, Master O'Duine," she said, and ind cated a place on the bench beside her.

"Master O'Duine?" he murmured as he seated himself. "You called me Tearlach but yestereve."

"In a moment of ill-advised forwardness. 'Tis hardly proper of me to address you with such indecent familiarity."

"I had hopes that ye would be addressing me with far more familiarity soon." He took her small hand in his and frowned when she tensed. "Mayhaps I go too quickly for ye. I have had little experience at courting a weel-bred lassie."

"You do it with great charm and skill. I have no complaint at all." Pleasance inwardly grimaced, for she knew she sounded as haughty and disdainful as her mother, but it was the only way she knew how to mouth the words her family was forcing her to say.

"Nay? Then why have ye become so cool and distant?"

Tearlach watched her look away, then shade her blue-green eyes from his inspection with partially lowered lids, her long dark lashes a perfect shield. Every instinct he had honed as a trapper was now telling him that something was very wrong. This was not the shy yet warm Pleasance he had first been attracted to. She was nervous, tense, even secretive. There was a cool, haughty tone to her voice that irritated him. Something had changed her, and in a way that he felt could only work against him. In fact, he was getting the alarming impression that he was about to be turned away, and he simply could not understand why. He began to grow defensive.

"I do not mean to act differently toward you, Master O'Duine." Pleasance sighed and twisted her handkerchief. "You have been most gallant, and I have no wish to repay that with unkindness."

"The more mealymouthed and polite ye become, the less I like it."

Tearlach rose to his feet and began to pace back and forth in front of her. Pleasance cursed silently. The man was too astute. She had hoped to dim his interest by acting cool and aloof, so that he ended this courtship on his own. Instead he had already surmised her intention. He was not going to play along and let her do what she must with gentle subterfuge. That meant that she would have to lie, for she could not tell the man that her parents had ordered her to give him to Letitia.

She did not want him to know that she was so weak as to obey such an absurd command just to please her family. There had to be a point where family loyalty ended, where meekly obeying every command became akin to slavery. She feared that her need to please her constantly critical parents was beginning to make her act the fool.

She cringed slightly when he stopped to stare at her. Then, suddenly, she was angry with him. If she had not met him, if he had not touched her emotions in a way no other man ever had, she would not be in this awkward situation now. A small inner voice told her she was being grossly unfair, even a little ridiculous, but it did not soothe her temper. If he had acted like all the other men before him and pursued the beautiful Letitia, she could have remained blissfully ignorant of the pain, loss, and confusion she was suffering now.

"Some of us, Master O'Duine, have been trained in civility to others." Pleasance did not need to see the way his eyes narrowed or the light flush that tinged his high-boned cheeks to know that she had spoken coldly and sharply.

"Something has happened between yesterday and now. When I brought ye a few posies yesterday and we sat right here and talked, ye were all smiles. Ye called me Tearlach and e'en allowed me a kiss. Aye, more than one."

"I acted without thought as to how you might interpret my behavior or even to the propriety of it. If I led you to believe my acquiescence indicated more than mere flirtatiousness, I sincerely apologize."

He flushed deeper with fury. "Ye are turning me away, shoving me aside like some bothersome child." He grabbed her by the arm and tugged her to her feet. "Ye have played me for a fool, havenae ye?"

"Nay, I have not! It is my right to decide to end the courtship when and if I see fit. There is no sense in wasting your time or mine any further. After weeks of your skillful and arduous courting I simply do not have the depth of feeling for you that I should have by now."

"No depth of feeling?"

The moment the words were out of her mouth, Pleasance knew that she had made a big mistake. She could hear in his reply that he had interpreted her words as a blatant challenge to prove her wrong. She tensed as he pulled her into his arms.

"Master O'Duine, release me. You can prove naught by failing to behave as a gentleman."

"I dinnae feel much like a gentleman at this moment. Aye, and ye have ne'er thought of me as one, have ye? That is what this is all about. Ye are as full of self-importance as the rest of your haughty family."

"You are mistaken."

"Nay, I think not. Ah, lassie, I really thought ye were one who would speak the truth."

"I *have* spoken the truth." But Pleasance could hear the lack of conviction in her own voice. She was a poor liar and the faint sneer that twisted Tearlach's fine mouth told her that he thought so too. "Now, release me or I shall have to call out for my father or my brother Lawrence," she threatened, thinking even as she said it that the portly Thomas and his lanky dandy of a son would be no match for Tearlach.

"And they will come hieing to your rescue, will they? I

dinnae think so. Since the verra first day I came courting, they have left us to ourselves. I surmised that such a lax guardianship was because ye are a spinster."

Pleasance felt her temper flare. She was weary of being called a spinster, a term she knew was never used kindly. This was Tearlach O'Duine's way of striking back at her.

Before she could respond in kind, however, he tightened his hold on her. Despite her valiant efforts not to let his nearness affect her, she immediately forgot what she had wanted to say. Being pressed against his hard, lean body stole nearly every thought from her head. To her dismay, she could see that he knew exactly what effect he was having on her. A distracting, captivating warmth seeped through her at every place he touched. She knew she should pull away before he beguiled her, but all she wanted was to get nearer. He was holding her scandalously close, yet all she could think about was how she wished to act even more wantonly.

He touched his lips to the hollow by her ear, and she, shivered as heat entered her veins, robbing her of all resistance. For a moment she almost hated him. He was showing her all too clearly what she would lose by rejecting him, and the realization was too painful for words.

"Oh, aye, no depth of feeling, she says. Ye are too poor a liar to try and tell such a big one, lassie."

"You have no call to insult me so, Master O'Duine."

"I have more call than most. Ye mean to cut my pride with your lies."

Tearlach was very angry. He had originally been drawn to Pleasance, instead of to her much prettier sister, for reasons some might call unflattering. Pleasance Dunstan was the older, plainer, and, rumor had it, the poorer of the sisters; therefore it would require less work on his part to win her. She might even be a more pliable wife, for she would be grateful for not being left ummarried.

It had taken very little time for Tearlach to realize that far more than those shallow reasons was attracting him to Pleasance, and he did not like it. He told himself to remain aloof, continuously warned himself against entertaining any more than the most superficial feeling for her, then ignored his own advice. That his original cynical mistrust was proving to be justified after all only added to his anger. So too did this proof that his judgment of women was seriously flawed.

This time he had really believed he had found a woman he could trust, one who would not look down her nose at a mere trapper from the western frontier. He wanted a woman who liked him for himself. He had let himself believe that Pleasance Dunstan was that woman.

He touched his mouth to hers and, when she meekly tried to turn her head away, caught her chin in his hand and held her steady. He savored the feel of her warm, soft lips beneath his, and that too increased his wrath. He wanted Pleasance Dunstan—badly—and he knew she wanted him. Yet still she was pushing him aside. There could be only one reason—she did not think he was good enough for her. Tearlach wished there was some satisfactory way to make her pay for that coldhearted snobbery. Instead, he would have to settle for making her fully aware of what she was denying herself.

He slid his tongue over her full lips, and she parted them for him. He held her as close as he could without hurting her as he stroked the inside of her mouth. A soft moan escaped her and he echoed it. He slid his hands down to her gently curved hips and pressed her loins against his, moving in an erotically suggestive way. It did not surprise him when she responded with an equally arousing movement. Their passion was perfectly matched.

But now he would never fully taste it, and that infuriated him.

It took all of his willpower, for Pleasance was so invitingly responsive, but Tearlach finally ended the kiss. He studied her flushed face, watched how her breasts rose and fell with her deep, unsteady breathing, and saw how desire had turned her blue-green eyes a deeper blue. She wanted him. Everything about her cried it out. He was nearly as caught up in his own need as she was, and he made no effort to hide it. Yet, despite the hunger that had them both trembling, she was going to reject him. Tearlach felt the urge to slap some sense into her and quickly stepped back.

"Despite all the heat we share, still ye will turn me away?" he asked, hating to ask yet tense with a need to understand her actions. "Why? It makes no sense to kiss me as ye do then tell me to go."

Pleasance fought to clear the fog of desire from her mind and answer him in some intelligible way. "The reasons why I am sending you away and asking you not to return are not your concern, sir."

"Nay? I am the one being shown the door."

"Aye, and you are very slow to go through it, if you ask me," she snapped, her temper frayed.

He stared at her long and hard. "Verra weel, mistress," he finally said. "Ye willnae be troubled with my company again."

Tearlach turned sharply and strode away. Pleasance sank onto the bench, still a little wobbly from the effects of his fiery kiss, and fought the urge to call him back.

"Why?" she whispered. "Why should I make this sacrifice, one that insults him and hurts me? 'Tis not as if Letitia has any difficulty attracting possible husbands."

She battled the sudden rebellion that swept through her, but it was proving far stronger than her sense of duty. Letitia had not wanted Tearlach until he had ignored her. It was plain selfishness that drove her, and Pleasance did not see why she should give up something she wanted so badly just to placate her sister's possessiveness.

Spurred by that outrage, Pleasance stood up and took one step after Tearlach before stopping abruptly. He was standing at the iron gate at the far end of the garden, the one that led into the front courtyard. Just as he passed through that gate, Letitia stepped up and slipped her arm through his. All the fight left Pleasance and she slowly sat back down. It was too late to take back her hurtful words now, and Letitia would never give her the chance to try.

The sudden appearance of Letitia Dunstan startled Tearlach. When the fulsome blond eased her arm through his, his first thought was to shake her off, but then he caught sight of Pleasance watching them. It was a petty act, and he knew it, but he turned his best smile on Letitita. He wanted Pleasance to feel the same pinch of pride that he did. A little voice in his head told him that it was far more than bruised pride he was suffering as a result of Pleasance's rejection, but he stoutly ignored it.

"Ah, Mistress Letitia, 'tis pleasant to see a welcoming face," he murmured.

"Oh, you poor man." Letitia smoothed her hand over his arm. "Pleasance told me what she planned to do."

"Did she." Tearlach did not appreciate that his humiliation had been made a topic of discussion amongst Pleasance's haughty family.

"I tried to counsel her against such a cruel rejection, but she would not listen to a word I said. Please do not think these are my words, and I do not wish to inflict any further pain, but— oh, dear, I am not sure I can speak such hurtful words aloud."

Watching Letitia, Tearlach decided she would make a fine actress. He wanted to tell her to keep her dirty little gossip to herself, but curiosity won out over good sense. If Letitia knew why Pleasance was sending him away, he wanted to hear what she had to say. It could be no worse than all the possibilities he was conjuring up in his own mind.

"The truth may be painful, Mistress Letitia," he said, "but 'tis always best to ken it."

"Please be assured that I do not share my sister's sentiments. I cannot understand how she came to think such things." Letitia sighed and shook her head. "I fear my sister suffers from the sins of pride and vanity, Master O'Duine. Quite simply, she is under the delusion that she can do much better than you. I fear she sees you as some ignorant backwoodsman, which is silly of her. Anyone can see that you are a man of refinement who is working hard to overcome the limitations of your birth. I will say no more. It can only upset you."

"Your kind heart becomes you, Mistress Letitia." It surprised Tearlach that Letitia's sweetly malicious speech should cut him as deeply as it did. He had suspected exactly what she was telling him. He had faced such snobbery before, endured that deep English prejudice against the Scots. That Pleasance Dunstan could cause that pain, that he had allowed her to penetrate his defenses to that extent, only angered him more.

He looked toward Pleasance. She was still watching him and Letitia closely, and he sent her a cold smile. It apparently annoyed her to see him with her sister, and he intended to make full use of that. Tearlach suspected that Letitia also considered him unworthy of her, beneath her in class and respectability, yet the smiling blonde was behaving quite flirtatiously. For a while, Tearlach would play along.

"Master O'Duine?" Letitia smiled up at him and lightly touched his cheek with her fingertips. "Allow me to try and make some form of amends. I feel so ashamed of Pleasance's harshness. Come, let us go into the parlor and I will have lemonade served."

"That sounds verra appealing."

And Tearlach allowed Letitia to lead him into the house.

Pleasance slowly unclenched her hands. She stared at the four half-moon-shaped gouges in each palm. She had the sinking feeling that she had just made the biggest mistake of her life. Worse, she knew she had only just begun to pay for it.

Chapter Two

"I want you to steal something for me."

Pleasance gaped at her fair-haired sister. A month ago, when Letitia had demanded that Pleasance reject Tearlach O'Duine so that she could have the man for herself, Pleasance had decided that nothing else her family could do would shock her. She was not pleased to be proven wrong. She also felt she had done more than enough already for them; Letitia was appallingly audacious to ask for more now.

"Steal? Did you truly say steal something for you?" she asked Letitia.

"Aye." Letitia pursed her lips in a sullen pout. "Why do you act so horrified? 'Tis not such a grand favor I ask of you. Why are you so reluctant?"

"Why? Because if caught, I would face hanging, the pillory, flogging, or virtual enslavement!" Pleasance paced her small, sparsely furnished bedroom before stopping to glare at her younger sister.

"I am well aware of the penalties for theft, Pleasance. There is no need to recite them," Letitia grumbled.

"Yet you ask me to risk them."

Pleasance frowned as she watched her voluptuous sister

shrink down in her seat. Letitia always stood tall, straight, and proud—perhaps too proud, blatantly displaying the curves so many men ogled. Yet now she looked defeated and just a little afraid. Although instinct told Pleasance that it would probably cost her dearly, she felt her heart go out to her young sister.

"What is it you wish me to steal and why must I steal it?"

"Oh, thank you, Pleasance. Thank you!" Letitia immediately sat up straighter.

"Do not be so hasty. I have not yet said I will do it. I simply want to hear more about it. If your answers do not suit me, then I shall not risk it." Pleasance moved to open a window, but it did little to ease the oppressive heat in the room, the late August night proving as hot as the day.

"I want you to steal some letters, some love letters."

"What harm or threat can there be in a few innocent billets-doux?"

Letitia grimaced and ran a hand through her thick golden hair in an uncharacteristic gesture of agitation. "A great deal of trouble when they are letters, and rather explicit letters at that, which were written to a man other than the one I plan to marry."

Nearly gaping, Pleasance sat down on her small bed. "You are to be married? Why have I heard nothing of this?" She feared her own agitation was revealed in the way she began to fidgit with a stray lock of her chestnut hair.

"Because it has yet to be announced. In truth, I have yet to be asked. But I shall be. I feel certain that Father has already been approached or will be within the next day or so."

It was an arrogant assumption, but Pleasance did not argue. If Letitia said the proposal was coming, then it probably was. Nearly a dozen men had been lurking around waiting for some sign of willingness from her, for some hint that she would accept a proposal. Pleasance hated to ask, and dreaded the answer, but knew that the question hovering on her tongue was the only logical thing to say next.

"Who do you intend to marry?"

"John Leonard Martin."

Surprise overwhelmed her relief, but was quickly followed by anger. John Martin had been their father's original choice, but Letitia had repeatedly demanded the right to choose her own husband. Several of the young men courting her had eventually tired of her fickleness and had ventured toward Pleasance, only to have Letitia immediately regain interest and pull them back to her. In every case their parents had sided with Letitia, ordering Pleasance to give her sister precedence.

Letitia had claimed to feel both love and passion for Tearlach O'Duine, but only a few weeks after Pleasance had given him up, the fickle girl had lost interest in him.

"I see," Pleasance murmured. "John—the man whom only a month ago you swore you did not want. The very man Papa wished you to marry from the start."

"Well, aye, but I had to see his worth on my own."

"Of course. And those torrid, impassioned love letters were not written to the most worthy John."

"Nay, of course not, or why should I wish them back?"

"Why, indeed. Letitia, if you felt strongly enough to write such letters to a man, why do you wish them back at all? Why, in fact, choose to wed another man?"

"Because I finally see that John is worthy," Letitia replied, staring up at the ceiling of Pleasance's tiny room.

"And this other man is not?"

"Not in the ways that matter. I had to gain the maturity to see beyond fine looks and pretty words, and at last I have."

"See beyond them to what?"

"To the future. To security and the manner of life I am most comfortable with. As I said, John is more worthy."

And John is so worthily wealthy too, Pleasance thought, then sharply scolded herself. Letitia was spoiled and vain, but the girl had never been otherwise. The results of all the pampering Letitia had received since birth could not be allowed to annoy Pleasance now. As always she had stepped aside for her sister. She could not fully blame Letitia if her own life was not to her liking.

"Well, who has these letters then?" Pleasance asked.

"Tearlach O'Duine."

Pleasance was not at all surprised, but she *was* dismayed. After she had turned Tearlach away, there had seemed to be something between Letitia and Master O'Duine. Pleasance hated to think that that something had gone beyond warm looks and pretty words. She also hated the idea of stealing from the man or, far worse, being caught as she attempted it.

"Have you tried asking him for the letters?"

"Aye," muttered Letitia. "Fool that I was. That cruel man laughed at me. He told me it might do me some good to fret a little."

That it might, Pleasance mused, but far worse than a few hours of worry for Letitia could result from those letters. Pleasance dreaded to think of the possible scandal. Letitia lacked the wisdom and foresight to temper her outpourings. When caught up in some fancied passion, she had even less sense than usual. If the letters became public, marriage with John would become utterly impossible.

Pleasance studied Letitia for a moment. She was probably not in love with John; Letitia was incapable of loving anyone but herself. With John, however, Letitia would have the society she craved and the wealth to become a leader within it. John would never trouble her to be any more than she was. Their father had clearly chosen the perfect match for her. Pleasance supposed it was a good thing that her sister had finally reached the same conclusion. The marriage might allow her to find her own happiness at last.

Pleasance quickly suppressed the unwelcome thought that she had lost her own chance for happiness when she had rebuffed Tearlach.

"You cannot expect Master O'Duine to be kind to you after you flirted so shamelessly with him only to toss him aside," Pleasance said, frowning. "Just what do you consider wrong with the man? I know of no great lack in him morally and he is not without an adequate income."

"He lives in the backwoods, far west of the Massachusetts colony, Pleasance, out on the fringes of civilization where there are only a few cabins and farms, mayhaps a small village."

"You intended to change his mind about where to live, if I recall."

"He is too stubborn. He insists that his home lies out there, and he wants no other. I am certain there are still wild, savage Indians there."

"I believe the recent war between us and the French with their Indian allies ended what Indian problem there was. And I would be much more wary of the French myself."

Letitia gave Pleasance a cross look. "He also has a sister. Did you know that?"

"Aye. A girl of but twelve or so, I believe. What matter?"

"He expected me to care for her."

"That is hardly unreasonable of him." Pleasance realized that Letitia's main complaint about Tearlach O'Duine was that she had been unable to get the man to do exactly what she wanted.

"Pleasance, the girl is part savage. She is the spawn of the rape of her mother by some heathen," Letitia whispered. "The woman survived the attack and kept herself alive until the babe was born. Why, I cannot say. Better to die and escape the shame than to live and bear the fruit of it. And Tearlach still keeps the creature, intends to raise her amongst civilized people. That man is not quite right in the head."

"The girl is his sister," Pleasance said. "They share a mother's blood."

Pleasance sighed and wondered why she even tried to explain such sentiments to Letitia. Her sister lacked the compassion to understand. Nevertheless, she felt a need to defend Tearlach. Before any further discussion could ensue, however—a discussion she knew would severely try her already waning patience—Pleasance forced her thoughts back to the matter at hand. She idly tugged on her full bottom lip as she tried to think of a less drastic, less criminal solution to Letitia's problems.

"Perhaps if I speak to Master O'Duine," she finally said.

"That will do no good. No good at all." Letitia got to her feet and began to pace the cramped quarters. "He is angry— with all of us. There is something else as well." She glanced nervously at Pleasance.

Unease rippled through Pleasance. "What?"

"I gave him a gift and that too must be returned."

"What sort of gift?" Since Letitia received only a small stipend from their parents, the gift could not have been too expensive or improper.

"A lovely silver tankard."

Pleasance gasped, astonished by the extravagance and the impropriety of such a present. "Wherever did you get such a thing?"

"From John. It was an heirloom of his family's."

For a moment Pleasance was too stunned to speak. Letitia was prone to doing things without thought, but this seemed too reckless and stupid even for her. It also presented a far greater problem than some ill-advised love letters.

"How could you have been so stupid?"

"It did not seem so stupid at the time. Tearlach much admired the tankard," Letitia said, outrage tinting her voice.

"So you gave it to him and then thought of John. How is it that John has not yet noticed it is gone?"

"Well, I have had to make an excuse or two. I cannot keep doing that for much longer." She fell to her knees before Pleasance, grasping her sister's hands. "Please, you must get it back for me. If John should ever discover what I have done, all shall be lost."

Staring into her sister's tear-drenched blue eyes, Pleasance resisted the strong urge to slap that perfectly oval face. Such stupidity was beyond understanding. She was sorely tempted to let her sister sink into the mire she had concocted. Unfortunately, that mire could touch their whole family. What she did not wish to do she would be forced to do to protect her family from scandal. She had herself to consider too. Her own future was at risk.

"And you did not ask Master O'Duine for the return of this gift?" Pleasance asked, fighting and failing to keep the fury from her voice.

"Aye, I asked him. I explained that I had been overcome by a generous impulse. I also explained that the impulse had been in error. He said I was indeed generous, that it was a fine gift he would long appreciate. As for the error in giving him such a gift, he simply remarked that I seemed to be making a great many errors of late. He hoped I would soon have a better turn of luck, then he literally pushed me out the door. The man is impossible." As Letitia spoke she rose to her feet and strode back to her chair to flop down in it, renewed anger evident in her every gesture.

"Oh, nay, Letitia. Master O'Duine is not the impossible one. 'Tis you. You insisted he was the man you wanted, even forced me to reject him. You flirted shamelessly with the man. He stayed on in Worcester far longer than he had planned because you gave him reason to believe that his interest was returned in full measure. Then you blithely cast him aside for John. You wrote Master O'Duine love letters. Now you want them back. You gave Master O'Duine a lavish gift which was not yours to dispense with, and now you wish that back as well. It would all make a fine comedy save that our family would be the butt of all the jests."

"So you mean to give me no help?"

"I am sorely tempted to let you fall, face first, into the mire you have stirred up."

"Pleasance, you cannot do that to me!" Letitia wailed.

"Nay, sadly, I cannot." Pleasance shook her head in a weary gesture of utter disgust, with herself as much as with Letitia. "I find John a very dull stick of a man, but he and his kin have been friends of this family for many years. You have set the stage for a monstrous scandal which would surely touch John as well. He does not deserve that."

"'Tis not all my fault."

"Then there is our own family to consider," Pleasance continued, ignoring Letitia's truculent interruption. "You seem to have thought little of them in your recent foolhardiness, Letitia. Mother would be destroyed. She could neither bear the ill talk which would result nor the estrangement from society that such scandal always brings. I dare not even think how Papa would react. Then there are our brothers. They would feel honor-bound to defend each slur aimed at us, and I do not have to tell you what tragedy could result."

"So you will do it?" Letitia said. "You are, after all, the only one who knows how to get into Tearlach's locked room."

"I truly regret the strange, unasked-for skills that I possess," Pleasance muttered.

"If you had not been such a bad child, you would not have been locked in the attic so much. You learned to pick locks so that you could sneak out. I have never told Mama and Papa about the times you did so. Nor have I told them about the times you picked the locks on the pantry to steal food after they had ordered you to fast." She looked at Pleasance meaningfully.

Pleasance ignored her sister's subtle threat of blackmail. "If I did not have the skill, I would not be in the middle of all this trouble you have brewed. Instead I must now put myself at risk because you acted without thought.

"Nay," she added when Letitia opened her mouth again. "I do not wish to hear any more excuses or explanations. Here is what you must do. Invite Master O'Duine to a little tête à tête in the garden for tomorrow night. Use any ploy you want but get him here and hold him here for at least two hours."

"What if he will not stay?"

"Make him. If you do not then I shall be caught and we shall both be plunged into scandal. Now, just tell me all you know of where Master O'Duine is staying and where that cursed tankard might be."

Well hidden beneath the voluminous folds of a large black cloak, Pleasance crept along the night-shrouded streets of town. The cloak was too warm, but it helped her blend into the shadows. She was already trembling with fright and the inn was only just now coming into view. With each hushed step she took, the urge to turn back grew stronger. She prayed she would be able to accomplish her goal before that urge to flee overcame familial responsibility. This was no time for cowardice. Letitia's folly could ruin them all.

She slipped down an alley that ran alongside the large wooden two-story inn to which Letitia had directed her. Her heart was beating so hard and fast she feared the sound was echoing off the walls of the narrow passageway. Her palms were sweating and she wiped her unsteady hands on her skirts. She knew she had to conquer her fear or she would fail. If she did not stop shaking she would not be able to pick open the lock on the door to Tearlach's room.

Pausing at the rear of the inn, Pleasance looked up the steep back stairs. She had crept in and out of the inn unseen once before when she had helped her brother Nathan play a jest upon his old friend Chadwick. That had been fun, with no threat of dangerous consequences if she were caught. The seriousness of what she was doing now seemed to add weights to her feet and she found it difficult to ascend the first step.

As Pleasance inched up the wooden outer stairway she became painfully aware of every creak, every groan. She had taken little notice of the inn's state of disrepair before. Now it threatened her with discovery at every turn.

Another thing that slowed her advance was the knowledge of whom she would be stealing from. Tearlach O'Duine had received shabby treatment from her family. Letitia had toyed with him. She herself had rudely snubbed him, painfully reluctant though the snub had been. Her brothers had been indifferent—unintentionally so on Nathan's part, but it was a slight nonetheless. Her mother and father, on the other hand, had made it abundantly clear that they hoped nothing would come of Letitia's fascination with the man. All in all, Tearlach O'Duine had every reason to loathe the lot of them. Pleasance hated to give him yet another reason to feel ill treated.

She also hated to consider the implications of Letitia's familiarity with Tearlach's room at the inn. Pleasance dreaded finding out exactly how often her sister had been there, and why. She knew Letitia was far too free with her favors, but she loathed the thought that Master O'Duine was one of the many men who had taken advantage of her sister's lack of moral rectitude.

Finally Pleasance reached the top of the stairs. After taking several deep breaths, she withdrew a long thin lockpick Nathan had had made for her and inserted it in the lock. Her first try resulted in utter failure. She cursed. Leaning against the clapboard wall, she forced herself to calm down. It took several more tries, but eventually she was successful. Slowly she opened the heavy iron-trimmed door, cursing every tiny creak it made. The minute there was enough room, she slipped inside and shut the door behind her. To her relief, the hall was empty, dimly lit by only a few wall sconces.

As Pleasance tiptoed down to Master O'Duine's room, she firmly cleared her mind of all thoughts save that of getting the job done and returning home. Letitia had sworn to keep Tearlach away from his room by luring him to their mother's garden, perhaps even attempting a little seduction, but Pleasance had little confidence in her sister's ability to keep her promise. Although Letitia was an expert at keeping men beguiled, Pleasance doubted that Master O'Duine was in any mood to be trifled with. In fact, after all that had happened, she felt sure he would view any such attempt with extreme suspicion. She was surprised he had even agreed to Letitia's pleas to talk. It would be gratifying to see her sister fail to hold a man's attention, but Pleasance decided she preferred to savor that defeat from a safer distance.

Finding the door to O'Duine's room securely locked, Pleasance cursed softly and set to work. In only a moment she had sprung the latch and was slipping into the room. She felt the usual twinge of pride tainted with guilt at her unusual criminal skill. Quickly but silently, she shut the door behind her, eager to leave the hallway where anyone might chance upon her. She crouched low and lit the shuttered lantern which one of Nathan's customs-eluding friends had given her. It provided enough light with which to search but, she hoped, not enough to alert anyone to her presence. She could hear the din of voices coming from the tavern below and hoped it would also help disguise any sounds she might make.

Once her eyes adjusted to the dim light, she looked around with some surprise. Despite the fact that Tearlach's room was located at the back of the building, where the steep slope of the roof made the ceiling low in places, the room was large. A big four-poster bed dominated, a linen-draped table beside it. A big chest had been pushed against one wall, a tall wardrobe filled one corner, and a small writing table and chair stood near the door. Rag rugs covered the wide-board floor. This was clearly one of the inn's better rooms.

Next she noticed that Tearlach was a very tidy man. He was also more comfortably financed than she had thought. Few people could afford a bed to themselves, let alone an entire room. She knew that the landlord, Thomas Cobb, would have carefully ascertained the man's ability to pay before letting him rent the room.

Sharply telling herself not to delay, she began her search. The first thing she found in a small stationery box on the writing table were the letters Letitia had written to him. Pleasance stared at them for a long moment before actually picking them up. She had tucked the letters into an inside pocket of her cloak before she finally lost the battle against her curiosity. Although a large part of her shrank from what she might discover, she took out one letter and began to read.

Two paragraphs were all she managed, and not just because of the near illegibility of Letitia's flowery handwriting. Pleasance's cheeks felt afire, she was blushing so deeply.

Torrid was the word for such prose. If Master O'Duine and Letitia were not lovers, it was certainly not for a lack of effort on Letitia's part. Since Pleasance could not envision any man turning aside an eager and willing Letitia, she was convinced that the pair had indulged in a fierce love affair.

As Pleasance returned the letter to her cloak pocket, she

noticed that her hands were trembling slightly. She sighed and shook her head. Her infatuation with Master O'Duine, which she thought had died, was clearly still strong. It hurt to think of Tearlach and Letitia making love. Foolish though it was, Pleasance had to admit that she still wanted the man herself.

"Well, Letitia had him, you idiot," she whispered as she began to look for the tankard. "And once Letitia decided she wanted him, you did not stand a chance. Letitia always gets what Letitia wants. And why would you want him after Letitia has sampled him anyway?" she grumbled. Then she briefly forgot her grievance when she found the tankard tucked inside Tearlach's carpetbag on top of the wardrobe.

It was no mere utensil but a work of art. She marveled that Master O'Duine had even accepted such a treasure. He had to have known it was worth too much to be a proper gift. He also should have guessed that no young woman could afford such a thing. It was unquestionably an heirloom, and that alone should have made him hesitate. Yet he had accepted the gift, and she could only wonder why.

There was no puzzle, however, she mused wryly, as to why he did not give it back. True, it was worth a great deal and was indisputably handsome, but Pleasance felt sure there was another reason. Revenge. The sad thing was, she had to admit the Dunstans deserved it.

"Hail and good evening, Tearlach. We had not expected you to return so soon."

Master Cobb's booming voice coming from downstairs pulled Pleasance from her dark thoughts. For a moment she stood frozen, in a panic-induced state of indecision. Apparently Letitia had not managed to hold Tearlach's attention after all!

"I was sent on a wild-goose chase," replied Tearlach. "'Twas not a complete waste of my time, howbeit, for I met

Corbin on my way back here. So, Thomas, set out some ale for me and my friend. I need to go to my room."

"Will do. You and Master Corbin can have the table near the window."

"Thank ye kindly. I willnae be but a moment, Corbin."

Those words finally drew Pleasance out of her dangerous state of motionless terror. She still had a chance to avoid capture. She put out the lamp and dove under the bed. It was an obvious place to hide, far too obvious for her liking, but she had no time and few other choices. The long bedcovers hung nearly to the floor and she hoped they would conceal her. She huddled beneath the bed, trying to make herself as small as possible, and struggled not to breathe as she heard the door open. Silently and fervently she prayed that she had left behind no telltale sign that she had been in the room.

Tearlach O'Duine was still chuckling over his friend Corbin Matthias's jest as he strode into his room. That lingering amusement faded as he moved to light a lamp near his bed. Cautiously he sniffed the air, then frowned. There was the scent of a recently snuffed candle in the room, yet he had only just lit his lamp and that used oil. There was another scent as well—faint and far more pleasant. His frown deepening, he sniffed again, and grew angry as he recognized the delicate, enticing scent of lavender. He remembered all too well where he had smelled it last. In truth, his memory of it was a great deal more vivid than he might wish.

Acting as if he was still unaware of anything odd, he warily checked for two specific items. He took a quick peek inside the stationery box on the writing table and then into his carpetbag. It did not surprise him to find the items they had contained missing. *The bird has probably flown already,* he concluded, then immediately questioned that assumption. There was a chance his prey might still be present.

There was only one exit and one window and he felt confident he would have seen someone slip through the door if she had done so in the last few minutes. He moved back to the small wardrobe in the corner and looked inside, but found no one. In hopes of deceiving anyone who might be watching, he took out a shirt and walked back to the bed. As he carefully placed the shirt on the bed, he stared down at the plank floor, then narrowly eyed the space beneath his bed. It was a painfully obvious place for someone to hide, but it was the only place left.

"Ye will come out now, Mistress Dunstan," he said.

Pleasance felt her heart stop. For a moment she forgot to breathe, then fought to do so without making a sound. How could he possibly know someone was there? How could he know it was her? She remained still and silent, the lantern handle slung over her wrist and the tankard clutched tightly in one hand, hoping he had just made a wild guess and would not pursue the matter. That hope was abruptly extinguished when a shaft of light penetrated the shadows under the bed as the hem of the coverlet was lifted and she found herself staring into Tearlach O'Duine's frighteningly expressionless face. With a soft cry of alarm, Pleasance scrambled out from under the bed, hit Tearlach in the knee with the tankard to knock him off balance, and bolted for the door.

Tearlach leapt to his feet, bounded to the door, and slammed it shut just as Pleasance started to yank it open. He was startled by her speed. He also noticed with some surprise that, despite her panicked haste, she had made little noise. Miss Dunstan clearly possessed a few unusual skills for a gently bred lady, he mused as he grabbed her around her tiny waist and tossed her over his shoulder. Ignoring her struggles and the way she kept hitting him with the lantern and tankard, he carried her back to the bed and threw her on top of it. In the brief instant when she was too winded to move, he used his body to pin her to the bed. He yanked the lantern from her hand and studied it.

"A custom runner's lantern, if I am not mistaken," he murmured. "'Tis a strange implement for a lass to possess." He looked down at her and saw that her fear had either been replaced, or was at least well disguised, by anger. Her wide eyes glowed with fury. "'Tis a useful tool for a thief though," he added.

"I am no thief," she replied, but the hard look on his dark face offered Pleasance little hope for mercy.

"Nay? Ye but crept in here to admire my tankard, did ye?" He looked at the tankard still clutched in her hand, which he held pinned to the bed.

"'Tis not yours, and well you know it, sir."

"'Twas a gift to me."

She wondered crossly how the man could be so many things at once—terrifying, irritating, and intriguing. "One that the giver requested you return."

"Ah, but I have grown verra attached to it." Easily keeping her slender form beneath him, he searched her cloak and was not surprised to find the letters Letitia had written to him. "These are mine as well," he said.

Since she could not deny that, Pleasance just glared at him. She had no defense so she struggled to maintain an air of righteous indignation, prepared even to attack him if it proved necessary. She sincerely doubted that the big dark man pressing her into the coverlet would give her the time to come up with something truly clever, however.

"You were also asked to return those letters to their rightful owner," she snapped. "I but came here to retrieve them."

There was such mockery and sneering in his smoky gray

eyes that she wanted to scream. "Did ye." He almost smiled at her. "Weel, I dinnae wish them to be retrieved. They are mine."

"Nay, they belong to Letitia."

"Ah me, it seems we will ne'er agree." He stood up, but with one large calloused hand wrapped around her delicate wrists he kept a firm grip upon her as he tugged her to her feet. "I think a neutral third party is required." He began dragging her out of the room. "Dinnae let my tankard slip from your wee fingers," he drawled. "I should hate to see it dented."

Pleasance was sorely tempted to dent it on his head, but the way he held her prevented her from fulfilling that wish. "Where are you taking me?" she demanded.

"To see Corbin Matthias. Ye are in luck, Miss Dunstan. He awaits me in the taproom."

The very last person she wished to face was the magistrate. Did Tearlach O'Duine plan to openly cry her a thief?

She tried to pull free, but his hold was firm. When she dug in her heels, he just yanked her along the hall. At the top of the narrow stairs leading down to the taproom, she hooked her arm around the stair post. Tearlach gave her a scowl of disgust, pried her arm free, and continued on. To keep from falling she was forced to stop struggling. The moment they reached the bottom she again tried to use the stair post to halt their progress, but he gave a sharp tug on her arm, causing her to slam into his body and putting the stair post out of reach. The door to the noisy taproom was now only steps away.

Pleasance inwardly cringed as Tearlach pulled her into the large room. Despite the dim light from the tallow candles, she recognized every man in the place. Far worse, they recognized her. Tearlach kept doggedly marching toward a table set before the front window. Corbin Matthias slowly stood up, his thin face revealing his surprise as Tearlach dragged her forward. Pleasance cursed softly when he shoved her toward Corbin and she barely stopped herself from careening into the young magistrate.

"Tearlach, what goes on here?" Corbin demanded.

"Miss Dunstan and I seem to differ in our opinion of ownership. The tankard she holds and these letters are the items in question. I say they are all mine. She says otherwise."

Corbin nervously cleared his throat and studied both items. "The letters are addressed to you, Tearlach, so they are indisputedly yours. That is true of the tankard as well, I believe, for I know you have had this tankard for a while and to give a gift is to imply a transfer of ownership. You showed it to me when you first received it."

"That settles that then," Tearlach said before Pleasance could attempt a defense.

"Is that all you wished of me?" Corbin asked.

"Nay, Corbin. I demand that ye do your sworn duty. This lass is a thief. Arrest her."

One look at Corbin's face told Pleasance that the man would reluctantly do as Tearlach O'Duine demanded; one look at Tearlach O'Duine's smug countenance and she felt the bite of rage. Before either man could stop her, before she could fully think through the consequences of her actions, she swung at Tearlach with the heavy tankard. Her aim was true and she hit him—hard—on the side of the head. He crumpled to the floor at her feet.

Numbly, Pleasance stared at Tearlach, blindly watching a trickle of blood run over his beard-shadowed cheek as Corbin grabbed hold of her. She had certainly solved Letitia's problems, she thought ruefully. Even if the town crier read each of Letitia's sordid love letters in the common at high noon, townspeople would be far more interested in the fact that Letitia's spinster sister was about to be hanged for murder.

* * *

Pleasance winced as the heavy iron cell door was locked behind her. She kept her back to Corbin, maintaining the cold silence she had adopted since the scene at the inn. The only good thing was that Tearlach had not ridden in the carriage with them as they had traveled to Corbin's house on the eastern outskirts of town. He had stayed behind to have his cut head bandaged by the doctor. The look of fury on his face as Corbin had led her away was not something she would soon forget. There would be no mercy from him.

"I will send word to your family," Corbin said, nervously jingling his keys.

"Why trouble yourself?" She sighed as she finally turned to face him, knowing that he did not really deserve her anger. Besides, her brother Nathan would be sure to help her once he returned from his business trip to Philadelphia.

"Your family needs to know. They can help you. I know there is more to this matter than it appears." He looked at her expectantly.

She had no intention of satisfying his curiosity. At first she had not wanted her family to be told, but she knew they must be. They might well be able to think of a way to free her without revealing the full truth. She felt a flicker of doubt and firmly suppressed it. After all, she had risked everything for Letitia. Her family could do no less for her.

"Mistress Dunstan?"

"Aye, you had better tell them, although they will not be pleased."

"As matters stand now, aye. Howsomever, I think it would help if you would speak to me. I simply cannot believe I have been told the whole truth. While 'tis true that I saw you strike Tearlach, I do not believe you are a thief."

"I suggest you talk to your friend Tearlach then. This is his doing."

Corbin Matthias sighed and shook his head. "As you wish. I hope your stay here will be a short one."

"So do I."

As soon as he was gone, disappearing up the stairs to the upper part of the house, Pleasance sat down on the narrow rope-slung cot and surveyed her quarters. It was a small cell, the middle of three, and was separated from the others by sturdy iron bars. She was glad she was Corbin's only prisoner, for her quarters provided no privacy. There was a small battered table in the middle and an unsteady chair. Her cot was placed beneath a tiny slit of a window with thick bars between her and the glass.

She gingerly pressed down on the mattress and grimaced. It was straw. The blanket folded at the end of the cot was made of scratchy homespun. She would find little comfort on this bed. She touched her fingers to the solid stone wall, which was cold from the seeping damp. She could not move the bed away from the wall, for it was chained in place. The coolness of the cellars was a welcome respite from the heat outside, but she knew the combination of the chill and damp could easily give her the ague.

She retrieved her lockpick from an inside pocket of her cloak. Tearlach had not searched her once he found the letters, and Corbin had been too polite to paw through her pockets. She went to the cell door and studied the lock closely. Nodding as she recognized her good chances for success, she slipped the lockpick into the mechanism, and an instant later heard the click of success. After briefly cracking the door open and shutting it again, she kept her gaze fixed upon the stairs as she practiced locking and unlocking the door again. She returned to the cot feeling in somewhat better spirits. If worse came to worst, she could always run away.

* * *

"Mistress Dunstan?"

Pleasance slowly sat up from her huddled position on the cot and looked out at Corbin. She had not seen him since he had first put her in the cell three days ago. Neither had she seen any of her family. When the first day had passed without sight of or word from them, she had kept up her spirits by telling herself they were making plans to help her. That excuse had not worked for long into the second day, and her hurt had grown. Now, at the end of the third day, she was forced to accept the truth—they had deserted her. The look on Corbin's face as he carried her meal into the cell and set the tray on the table told her that she was right to feel abandoned. She suspected he had dreaded telling her, and that was why he had avoided her, sending his elder manservant to see to all her needs.

"You can tell me, Master Matthias. I will not crumple into a weeping, wailing mass of self-pity," she said as she stood up and fruitlessly tried to smooth out her dress and tidy her hair.

"Tell you what?" Corbin nervously fiddled with her eating utensils.

"That my family has decided to throw me to the wolves." She sat down at the table and gave him a weary smile.

"You cannot be certain of that." He began to pace the cell as she ate.

"Oh, aye, I can, and you know it too. You sought them out, so you must have their reply."

He stopped pacing and rubbed his hand over his chin. "It could be shock. They will come around soon, before the trial."

Pleasance told herself she was glad he had not revealed exactly what her family had said. His words had confirmed her worst fears and that hurt enough. She ate the thick fish stew, but tasted very little of it, as she fought not to give in to her despair.

"If Master O'Duine insists upon pressing charges, then the trial will go on," she said.

"Once the charges were made, 'twas mostly out of his hands."

"Of course. And when is the trial?"

"In four days. There is yet time for your family to come to your aid, perhaps even to come to some agreement with Tearlach, or myself and the other magistrates."

"The magistrates? I am to have a trial before just the magistrates? No jury? No one to speak in my defense?"

"Nay. That requires coin, you know."

"And no one is willing to pay it." Although she heard herself say the words, she found them hard to believe.

Corbin cleared his throat. "Well, the cost of your imprisonment is being paid."

"I see. No help to free me, but they condescend to assure that I am properly imprisoned." She pushed the bowl away, surprised to see that it was almost empty. "I guess I am to be left to hang."

"We no longer hang thieves, Mistress Dunstan."

"But you do a lot more I shall undoubtedly find uncomfortable. And I am not a mere thief. I also attacked a man."

"Tell me what really happened, what the full truth is, and I can help you," Corbin pleaded.

He sounded so sincere, she was tempted. Her family had deserted her and thus forfeited her blind loyalty. Two things held her back—her own sense of honor and a need to protect her brother Nathan from the scandal. She glanced toward her cloak draped over the end of her cot and thought of the lockpick. She would remain silent. If all else failed, she still had the option of escape.

"There is nothing to say," she murmured, and concentrated on drinking her cider, thus avoiding Corbin's look of frustration. "When is the trial?"

"I told you—in four days."

Pleasance sighed. It would be a long wait, especially if her family continued to ignore her plight. Corbin left and she returned to her cot and laid down, finally giving way to the tears she had held back since her arrest.

She was alone, utterly alone.

Chapter Three

A shiver went through Pleasance as she washed her face. The hot water Corbin had brought her had quickly lost its warmth in the cool cell. She hurriedly dried off and redonned her clothes, grimacing over their sad condition. A week in the cell had ruined her dress, and she had been given no other clothes. She would present a rather pathetic sight when she stood trial.

She still found it hard to believe she was in this situation. Her family was sacrificing her to save themselves and their precious Letitia. Pleasance's hurt had changed to fury days ago. That emotion flickered through the deep chill that had invaded her body, and she would try to keep it to the fore. It would help her endure the ordeal ahead of her.

When Corbin arrived to take her to the courthouse, she slipped on her cloak. As he led her out of the cellar to the rear drive where a carriage waited, she covertly eased her hand into the pocket where she had hidden her lockpick. Her fingers curled around the cool iron pick, and she felt some of her fears ease. She was not completely without hope. As Corbin helped her into the carriage, she told herself that the option of escape and flight would help her remain strong in the face of her family's indifference.

It took every ounce of strength she possessed, but Pleasance forced her weary, cold body to remain upright as she was brought before the magistrates. Her confidence had left her the moment she had faced the huge crowd in the meetinghouse. Now she only felt the numbness that a week in the chill, dank cellars of Corbin Matthias's home had left her with.

Pleasance slowly lifted her gaze to her family. Her father, mother, Letitia, and Lawrence sat in the front pews of the large meetinghouse next to John Martin and his parents. All of them blatantly ignored her. Despite her desperate situation, she felt a flicker of hope. Her brother Nathan was not among them, which meant he had not yet returned from his journey to Philadelphia and possibly knew nothing of her plight. She could continue to hope that at least Nathan might still care. That was enough to help her regain a little calm and an air of dignity.

She stood perfectly erect in a small enclosed area just to the right of the long table at which the four magistrates sat. The meetinghouse was full, every seat on the hard wooden pews taken. There were even a few people standing at the far back near the doors. Many people idly fanned themselves, for this first week of September was proving to be uncomfortably hot.

Pleasance suspected it was the Dunstan name that had brought so many people to her trial. Everyone except her own family was studying her carefully. She knew they wondered— as she did—why she was not having a trial by jury and why there was no one to defend her, as was usual for the wealthy. No doubt it surprised more than a few citizens to learn that she was being treated like an indigent criminal. Her family was not expending any effort or coin on her behalf.

Taking a deep breath to steady herself, she covertly glanced at Tearlach O'Duine, who sat tall and expressionless in front of the fascinated crowd. She knew she ought to be glad she had not killed him when she hit him on the side of the head, but at the moment she was not.

Her anger at him was nearly as great as her fury at her family. True, she had treated him poorly, but she did not deserve this humiliation. Nothing her family had done to him warranted such revenge. At best he had suffered stung pride, perhaps a little heartbreak. His accusations and this trial were going to ruin her entire life. He could go home and soon everyone would forget his part in it all, if they had not done so already. But she would be a pariah, a leper, cast out by even her closest relations.

Tearlach suddenly turned and their gazes met. He held her look and she briefly softened. There was regret, even sympathy, in his expression. Then she sternly reminded herself that he was the one who had had her arrested. She sent him one cold, hate-filled glare and turned away, thinking bitterly that facing him as her accuser before the magistrates was a drastic way to be cured of her infatuation with him.

Inwardly, Tearlach winced when he caught her glare before she presented a very stiff back to him. He had never intended to take his accusations so far. He had expected her family to extract her from this brangle, yet they acted as if she were a stranger to them. They had inquired after her only once, immediately following her arrest, and that had simply been to ask what her story was. Told that she had yet to explain herself, they had urged Letitia forward and the girl had spun a tale that had left him gaping.

Tremulously, with an admirable show of regret, Letitia had libeled Pleasance. She had insinuated that Pleasance was no better than a common slut who had stolen the tankard to give to Tearlach to win his affection. From that point on, there had been no way to stop what Tearlach had started. His little game had become tangled up in a far more complex one being played out by the Dunstan family.

Once the Dunstans and the Martins put their power and prestige behind condemning Pleasance, he could do nothing. No one would listen to him now and he did not have the time to get the help he would need to fight such high standing Worcester citizens.

He did have one plan, but he was loath to use it. Pleasance would hate him even more. It would, however, save her from public humiliation or corporal punishment. She might not think so at first, but it would be far better than any of the alternatives if her family continued to ignore her.

She looked wan and tired. The dark gray gown she had worn the night of her arrest was now wrinkled and stained. Her ivory skin had lost the healthy warm glow he had always admired. All the color was washed from her bright blue-green eyes, and her rich chestnut hair was dull. There was a bruised look to her eyes, dark shadows encircling them. The sight renewed his anger at himself for even starting the game. It also increased his fury with her family. He found their behavior not only hard to comprehend but also deeply distasteful.

His fury at the Dunstans grew when John Martin, the epitome of a fine respectable gentleman from the top of his crisp white wig to the tip of his silver-buckled shoes, stepped forward. The man's claim that he would speak for his fiancée, Letitia, because she was far too delicate to endure the questioning, and much too distraught over her sister's actions, nearly made Tearlach gag. He wondered if John truly believed the lies he was telling or had joined willingly in the Dunstans' conspiracy to ruin Pleasance in order to save Letitia from scandal. And he wondered how Pleasance felt about it all.

Pleasance nearly gasped aloud as John began to speak. Her

attempt to rescue Letitia from the mire was to be rewarded by her being tossed into it so deeply she would never be clean. This was a betrayal beyond her comprehension, beyond her ability to forgive.

"This tankard is yours then, Master Martin? You are certain?" Corbin Matthias pressed.

"Aye, very certain. My fiancée reported it missing a fortnight past."

"At that time did she explain how it had come to leave her keeping?"

"Nay. She wished to protect her sister."

With such protection, Pleasance mused bitterly to herself, I will have a very short life.

"You are saying Mistress Pleasance Dunstan had taken the tankard?"

"Aye. She gave it to Master O'Duine, calling it a gift."

Dully, Pleasance listened as John accused her of being a thief—and worse, a woman of no morals—implying that her chastity had been discarded years ago. He made her sound like a whore, a burden her family had endured for years. He described her rash action as a desperate need to impress Tearlach O'Duine since, at one and twenty, she was still lacking any marriage prospects. Pleasance found that being portrayed as a spinster so desperate for a man that she would stoop to stealing from her own family was almost as painful to bear as being called a thief. It hurt to see so many people nod in agreement.

She suffered yet another devastating blow when other people rose to testify against her; they also depicted her as loose of morals. Various patrons from the inn testified that she had been carrying on a torrid affair with Tearlach. In her trysts with him, Letitia had made everyone believe that it was actually *Pleasance* Dunstan creeping into Tearlach's room at the inn. Pleasance was stunned to realize that her sister had protected her own name by thoroughly blackening hers.

The trial was halted so everyone could eat their midday meal. Pleasance was escorted to a small room at the rear of the meetinghouse. Young Luther Cranston was left to stand guard over her as she ate. Although the cold pigeon pie and cider tasted like ashes in her mouth and her bound wrists made it difficult to eat she forced the plain but hearty fare down her throat. It would give her the strength that she would need.

When the trial resumed she was confronted with more lies. Several of Letitia's friends dutifully repeated the lies Letitia had told them. It was all hearsay, but Pleasance could see in the faces of the listeners that they believed this libel. These witnesses were followed by the people who had been in the tavern the night she had been arrested, who luridly related how they had seen her viciously attack Tearlach O'Duine. She numbly wondered why they were bothering with the ceremony of a trial, since she had been caught red-handed. They could have declared her guilty without all the damning speeches and hurtful lies. It seemed an added cruelty to make her endure it all.

Throughout the trial Tearlach remained silent. She knew he could dispute every lie being uttered, but he made no effort to do so. He had obviously decided to let her family destroy her. Since her own family had decided to let her take full blame, he was not going to dispute it. The letters Letitia had written could probably have saved her, but they had disappeared. Despite the way her family had turned against her, she began to worry that Tearlach O'Duine planned even more trouble for them. Perhaps he considered her ruin as but one step toward the ruin of her entire family.

The time for her to say something in her own defense finally came. She lifted her eyes toward her family. For the first time since the trial had begun they were all looking at her, as were the Martins. Pleasance fixed her gaze upon her parents.

"Do you intend to completely desert me then?" she asked them.

"You must face the punishment you deserve," her father replied.

"*I* deserve? Yes, perhaps I do deserve some punishment. Stupidity might not be a crime, but I begin to think it should be." She looked at Letitia. "And you? Is this how you mean to play this game?"

Letitia's expression was one of deep sorrow. "How can you call this a game? I fear that reveals your contempt for the law. We cannot protect you any more. Just know that I forgive you."

"How kind."

"Mistress Dunstan?" called Corbin, bringing her attention back to him. "Do you have anything to say in your own defense?"

It was on the tip of her tongue to spit out the whole truth, but she did not. She doubted that anyone would believe her anyway. The Martins and the Dunstans had spoken out against her, and their words would be the ones taken as the truth. Since the plan she had devised with her sister was known only to her and Letitia, there were no witnesses she could call in her own defense. For one brief moment she thought to demand that Tearlach tell the truth, then decided against it. People would not heed the word of a poor trapper and fur trader over that of Worcester's more prominent citizens. Despite what they had done to her, she could not bring herself to speak the words that would free her. Although her family had shown little loyalty toward her, there was her brother Nathan to consider. He had not turned against her, and, although she felt sure he would urge her to tell the truth if he were there, he did not deserve to be dragged down with the others.

As Corbin Matthias questioned her, she replied evasively, further convicting herself. As a clearly uncomfortable Corbin began to pronounce sentence upon her, Tearlach O'Duine finally stepped forward, and she wondered sadly what further blow he might strike against her.

"What fine do ye mean to levy?" Tearlach demanded of Corbin.

"I hesitate to levy a fine, for the girl has no funds. Unless"—Corbin looked toward the Dunstans—"you are willing to pay any penalties, Master Dunstan?"

"Nay, sir, I am not willing," her father replied.

Corbin sighed. "Do you possess any funds, Mistress Dunstan?"

"Not a farthing."

"Then it seems a useless gesture to impose a fine," Corbin began.

"I will pay whatever fine ye levy," Tearlach offered.

Pleasance's astonishment was followed by a swift flare of anger. "I wish no charity from you. You have done more than enough for me, thank ye kindly."

"I dinnae speak of charity, Miss Dunstan."

"Neither do I possess the means to repay a loan."

"Neither is it a loan I speak of. Not exactly." He turned to Corbin. "Set your price and I will pay it. I will then collect my due through Mistress Dunstan's labor."

Nearly gaping, Corbin took a full moment to regain his composure. "I am not sure we can do that."

"'Tis the law. The person wronged may pay the fines levied upon the guilty, then take recompense in labor."

"I know the law, but"—Corbin again looked to Pleasance's father—"surely you cannot condone such an arrangement, sir?"

Standing and signaling his family to do likewise, Thomas Dunstan said coldly, "Do as you please. I renounce all claim

and responsibility for the girl." He then walked out, his
family and the Martins hurrying after him.

Pleasance prayed her ordeal would reach a speedy end.
She had never felt such hurt, such utter betrayal. The effort
it took to keep from crumbling to the floor and weeping was
growing to be too much for her. She dreaded the thought of
breaking down before all the people staring at her, and so
she prayed Corbin would hurry.

"The fine, Corbin," pressed Tearlach.

"I am not certain," Corbin faltered.

Tearlach moved closer to his friend and the pair began a
low, murmured discussion. Pleasance watched them as they
discussed her future. At any other time she would have
pushed her way into the very midst of such a conference.
Now she only wished it finished. When Tearlach stepped
away from Corbin, she tensed slightly.

"Pleasance Dunstan, you are found guilty of the crimes
of theft and assault. For the period of one year you are to be
placed in service to Master Tearlach O'Duine, who has seen
fit to pay your fines. One year from this date you and
Master O'Duine shall come before me once again, whence
we shall determine whether or not you have dutifully made
all recompense for your crimes against him." Corbin stood
up and looked at Tearlach. "Until you depart, Master O'-
Duine, Miss Dunstan will remain secured in her cell."

Left alone in her small dark cell, Pleasance sank into a
black depression. It was many long hours before she began to
pull free of it. She thought of all that had happened to her but
could make no sense of it. The sound of someone approaching pulled her further out of her gloom. She realized it was
time to eat, but doubted she would be able to take a single bite
of food. When she saw that Corbin Matthias himself had

brought her meal, surprise and curiosity made her rise to her feet. Silently she watched as he entered the cell, set the tray down upon the battered small table at which she sat, and took a seat on the three-legged stool opposite her.

"Eat, Mistress Dunstan," Corbin politely ordered. "You will need a full stomach to fight the chill and damp. I have tried to rid the place of it but without success."

"All cellars suffer from it, sir. For what it is, this place is most comfortable." She forced herself to eat the rich venison stew and wondered why he stayed.

"I am sorry for all of this—the trial, the sentencing, and the humiliation you must feel."

"You did only as the law required of you." She found that she honestly felt no anger toward him.

"Well, I believe you shall be my last case. I but wish it could have been a more pleasant one."

"You have found a better position?"

"Nay, but I shall leave this one."

"Why? 'Tis a good one."

"Aye, but there blows an ill wind over this land. Many set themselves against the king and his laws. The trouble began with the Stamp Act of '65. It was further aggravated by the Townshend Acts of '67. Lord help us, the king's agents even halt and inspect chickens being ferried over a river by a farmer. Tempers in the Colonies are high. There is rebellion in the air."

"I have heard the murmurs. Well, some murmur rather loudly."

He smiled briefly and shook his head. "I am torn. Each side sounds right. I do not wish to be in the position to have to pass judgment, a judgment of traitor and treason no less, upon friends and neighbors. Today showed me most clearly that even when I act rightly I can be wrong—very, very wrong."

His serious hazel gaze fixed upon her made Pleasance nervous. He was a clever man. Although she did not know him well, she was sure of it. He also knew a great deal about everyone in town. She felt certain he had, more or less, guessed the truth. While it was comforting to know that someone did not believe her accusers, at least not wholly, she could not tell him the truth. She was not sure it would do her any good anyway.

"You were there when I was caught. You saw me strike Master O'Duine. How could you think yourself in error?"

"I have no doubt that you hit the man. Howbeit, I am certain you did not give that tankard to Tearlach."

Of course, she thought, and inwardly sighed. If Tearlach had showed him the tankard, then he undoubtedly had also told him where it came from. "You doubt the tale John Martin and the others told in court?"

"I doubt it indeed. I heard naught but lies, those spoken and those bred of silence. You said nothing in your own defense. Tearlach said nothing. Yet I know that each of you could have proven it all lies."

Although she would not agree to his surprisingly accurate assessment, neither could she bring herself to deny it. She had decided not to defend herself, but she could not speak lies to condemn herself. Corbin might simply be curious; then again, he might feel honorbound to correct the miscarriage of justice. She had decided to remain silent, to evade any further scandal for the sake of her already questionable future and to protect her brother Nathan. Despite the hurt and bitterness that was a hard knot inside of her, she would hold fast to that decision. Her family might have sacrificed her to protect themselves, but she would not add to that crime by returning that slap in kind.

"And mark my entire family as liars, perjurers? Ones who would cast their own flesh and blood to the wolves? If I did as you are suggesting, I would reveal that the oaths my parents, Letitia, and Lawrence spoke upon the Bible itself were just empty things. I could never do such a thing to my own kin."

"You do by them far more honorably than they did by you."

She said nothing, then, "Master O'Duine had no such reason to remain silent." Petty revenge tied his tongue, she thought sourly, then fought to convince herself that his lack of defense had been for the best.

"He never expected his accusations to result in a trial."

"Is that so? Once I was arrested where else was it to go, may I ask?"

"Your family could have extricated you. O'Duine only intended to frighten you, perhaps sting your pride." He shook his head. "When your family did absolutely nothing, we were all stuck firm in a trap of our own making. There was no turning back."

It sounded reasonable, yet she was reluctant to believe it If Tearlach O'Duine had not intended her to be tried and sentenced, then he should not have had her arrested, especially so publicly. It had been an unnecessarily cruel game to play. The revenge had far outweighed the crime even at the beginning. There was also the fact that he now demanded a full year of servitude from her. If he had intended little more than a slap on the wrist, he would have paid the fine and released her. The law did not say he *had* to make her work off the fine, only that he had the *right* to do so.

"I can see by your face that you doubt my words. Do not let bitterness and anger cloud your mind," advised Corbin. "Tearlach O'Duine is a good man. I have known him since he arrived in this land."

"So you wish me to smile as I slave for him for one full year."

Corbin sighed. "He sought to save you from harsher punishment, from greater public humiliation."

"We will wait and see if he succeeded." She pushed her plate aside, indicating that she was finished.

Nodding sadly, Corbin stood and collected her plate and cup. "Try not to let your anger, an anger you have every right to feel, make the situation more difficult. Tearlach is a fair man. He needs a woman to help raise his sister. I may not agree with the manner in which he has gained a teacher for her, but I can understand what motivates the man. If you cannot still your anger at Tearlach, I but ask that you keep it aimed at him alone and do not prick the child with it."

She could agree to that without qualm, and she nodded. When he was gone she immediately wished him back. Talking with Corbin had diverted her, had kept her mind from preying upon all the hurts she had been dealt.

She retrieved her lockpick from the hidden pocket in her cloak and stared at it. It was still possible for her to escape. The question was—to where? Nathan had said he was going to Philadelphia, but she knew that once he met up with his customs-running friends he could have gone anywhere. There was also the fact that she had no coin, no clothes, no food, and no horse. Neither did she know anyone who might be willing to help her escape.

With a heavy sigh, she put the lockpick back in her pocket and sat down. The best thing to do was to stay where she was. The thought of escape had helped her survive the ordeal of imprisonment and trial, but she now accepted that it had been a foolish idea. When she thought of what the people of Worcester now believed about her, escaping into the wilderness was almost an attractive prospect. And eventually Nathan would find her and help her. The minutes dragged by and she found herself hoping that Tearlach O'Duine would not take too long to carry her off into servitude.

* * *

Two days after the trial, Tearlach eased his long frame into a heavy oaken chair in Corbin Matthias's parlor and smiled crookedly at his friend. "I am here for my servant."

Corbin served them each some wine before sitting opposite Tearlach. "Do not taunt her by calling her servant, Tearlach. She has some pride. Neither does she deserve such humiliation. She was wrong, even though her reasons for doing all she did were most admirable, but this punishment is harsh."

"She made no attempt to elude it."

"Aye, I know. That tiny woman has more honor and loyalty in her heart than her whole family plus John Martin combined. Well, save for her slightly younger brother, Nathan. He has yet to hear what has befallen his sister. I do not believe he will turn his back on her. You would be wise to keep that in mind."

"Ye mean I might have some outraged pup pounding upon my door?"

"It is possible. Tearlach, can I not dissuade you from placing her in servitude for a year?"

"Nay."

"But you have enough coin to hire a dozen servants."

"No one here kens that. Ye swore ye would tell no one."

"And I kept my word," Corbin assured him, "although you never explained the need for such secrecy."

"The first time I had a full purse I thought of marriage and sought out a bride. The jingle of coin in my pocket made me very popular, but I was fool enough to think that I alone drew the admiration. One woman soon showed me what a vain idiot I was. I made a complete ass of myself for her, love and lust blinding me to her true nature—that of a mercenary tart. The awakening she forced upon me was cruel, but I learned from it. Without coin I draw little interest. With it I gain the sort of attention I am better without."

"You should not allow one bad experience to sour you."

"One bad one and a dozen lesser ones."

"Fine. Keep your wealth a secret, but it does not require any great wealth to hire a woman to care for your sister, one who is willing to go with you, and leave Pleasance behind."

Tearlach leaned forward. "What if I let her stay here? What would she face? Her family has cast her aside. The whole town believes her a thief. After she spends a year away, folks' memories mightnae be so strong. The truth could yet come out." He leaned back, relaxing again, and sipped his wine. "She willnae come to any harm."

"Nay? Can you swear that you will not approach her in a lustful manner? The winters can be long and cold in the Berkshires, and she is a fair little thing."

"I dinnae consider that sharing my bed would be doing her harm, Corbin. Neither have I indentured her to me for that purpose."

"Neither have you sworn that you will leave her be."

"As ye say, the winters in the Berkshires can be verra long and cold."

"Curse it, Tearlach! I ought to declare the girl innocent and set her free."

"Ye cannae for the same reason I sat silent at the trial. Once her family decided to let her take all the blame, it became a matter between them and her, and no longer our business. She set the course for all of us when she didnae defend herself. If she chooses to protect those ungrateful fools who are her family, who are we to say nay? To allow her to go free ye must paint the others black. She doesnae want that, 'tis clear. She chooses to take it all upon her own slim shoulders, so let her. She willnae appreciate ye exposing all she has fought to hide. I kenned that. 'Tis why I said nothing."

"How could they do that to her?" Corbin shook his head.

"She will not admit it, but she stays silent about the truth to protect that ungrateful lot. You have said little as well, yet I cannot think you mean to protect that blond wench Letitia."

"Nay, not I. I told you, once Pleasance did not dispute her family's tale, I chose to follow her lead. And with so many witnesses confirming the tale the Martins and the Dunstans told, how could either of us dispute it and be believed? I may have the power and wealth to fight them, but by the time I mustered them, Pleasance would have been imprisoned for weeks. As for Letitia, she can go to hell in a handbasket for all I care. Letitia is spoiled and vain. 'Tis clear she is the favored child, but I fail to see her charm. She pursued me so vehemently simply because I chose to cast my eye toward the elder first."

Corbin was surprised and made no effort to hide it. "You never spoke of this before."

"After courting Pleasance for a fortnight, I was coldly pushed aside." Tearlach found that the admission still stung him. "Rudely pushed aside, in truth."

"Nay. Pleasance has been known to have a sharp tongue, but she is never cruel or rude without good reason or strong provocation."

"The reason is plain. The Dunstans want little to do with a poor Scotsman, a mere farmer and one they think is poorly funded and settled far from civilization."

"I still cannot believe Pleasance felt that way. Nay, do not take offense. I do not cry you a liar. I but say that you guess her reasons wrong. Pleasance Dunstan does not have such vanity or airs. Try to find out why she treated you so. Do not sit back and assume you know. I may not know the young woman well, but I believe she is neither shallow nor as simple to decipher as that. She is much like her brother Nathan, and him I do know well. Nathan treats each man as an equal, be he in rags or fine lace. Nay, I will not believe that Pleasance turned you away because she thought you too common."

Tearlach wanted to believe that, but he remained distrustful. For the first time in his life he had honestly been interested in a woman for more than what lay beneath her skirts. Although he had been interested in that as well, and still was, he thought with an inner smile. He had sought after Pleasance for more honorable and lasting reasons, however, and had been surprised at himself even as he had done so. Her initial elusiveness he had attributed to shyness, but she had soon ended that misconception. His pride, which he knew could be too strong, had been badly stung. He was also angry at her for not being what he had thought her to be and angry at himself for being so mistaken about her.

He had grown even more angry when he had discovered, in an embarrassing way, that she had somehow made captive his lusts. To ease his stung pride, he had tried to bed one of the tavern wenches, only to have his body refuse to cooperate. Pleasance Dunstan had captured his passions in a way that made it impossible for him to satisfy them elsewhere.

So, he thought with a sly glance at Corbin, I will satisfy them with her. It was one of the real reasons he had paid her fine and so indentured her to him. A part of him had wished to see her rescued from the heartless disloyalty of her family—in fact, a large part of him, which troubled him a little. But he had also been quick to see the advantages of the arrangement for himself.

He and Pleasance would be together for a full year. In that time he felt sure that he could get a clear picture of her character. She would not be able to maintain any airs and elegance in the hills. He had a good life, far better than she probably suspected, but it was a hard one, and the place where he had chosen to live was still sparsely settled. He could not even be certain that the recent peace with the French had truly ended all the Indian troubles.

"You have become very quiet, Tearlach," Corbin observed.

"Merely pondering all ye have said. I will keep it in mind. I dinnae wish to let the sin of pride blind me. Did ye gather up all of her belongings?"

"Aye, but with some difficulty. I cannot think what the Dunstans meant to do with her clothing, since she is so much smaller than her sister and mother. Howbeit, at first they refused to turn her belongings over to me."

"Thomas Dunstan is a merchant to the verra marrow of his fat bones. He probably thought to sell her clothes."

"Well, I exerted what meager power I have and forced him to pack up her things. That allowed me to offer her the luxury of a bath and some clean clothes. You will find her looking much improved."

Finishing off his wine, Tearlach stood up. "I will set her belongings in the wagon and then collect her."

Pleasance tensed when she heard two sets of footsteps approaching. Corbin had told her that she would be leaving with Tearlach O'Duine this morning, but she had hoped that some intervention of Providence would prevent it. It was clear that Providence was not on her side at the moment.

When Tearlach came into view she felt a resurgence of her anger. He might not have intended to bring her to this pass, but he had. What truly fed her anger, however, was that, despite all he had done to her, she still found him attractive. Tall, dark, and with strongly hewn features, he twisted her insides with wanting. She hated him for that even as she savored the feelings he aroused, feelings that, before she met him, she had begun to believe herself incapable of.

He wore tight buckskin breeches that revealed long, well-shaped legs. His loose buckskin shirt was not fully laced and revealed some of his smooth, dark chest.

Pleasance felt a flicker of desire and firmly repressed it.

"'Tis time to leave, Mistress Dunstan," Tearlach said as Corbin unlocked the door to her cell. "I am a little surprised to find ye still here. Ye have shown a true skill at slipping in and out of securely locked places."

She donned her cloak as she looked at him. "I would never be so inconsiderate as to deny you your full victory, sir."

"A few days of hard work, away from all the luxuries ye are accustomed to, and ye might regret that decision."

"Quite probably, but I should not worry yourself over that. I am becoming accustomed to making decisions I regret."

"Shall we go?" urged Corbin.

"Aye," Pleasance replied. "There is no reason to stay here."

As she, Corbin, and Tearlach ascended the cellar stairs and stepped out into the drive that curled around to the back of Corbin's house from the main road, Tearlach took her by the arm. She almost yanked free of his hold. His touch, light and impersonal though it was, caused the heat of desire to flicker through her veins. That frightened her. One long year of living close together stretched ahead of them. Such wild feelings could easily bring about the completion of her downfall. She knew she had to fight them, yet she was not sure how.

Tearlach's large freight wagon and its double team of horses loomed up in front of her. Before she could succumb to a flash of panic and try to flee, Tearlach grasped her firmly by the waist and lifted her up on the high wagon seat. As if he sensed her urge to run, he kept a gentle but firm grip upon her wrist as he stood beside the wagon and took his final farewell of Corbin.

By the time she and Tearlach started on their way, Pleasance had calmed herself somewhat. She sat stiffly, her gaze fixed on the horses' ears as they drove through town. It was not until the houses began to grow farther apart as they neared the western edge of town that she began to relax. As the stiffness began to leave her body, she suddenly realized where they were and tensed again. Her house loomed up ahead of them.

Despite her best efforts not to, she glanced toward her home as they drove past it. There was no one outside of the two-story gray-shingled garrison house to watch her leave or answer her faint hope that her family might still step forward to help her. There did not even appear to be anyone watching for her from inside the house. Not one face appeared in the multipaned windows. Staring down at her tightly clenched hands, Pleasance fought back her tears and swore to herself that she would never let her family's betrayal break her spirit.

Tearlach watched her covertly. He saw the hurt she struggled to hide, and he felt a strong urge to stop the wagon, march inside the Dunstan home, and beat Thomas Dunstan soundly. John Martin and the spoiled Letitia were deserving of a good thrashing as well. This strong surge of anger and outrage on Pleasance's behalf troubled him. He recalled her ability to stir a lot of puzzling emotions in him. Tearlach began to wonder if he was making a very big mistake, if perhaps he should have released Pleasance after he paid her fine.

He quickly shook his doubts aside. In several ways, some righteous and some not, he needed her. She stirred a desire within him—one that possessed him to the point of denying all others—that demanded satisfaction. Society might frown upon his fulfilling that desire outside of the bonds of marriage, but the society of Puritan-born Massachusetts still frowned darkly on a great many things. He was past caring. In the wilderness one played by different rules. He also needed Pleasance Dunstan to help care for Moira, his rebellious half sister. Moira needed the guiding, gentling touch of a woman.

The girl would turn thirteen soon, and full womanhood was not far away. Moira was too wild, too rough, and now that she was getting older she must be tamed. Tearlach grimaced as he recalled the incident that had brought him to Worcester looking for a wife. Even in the wilderness there were things a young woman could not do without stirring up a scandal, and beating a young boy with her fists was one of them.

Yes, Pleasance Dunstan would fulfill his needs for the year to come, in his bed and in helping Moira. But he would make certain that she never had the chance to use those needs against him.

Chapter Four

Pleasance grimaced and glanced around to be sure that Tearlach was not watching her. With an inner sigh of relief, she rubbed her aching backside. Her petticoats did not provide as much padding as she had hoped. She suspected that the road they were traveling on was the only usable route to the far western settlements of the colony, but it had to be the worst road in all of the northern colonies. Just traveling on it should be considered punishment enough for the crimes she had been accused of. The only thing she had to be thankful for was that the September heat was eased.

The lack of any good inn did not help matters. Either Tearlach was avoiding the places or there were not any. After all, until the recent war's end, the Indians and the French had kept the western lands in utter turmoil and the roads had remained little traveled. A man would not set up an inn unless he felt assured of some commerce.

So, instead of finding herself at a warm, welcoming inn at the end of the long, exhausting day, she arrived at a small, one-story log outpost around which lounged a few slothful soldiers. Peace had made them lazy, she mused. She would not be surprised to find that a posting to one of these remote fortified waysides was now considered a form of punishment. The way the soldiers eyed her made her begin to think that the last thing she would find here was safety.

When Tearlach returned from unhitching the horses and securing them for the night, she almost shared her concerns with him. She quickly shook that urge away. Just because the soldiers were slovenly, sullen, and eyed her lecherously did not mean that they were actually dangerous. They might be merely ill-mannered and badly trained. The very last thing she wished to do was appear to be a timid female who saw threats and peril lurking all around her. She would not have Tearlach thinking she was a burden or that she looked to him for her protection. Straightening her spine, she faced the soldiers with a bravado she did not feel, an attitude that was hard to maintain beneath the soldiers' sneering contempt. They clearly considered her beneath them, which might make them dangerous indeed.

Inside the tiny blockhouse she found little to allay her concerns. The only amenity the damp, badly lit place offered was possible safety from attack. Tearlach picked out what appeared to be the cleanest corner in the ill-kept place and started to lay out bedding for himself. Her thoughts were diverted from the sullen soldiers and the dirty shelter when she saw that no bedding was being prepared for her.

"And where am I to sleep?" she demanded.

Sitting on his pallet of blankets, Tearlach began to open the sack he had brought with them. "Between me and the wall."

"You mean to force me to share your pallet?" She was not sure whether she was shocked or angry or both as she snatched the johnnycake and pemmican he handed her.

He poured some cider into a tin cup and leaned close as he handed it to her. He wanted to speak without the soldiers' overhearing them. Despite the dusty ride, she smelled of fresh clean skin scented with lavender. He struggled to ignore the lure of her wide eyes sparkling with anger. It was a look he found dangerously alluring, but they had been together for barely one full day. It would be folly to push his attentions on her so soon.

"Listen to me, woman," he hissed. "Do ye see those Sassanach soldiers?"

"Of course I do." Her anger began to ease as she realized that he had also sensed the threat they presented, and she idly wondered if *Sassanach* was a curse word. "Sassanach?" she finally asked, driven by curiosity.

"English soldiers, and these are the verra dregs of the kings army. That is all that can be spared for these rotting outposts now, outposts the authorities are beginning to consider useless. The good soldiers are kept busy hunting the customs runners, smugglers, and agitators. These men arenae to be trusted. Look at how they watch us yet offer us no hospitality. They think we are no better than the dirt beneath their boots. As long as we must seek shelter here, ye are to stay close by me."

"And your bulk will be all that is required to save me, hmm?"

"My bulk and one eye opened all night—aye. Eat and then get some rest. Oh, and dinnae even loosen one button on that pretty blue gown of yours. We dinnae want to tempt the buggers. We will leave this cursed place at first light."

She shut her mouth and obeyed him. He was right. And his words were proof enough that she had good reason to be afraid. There was also the fact that he was the best protection she had against the threat she read in the soldiers' eyes.

Handing him back the tin cup after she finished eating the thin toasted cake of Indian meal and the strip of dried meat, she curled up on the rough pallet he had spread out for them. Not even bothering to be subtle about it, she pressed as close to the wall as she could get without completely forfeiting her own comfort. It was a long time before she felt Tearlach lie down at her side and spread a thin blanket over them. She thought it a little strange that his presence was what allowed her to finally smother the last of her nervousness and fall asleep.

Tearlach curled up on his side, his back to Pleasance and his eyes on the soldiers. Subtly he slipped a knife beneath the folded sack that formed their meager pillow. As he breathed deeply of Pleasance's gently alluring scent, he knew that the need to keep a close watch on their sullen, narrow-eyed hosts was not the only reason it was going to be a long, long night.

Pleasance murmured crossly, not eager to relinquish her sleep, but something nudged her awake. Even as she stretched out her hand, she realized what it was. Tearlach was gone. It was another moment before she recalled why that should trouble her, before she remembered the threat of the soldiers. She quickly opened her eyes, but was too late to elude the hand that clamped over her mouth or the ones that pinned her to the blankets.

A soft, triumphant chuckle sent the chill of terror through her. She began to struggle, but that only amused her captors and did little to slow the rough loosening of her clothes. The man on top of her halted the thrashing of her legs, using his own legs to pin hers down. He then began to tug up her skirts. Despite an occasional grunt or soft curse, the soldiers were coldly, horrifyingly silent.

Even her attempt to bite the hand covering her mouth proved fruitless, for the soldier wore thick deerskin gauntlets. By the time Pleasance managed to get a grip, he yanked his hand away. She opened her mouth to scream and a dirty linen rag was stuffed in it, gagging her. Her desperate call for help was forced back in her throat, becoming a low moan of fright. All she could do was twist her body and buck uselessly as the assault continued unhindered. Nausea stung the back of her throat. She frantically wondered what had happened to Tearlach, the man who was supposed to protect her.

After a final check on the team and the wagon, Tearlach looked around and cursed. He had let his attention wander for only a moment, but that had been a moment too long. The soldiers were no longer outside, save for two stationed on either side of the doorway, and those two were peering inside the small stockaded cabin. Tearlach immediately knew what must interest them so much. He cursed again, silently and viciously, as he grabbed his musket, stuffed his pistol into the waistband of his breeches, and made sure his knife could be quickly withdrawn from the sheath on his belt.

Fury and fear tore through him, but he fought to keep them under control. He understood his fury. These men were the dregs of the army, little better than criminals. They also shared a common arrogance, a contempt for "Colonials." He had seen it in their sneering glances from the very first. It was an attitude too many Englishmen held, an attitude he knew was contributing to the growing rift between England and her colonies. It was an attitude that allowed those men to think they could brutally rape Pleasance with impunity, without fear or reprimand and certainly without fear of intervention from him. He smiled grimly as he thought how he would prove them wrong.

Tearlach cracked the first guard at the entrance over the head with his musket butt and the man went down with barely a grunt. The second guard had only enough time to register his surprise at this unexpected attack before Tearlach slammed his gun butt into the man's jaw, sending him catapulting backward, unconscious before he could cry out a warning. As Tearlach stepped over one guard's body, he wished he had time to tie the men up, but he felt confident it would be a goodly while before either would again be a real threat. If he was lucky and could move fast enough, he and a hopefully unscathed Pleasance would be well on their way before either man stirred.

No one saw him as he stepped inside. The sight that greeted him filled him with such rage he nearly shot the man crouched over a silently, frantically struggling Pleasance. Her bodice was open and her full skirts were pushed up to her thighs. The man on top of her was already unlacing his breeches as his friends held Pleasance captive. Tearlach heard her moans as she arched her body in a fruitless attempt to throw off her attackers.

It took him a moment to still the searing fury ripping through him, to silence the instinct to kill. He needed loaded guns to threaten the men. If he shot now, at best he could kill two men, and those left standing would kill him long before he could reload.

His only choice was to bluff. "Let her go. Now."

Pleasance almost fainted with relief when that icy but already familiar voice broke the silence. Her attackers stiffened, then slowly edged away from her. Although she felt weak and was shaking badly, she managed to yank the gag from her mouth and haphazardly pull her clothes together. The need to run, far and fast, gave her the strength to move.

"Take the blankets and get in the wagon." Tearlach saw that the man who had been crouched over her had his breeches undone. "Did he succeed?"

"Nay," she rasped as she scooped up the blankets.

"You cannot shoot all of us," one of the soldiers growled, a tentative bravado replacing his surprise.

"Nay, only two. Do ye wish to be one of those two?" When Pleasance stumbled up to him, he nudged her toward the door. "Get in the wagon. Can ye manage a team?"

"Aye, but not expertly."

"No matter. Get in the wagon, take the reins, and be ready. Hold, I need a moment's assistance." Slowly he backed closer to the door. "Throw your weapons toward me," he told the soldiers. "Carefully."

After a moment's hesitation the soldiers obeyed. Keeping an eye on them, Tearlach ordered Pleasance to put the weapons in a sack. He was relieved to see that, though she was trembling badly and looked ready to faint, she set down the blankets and obeyed his command with admirable haste. The moment she set the filled sack at his side, he ordered her to grab the muskets and put them into the wagon. The weight of the weapons forced her to make two trips. Tearlach was beginning to worry that the guards outside would rouse before they could leave when he heard two soft but ominous thuds. When Pleasance returned to his side he chanced a fleeting glance her way.

"The guards were stirring. They are still again," she said, hurriedly collecting the blankets.

"Good lass. To the wagon." He heard her soft retreating footsteps and picked up the sack holding the soldiers' small arms.

"That there's the property of the Crown. It be agin the law to steal it," cried one of the soldiers.

Backing out of the door, Tearlach smiled coldly. "Oh, I dinnae intend to steal it. I will toss it out along the road somewheres. Ye whoresons can look for it." Even as he bolted for the wagon, Tearlach yelled, "Move, Pleasance."

She snapped the reins. The team was just leaping forward

when Tearlach hurled himself into the back of the wagon. She chanced one quick look over her shoulder. Tearlach kept his musket aimed at the soldiers, now stumbling over the unconscious guards at the door. She then concentrated on keeping the wagon team moving as fast as possible without risking a spill.

When they had gone a few miles Tearlach began to toss out the soldiers' weapons one by one. They would have to halt to collect them. Once they had gotten all of them back, he hoped they would decide not to continue the chase. If nothing else, they would waste so much time picking up the scattered weapons they would begin to worry about having deserted their post.

To Pleasance, it seemed like hours before Tearlach ordered her to slow the team and climbed forward to take the reins from her stiff fingers. She bit back a groan as she released the reins to him, all too painfully aware of just how great a strain it had been—not something she wished to reveal to Tearlach.

Trying to ignore the ache now ripping through her arms, shoulders, and back, she turned her attention to tidying her disordered clothing.

Nausea welled up inside of her, but she fought it down. There was no time to indulge in weakness. Somehow she would have to put the assault out of her mind, would have to cling to the knowledge that the attack upon her had ultimately failed.

The sun had nearly set by the time Tearlach drew the wagon to a halt and pulled it off the road as far as the thickening trees of the surrounding forest would allow. They had made only the briefest of stops at midday, mostly for the benefit of the horses. Pleasance watched as he worked to erase the tracks of the wagon back to the road and several yards down it with some brush.

They worked silently to set up camp. Tearlach doubted the soldiers were following them, but decided against a fire just in case. Their meal was a simple one of johnnycake and pemmican again.

As he laid out the blankets that constituted their pallet he covertly watched Pleasance. Her silence was troubling. Although she had said that the soldiers had not accomplished the rape, they had nearly done so. Too nearly. He had seen the scars left on a woman's heart, mind, and soul by the brutal taking of her body. He had seen it in his own mother. He did not wish to see it in Pleasance.

The depth of concern he felt for her made him frown. The wench was arousing far too much emotion in him, he thought crossly with a sigh.

"Come, Pleasance, ye need to rest."

Even as she moved to curl up on the makeshift pallet, she murmured, "As do you."

He covered her with a blanket. "I will get some. Enough to last me until we reach a safer place."

When he crawled in beside her she tensed, then immediately felt guilty. He had done her no physical harm. He did not deserve her fear. She moved to get more comfortable and could not suppress a groan at the wrenching ache in her shoulders.

Tearlach immediately reached for her. "They did hurt ye."

The touch of his hand, the concern in his rich voice, seriously undermined her efforts to be strong. She did not want to give in to weakness. Neither did she want to seek comfort from him. He touched her feelings in a way that could only prove dangerous in the year to come. Keeping some distance from him would be essential.

"Nay, not truly. A few bruises, 'tis all. I fear it was driving the team that brought a real pain or two."

"Ah, of course."

She frowned as he suddenly left her side. Peering through the darkness, she tried to see what he was doing, but could only make out his shape by the wagon. She tried to hide her interest by quickly turning her back to him when he returned to their pallet.

"Loosen your bodice."

"What?"

"I have a salve that will help that ache, but I need to rub it into your shoulders and back."

"Not a horse liniment? They are the foulest-smelling things. I think I would prefer to endure the pain."

"Fear not. No unbearable stench shall touch your pampered skin. Aye, 'tis horse liniment in a manner, but 'tis gently scented. A wife of a friend of mine prepared the salve, and I purchase a pot or two whenever I can. Come, loosen your bodice."

Her embarrassment eased by the cover of darkness, slowly she obeyed him. As she did so she puzzled over his reference to her "pampered skin" and the tone he had used to speak those words. She was no Letitia, given to milk baths and other such nonsense, yet he apparently thought she was. How he could have come to such a conclusion puzzled her.

"Turn onto your stomach."

When she did as he asked, he brushed aside her hair and began to massage the liniment into her back. He fought to ignore how it felt to touch her slim back, the faint light of a half-moon making it glow a soft ivory. Although he still had every intention of feeding the hungers she instilled in him, he knew this night was not the time to begin his seduction. He did not want her thinking him one of a kind with the soldiers they had fled.

"I should have thought of this. Should have realized such honest hard work was not something ye would be accustomed to. Weel, that shall soon change. Ere the year is out ye will come to understand that there is more required of a woman than kenning how to pour tea or play callous, flirtatious games with some poor fool." He bit his tongue and silently cursed his blunder, hoping she did not guess that he considered himself one of those poor fools.

At first his words stirred Pleasance's anger, but his final words brought realization. He *did* think her of the same ilk as Letitia. Despite the month he had spent courting Letitia, the fact that she, Pleasance, had rejected him obviously still pinched. Clearly his pride had been badly stung. She quickly told herself not to be fooled into thinking there was anything more than his pride involved.

The words required to forcefully defend herself were on the tip of her tongue, but she bit them back. He was clearly still angry and in no state of mind to listen to reason. She was also not sure what she could say to ease that anger. How could she explain that she had hurt him because her parents had told her to, because they had ordered her to cast him aside so that Letitia could have him? That would make her look like a fool, and she did not want Tearlach to know how spinelessly she had acted. She would have to show him the error of his assumptions about her through her actions. In fact, it would be a pleasure to prove him wrong.

Her thoughts were disrupted by a growing warmth spreading from his hands throughout her body. It felt good—warm, soothing, yet enticing—to have those strong, calloused hands moving slowly over her skin. He pulled from her feelings she had thought herself incapable of having, feelings so strong and tempting she knew they would be hard to fight. Even now, although she felt soiled by the mauling of the soldiers, she had to fight the urge to turn toward him, to throw herself into his arms.

"The ache is gone. The salve has done its work," she said.

Tearlach blinked, her hoarse, clipped words drawing him back as if from a dream. Reluctantly he withdrew his hands and watched her hastily do up her bodice as he wiped his hands on his handkerchief. Another moment and he knew he would have been trying to touch far more than her slim, silken back. When she had spoken up, he had been staring at the nape of her slender neck, thinking how it would feel beneath his lips.

"Ye may find ye need more on the morrow."

Curling up at the very edge of their rough bed, she murmured, "I may. Thank you."

"My pleasure." He set down the pot of salve and slipped beneath the blanket "Any other aches I might doctor?"

She was glad of the dark, for the answer that popped into her head was so wanton it made her blush furiously. "None that salve can heal. No amount of doctoring can rid me of the feel of their filthy, grabbing hands."

Turning onto his side, he gently smoothed his hand over her hair, enjoying the feel of it. "Ye said they didnae accomplish what they had intended."

Although she did not wish to discuss what she had endured at the outpost, she hoped talk would keep her from thinking of his disturbing nearness, of how stirred she was by the simple touch of his hand on her hair. "Nay, and that is what I must try to remember."

"Aye. Ye must remember that, despite all, ye werenae raped."

"Yet I feel as if I have been." She tensed slightly when he slipped his arm around her waist and tucked her up against him. Her errant desire immediately stirred to life, and she dreaded that he would discover that she still wanted him.

"I dinnae intend to hurt ye, Pleasance. Merely comfort ye. The distaste of an unwanted touch can fade; the brutal invasion of your body would never have left your thoughts. 'Tis hard for a mon to say the words needed at such a time.

"Have you heard what happened to my mother?"

"Aye, Letitia told me."

"I had no words to ease my mother's horror, and eleven years of living since then hasnae given them to me. Ye were mauled, your body insulted by their rough, unwanted touch. Just now it seems the worst of all crimes, but, believe me, if they had gained what they sought, ye would have wounds that might never heal."

That he could insult her so easily one moment and try so hard to comfort her the next puzzled her. "I do understand that. It but takes a while for such knowledge to be set firm in mind and heart."

"Mayhaps if my mother had lived longer she too would have healed, at least in some ways. She couldnae fully bear even my affectionate embrace after she was raped."

"But you had naught to do with it." She sensed that he found it hard to speak of the crime done to his mother, and she was moved that he did so in an attempt to help her overcome her own horror.

"I was a mon. Seventeen only, but still considered a mon. She hurt herself as much as I was hurt when she flinched at my touch, but her tortured mind made her see all men as a threat, made her tense warily at even the gentlest of caresses. She wanted death, though she denied it. Though she was nearly past childbearing age, Moira's birth didnae harm her that much. She simply refused to fight for her life when she got a fever. And that fever was brought on because she wouldnae eat, wouldnae do anything to regain her strength. Those are the scars, the hurts, that rape inflicts upon a woman." He sighed. "I cannae begin to understand how ye feel."

"Dirty, soiled, violated."

"Can ye not feel anger and outrage instead?"

"What?"

"They had no right, no right at all. Only fools think otherwise and try to blame the woman for their own crimes. Only animals have a blind need to rut. A mon should be beyond that no matter what the provocation."

"I gave them no provocation. I was asleep when they sprang." She discovered that she did feel anger, even outrage, at what had occurred. "I barely even glanced their way since arriving at that outpost."

Hearing the anger in her voice, he smiled faintly. "That is the truth. It was their crime only. Their fault. Not yours. That is where the healing will come from. Now, best to get some sleep. We leave at daybreak."

After a moment of silence, she whispered, "Thank you for telling me of your mother. It helps."

"Ye had become too quiet. I feared ye had slipped into a darkness of the mind. Now I can see ye werenae afflicted as I had thought. Ye dinnae flinch from my touch." He moved his hand in a small circular motion over her stomach.

For a moment the feel of that subtle caress held her still. Heat flared in her abdomen and spread quickly throughout her body. The man was truly dangerous, she thought with a touch of exasperation. She grasped his hand and moved it aside, noting idly that he made no effort to resist her abrupt rebuff.

"Since you know that I can abide your touch already, there is no need to further test me."

Chuckling softly, he sprawled on his back, crossing his arms beneath his head. He had felt the softest of ripples beneath his hand, had heard the hint of huskiness in her voice. She was not averse to his touch. The fact that he could draw a response from her despite her recent ordeal suggested to him that she still felt as strongly drawn to him as he did to her. He did not intend to wait long to test out his theory.

"Just making sure."

"Fine. Now that you are sure, you may keep your hands to yourself."

"I may, may I?"

"Aye, you may. In fact, you had better."

"Mayhaps."

"Master O'Duine, I am an indentured servant, not a leman."

"As ye wish. Leman, eh? There is a fine old word."

"Oh, hush. I need my sleep."

She heard him laugh softly again and almost struck him. He knew what she felt when he touched her. She was sure of it. Worse, she had the distinct impression that he meant to take advantage of her weakness. She did not feel confident she could fight the feelings he stirred if he intended to tug at them constantly.

Mentally cursing him, Letitia, and everything that had led to her being there, Pleasance closed her eyes and tried to go to sleep. She would need all the rest she could get.

Pleasance cautiously sat down before the fire Tearlach had built. She did not think her backside would ever stop hurting. After six long days on the hard wagon seat she suspected she had bruises that would never heal.

"We will reach my cabin by day's end tomorrow," Tearlach said as he handed over her share of their food. "Soon we will be able to eat something besides pemmican."

"And sit on something besides that cursed wagon seat," Pleasance muttered as she chewed the strip of dried meat and washed away its taste with cider.

"Sore, are ye? I have a salve for that." He laughed at the disgusted look she gave him.

The moment she had finished her meager meal, Pleasance decided to go to sleep. Using a little of their water, she rinsed out her cup and then lightly washed up. She stepped over to the bedding Tearlach had spread out near the wagon and silently cursed. One bed, one blanket—again. The man was incorrigible, she grumbled to herself as she laid down.

She was groggy with approaching sleep by the time Tearlach joined her. Although she muttered a curse as he curled his arm around her waist, she was too tired to fight him. He touched his warm lips to the hollow near her ear and she shivered, desire seeping through her body. She struggled to grasp at the resistance she needed to push him away, but exhaustion made that impossible. A flicker of that resistance finally appeared when he gently turned her to face him, but it quickly vanished when he placed his mouth on hers.

A soft moan escaped her as she slid her arms around his neck and gave herself over to his kiss. She parted her lips to welcome the invasion of his tongue, pressing close to him as he slowly stroked the inner regions of her mouth. Her passion flared to life, banishing her weariness and making her forget all her aches and pains. The heat of her desire made her feel renewed, strong, and vibrant.

"Ah, lass," Tearlach murmured as he kissed the pulse point in her throat. "We shall have some verra warm nights while ye are in the Berkshires with me."

His soft words were like a splash of icy water in her face. Pleasance cursed and pushed herself out of his arms. She clenched her hands into tight fists as she fought the urge to slap him.

"So you think to use me to warm up your nights, do you?" she snapped.

"I didnae notice any great resistance from ye. Nay, none at all, in fact."

"'Twas a brief error in judgment on my part. I seem to be having a lot of them lately. May I remind you that I am to be your servant, not your whore." She flipped onto her side, showing him her back.

Tearlach turned onto his own back and crossed his arms beneath his head. "I didnae hear myself ask ye to be my whore."

"Oh, you asked it clearly enough."

"Nay, I thought we were becoming lovers."

"Well, whatever your twisted mind thought, 'tis not to be. I may be reduced to servitude in your home, Master Tearlach, but I will never be reduced to servitude in your bed."

"Good, because servitude isnae what I was seeking. Nay, I want that passion ye just revealed in my arms."

"You imagine things. And your arms will remain empty."

"We shall see."

Pleasance silently cursed. The man had a right to his cockiness. She found resistance a difficult thing to muster when he held her in his arms. She closed her eyes and cursed again. It definitely looked to be a long year ahead.

Chapter Five

"I had best tell ye something of what to expect."

Pleasance rolled her eyes heavenward and bit back a tart retort. They had just spent seven long exhausting days on a rough, dirty journey—just the two of them. He had had plenty of time and privacy to tell her what lay ahead down to the smallest detail. Instead, he had waited until his cabin was in view. How typical of a man. Tearlach would now try to cram hours worth of information into a few terse sentences before they pulled up before his door.

"Oh, do you think that necessary?" she said. Well, so much for not being snide, she mused.

He shot her a quick glance, certain sarcasm had dripped from her every word, but she met his gaze with a look of calm interest and sublime innocence. "Aye. Moira is twelve, nearly thirteen. She has a few, er, difficulties." Inwardly, he winced over those inadequate words. "The facts that she is illegitimate, the product of rape, and has Indian blood have proven a hard burden to bear at times. Having no woman about has led to her growing up a wee bit wild."

"And you expect that one year of having me muddling

about will cure her of these problems?" Typical male idiocy, she thought.

"Nay, not fully, but I do believe ye can help her, temper her. She will soon be a woman, and she cannae be running about as free and wild as some lad. Howbeit, ye arenae to teach her to be some useless society miss. That willnae do her any good at all. I willnae have her made into some flirtatious gossip who willnae set her soft hand to any work and turns her little nose up at neighbors and friends."

It took a great effort of will, but Pleasance restrained herself from shoving him off the wagon seat as they came to a halt before his cabin. She was dismayed at his low, unfair opinion of her. His anger was not easing as she had hoped it would. It was going to be very hard not to defend herself against such slurs, but she did not believe the truth behind her rebuff of his courtship would ease his anger either.

"I assure you, Master O'Diune, I shall do my best not to infect your sister with the ills of my class."

Scowling, Tearlach helped her down from the wagon. Before he could reply to her sharp words, Moira emerged from the cabin, ran down the neat path, and hurled herself into his arms in greeting. Behind her strolled the gangly, aging Jake, an old fellow trapper who often watched Moira for him. A little cautiously he introduced them to Pleasance.

Jake was tall, slim, and white-haired, a rough character who had spent most of his life isolated from civilization. Moira was dressed tidily enough in a blue linsey-woolsey dress, but her Indian heritage was clear to see. Both were people that those of Pleasance's upbringing would consider far beneath them. Tearlach watched Pleasance closely for any sign of insult or contempt, but her response was faultlessly polite and warm. Moira's reaction caused him to frown, however. The girl was eyeing Pleasance coldly.

"Ye didnae need to bring her," Moira grumbled as Jake and Tearlach began to unpack the wagon.

"Oh, but he did," Pleasance answered before Tearlach could speak up. "He paid good money for me." When Moira's light brown eyes widened, Pleasance was glad to see she could startle the girl out of her sullen state.

"Ye *bought* her, Tearlach?"

"I didnae buy her, Moira. I paid her fine."

"Fine? Fine for what?"

"It doesnae matter."

Pleasance was a little surprised to see that Tearlach felt uncomfortable discussing the subject. Serves him right, she thought, then smiled at Moira. "My crimes were theft and assault with an absurd weapon." She ignored the glare Tearlach sent her way.

"Assault with a *what?*"

"A tankard. I struck your brother a telling blow over his enlarged head with a silver tankard."

"Which ye had stolen," Tearlach added. "Enlarged head?"

"It sounded kinder than 'fat' or 'swelled.' And I repossessed that tankard."

"So, ye are a common thief," Moira drawled. "That is why your own kin has turned their backs on ye."

Shocked, Pleasance stared at the girl before she was able to ask. "How did you know that?"

"'Twas just a lucky guess," Tearlach said quickly.

There was such a look of uneasiness on his face that Pleasance knew he was not telling the truth. And yet if it was not a lucky guess, then what was it? Tearlach turned to his sister before Pleasance could question him further.

"Moira, 'tis too complicated to explain. Ye willnae refer to Pleasance in that way, ever." Tearlach gave his sister a stern look and, after glaring at him for an instant, she finally nodded obedience.

"Such stout defense from my accuser," Pleasance murmured. "The world is truly a strange place."

"Ye have grown verra saucy these last few days, Pleasance Dunstan."

"So she is an indentured servant?" Moira asked before Pleasance could answer.

"Aye, for one year."

"So I can order her around."

Before Tearlach could say a word, Pleasance faced Moira squarely. "Nay, you cannot."

"But ye are our servant."

"I am indentured to your brother, not to you."

Pleasance was pleased when Tearlach nodded in firm agreement. Although, as a servant, she should take orders from most anyone who felt inclined to give them, she could not allow that to happen. Tearlach wanted her to help his sister. If Moira was allowed to wield absolute authority over her, that help would be impossible to give. She had to have some control over the child. Hearing Tearlach support her in this matter relieved Pleasance immensely.

As Tearlach and Moira continued to argue, Pleasance studied the girl. She was a beautiful child. There was a hint of copper in the girl's brown skin. Moira's thick dark hair, revealing a natural tendency to curl, fell in waves to her waist. Her features were finely drawn and her eyes, her best feature, were huge, heavily lashed tawny pools. The girl showed true promise of becoming a lovely woman.

Picking up the smaller of her bags, Pleasance followed the men as they went into the cabin. She could hear Moira hurrying after her. The interior of the cabin was a surprise. Finely scrubbed wood floors and animal pelt rugs gave it a wild yet warm look. Pleasance set down her bag and, as the men continued to bring in the things from the wagon, she decided to have a good look around. Moira shadowed her as she began her explorations.

"I may have to obey ye, but ye best be careful about telling me what to do."

"Oh, and why is that?" Pleasance noticed that the large main room had been subtly divided into a living area and an ample kitchen, beside which was a small enclosed room that was obviously a spare sleeping area.

"Because I am a witch." Moira hurried after Pleasance as she started up the stairs to the loft.

"How interesting." The loft was divided into two rooms, with a small hallway running between them.

"I am. If ye do something I dinnae like, I shall put a spell on ye."

"Moira." Tearlach's stern voice nearly made Pleasance jump and she backed out of the large, well-furnished room that was clearly his.

"You did not tell me your sister had such skills."

Although Pleasance did not believe the girl's claim that she was a witch, she did think there were a few things he had neglected to mention about his sister. After all, Moira had known how her family had deserted her, yet no one could have told the child.

"She deludes herself." Tearlach opened the door to Moira's room so that Pleasance could have a good look around, then ushered her and Moira down the stairs. "'Tis a dangerous game she plays that I grow verra weary of."

"I can afflict ye with something truly revolting," Moira threatened, glaring at Pleasance.

"Can you now?" Feeling weary, Pleasance sat down on a bench at the table that dominated the kitchen area, and Jake, who was already sitting at the table, hurriedly poured her a tankard of mead. "Thank you, sir." She looked at Moira, who was clearly trying to look malevolent but looked simply sulky.

"'Tis hard to believe in witchcraft in this age of reason. Perhaps you can demonstrate."

"Demonstrate? What do ye mean?"

"Put a spell on . . . on your brother. Turn him into a snake. That should not be difficult. He is as near to being one already as I have ever had the misfortune to meet."

"Tearlach, she just insulted ye. Ye had better beat her." Moira sat at the table looking expectant.

"'Tis sorely tempting." After glaring at Jake, who did a poor job of hiding his amusement, Tearlach sat down at the table and poured himself some mead.

"Weel? Do it then."

"Nay, Moira."

"She is a servant. 'Tis allowed."

"'Tisnae allowed—or, if it is, 'tisnae right. And Mistress Dunstan isnae just any servant."

"Nay? There are special kinds, are there?" Moira asked, her sarcasm bordering on impudence.

"Pleasance isnae someone ye can beat. Just leave it be."

"I am just trying to understand."

"Oh, aye? I think ye are being stubborn and trying to irritate me. Weel, lassie, ye are certainly accomplishing the latter."

The argument between sister and brother continued, but Pleasance lost interest. If she were not so tired, she would have found it amusing to hear Tearlach trying to explain how she was a servant yet not a servant. Jake set before them each a bowl of the hearty venison stew he had prepared for Tearlach's return, and Pleasance turned her attention to him as she ate.

"How long have you known Master O'Duine, sir?" she asked.

"Call me Jake. Everyone does. Ah, well now, I have known the boy for years, since he first tried his hand at hunting." Jake chuckled. "The lad could not creep up on a deaf mule back in them days."

"Do tell." Pleasance saw Tearlach scowl at Jake, but Moira required his full attention so Jake kept right on talking.

The wiry, white-haired Jake proved to have a good sense of humor and a real skill at storytelling. His account of Tearlach's first hunt made her laugh several times. She was sorry to see him go when, before it grew too dark, he finally left for his own cabin a half mile away.

A few moments alone with a pair of bad-tempered O'Duines made her decide she had far better things to do. Tearlach clearly felt in no mood to describe what chores were expected of her, and Moira was being openly belligerent. Pleasance decided to leave them to their own poor company.

Toting her bags into the little room by the kitchen, which Tearlach had indicated was hers, Pleasance unpacked and put her clothes away in the small chest of drawers. She returned to the main room and her inhospitable hosts only long enough to get some hot water to fill the washbowl set on a table next to her narrow bed and then she indulged in a thorough sponge bath. After slipping into her nightdress she got into bed, sighing with pleasure at having a real bed to sleep in again. To her surprise sleep came quickly, and her last clear thought was the hope that plenty of rest would give her the strength to deal with the cantankerous O'Duine siblings in the days ahead.

Pleasance grimaced as Tearlach dragged her out of the cabin. It was cruel beyond words to force her out of bed so early in the morning after the long, arduous journey from Worcester. One night of sleep in a comfortable bed was not enough to help her recover. She winced as the bright sun stung her tired eyes.

"I thought breakfast would wake ye up," Tearlach

murmured as he led her to the log stable a few yards from the cabin. "Ye had best get used to these early hours."

As they walked past a pitchfork standing in a pile of hay near the wide stable doors, Pleasance indulged in a brief thought of murder. She could see herself picking up the pitchfork and sticking it in Tearlach's broad back. The thought helped her get over her spurt of anger.

"Now, listen carefully as I tell ye how to tend to the animals."

"How delightful." She warily eyed one large cud-chewing cow as they walked past the half dozen head in the stable.

He ignored her sarcasm. "I will do these chores when I am here, but when I am out hunting ye will have to see to the care of the beasts." He stroked the nose of a large roan gelding. "They are vital and should be treated as kindly as ye would treat your own kin."

He cocked one dark brow. She rolled her eyes and looked away. As he continued to tell her how to feed and water the animals, when to do it, when to let them out to pasture, when to milk the cows, and all the rest, she listened closely. He spoke to her as if she were slow of understanding, but she made no complaint. She did not like the idea of tending to the animals, but she would do her best when the time came. Her revenge for his snide remarks and condescension would be to prove him embarrassingly wrong in his poor judgment of her.

Next he took her on a tour of his land which was within a comfortable walking distance of the house. They tramped over the field he was clearing for new crops next spring, then passed through the nearly mature apple orchard he had planted on land stretching out behind the cabin. When they returned through the kitchen garden, she sat on a water keg near the back door as he identified each plant and explained when each herb and vegetable should be harvested.

She assumed that was the end of it, but he led her back into the cabin. There, he described each and every chore she was expected to do—from breadmaking to candlemaking. Pleasance inwardly sighed when Moira joined them. The smirk on the girl's face only aggravated Pleasance's rising temper.

"Is that all of it then?" she asked a little testily when Tearlach finished explaining how to use the butter churn.

He saw the anger glittering in her eyes and almost smiled. Within moments of the start of his litany of instructions, he had known he was irritating her. He wondered how long he could keep it up before she lost her admirable control on her temper.

"Nay, not all. Now we will travel to Durham, a town just down the road. I need a few supplies and 'tis time ye kenned what and who is in these hills around us." He started out the door. "We willnae be long, Moira."

"Cannae I come?" Moira asked.

"Not this time, lass."

"Ye cannae leave me here all alone."

He grimaced then waved toward the door. "Saddle your horse then." He glanced at Pleasance as he started out of the door. "Coming, Mistress Dunstan?"

Pleasance gritted her teeth and followed him out of the cabin, waiting on the large veranda as he and Moira went to get the horses. She muttered a curse when he led only one saddled horse out of the stable. He mounted, ambled up to her, and held out his hand.

"I know you have more than two horses," she said.

"Aye, but I dinnae see the need to tire out two just for a wee ride to town."

"I can ride with Moira then."

"Nay, her mount doesnae take weel to strangers on its back."

She suspected that was not the truth, but did not question him further as he helped her mount behind him. He simply wanted to force her into intimate proximity with him. At the moment, however, he looked to be far better company than the scowling Moira, and Pleasance knew that arguing would only reveal how much she was trying to avoid being close to him.

As they rode along, a pouting Moira trotting her horse behind them, Pleasance breathed deeply of the fresh forest air. It was easy to see why Tearlach wanted to live in such a sparsely settled area. If a person was strong enough to face the hard work and danger, the reward was to be surrounded by the full bounty of nature's beauty. She found herself hoping that the area did not become too heavily settled.

Only one cabin stood between Tearlach's land and the town. Tearlach told her that the cabin belonged to Mary and Henry Peterson, but there was no one in sight. Pleasance was a little relieved. She was not looking forward to explaining her presence there.

Once in town, she stood quietly with Moira as Tearlach left their mounts with the blacksmith. Durham was a small village with only a few buildings. Next to the blacksmith's stable was an inn and tavern. A little farther on was a large trading post and general store. Across the street was a cooper's shop with the man's barrels on display outside his door. Another inn lay just beyond that. There were several buildings, of both logs and framework, which showed no clear visible signs of business. At the far western edge of the rutted dirt road a new building was going up; the framing strongly suggested it would be a church. The little village was on the brink of growth. Since it was one of the few settlements on the main road into the frontier, she was not really surprised.

As she, Moira, and Tearlach made their way to the general store, Pleasance found herself subtly pushed behind Tearlach and Moira. The way the girl glanced back at her was enough to tell Pleasance that the separation was intentional on Moira's part. She began to understand Moira's animosity. The girl feared being set aside. She was protecting her territory.

Inside the general store, Tearlach tugged Pleasance and Moira over to a long table where bolts of cloth were on display. "I want ye to pick out something to make Moira a few pretty dresses."

"After I tend the livestock, cook the food, scrub the floors, harvest the garden, make candles, and chop wood," Pleasance said.

"Aye, after all that, though I didnae ask ye to chop wood."

"Obviously an oversight. How many dresses do you want for her?"

"I dinnae ken. Get enough for what ye think she will need." He started to move away. "I will be over here talking to Ben Tucker as he fills my order."

"He did not even ask if I can sew."

"Can ye?" asked Moira.

"I can, and very well too, if I may be so immodest."

Pleasance looked Moira over carefully to judge the slender girl's size, then began to inspect the bolts of cloth. Moira dutifully stood still as Pleasance held various lengths of cloth against her to see how well the color suited the girl. Evidently Moira was willing to briefly set aside her animosity for the sake of a few new dresses. Pleasance was just about to take her choices to Tearlach when three women stepped up to her. The tight, prim looks on their faces made her wary.

"You are Master O'Duine's new servant?" the tallest of the three women asked.

As she hugged the bolts of cloth a little tighter, Pleasance nodded. "My name is Pleasance Dunstan."

"I am Martha Teasdale, this is Elizabeth Chadwick, and this is Charlotte Holmes," she said, indicating the shorter, plumper women on her right and left respectively.

"I am pleased to meet you." She noticed that all three women kept glancing nervously toward Moira. "You know Moira O'Duine, of course."

"Aye, we know the child. I wonder if *you* do."

"I beg your pardon?"

"She is a witch," Elizabeth Chadwick hissed, fidgeting with the lace on the sleeves of her too snug gown.

"Do not be so foolish," Pleasance said, unable to keep the tartness from her voice.

"Foolish?" Martha straightened her bony shoulders. "'Tis not foolishness. We have proof that the girl spelled Truth MacGovern's cow just as she had threatened to do."

"Did it grow another head?"

"You mock me. The cow died. It had been strong and healthy for twenty-odd years, then suddenly dropped dead in the pasture." She pointed a long finger at Moira. "It died the very day this child cursed it." Martha's two companions nodded vigorously in agreement.

"Twenty-odd years? The cow died of old age. 'Tis just coincidence that this obstinate child spoke against it on the very day it decided to die."

"You should take heed of Martha's warning," said Elizabeth, cringing closer to Martha when Moira took a step toward her.

"Martha's warning is pure codswallop." Pleasance was unable to hide her anger. "You feed the child's sense of importance by believing her fantasies. I suggest you find something to keep yourselves busy. Such tongue-wagging results from having too much idle time."

It did not surprise her when all three women looked at her with openmouthed outrage before marching out of the store. She sighed and shook her head. Moira was staring at her in some surprise.

"You are treading a very rocky path with all this talk of spells, Moira."

"They are stupid women. No one will listen to them."

"Moira, you will not win their respect or friendship by playing upon their superstitions."

"Ye dinnae ken anything about it," Moira snapped.

Pleasance muttered a curse when the girl strode away, hurrying to join her brother. It was going to be difficult to make Moira see the error of her ways, but Pleasance knew she would try. The games the girl was playing were dangerous ones, and she had to be stopped. Still pondering how to accomplish that, Pleasance took the cloth she had chosen over to the counter.

Tearlach took a deep breath as they rode back to the cabin an hour later. "Ye cannae find this beauty in Worcester, Pleasance."

"Nay, that is true." Pleasance tried to imagine how it would look when the leaves began to turn in the approaching fall. "'Tis very lovely."

"Aye, and it isnae crowded. Ye willnae find your teas and balls out here. Ye will be doing honest work now, not frittering away the hours in idle gossip."

"You have a very low opinion of me, Master Tearlach. I grow weary of it and I do not know why you should think such things about me."

"Come now, I ken verra weel what ye are."

"You know nothing about me."

"Nay? Ye are the daughter of a rich merchant, a pampered creature used to idleness and gossip. And ye are English, one of a people who have never tried to hide their contempt for others. The Scots and, the English may share a king, but you English have always considered us beneath your notice."

Pleasance leaned away from him and studied his broad, stiff back. "I am not English, Master O'Duine. I was born and raised here. I am a Colonial. Those from England treat me little better than you claim they do the Scots. It appears that you have judged me without cause or a hearing."

"Have I now."

"You presume to know all about me, yet you know nothing."

"Then ye shall have to tell me all about yourself." When a full minute passed and she said nothing, he prodded, "Well, I am listening."

"Nay, I do not believe you are."

He looked over his shoulder at her. "What do ye mean?"

"You have already made up your mind about me. Words will not be enough to change it. Considering your low opinion of me, you would probably think I was lying. So, I shall not try to change your stubborn attitude with words. Nay, Master O'Duine, I intend to *show* you just how wrong you are about me."

Tearlach's mouth curved in a smile. "I accept the challenge."

As he turned away, Pleasance grimaced at his back. She prayed she could live up to her lofty promise.

"I refuse to stay here with ye."

Pleasance paused briefly in kneading bread dough on the kitchen table to look at Moira. In the week since her arrival she had reached the conclusion that the girl had only two expressions—sullen and angry. The latter twisted the child's pretty face now. Pleasance hid her own anger. Moira's troubles would not be cured with a display of temper, she was sure of it.

"Fine." She returned to kneading.

"What?"

"I said fine. Where will you go?"

"I will camp outside this cabin until Tearlach returns ye to Worcester. I will put a spell on ye."

"So you keep threatening."

"I put one on Truth MacGovern's cow."

"Truth MacGovern's cow died of old age."

Pleasance sighed as she recalled the unpleasant confrontation six days ago in Durham, a confrontation which had thrust her firmly into the middle of the O'Duines' troubled lives just one day after she had arrived. Moira clearly had many of the people in the area believing she was a witch. The girl did have an unsettling insight, but it was hardly sorcery. Pleasance was surprised anyone still believed in such things or would allow a troubled, angry little girl to frighten them so.

"Moira, I am not trying to take your brother away."

"Ye couldnae do that if ye tried."

"Nay, for he loves you."

"Aye, he does, and I will get him to make ye leave. Ye wait. Ye just wait." Moira stomped away.

"Best take plenty of blankets, for the nights grow chill."

A moment later Pleasance heard the cabin door slam shut. As always, Moira responded to Pleasance's attempts to reach out to her with anger. She hurried to finish her bread. To some extent Tearlach allowed her a free hand with Moira. There were times, however, when he felt compelled to speak out. Pleasance had a strong suspicion that this would be one of those times. She did not wish to be elbow-deep in bread dough when the confrontation came.

Fifteen minutes later, the shuddering bang as the heavy door was flung open made her jump. Clearly this time Tearlach was not confused or merely annoyed, he was furious. She hurriedly finished washing her hands and dried them.

All the while she listened carefully to the thud of Tearlach
boots as he strode toward her. When she finally turned
face him, he was coming to a halt a few inches away fro
her. She inwardly winced when she saw his furious face.

"What the hell are ye playing at, throwing Moira out
her own home?"

"Did she say that?"

A little taken aback by her calm, Tearlach frowne
"Weel, nay, not exactly. She informed me she is going
sleep outside because of ye. 'Tis much the same."

"Nay, 'tis *not.* much the same, although Moira would li
you to think so. She means to stay out of the house until I lea
it. She means to force you to take me home, to choose betwee
her and me." Half smiling, Pleasance added, "She also inten
to put a spell on me. An added precaution, no doubt."

"Foolish lass. I will drag the brat back in here by her ea

"Nay." The way he looked at her, as if she had lost a
good sense, made Pleasance a little less confident of h
ability to explain her reasoning. "Leave her where she is.

"Are ye mad? I have allowed ye your way, for I thoug
ye kenned what ye were about. This foolishness clear
shows ye dinnae." He began to think he had erred badly
allowing her such a free hand with Moira. "Ye cannae allo
a child to camp out alone. Aside from the threat of anima
and humans, there is the bite of fall in the air."

"True. Howsomever, I do not believe she will last the nigh

"Nay? Moira can be most stubborn."

"If you bring her back in, you might as well send me ba
to Worcester."

"Nonsense. I have no intention of giving in to her blac
mail."

"Ah, but you will be, in a way. I may still be here, but yo
will have shown her that, if she pushes hard enough, she ca
force you to countermand me. She will then keep pushing ju

so hard until nothing I do or say carries any weight. Unless she gives up this scheme on her own, she will win. Perhaps not as resoundingly as she would like, but she will win."

Tearlach considered her words and sighed. "Ye may be right. Nevertheless, I cannae leave a child outside at night, alone and unguarded."

"I did not say she should be left unguarded. I am sure we can think of a way to keep a close watch on her without her knowing it. As I said, I doubt she will last a full night."

"I dinnae understand what has come over the child. She has never been so difficult."

"She is angry. Angry children tend to lash out. Moira has a lot of anger in her, although she might not be able to tell you at what or at whom. She is also jealous."

"Jealous? Of what?"

"Moira feels an outcast with everyone but you and Jake. You have seen how the people in the village treat her, just as I did the day you took me to town. She sees me as a threat. She fears that I will come between you."

Tearlach was not sure Pleasance was right but he did not argue. From the beginning she had seemed to understand Moira, to know how the child felt and thought. Since a lot of what she said made perfect sense, and he knew of a way to keep a close eye on Moira while she slept outside, he decided it was a small risk to trust Pleasance's judgment in the matter. Moira might well accept defeat when her grand gesture failed to gain anything. Then there might be some peace in his house again.

His attention turned fully to Pleasance. The hunger he felt for her ate away at him night and day, and his subtle attempts to seduce her did not seem to be getting him any closer to the prize he sought. Perhaps it was time for a less subtle approach.

He edged closer to Pleasance. Although she wore a simple,

tightly laced bodice and a skirt of a dull blue color, he still found her very attractive. She had done her hair in one long thick braid that hung down her back, not hidden by the lacy mobcap she wore. He took the thick braid in his hand.

Pleasance tensed. Tearlach was at it again. The light brushing of his body against hers, the brief caresses of her hair, and the way he constantly touched her—he had but one purpose in mind. What truly annoyed her was that she was succumbing to his seduction. It had been going on since they arrived at the cabin, perhaps even before that, if her memory did not serve her false. There had been a few times during their journey when she had seriously questioned the need for them to share a bed. Each day she weakened just a little more. A faint smile from him could make her knees weak. She was disgusted with herself.

"Well, now that we have that problem settled, I best get back to my work." She attempted to move away from him, but his hand on her hair held her in place. "I am really quite busy. I am making bread."

"Ah, that explains the spot of flour upon your nose." He gently rubbed it off, then moved his hand to her cheek, softly tracing the delicate bone structure. "I hadnae expected ye to be so domesticated, Pleasance Dunstan."

There was the hint of insult in his words, but she ignored it as she had so many other times. That was not important at the moment. What was important was the fact that she was letting him tug her into his arms. In fact, she thought with additional self-disgust, she was positively melting in his embrace. She did not need the way she trembled as his hand traced her spine, then came to rest at the small of her back to tell her that in his arms was a dangerous place to be. It was dangerous to her heart, to her morals, and, she mused as she stared into his darkening gray eyes, to her very sanity.

Tearlach kissed her forehead, then each cheek, and felt

her sigh. She was soft and pliable in his arms. As her eyes turned a rich warm blue and grew heavy lidded he read desire in them. Her full lips were moist and slightly parted. No man should be expected to resist such temptation.

When his mouth brushed her lips, Pleasance briefly tensed, knowing she should immediately and forcefully resist. But as his mouth continued to play over hers, good sense was swept away by mind-clouding sensation. Her lips tingled and the feeling soon spread to the rest of her. His arm tightened around her waist, and he lifted her off the ground, pressing for a fuller, deeper kiss. What thoughts of resistance tickled the corners of her mind were abruptly dissipated. She flung her arms around his neck and surrendered.

A groan escaped Tearlach when she opened her lips to welcome the probing of his tongue. She was sweet and warm. He felt her arms tighten around his neck and pressed her body even closer to his. He wanted to devour her.

"I kenned it. I kenned it all along. That is why ye brought her here."

Moira's voice cut through the haze of desire that enveloped them. Despite the tremors rippling through his arms, Tearlach managed to set Pleasance away from him with some grace. As he fought the urge to strangle his sister.

Pleasance's desire was swept aside by embarrassment, then a burgeoning shock heavily laced with anger. Tearlach made no move to immediately and pointedly deny Moira's assumption. She considered how steadily he had been working at his gentle seduction of her.

"Is Moira right?" Pleasance demanded.

Frustration twisting his insides, Tearlach tried not to give in to his anger. The way Pleasance was looking at him, as if he had just crawled out from under a rock, fractured what little strength he had to remain calm. She had just been clinging to him like a limpet, turning to living fire in his

arms. She had no right to look at him now as if all the f
should be thrown at his feet, as if he had been trying to t
her out of something she had not wanted to give.

"Not completely. I needed someone to help care
Moira. Howbeit, I see no harm in gaining an extra ben
or two from the arrangement."

A sharp pain tore through Pleasance as she came to
cold realization that she was an even bigger fool than
had suspected. She had let herself think that his passion
stirred by something deeper than mere lust. His wo
showed her how stupid she had been. That hurt was
lowed by blind fury. She grabbed the closest thing at ha
a cast-iron skillet, and swung it at him.

Ducking barely in time to avoid being smashed in
head, Tearlach backed away as she swung at him aga
"What is the meaning of this display of righteous fury
made no protest when I kissed ye. Fact is, I have ne'er h
a woman who grew so warm so fast."

She gave an inarticulate sound of rage and swung at l
again. The curse he bellowed when she hit his arm was
music to her ears. A small part of her mind was aware t
Moira was standing by the door, openmouthed and wi
eyed, but Pleasance was too furious with Tearlach to c
what the girl saw or heard.

"You swine! You worm! You slug! I wish you wo
return to whatever hell pit you oozed out of." She cried
in frustration when she caught him, backed up again
wall, only to have him grasp her wrist and wrench the s
let out of her hand, tossing it out of her reach.

"That wasnae what ye were wishing but a moment a
when ye were moaning softly in my arms."

She tried to kick him, but he held her by the wrists
kept her at arm's length. "You heartless pig. Did you th
you had not already done enough to hurt me?"

"Hurt ye? I but kissed ye, ye mad woman."

"With all the intention of making me your whore. That is what game you played. That is the game ye have played from the moment we left Worcester." Since she had ceased trying to kick him, his grip had loosened and she yanked herself free of his hold. "You have branded me a thief in my town, caused me to be cast out by my own family—"

"I had naught to do with that. Ye cannae lay the blame for that at my door."

"Mayhaps not fully, but you are far from free of blame and well you know it. If not for your foolish games, I would not have seen the truth of what I had only suspected on my darkest days—that my own family cared not a jot for me. I could have continued in blissful ignorance if you had not sought to soothe your poor wounded pride or whatever it was that ailed you.

"Now, as if that is not a big enough stick to beat me with," she continued, "you try to steal what few scraps of honor I have managed to cling to. You play the libertine with me, try to make me your indentured light-skirt. That will never happen. Never—do you hear me? Best you find some other fool to warm your sheets, for I will not crawl between them."

Seeing her about to slip right through his fingers revived the anger Tearlach had begun to get under control. "Just moments ago ye didnae care if I even offered ye a bed. I could have had ye upon the chopping block." He did not have to see how all the color fled her face to know that his words had not only been unnecessarily cruel but very stupid as well.

Hissing a curse, Pleasance swung one small, tight fist at Tearlach's stubborn jaw and coldly watched him slam up against the wall, as much in surprise as from pain. "You can go straight to hell, Tearlach O'Duine." She raced to her chamber and bolted the door. She needed to be alone, to escape him before he continued to tear at her heart and pride with his cruel words.

Even as Tearlach pondered the wisdom of going after her, he sensed Moira standing at his side. He flushed slightly as he realized what she had heard and warily met her stare. For the first time in a long while Moira looked neither sullen nor angry, but for the life of him, he could not read what emotion did sit upon her small face.

"Did ye really do all that to her?" Moira asked.

"She twists the truth some."

"But I was right—her family really did turn their backs on her."

"Aye. They threw her to the wolves without pausing to blink." He frowned when Moira turned and walked out of the cabin, only to watch in growing surprise when she returned a moment later with the blankets and food she had intended to make camp with. "This fight with Pleasance doesnae mean I will be sending her back to Worcester," he said.

"I ken it."

"Yet ye are giving up your scheme to sleep outside."

"Aye. One thing that troubled me about Pleasance was that she seemed to ken all about me, could see into my verra heart. I hated that. I truly did. Why should she ken what I feel? Now I see why she could. She kens how it feels to be shunned. Aye, and to live amongst folk who treat ye coldly no matter how hard ye try to please them."

After watching Moira take her things back to her room, Tearlach took one last long look at Pleasance's door, then cursed and went outside to finish fixing the paddock fence. He had stepped wrong and had said all the wrong words. It would take more than a few calming gestures to soothe her now. In fact, he thought crossly, he had probably insured that

Pleasance Dunstan would stay as cold toward him as the worst winter's day for many months to come.

It took a long time for Pleasance to put aside her hurt and anger, an anger directed at herself as well as at Tearlach. His ploy had been despicable, but she had been as ready to fall for it as ripe fruit was to drop from the tree. As she peeked out the door to be sure he was gone, then returned to her work, she vowed that such a thing would never happen again. No matter how much she wanted to learn what it meant to be a woman in his arms, she would hold firm to her innocence. She would not be the plaything Tearlach O'Duine wished to make of her.

When, a few moments later, Moira appeared and quietly began to work at her side, Pleasance hid her surprise. It seemed that something in the set-to she had had with Tearlach had caused Moira to change her mind about her. Pleasance was delighted. If only this small success could be enough to ease the hurt and sadness that choked her heart.

Chapter Six

Tearlach stepped up behind Pleasance and smoothed his big hand down her back to rest it on her waist. Her knife faltered as she continued to chop carrots for the stew she was making. She briefly savored the idea of sticking the blade in him. It had been exactly twelve days since their previous argument. She had had three days of peace during which he never touched her, even barely spoke to her. Then he had started his seduction of her all over again. The constant touching, even the occasional stolen kisses on the back of her neck, her cheek, and on the hollow by her ear were driving her to distraction. He always approached her when, as now, she was busy and could not easily elude him. When she did lose her temper and try to confront him, he quickly fled. The coward, she thought.

"Ye are proving to be a fine cook, Pleasance. Where did ye learn?" He touched a kiss to the top of her head.

"In the kitchens at home. I was often sent to help the cook." She tensed when he slid his hand down to lightly caress her hip. "You are in danger of losing those fingers, Master O'Duine." She whirled to confront him, only to find herself neatly pinned against the table.

Tearlach easily took the paring knife from her hand and

tossed it on the table before he tugged her into his arms. "How ye do squirm, wee Pleasance."

She knew it was useless, but she continued to try to wriggle free. "I but try to escape a blackguard."

"This blackguard is leaving in the morning."

She was so startled by the abrupt announcement she stilled and stared at him. "Leave? To go where?"

"Hunting. 'Twill be a short trip—about a week."

"Why do you keep hunting? You have enough land cleared to plant a crop."

"'Tis too late in the year to plant. And I like the hunting. 'Tisnae often that a mon can do what he likes and make some profit at it. I dinnae love it enough to travel too far from home, which I shall have to do soon, as the game around here is growing scarce. For now, though, I can still wander through my hills here and 'tis a pleasure, a pure pleasure." He pressed her closer to him. "There is only one thing I could take more pleasure in."

Lulled by his talk and by the way he rubbed her back with his big hands, she was slow to guess his intentions. Just as she realized what they were, he covered her mouth with his and kissed away all her resistance. She curled her arms around his neck and heard herself moan softly as he stroked the inside of her mouth with his tongue. The way he smoothed his hands up and down her sides soon had her trembling.

She tilted her head back, allowing him free access to her throat. Her eyes closed as she savored the hot, moist touch of his lips. It was not until his hand slid up her ribs to cup her breast that she shook free of passion's tight grip. At first the intimate caress sent waves of heat roiling through her, but the sensation was so new, so intense, that it made her sharply aware of how far their intimacy had progressed. Pleasance gave an incoherent cry of rage and twisted free of a startled Tearlach's loosened grip. Unable to articulate her feelings, and a little afraid of finding herself back in his arms, she gave him one fulminating glare and fled.

Once safe in her room, she sagged against the rough plank door. It took several deep breaths before she could calm herself. She could not believe she had let his lovemaking go so far. It was clear that Tearlach was very close to getting her into his bed. Perhaps it was a good thing the man was leaving in the morning after all. She needed time to shore up her crumbling defenses.

She heard the cabin door shut and cautiously left her room. When she saw that he was gone, she breathed a sigh of relief and returned to preparing the venison stew. Pleasance knew it had been cowardly to run away, but it would have been stupid to stay. The man swept away her resistance with one kiss. She needed to put distance between them to regain some common sense. As she hefted the iron stewpot onto the hook over the kitchen fire, Pleasance decided that a little cowardice was not such a bad thing at times.

As she tidied up the kitchen area, she looked around for another chore. There was nothing else to do in the cabin for the moment, which meant she had to tend to the animals. She wished she had not agreed to it when Tearlach had asked her at breakfast, but since he had planned to spend the day clearing his field, she had not been able to refuse. He had seen to them after breakfast, but now it was her turn and she dreaded it, for it was not something she did well.

"Cease this dithering, Pleasance," she scolded herself as she started out of the cabin. "They are only dumb animals."

Her brief bravado faded quickly as she opened the barn door, retrieved the stick she had seen Tearlach use to herd the animals and entered the enclosed pasture where they were grazing. From where she stood she could see Moira and Tearlach working together to clear the field of the rocks that seemed to be in endless supply, using them to build a low encircling wall. Tearlach was shirtless, his dark skin looking warm and inviting. Pleasance felt rooted to the spot as she watched him heft up a large stone, take it to the growing rock wall, and set it into place. She thought it a little curious that simply looking at him without his shirt on should make her feel so flushed and breathless.

Then suddenly he was looking at her. Pleasance hastily turned away, only to come face-to-face with Tearlach's horse. She screeched in surprise and stepped back so quickly that she stumbled. She grabbed one of the split rails to keep from falling, but a huge splinter embedded itself in her palm. She set the herding stick aside and worked the splinter out, cursing softly for she knew Tearlach had seen her bungling.

Once the splinter was out, she picked up the stick and started to herd the animals back into the stable. The horses gave her no trouble, but the cows proved obstinate. Her nervousness over being among so many large animals began to fade and irritation took its place. One cow in particular proved to be very obstinate. She finally ignored it, shooed the rest of the animals into their stalls, and went back for the stray cow.

"Now, Mistress Cow," she said as she approached the cud-chewing animal, "you will get into your stall so I can get the cursed milking done." She poked the cow with the stick, but the animal simply looked at her.

Pleasance moved to grab the cow by its rope collar, only to fall back with a screech of alarm when the animal butted her with its head. She quelled her sudden fright, straightened her shoulders, and approached the cow again. When the animal started to move toward her, she lost courage and began to back up. The cow advanced faster, her head lowered. Pleasance turned, hiked up her skirts, and ran. She was not sure what a cow could do to her, but she had no inclination to find out.

A quick glance over her shoulder showed her that the cow was indeed chasing her—and gaining on her. She bolted out of the pasture, realized she did not have time to close the big gate on the fence, and headed into the stable. There was only one open stall and she dashed into it, slamming the door behind her. The cow halted and thrust its head toward her. Pleasance moved out of its reach just as Moira and Tearlach burst into the stable. She groaned, realizing that they had seen the whole fiasco. When Tearlach started to chuckle, she wanted to slap the expression off his face.

"Weel, ye got the obstinate beastie to the stall, lass, but the idea is to put *her* in it, not you."

"How very astute of you, Master O'Duine." She scowled at him when he pressed his lips together tightly. "I believe laughing would be very illadvised," she warned.

"I will wait until I get back out into the field."

"That would be wise. Now, do you think you can get this murderous beast away from me?"

He grabbed the cow by the rope collar and pulled it away from the stall so that Pleasance could get free. As soon as she had scrambled out, he dragged the stubborn cow in and latched the door. He leaned against the wooden planking, crossed his arms over his chest, and watched as Pleasance spent a great deal of time straightening her skirts. When she finally glanced up at him, he grinned, still stoutly resisting the urge to chuckle.

"Weel, there ye be, lassie," he said. "The beast is caged and ready to milk."

"Thank you kindly."

"Ye should have told me that ye didnae ken how to handle the animals."

"I know how to handle horses, not unreasonable, vicious cows."

"Ye do ken how to milk these vicious beasts?"

"Of course."

"Then we will leave ye to it. Come along, Moira," he said as he started out of the barn.

"If ye dinnae mind, Tearlach, I think I would rather stay here and help Pleasance," Moira replied. "'Tis a lot less work milking cows and ye have to admit I cannae lift the larger rocks anyway."

"Fine then. Give me a holler when dinner is ready."

The moment Tearlach was gone, Moira put her hands on her hips and grinned at Pleasance. "Tsk, tsk. Such a liar. Ye dinnae ken a thing about milking, do ye?"

"I have seen it done once or twice. I am sure I could have figured it out." Pleasance stepped toward the stall, only to have the cow lower her head again.

"Ye can do the feeding and watering and I will do the milking," Moira offered. "When I get to the last cow, ye can join me if ye want to." She picked up the milk bucket and the stool. "Let me in there."

Even as Pleasance opened the stall, she asked, "Is it safe?"

"Aye, she kens who I am."

Pleasance nodded and, once assured that the cow was not going to attack Moira, moved to feed and water the livestock. She was just finishing when Moira started to milk the last cow. Pleasance found another three-legged stool and cautiously sat down next to the girl. Although she caught on to the process of milking quickly, she did not really like it. Such proximity to a large animal made her nervous.

"Ye really dinnae like this, do ye?" asked Moira.

"Nay, but I can do it."

"Aye, ye can, but ye dinnae have to. We can make a trade."

"But then your brother will think I could not do it, or even that I made you do it."

"Nay, and dinnae forget, he leaves to go hunting in the morning. By the time he returns, he will have forgotten all of this and just think that we divided up the chores. After all, ye willnae be idle."

"True." As Pleasance dickered with Moira about how to divide up the chores, she tried hard not to think about the fact that, as of dawn on the morrow, she and Moira would be on their own.

"I tell you, that child is a witch." Mary Peterson stabbed a long bony finger toward a bristling Moira.

"Point that finger at me again, ye old crone, and I will change it into a snake."

"That is enough, Moira." Pleasance yanked a silent but glaring Moira behind her back and turned her full attention to Mary Peterson.

She supposed it had been foolish to think that getting Moira to stop declaring herself a witch would stop people from believing she was one. It had been nearly a month since Moira had sworn to stop saying it, but it had made no real difference. Pleasance almost wished she had not come to the general store until Tearlach returned, but he had been gone for nearly two weeks and she needed a few supplies.

Although she was meeting people without Tearlach looming nearby, it was not always in the cordial manner she had hoped for. The aging Mary Peterson was the third person to complain about Moira's spells and wildness. For the first time in the five weeks since her arrival, Pleasance actually wished Tearlach was around. People would not dare cast aspersions on Moira in his presence.

"Moira is no witch, Mistress Peterson." She wondered how many times she would have to say that. "Has she ever accomplished one of her threats?" Inwardly nodding at the woman's arrested expression, Pleasance wondered a little crossly why none of Moira's accusers had the wit to see the truth for themselves. "You have let her play games with you. She is naught but a child."

"I am nearly thirteen," Moira grumbled.

"Exactly."

"She sees things," Mary Peterson said.

"Pardon, Mistress Peterson?" asked Pleasance.

"She sees things little girls should never see. And understands things she should not understand."

Pleasance took pity on the woman as she floundered to explain what troubled her. "I understand what you mean, Mistress Peterson. 'Tis intuition, that is all. We all have it. That prickle of warning when danger lurks close at hand? Moira's is but a little keener than most people's. Now, it has been most pleasant to meet you, but I must get back to the cabin. Master O'Duine is due to return from trapping any day now, and I have a great deal of work to finish."

"For Master O'Duine?"

"Aye, and for Moira."

"Master O'Duine is a very handsome man and he is unmarried."

"True."

"Does he stay in the cabin with you?"

"'Tis his cabin."

After enduring a few more far from subtle questions and remarks from Mistress Peterson, Pleasance and Moira managed to slip away. They headed straight to the wagon. Getting to know Tearlach's neighbors and friends was clearly something Pleasance would have to do in bits—very small bits—until a few things were clarified. If she was not sorting out some trouble concerning Moira, she was trying to adroitly evade questions concerning the relationship between herself and Tearlach.

It would serve them well and proper if I told them the truth, she thought sourly as she climbed into the cart and urged the horse into a quick trot. All that existed between her and Tearlach was a strange form of madness. He had resumed his attempts to seduce her within days of their violent confrontation. To her disgust, the revelation of his true intention to merely bed her had not given her the strength to completely resist him. She had even found herself kissing him back on the night before he had left on his hunting trip. Fortunately good sense had returned to her and she had fled to the safety of her room.

She was doing a lot of that lately. He approached. She weakened, He drew closer. She pushed him away. He got angry. She got angry too and then ran. *Madness* was the only word for it.

"That nosy old corbie—"

"Corbie?" Pleasance asked.

"A crow, a raven. That nosy old crow was trying to find out if ye were bedding down with Tearlach," Moira said, abruptly breaking the silence they had maintained on the ride back to the cabin. She hopped down to help Pleasance put away the cart and horse.

"Moira!" Pleasance blushed, then inwardly scolded herself for such sensitivity. "You should not speak of such things."

"Why? I ken all about them. It willnae be so very long before I am a woman. I will turn thirteen soon." Moira assisted Pleasance in taking their purchases from the cart and fell into step beside her as they walked from the small stable to the cabin.

"Let us compromise. Aye, talk about the things you know, but be very wary of whom you talk to."

"Ah. That is a lesson in good manners, is it?"

"Aye, partly. 'Tis also a lesson in how to keep hold of your good name. I fear a woman can never speak of such things or those who hear her think that she has learned about them by doing them."

"That seems most unfair. I can speak of Italy and Spain yet have never seen either place."

Pleasance urged Moira inside the cabin. "There is no way to explain such things. No way that makes sense, leastwise. 'Tis one of those rules you obey because the cost of fighting it is too high."

"Too high?" Moira hurried to help Pleasance put away their few purchases so that they could begin preparing their evening meal.

"Aye, much too high. A woman's good name is of great value. Once lost, 'tis hard to gain it back. Most times 'tis lost forever. Fair or not, there it is. If a woman loses her good name, she becomes shunned by most and may never find a husband. Do you understand what I am telling you?"

"Some. Tearlach is taking away your good name. That is why that old corbie felt she could ask ye those rude questions."

"I think Mary Peterson simply likes to ask questions. As far as my good name is concerned, my sister Letitia damaged it far beyond repair before I even came here. She met men alone at the inn in town and said she was me." Pleasance did not tell Moira that the only man she was sure Letitia had met was Tearlach. "Then there were the accusations and trial which brought me here. I doubt I have a shred of a good name left to me. Enough of this. 'Tis far past time for us to begin preparing our meal."

"Do ye think Tearlach will be home to eat this one?"

"Who can say, Moira? Now, do not look so downcast. I am certain your brother is fine."

Pleasance hoped she sounded more confident than she felt. Tearlach had said he would be gone for only a week. He had now been gone for eleven days. Moira had begun to worry on the eighth day. Pleasance ruefully admitted that she had begun to worry on the ninth. The very fact that Moira was concerned added to her own fear; clearly Tearlach was not one to make a habit of tardiness.

She spent the evening trying to keep Moira's mind off Tearlach's continued absence. It was a relief when the girl finally went to bed. After securing the cabin for the night, Pleasance sought out her own bed. She hoped she would be able to sleep. It had become harder and harder the longer Tearlach stayed away.

It seemed that she had only just shut her eyes when someone was shaking her awake. It was a moment before she recognized a pale Moira leaning over her, a flickering candle in her hand. Pleasance tried to shake sleep's grip from her mind, for the child looked very upset.

"What ails you, Moira? Are you sickening with something?" she asked as she struggled to sit up.

"'Tis Tearlach."

"He has returned? I heard nothing." Pleasance tried to find her robe in the darkness.

"Nay, something is wrong. Terribly wrong. I feel it"

Having already had some hint of Moira's strong intuition, Pleasance felt her alarm grow, but she fought to keep her voice calm. "Now, Moira, I have begged you not to worry. I know 'tis hard, but Tearlach is—"

"Please. Please, Pleasance. I feel it strongly. I feel it so very strongly."

"Child, what can we do even if your feelings are right? We do not even know where he is."

"Cannae we look about outside? Just around the cabin? Please? Just a quick wee look?"

Although she knew she ought to say no, Pleasance nodded. Moira was nearly frantic. It would be dangerous to go outside at night, but Pleasance felt certain that Moira would do it with or without her. It would be far better if she and Moira went together.

They threw their outer clothes on over their nightdresses. Pleasance had Moira carry the lantern while she carried the heavy musket. They cautiously slipped out of the cabin. In an ever widening circle they searched the surrounding area. Pleasance was just about to put an end to the search when the soft whinny of a horse broke the quiet of the night. She and Moira tensed with fear and anticipation.

"What the blazes are ye two fools doing out in the middle of the night?" rasped a voice that was both recognizable and unfamiliar.

"Tearlach?" Moira whispered. "Is that ye out there?"

"Aye."

The moment the rider appeared out of the shadows, Moira and Pleasance ran to him. Immediately Pleasance knew that something was terribly wrong. He was having difficulty simply staying in the saddle.

"Is something amiss?" Even in the dim light of the lantern Moira held up, Pleasance could see how white he was.

"A bear had a wee nibble of me." Tearlach struggled to loosen his frozen grip on the reins.

"Oh, dear God. Badly?"

"Bad enough."

"Can you make it to your bed if Moira and I help you?"

"Aye. Aye, I believe so."

After handing Moira the rifle, Pleasance helped Tearlach dismount. With her arm about his trim waist and his arm draped over her shoulders, she began to help him up the porch steps, while Moira hurried to see to the horse. It took only a few steps before he was leaning on her heavily. By the time Pleasance reached the base of the steps to the loft, she feared she would never get the man to the top of them. She was certain that she was the only reason he was still upright.

At that moment Moira returned. The girl barred the door and hurried over to help Pleasance. Between the two of them they managed to get Tearlach to his room and onto his bed.

He was barely conscious as they tended him. Moira collected hot water, bandages, and other essentials to treat him while Pleasance fought to get him out of his clothes. When his wounds were fully revealed she had to fight for calm. The bear's huge claws had left a deep gouge across Tearlach's chest and there were several smaller ones on his arms, shoulders, and back. She tore off the dirty, blood-encrusted strips with which he had bandaged himself. That roused him a little even as Moira returned to the room with everything Pleasance had requested.

"Can ye do anything to fix this mess?" he asked in a raspy whisper as he stared up at Pleasance. "Do ye even ken what ye must do?"

"Aye. My brother and some of his friends have appeared with wounds they wished to have tended in the utmost secrecy. I was forced to learn some doctoring skills."

"Ah, aye. That custom runner's lantern ye had. I recall it now. Moira, I need some brandy."

Pleasance frowned as she washed her hands and Moira helped her brother drink the fiery liquid. "Are you certain you need that?"

"'Twill ease the pain."

She doubted he had enough brandy for that, but said nothing. Instead she forced all worries and fears from her mind and set to work. By the time she had cleaned and stitched all of his wounds he had fallen unconscious. She was glad to see that, although pale and wide-eyed with fear for Tearlach, Moira was holding up well enough to help. The girl proved to be an immense aid in shifting her brother's limp weight so that the bandaging could be done correctly. When she was finally finished, Pleasance poured herself a small drink of brandy, pulled a rocker to the side of his bed, and wearily sat down. After a sip of the bracing drink, she looked at Moira. The girl looked as exhausted as she felt.

"Go to bed now, Moira. There is naught left to do but wait."

"Will he be all right?"

"I think so. He has lost a lot of blood, but he is a strong man. Go to bed, child. If he takes a fever, I will be in sore need of your help, and it will be best if you are well rested. Do not fret. I will call if I have need of you."

Moira impulsively kissed Pleasance on the cheek and hurried off to bed. Pleasance turned her full attention on Tearlach. His wounds were bad, but they need not be fatal. She closed her eyes and prayed. The mere thought of him dying left her chilled to the bone and shaking with fear. She prayed with all her heart that he would recover.

By morning, a fever held Tearlach firmly in its grip. Pleasance did all she could by herself, for the sight of Tearlach fevered and delirious deeply troubled Moira. At times, however, Pleasance had to ask the girl for help. When Jake appeared and offered to lend a hand, Pleasance wept with relief. He immediately urged her to get some rest. It did not take much argument to persuade her.

The three of them worked continuously, but it was two long days and nights before Tearlach's fever finally broke. Once assured that he was on the mend, Pleasance again sought her bed. She knew she had to be well rested for what would come next. Tearlach was going to be in need of constant care, not only so that he could regain his strength, but also to ensure that he did not try to do anything too soon and thus hinder his recovery.

The moment she got into her bed her eyes closed. This time she felt no guilt about sleeping and knew that worry would not disturb the rest she needed so badly. She briefly wished that she could be at Tearlach's side when he first awoke, clear-eyed and aware, but knew that it would be best if she was not. Her emotions were too near the surface for her to face him now.

During the heart-wrenching period when he was so badly ill, weak and delirious with fever and fighting for his life, she had been forced to face a cold hard truth. It was a truth she had been battling to keep hidden from herself. She was in love with the man, deeply and perhaps a little blindly. Despite all the trouble he had caused her, despite how he intended to take advantage of her indenture to him, she had stepped beyond the bounds of good sense and fallen in love with him. It was not something she wished him to know, however, and she prayed that by the next time she faced him, she had the errant emotion well hidden.

Pleasance finally ventured in to see Tearlach late the next evening. Once Moira was settled in bed for the night and Jake had gone home, Pleasance took up her post at Tearlach's bedside. It had been agreed that for at least one more night he should be very closely watched. She had barely finished reading a poem in the small book of poetry Nathan had given her on her eighteenth birthday when she sensed that she was being watched. Cautiously, she looked up and met Tearlach's steady gaze.

"Ye learned your doctoring skills weel, lassie," he murmured.

"Thank you."

"Where is Moira?"

"In bed—asleep."

"Good. We need to talk."

"Now? You need to rest."

"I must say my piece while there is little chance of

Moira's overhearing it." He tried to sit up, but the small effort brought a wave of pain that left him awash with sweat and gasping out vile curses.

After fetching him some ale to drink and gently bathing the beads of sweat from his face, Pleasance returned to her seat. "You really must lie still or you will pull all those stitches out. They have not had time to set properly. Your wounds may not be bleeding, but they have not closed either."

"I ken it." He paused, then added, "That bear was a trap."

"Pardon? How can a bear be a trap?"

"When someone has purposely wounded the poor beast enough to madden it and then led it straight to me."

"Nay, 'tis impossible. Who would do such a thing? If naught else, the bear could easily have killed the one who hurt him. It seems a mad plan to me."

"Oh, aye, mad indeed, for 'twas a madman who thought of it—Moira's father, Lucien. I saw the man's tracks. He didnae chance staying around to see if his crazed plot had succeeded."

Pleasance was stunned. "The man who fathered Moira is still alive?"

"Aye—to my shame. In all these years I havenae been able to make him pay for his crimes. He runs free, appearing at odd times just to plague me."

"Or to try and murder you, by the looks of it."

"Aye, that too. He has tried more times than I care to count. Aye, as I have tried to kill him."

There was such hatred in Tearlach's voice that Pleasance shivered. "Is he after Moira? Is she what he is seeking?"

Tearlach was a little surprised at what sounded like honest worry in Pleasance's voice, but he hid that feeling. His surprise could insult her, and he did not want to stir up what had proven to be an impressive temper. It was important that she listen to him and listen closely.

"Nay, not truly. He kens about her and she kens about

him. She has even seen him. Once, two years ago, I finally caught him and brought him to face justice. The fool set to keep him prisoner didnae heed my warning about how sly and deadly Lucien can be. Within two days the guard was found with his throat cut and Lucien was gone."

"And you still hunt him."

"I do, and I will continue to do so until he is dead. He hunts me as well. This"—he touched the bandages on his chest—"is but the latest in a long line of attacks and counterattacks." He frowned, the simple chore of talking making him tire already. "I always thought him mad, more a beast than a mon, and I fear he grows more so."

"Mad enough to attack your home?"

"Not yet I think." He sighed. "Though I no longer feel as certain of that as I once did. Lucien avoids the settlements. To ye this area must seem sparsely peopled, but to Lucien 'tis crowded. Our game is played whenever I go hunting, whenever I enter the forest."

Then stay out of it, fool, she thought, but bit her tongue. Hunting and trapping were his livelihood, something he deeply enjoyed doing. If he allowed Lucien to take them away from him, to force him to give them up, then he would be handing him a victory of sorts. She knew no man who would easily settle for that.

She realized she was in the midst of a feud, a deadly battle between two men. Tearlach said Lucien had never come near the cabin, yet she knew he worried about it now. That was why he was telling her. He wanted her to be aware of the dangers that lurked in the untamed forest around them.

"And what do you suggest I do about this lunatic?"

"Just be wary. Ye dinnae wish to be far from others. And dinnae let anyone ye dinnae ken get too close to ye. The mon seeks me, and for eleven years that is all he has done. 'Tis just that his strikes are coming more often now. And are much more vicious." He closed his eyes, not sure he had made himself clear but too weak to continue discussing the matter. "Just be verra careful."

Once he was asleep she checked his forehead and found it cool, but her relief was not able to push aside the worries he had roused in her. She had known that dangers abounded in this part of the colony, dangers people no longer had to worry about in well-settled towns like Worcester. A lunatic and a battle to the death between two men, a battle that she and Moira could well be dragged into, had not numbered among those recognized perils. She almost wished Tearlach had not told her.

Sprawling in her chair in a most unladylike manner, she stared at the sleeping Tearlach and wondered crossly why he could not have been the common, plodding—if extremely attractive—farmer she had first imagined him to be. A simple farming life could be boring, even tedious, but it was more or less safe. Instead he tried to seduce her, left her alone for long days and nights while he went off hunting, and he indulged in a deadly feud with a madman.

Yet she must be nearly as mad as Lucien, for she could not honestly say that she wished herself back home.

"Curse all ye females! Do ye mean to leave me here to rot?"

Pleasance rolled her eyes as Tearlach's bellow echoed through the cabin. "'Tis a pleasant thought," she murmured, and grinned across the kitchen worktable at a giggling Moira. "I think that the bear gave your brother some of its bad temper." She stuck her hands in a large bowl to mix up the herbal stuffing she was preparing.

"Aye, Tearlach has been acting verra poorly." Moira added a little milk to her biscuit mix.

"True, but we should try to understand. He has recovered

enough to want to do things, but has not regained the strength to do them. And the man has been stuck in that bed for a little over a fortnight."

"Do ye hear me down there?" hollered Tearlach.

"Then again," Pleasance said, scowling toward the stairs, "one cannot be expected to be too saintly." She took a deep breath and yelled, "I suspect they can hear you in the village."

"Then why hasnae one of ye come up here? I need some water."

"I will bring it up when I am finished with my chores here." She shook her head. "His voice is strong again. 'Twill be good when the rest of him is as strong so that he can take care of himself." She started to stuff the chicken she intended to roast for dinner. "I suppose I will have to go up there when I am done with this."

"Do ye want me to go?" asked Moira.

"Nay, you have some other chores to do." Pleasance smiled crookedly. "Besides, I feel inclined to let him know just how irritating he is." They both laughed.

Pleasance had set the chicken over the fire to roast, washed her hands, and was just filling a jug with water when there was a loud thump from upstairs. Even as she set the jug down, Moira was bolting up the stairs. Pleasance quickly followed and was not surprised to see Tearlach sprawled on the floor just outside his bedroom door. Shaking her head, she helped Moira get him back into bed, then sent her to get the water while she checked to make sure Tearlach had done no damage to himself. She said nothing until Moira had brought the water and left again.

"How could you be so stupid?" she demanded even as she poured him a tankard of water and handed it to him. "Did that bear knock the sense right out of you?"

"I cannae abide just lying here," he snapped.

"Well, you had better learn to abide it. If you keep trying

to do things when you are still weak and when your wounds are so newly healed, they could break open, and then you will find your stay in this bed becoming even longer."

"It has already been too long."

"Barely fifteen days." She snatched the empty tankard back and slammed it down on the table by his bed. "I suggest you use some common sense, Master O'Duine. Your sister and I have far too much work to do to keep running up here just because you feel a touch of boredom."

"Ye are right." He shifted in his bed, wincing a little, and combed his fingers through his hair. "'Tis just that I feel I shall go mad if I must lie here idle for even one more hour."

"I believe a little madness is better than killing yourself through sheer obstinate stupidity."

"Blunt and impertinent, but true. I shall endeavor to be a better patient." He held up his right hand. "I swear to it."

"Be careful what you swear to."

"Ye dinnae think I can do it."

She started toward the door. "For a day or two, and I shall revel in that brief respite. I shall return later with your supper."

"Am I to be shut up in here—alone—again?" he yelled as she closed the door.

Pleasance laughed softly and shook her head as she went back to the kitchen. She knew he would still be impatient and irritating, but he would stay put now. That was a victory in itself.

Pleasance worked the butter churn with vigor and wished she was pounding Tearlach. His stitches were out and his strength was rapidly returning. It had taken nearly a month, but she knew that it had been a speedy recovery considering the severity of his wounds. She should be overjoyed that the man she loved would fully recover. However, he was short of temper, impatient to return to work, and he had to be the worst patient anyone had ever had the misfortune to deal with. His promise to be a better one had not lasted long.

"Making cheese?" Moira moved closer to Pleasance, eyeing her warily.

"Butter."

"Um, I think it might be cheese if ye keep on churning it so hard."

Sighing, Pleasance reduced the strength of her churning. "Did you finish your chores?"

"Aye. I even filled the wood box."

Although she still found it pleasing to see a smile on the girl's face, Pleasance viewed this particular smile with deep suspicion. Moira was a hard worker and, on occasion, had become the teacher when Pleasance faced a task she had never done before. She had learned quickly, however, that when Moira did something extra, something unrequested, it was because the girl wanted something. And Pleasance had not asked the girl to fill the wood box.

"That was very good of you," she murmured.

"I ken it."

"Moira, best ask me now before your dallying puts me into a more foul temper than I am already."

"Jake is leaving to visit his sister Elizabeth. She lives about three days' travel from here. He has asked me to come along."

"Have you asked your brother if you can go?"

"Aye, and he said I can go only if ye can manage without my help for a fortnight. Maybe less. Can I?"

She probably could manage on her own, Pleasance thought, but she was not sure she wanted to. She would be alone with Tearlach. The man had recovered from his wounds enough to begin trying to seduce her again. Moria's presence was a crucial line of defense for her.

"Do you really wish to go?"

"Aye. I dinnae go many places. 'Tis fun traveling with Jake, and I like his kin weel enough." She grimaced. "Mayhaps by the time I get back Tearlach willnae be such a growling soreheaded bear."

"He has been a real miserygut, true enough. There are a few things I will need your help for, such as the candlemaking, but they can easily wait a fortnight. Go on then. No need for both of us to suffer your brother's snarling."

"I will just tell Tearlach and then gather up my things," Moira said, excitement in her voice even as she raced off.

Shaking her head, Pleasance decided she was reckless to let the girl leave. Unfortunately there was no good reason she could give Moira for saying no. She could hardly admit the truth.

She stiffened her back and firmly told herself not to be such a coward. What was or was not happening between herself and Tearlach was solely their concern. Moira should not be involved in any way. Pleasance told herself she was a grown woman and ought to be able to manage a man. If she could not, then she ought to be adult enough to suffer the consequences.

Her strength and determination wavered badly when she saw Moira off a few hours later. She waved at the girl and Jake until they were out of sight. No longer could she rely on Moira to bring Tearlach his meals or to keep him company while Pleasance finished her chores and then escaped into her bedchamber.

"Well, you will just have to find the strength," she told herself.

Some common sense and willpower would not hurt either, she mused as she returned to work. She seemed to be sorely lacking in both when it came to Tearlach O'Duine. When he applied his wiles, she melted. Recalling that he had come so close to dying only made it harder to say no. She did not want to be used and then cast aside, but a voice in her head kept reminding her she was turning from something that would never come again. Perhaps she should take what he offered and enjoy it for as long as she could. That. voice was growing louder every day.

She tried to ignore the part of her that wanted to toss aside all restraint and take what she craved. She tried to recall all the consequences of such recklessness. Unfortunately, the threat of a blackened reputation did not carry the weight it once might have. She knew her name in Worcester was already thoroughly ruined. It was not faring too well in the Berkshires either. Being the indentured servant of a bachelor for one long year would only add to that, whether she did anything wrong or not.

As the day wore on and she thrashed out all her problems in her mind, she still came to no firm conviction. She also realized that Tearlach was being unusually quiet. He was not bellowing for assistance or simply demanding attention as had become his habit during his convalescence. It began to seem very suspicious to her.

By the time she had prepared his evening meal, she was a little worried. He had not been so quiet for days. It was hard to believe he had suffered some relapse, but she could not shake that fear.

"Maybe he has finally realized what a nuisance he has been and has decided to behave," she murmured as she started up the stairs.

Outside of his door she hesitated, frowning a little when she thought she heard a scuffling sound. Listening carefully, she heard no more and shrugged. Her frown deepened when she found herself reluctant to enter his room.

"This is foolish," she muttered. "He is just a man."

The man you love, an inner voice reminded her. The man

who makes you melt with one warm glance. The man you desire so much that you lie awake at nights aching to go to him.

"Oh, shut up," she snapped, then felt a little foolish for arguing with herself.

Straightening her shoulders, she reached for the door latch. All that was true, but she need not let that truth direct her steps. It need not make her afraid to face the man. Besides, she told herself firmly with a wry inner smile, he had to eat.

Chapter Seven

Tearlach fought to restrain his smile when Pleasance entered the room. He wanted to look weak and helpless, and a wide grin would ruin the effect. For a moment, when he heard her hesitate outside his door, he had thought she would balk and run. For a brief instant he had feared that all his plotting would be wasted.

"You have been quiet today," Pleasance said as she set the tray on the table by the bed. She moved to help him sit up against the pillows when he appeared to be having some trouble doing it on his own. "Are you feeling poorly?"

"A mite weak, aye."

Setting the tray on his lap, she frowned, then looked closer at his hair. "Your hair is damp."

Inwardly he cursed, but fought to look innocent. "Is it?"

"Aye. Did you have a bath?" She straightened up, her hands on her hips.

"As much a one as is possible with naught but a sponge and a bowl of cold water." He began to eat. "I stank."

Although she could sympathize, and approved of his penchant for cleanliness, she thought he had been somewhat foolish. "So badly it drove you to risk pneumonia? Look how weak it has left you."

"I shall recover. I will rest easier now without having to endure my own stench."

"You did not smell as bad as you seem to think," she murmured as she sat down.

He smiled faintly over that backhanded compliment. "Bad enough. Did Moira set out without mishap?"

As she described Moira's leavetaking, he watched her. His pretense of weakness had worked just as he had hoped it would. She had lost her wariness, that tense watchfulness that kept her at a distance. It would be easier to draw her close now, close enough to kiss away her resistance.

A ripple of guilt assaulted him. He frowned, for he had thought he had rationalized all his guilt away. Inwardly, he shrugged. He wanted Pleasance too much to worry about a little guilt over his less than honorable intentions. She wanted him too. He was certain of that. She would not fight so hard to turn him away unless she felt the temptation to succumb to his blandishments. A simple, heartfelt *no* would do. He was no rapist. Pleasance, however, went to great extremes to avoid his touch.

Thinking of the few times she had lagged in her resistance to him caused his body to harden with desire. He could almost taste her kiss. This time he would not let her run. This time he would taste the full promise of those kisses.

"A fine meal," he said as he relaxed against the pillows. "'Tis glad I am I wasnae kept on a diet of broth and gruel for too long."

"Broth and gruel can serve a fine purpose."

"Aye, they can kill the patient. They killed my father."

"Broth and gruel cannot kill anyone."

"My father was shot and after his wound was tended he was fed nothing but broth and gruel for a week. He died."

"How can you make light of such a thing? Who shot your father?"

"The English soldiers. He was on a hunt, met a small group of Sassanachs and there was some sort of confrontation. Father couldnae speak English very well and the soldiers claimed they thought he was a Frenchmon. His hunting partner brought him home to die. Ye are right," he added. "'Tis a poor subject for jest, although I was but quoting the mon himself."

"You lost both your parents out here then. How can you still love this land?"

"'Twasnae the land that killed them. My mother and father loved this land and they are buried here. 'Tis now O'Duine land."

She stood, took the tray, and set it on the bedside table. Even as she turned back to him, intending to help him get comfortable for the night, a surprisingly strong arm curled around her waist. She gave a soft cry as she was yanked into his arms and lay sprawled on top of him. Before she could voice a protest, he was kissing her.

Her mind seemed to go blank, emptied of all thought by his tongue stroking the inner recesses of her mouth. Try as she would, she could not form a coherent thought. The sudden attack on her senses was all she had feared and desired. She had had no warning, no time to shore up her defenses. With each stroke of his tongue, the walls of her resistance were further breached. Even the realization that he had planned it so only brought forth a flicker of protest.

"You are not ailing, as you led me to believe," she accused him when he finally released her mouth, only to send her pulses racing with soft, heated kisses over her throat. "Not sick at all."

"Oh, but I *am* sick." He neatly turned her so that she was pinned beneath him.

"Nay. Nay, you are most definitely not." When he kissed the hollow by her ear, she shivered.

"Ah, but I am. Sick with wanting ye."

She was startled to hear the soft thud of her shoes hitting the floor, for she had not realized he had been taking them off. Weakly she pushed against his chest, but he paid no heed and tugged her beneath the covers.

"Nay, Tearlach O'Duine, I have said—"

"Ye talk too much, Pleasance Dunstan."

Tearlach kissed her again. Her hands stopped pushing against him, then slowly slid up around his neck. Pleasance scolded him for his forwardness and sighed in a decidedly wanton way before returning his kiss, only to complain again about his actions in her next breath. Tearlach grew even hungrier for her. He struggled to keep his mind clear of passion's drugging grip so that he could think straight. He wanted to be sure she felt the same blind need that he did.

Pleasance made only one attempt to halt the removal of her clothes, an attempt Tearlach easily ignored. He kept her complaisant with kisses and she found it impossible to fight him. It was not until she wore only her shift and stockings that he paused. She stared up at him as he crouched over her and slowly unlaced her thin linen shift. His eyes had grown dark and heated. Desire tautened his features. She felt spellbound by this evidence of what she aroused in him.

"Must you play these games with me?" she asked in a near whisper.

"I play no games, Pleasance. I am most earnest." Her shift undone, he eased it off her shoulders, drawing in a slow, shaky breath as her firm breasts were bared. "I have thought of little else for more days and nights than I care to count." He paused in removing her shift to cup her breasts in his hands, savoring the way their gentle curves filled his grasp so perfectly, the hardened tips brushing against his palms. "Ye want me," he said when he felt her tremble.

Since he made it a statement of fact, she gave no reply. She wondered why she made no move to halt him as he continued to ease her shift down her body. Instead of fighting him, she lay still and let him look his fill of her even as she looked her fill of him.

The wounds the bear had inflicted were puckered red scars across his strong torso, but they failed to dim his beauty in her eyes. Though lean, he was broad of shoulder and his strength was clear to see beneath his taut dark skin. A thin line of black hair began at his navel and led to his groin, thickening around his jutting manhood, which he made no effort to conceal from her. His legs were long, muscular, and lightly coated with hair. They had looked well shaped when he was clothed and she could see now that she had not been deceived. He had no need to enhance their form with pads or other artifice as some men did.

Tearlach found himself fighting desperately to maintain control over his desire. He must move slowly, gently. He removed her stockings and lingered over the feel of her soft skin as he bared it. The way she watched him as he did so made his blood run dangerously hot. The warmth in her eyes grew stronger with his every touch.

After tossing her last piece of clothing aside, he remained kneeling between her slim legs to look at her. She was so small, so pale and slender, he wondered if she had the strength to accommodate the fierce need she instilled within him. A faint blush touched her cheeks and spread down to the swell of her breasts, revealing her embarrassment, yet she made no move to cover herself.

"Ye dinnae mean to fight me this time, Pleasance?" He slid his hands up her sides as he slowly eased his body onto hers.

"I have lost the will. 'Tis as you planned it."

He brushed a kiss over her mouth. "Aye. The constant to-and-fro was driving me mad." He cupped her breasts in his hands, brushed his thumbs over the taut ends, and watched her eyes slowly close with pleasure.

"How you must gloat over my weakness."

"Nay, little one." He slowly drew his tongue over one nipple and she arched toward him. "No gloating. Only pleasure."

"Yours," she rasped, the feel of his flesh nearly robbing her of the ability to speak.

"Oh, I believe I may be able to make ye like it just a wee bit."

When his mouth enclosed the aching tip of her breast and he began to suckle gently, she could not stifle a soft moan of pleasure. She gripped his shoulders as she arched her body toward that delight. The feel of his skin beneath her hands made her bolder. She began to return his caresses, the faint tremors beneath her hands only adding to her pleasure for they told her she was pleasing him.

Her desire reigned unchecked until his hand slid up her inner thigh. Such an intimate touch startled her. The feel of his hand there, stroking her, sent her reeling, yet she could not feel it was right.

"Nay, Tearlach." She grasped his wrist but lacked the strength to tug his hand away.

"Hush, sweet Pleasance." He kissed her. "Such warmth. Such welcome. Dinnae let fears and modesty steal them away. 'Tis to be enjoyed, shared."

His hoarse words and gentle kisses kept her from stopping him until eventually she no longer wanted to. Her legs grew heavy, yet she felt compelled to move them with an increasing restlessness. She had thought she knew all the wanting any woman could, yet his touch was strengthening that ache until it was nearly painful.

Her restless stroking of his body reached his taut backside and he groaned. He could wait no longer. Slowly he began to ease himself into her, gritting his teeth as he fought for the strength of will to move carefully. He echoed her soft cry as he felt her warmth surround him. A purely male joy surged through him when he met the barrier of her maidenhead, the final proof that he was the first to possess her. She gave a brief startled cry of pain when he pushed all the way into her. Although panting from the effort, he grew still.

Pleasance clung to Tearlach as the short-lived stinging pain began to ease. She wondered why he did not move. It was an effort to open her eyes, but she managed to lift her heavy lids enough to see him. The strain upon his face was clear to read. Her body told her that he wanted still more, but her lack of knowledge left her wondering exactly what that more was.

"Is it accomplished with such calm?" she whispered.

"Nay, sweet one." He gently kissed her. "I but wait for the pain ye felt to ease."

"Oh. 'Tis gone. In truth, it came and went quickly."

"Good. Now we are free to reach for what we both want."

Even now she wanted to deny that, but she lost all power for coherent speech when he began to move. He only had to slightly coax her to get her to wrap her limbs around him. She wanted to cling to him, needed to, as she was plunged deeper into a maelstrom of sensation with every stroke.

At first, Tearlach strove to thrust slowly and gently. The way she clung to him, the soft noises of pleasure that escaped her kiss-swollen lips, and the way she arched to allow him to plunge deeper into her heat all combined to snap the restraints upon his passion. He muttered an apology as he grew fiercer and his needs drove him to toss aside all delicacy. Pleasance met and matched his pounding thrusts. Even as his release tore through him with a power he had never experienced before, he felt her own release seize her. His hoarse cry blended perfectly with hers.

She held him close when he collapsed in her arms, his body echoing the tremors that still rippled through her. A strange tingling warmth lingered in her veins for several moments before it began to fade. When he eased away from her, she was forced to face the hard, cold reality of what she had just done.

Her eyes tightly closed, Pleasance lay still as Tearlach cleaned them both off. She could hear by the heaviness of his steps that he had weakened himself, but she made no move to assist him. Despite the lingering pleasure that still warmed her, despite her reluctant acknowledgment to herself that she had enjoyed their lovemaking, embarrassment held her firmly in its grip. While she had been caught tightly in passion's hold, she had not minded the intimacies they had shared. She had savored them. Now, all she could think was how shamelessly she had acted, how much of her naked body he had seen and of all he had touched.

Tearlach watched her closely as he slid into bed at her side. He could easily read her embarrassment. He suspected she now felt ashamed of how she had come so completely alive in his arms. Gently tugging her tense body into his arms, he thanked God she had not started weeping or become hysterical. He hoped he could avoid recriminations and anger. What had passed between them would only be spoiled by such things.

"Are ye sore, little one?"

"Nay. I had best get dressed now."

He tightened his hold on her. "Ye will stay."

"You have gained what you sought. There is no need for me to remain here."

"Ah, but there is. I have learned this night what I suspected soon after setting eyes upon ye. A hunger the like of which ye have stirred in me cannae be fed with but one toss between the sheets. Nay, no matter how fiery that toss was."

He saw her wince slightly. His words had been blunt, but he did not apologize for them. He did not possess prettier ones, nor was he sure he wished to give her too many sweet words. She had given him more pleasure than he had ever known, but he was determined to keep some distance between them. They would share passion, but no more than that.

Corbin's words flicked through his mind and he inwardly sighed. *Do not sit back and assume you know,* Corbin had warned. *Pleasance Dunstan does not have such vanity or airs.*

So far she did not seem the snobby woman Tearlach had judged her to be, but his wariness lingered. He was not fool enough to keep putting his hand in the fire, to keep giving her opportunities to strike at his pride. She had not been with him and Moira for so very long. The haughty Pleasance who had cast him aside for no apparent reason might yet reveal herself. He would not trust her with any more than the knowledge that he desired her. If she rebuffed him yet again, she would never know she had denied him anything more than sexual easement.

"I have let you make me your whore," she finally whispered.

"Nay, my lover."

"The world will fail to see the distinction."

"The world is full of blind hypocrites. Why do ye care what they think?"

"One must live in that world. To flaunt the rules makes that all the more difficult. In this one moment of weakness I have tossed aside the little respectability I had left."

"That was done in Worcester when ye were marked as a thief and slandered by your own family." Even in the dim candlelight he could see her pale and felt badly about reminding her so bluntly of her ill treatment at the hands of her own kin. "We both ken that most everyone will assume ye have shared my bed. Why deny yourself pleasure for the sake of people who have already condemned ye? They willnae listen if ye say what they believe isnae true."

He felt the last of her tension leave her in one soft sigh. "I know that." She shyly cuddled up to him, resting her cheek upon his chest. "They will believe and say what they please. But that does not make my doing it right or for the best. Now I cannot even deny their lies."

"As I said, 'twould matter little if ye did."

"Mayhaps, but at least I could look them square in the eye and know I spoke the truth."

She did not appreciate his reminder of the truth of her position. Yet he spoke only the truth. Too few people did anymore.

"Dinnae worry the matter so. Ye will steal the pleasure from what we share." As Tearlach ran his hand down her back, caressing his way to her slender rump, he asked, "And can ye deny there was pleasure in it?"

"Why deny it?" Pleasance shrugged. "I am sure ye are so well versed in such things ye could discern it for yourself."

"I begin to think ye envision me as a great rogue and seducer. I am neither."

"You seduced me. Do you deny that?"

"Nay. I hope ye dinnae plan to blame it all on me."

"Nay. You could not have seduced me if I were not so weak, if I had not allowed you to."

"Exactly. Although I prefer to think of it not as a weakness that led ye here but as a strength, a strength of passion."

"Do you press me to admit to something?"

"Aye. I want to hear ye admit to what ye just felt whilst in my arms."

That was something Pleasance had no intention of doing, at least not fully. She was sure Tearlach did not seek words of love from her. He himself had made no mention of any feelings deeper than lust. She was not ready to open her heart to him until there was some hint that he felt something greater than desire. If he demanded she put voice to the passion he stirred in her, she supposed that could cause no great harm. She had already shown it clearly enough.

"I am here. I have let you have what you pestered me for." She idly smoothed her hand over his broad chest.

"Pestered ye?"

"Aye—doggedly."

"Ye do blame me."

"Nay. Only a fool fails to go after what he wants, especially when he can see there is a chance to gain it. I was unable to hide what you could make me feel." She shrugged. "So you took what you wanted. I wanted it too. I tried to cling to the rules. Clearly I did not try hard enough. Mayhaps I but desired you too badly."

The way she put it made him wince. She placed no blame except to fault herself for not being strong enough to resist him. Nevertheless, it made him sound callous, selfish. He had felt neither. Hunger and need had ruled him. He would silence that part of him that was troubled by her description of him.

Tracing one of his scars with her finger, she asked, "Do they hurt? Mayhaps I should move?"

When she started to edge away, he tightened his hold on her. "Nay. I daresay if I was struck a blow there, I would be ill pleased, but otherwise nay. The scars itch some, but there is little pain."

"You healed quickly."

"My wounds did. I am slower to regain my full health. I curse this lingering weakness."

"I did not notice so great a weakness," she murmured, and felt him laugh softly.

"I have been strong enough for that for days, but ye never seemed to draw near enough for me to grasp hold of you."

"That was an act of great wisdom upon my part, as has just been proven."

"Ye just meant to torment me."

"Ah, alas, my secret is out."

He smiled faintly, enjoying their quiet banter. "I do suffer some weakness. If I was back to my full strength we would-nae be spending so long resting before seeking our pleasure once again."

"Before? You mean to . . ." She hesitated as she groped for words and failed to find the right ones. "Again?"

"Do ye think a mon as hungry as I am could be satisfied with but one taste of what he has craved for so long?" He ran his hand down her side to caress her smooth hip. "Nay, little one. I kenned when I finally got ye into my bed that I would wish to glut myself. My body had denied me that indulgence. Howsomever, I feel my strength returning even now."

She gave a soft squeak of surprise when he dragged her body on top of his, pressing their loins together so that she could feel the proof of his claim. When that caused the warmth of desire to return to her own blood, she was even more surprised. Here was the proof that Tearlach O'Duine had the skill to turn her into a wanton.

"Mayhaps you should conserve your strength," she suggested.

"Nay. There is nothing better than this to put strength back into a mon."

"I have never heard a physician recommend such . . . er, treatment."

"'Tis a closely guarded secret."

He grinned at her and she felt the warmth of that smile

flow through her veins. She found his cheerful, friendly banter very attractive, but fought its pull, warned herself sternly against reading too much into it. He had gotten what he had wanted, could easily see that all their fighting was over. That could well be the source of his good cheer. Success put him in a good mood, not her, not the presence of any of the deeper emotions she craved from him. She would be a fool to think otherwise without more solid proof than a smile.

Pleasance sighed as she settled herself comfortably, welcomingly in his arms. She recognized her own weaknesses. She would take the passion he offered. It was not the love she craved, but it might lead to love. Hope springs eternal, she mused.

Tearlach brushed kisses over her throat and moved his hands over her backside. Closing her eyes, Pleasance wished his touch did not feel so good. She wished she did not want him. She wished she did not love him. She wished she had the strength to punch him in the nose, as he so richly deserved, and then walk away.

She soon cast aside those thoughts as she succumbed to the passion he so expertly aroused in her. It was so much easier to let the delicious feelings wash over her, so much easier to close her mind and let her love for him flow freely.

This time she was not so passive, returning his kisses vigorously and matching him caress for caress. When he finally turned, rolling so that she was beneath him, she was blindly eager for him. She wrapped her legs around him and held on tightly as he drove them both to the release they craved.

But when she finally lay still and sated in his arms, her worries returned. She was giving him everything she had to give, but in return he gave her only his desire, his hunger of the flesh. It was hard not to fret over that.

Replete and content, Tearlach rested his cheek against the top of her head. "I knew it would be good."

"I suspect you have a past rich enough in experience to be a good judge." It hurt to think of the other women he had known, but she recognized that she would be a blind fool to think he came to their union as innocent as she was.

He laughed softly and pressed a kiss to the top of her head. "Ye really do see me as some great Lothario. I have been too busy with the hard work of living, of trying to better my lot in life, to dabble long or heartily in the arts of love. The women I have kenned number barely as many as the fingers on my hands, and I can put name or face to verra few of them. Ye I will remember."

"That is something," she murmured. "I had best make my way to bed."

He easily held her in place. "Here is your bed. Ye will abide here now."

"Moira . . ."

"Will see naught wrong with it and will say nothing."

"How can you be so sure of that? This is something that everyone says is wrong."

"Moira hasnae been raised by everyone. *I* raised her and I havenae filled her head with the unbending rules that so many others hold to. She willnae tell anyone about this and she will-nae condemn ye. I ken how my sister thinks and feels."

Pleasance could not argue with that, but promised herself to see that Moira understood such freedoms were not right or wise. She did not want the girl to chance the same heart-break she herself now faced. There was little doubt in her mind that Tearlach would also speak to the girl. He would not want his sister to become some man's lover.

Closing her eyes, she waited for sleep to conquer the troubling thoughts whirling in her head. She did not want to think. She simply wanted to feel and act upon those feelings. Unfortunately, there was a part of her that refused to allow her such unfettered recklessness.

He had said he would remember her. They were simple words, even flattering, but they suggested that he foresaw no future for them, that he planned no more than a mutually pleasurable interlude. She wanted love. She wanted his name. She wanted to bear his children and keep his home. He simply wanted pleasant memories.

Well, she mused, even Tearlach O'Duine's plans could be set awry.

She would do her best to change his mind, she decided as she felt his body grow lax with sleep. They shared a fierce passion.

It was a start, she told herself as she finally felt the tug of sleep. Passion opened him to her in ways she would be a fool not to take advantage of. Somehow she ought to be able to slip in under his guard, to touch his heart, not just his loins. She had almost a year in which to accomplish her goal. As long as he felt desire for her, she had a chance to make it more. Passion could become a deeper, richer emotion as easily as it could dim or fade. She would do all she could to gain the former.

If she had her way, by the end of her indenture Tearlach O'Duine would not only remember her, he would also love her.

Stretching, Pleasance reached out, but Tearlach's side of the bed was cool and empty. She opened her eyes and found him standing by the bed, fully dressed and frowning at her. Gone was the soft desire in his smoky gray eyes. Gone was any warmth at all. He looked as remote as he had in the first days of their time together. A chill went through Pleasance, and she hugged the sheet closer to her as she sat up.

"'Tis morning," he said. "I believe ye have work to do. This isnae Worcester. Ye cannae lie abed all day." He started out of the room. "I will see to the livestock and I shall want my morning meal when I am done."

"But—" Pleasance began, though she was not sure what she would say.

"Ye didnae think this would change anything, did ye?" Tearlach saw her face grow pale and almost wished his words back, but he stoutly retained his aloof air. He felt strongly that there had to be a strict division between her roles as his lover and as his servant. Pleasance must not think her work could now end.

"Nay, I did not think things would change," Pleasance replied, determined not to let him know how much he was hurting her.

"Good. Then we shall go along fine."

The moment the door shut behind him, Pleasance sank back against the pillows. She still felt the chill of his words. She took a deep breath to steady herself and got out of bed. As she washed and dressed she continued to muster her strength. To her shame she found herself making excuses for the way he had acted.

She glanced back at the bed and knew she could not simply walk away from the passion she had found there. While the desire she had tasted was not the love she craved from Tearlach, it did feed a deep need within her. She vowed that she would not let the man use her too shabbily, but she would give him a little time.

"Perhaps he is always so ill-tempered before he eats. I just never noticed before," she said as she hurried downstairs to begin the morning meal.

"Ye gave the animals too much fodder," Tearlach said that night even as he sat down to help himself to the meal Pleasance set before him.

She placed the venison pie on the table and looked at him. "I fed them as you told me to." She sat down opposite him and, once he was finished serving himself, helped herself to some of the meat pie.

"Ye fed them too weel. 'Tis taking ye a long time to get that chore right." He poured himself a tankard of cider. "I realize that back in Worcester ye wouldnae have stooped to doing such hard honest work, but ye shouldnae need so long to learn such a simple chore."

"Perhaps you are just too particular."

"Nay. Animals are very valuable. I suggest that ye try harder to treat them weel."

"As you wish."

Pleasance quelled the urge to pour the entire contents of the cider jug over his head. She was trying so hard to be patient and understanding. A little voice in her had kept asking her if she was just being weak, as weak as she had often been with her own family. She did not want to be spineless, but she did not wish to act so hastily that she ruined all hope of being more to Tearlach than a convenient bed partner.

She was still wrestling with that problem as she scrubbed down the kitchen table after supper. Tearlach came up behind her and slipped his arms around her waist. Her body tensed. He began to kiss the nape of her neck. She felt her anger and hurt start to fade as the heat of his lips seeped through her body and awakened her desire for him.

"Are you here to tell me that I scrub the table the wrong way?" she asked.

"Nay, lassie." He took the scrub brush from her hand, turned her around to face him, and held her close. "The day is at an end, our work is done, and now we can play."

"Play?"

He kissed her, silencing her questions and banishing her doubts. She made no protest as he swept her into his arms and carried her to his room. He kept her drugged with kisses and she made no attempt to fight the headiness of the passion flowing between them. For just a little while she would play the game his way. Surely a man who could desire her so much, who could make her ache for him, had to feel more for her than lust. As he laid her down on the bed, she welcomed him into her arms and prayed that she was not lying to herself.

Chapter Eight

Tearlach shut the cabin door behind him. Through the window, Pleasance watched him ride toward the village until he was out of sight. There did not seem to be a part of her that the pain in her heart did not reach. For three days since she and Tearlach had finally succumbed to their hunger for each other she had fought to deny the truth that was slapping her in the face. She had tried desperately to convince herself she was imagining things. She could not fool herself any longer. She had run out of excuses for his behavior. The man who held her so tenderly and whispered sweet words in passion then treated her like the lowest servant. It was as if she lived with two different men—a gentle lover at night and a stern taskmaster during the day.

She closed her eyes tightly as she fought an urge to weep. "How could I have been such a fool?"

Warm lips that turned her mind to cornmeal and a touch that set her blood afire had brought her to this sorry pass, she told herself in rising anger. They were the temptations to which she had succumbed. Lust had vanquished her morals and common sense alike. Her own foolish heart had dimmed her wits, had caused her to be woodenheaded enough to think the act of love meant more to Tearlach than it did simply because it meant so much to her.

What hurt the most was the knowledge that she had no hope. She had thought to gain his heart through his passion. That was impossible when it could be lit and snuffed like a candle. The softness she had hoped to take advantage of was only there at night, when she was too caught up in her own desires to try to make some small niche for herself in his heart.

Nothing else he could have done, she decided, could have so successfully made her feel the whore. He claimed that was not what he wished to make of her, but his actions denied his words. And there was not even any profit in it for me, she thought bitterly. I work for his comfort all day and now all night as well.

Well, she vowed, she would not do so any longer. She knew it would be akin to cutting her own heart out, but she would leave Tearlach. That she would be breaking the law, would become a runaway, troubled her only briefly. She would find Nathan and he would help her break the legal bond that chained her to Tearlach.

It would be difficult to find Nathan, but not impossible. Pleasance decided to go back to Worcester. If she was careful, she would not be caught and she could try to find one of Nathan's many friends. This late in the year at least one of them should have returned home and might know where Nathan could be reached. There was even a chance that Nathan himself had already returned from his secretive business in Philadelphia.

Leaving immediately presented her with a few problems. She could not carry all her belongings, not even if she took a horse. And taking a horse would be theft. But she would not get far on foot; it would be winter before she got even halfway home.

After carefully sorting through her things Pleasance

packed one bag of what she considered essential. She packed a sack with food and collected some drink as well. Just as she started out the door she turned back, deciding to leave a message for Tearlach.

It took her several moments to think of the right words, but finally she wrote: *I am returning to Worcester. Added to the debt I already owe you is one horse, a saddle, and a small cache of supplies I have taken. I will see that you are fully reimbursed. Even if my brother Nathan cannot or will not aid me, I will gain the money. You have taught me some marketable skills. At least elsewhere I shall get coin for what I do and need not work both day and night. Pleasance.*

As she quickly wrote the terse note, she hoped that telling him where she was going would stop him from coming after her. He would not be left to think she had been carried off or had run blindly into the forest. Briefly rereading her missive, she wondered if she had revealed her hurt and anger too clearly, then decided it did not matter. At least he would know she had the wit to see how shabbily he was treating her.

The thought of riding off on one of Tearlach's horses, having taken a saddle as well as a fair quantity of his food, made Pleasance feel uncomfortable. No matter how she tried to justify her actions, it still felt like theft to her. She comforted herself with the assurance that she would pay him back in full for every item she took. If it was at all possible, she would even see to the return of his horse.

Pleasance picked a sweet-tempered roan mare and saddled it. She tied her small sack of supplies to the pommel, led the horse out of the stable, and mounted. She patted the mare's neck as she looked toward the village, down the road Tearlach had ridden earlier. There was no sight of him, and she quickly rode in the opposite direction, toward Worcester.

Suddenly she thought of Moira and almost turned back again. She and the child had become friends. Moira had put her trust in her. Pleasance could not be sure the girl would understand why she had left. Once she was settled somewhere, she promised herself she would write to Moira and try to explain.

By the time she stopped for a noon meal she was exhausted. She had not ridden a horse for so many hours without rest before. It made the wagon she and Tearlach had traveled in seem like the most luxurious carriage. After finishing a sparse meal, she relaxed against a tree. It would probably be to her advantage to take a short rest. The emotional turmoil she had experienced in the last three days had sapped her strength. She briefly worried that Tearlach would catch up to her, but shrugged that fear aside. Once he read her note he would consider himself well rid of her.

Tearlach slowed his steps as he approached the cabin. He had hurried to finish his business in town in order to get back home in time for the noon meal, but now he made an effort to move at a more casual pace. He did not want to appear too eager. It had not been easy, but he felt he had done a good job of letting Pleasance know the boundaries of their new relationship. He was confident he had shown her that her place in his bed changed nothing. Running eagerly up to the cabin in the middle of the day like some lovesick youth would undermine that careful structure, he told himself as he schooled both his step and his features.

"Pleasance," he called as he entered the cabin. "I have brought some supplies."

The silence immediately told him that something was wrong. He had not seen Pleasance outside, so he knew she had to be in the cabin, yet the place was too small for all hint of her presence to be hidden.

"Pleasance?"

Scowling, he moved to set the sugar, tea, and flour he had purchased on the table. When he saw the message he swore. His curses grew more virulent as he read it.

"Marketable skills?" he bellowed. "Curse the woman. Does she mean to become a courtesan?"

He read the note again and shook his head. "Sweet Mary, how could she be so stupid?"

Tossing the missive aside, Tearlach wasted no time in setting out after her. As he collected his weapons, he realized she had taken none with her, and again he cursed her stupidity. When he went to saddle a horse he saw that she had taken his best saddle, and he cursed her some more. Knowing what drove him so hard, why he was as near to frantic as he had ever been in his life, only added to his anger. He was worried. More than worried, he was scared. He knew only too well all the dangers she faced out in the forest. And she was unarmed. He was afraid he would be too late to save her.

The sound of approaching horses awakened Pleasance with a start. She had not intended to fall asleep. The thought that it was good something had roused her before she had slept the day away was immediately replaced by the realization that she was no longer alone.

The stench of unwashed bodies wafted toward her. It nearly made her gag. The two men standing before her wore buckskins darkened nearly to black with accumulated filth. Their hair and beards hung past their shoulders in greasy strands. It was not their filthy state that really troubled her, however. Although she thought they were probably the dirtiest pair of men she had ever seen, people who were reluctant to employ soap and water were no strangers to her. What set her heart racing with fear was the identical leers on their faces.

"Well, now, will you lookee here, Sep."

"Aye, Dec. There's no end to the bounty God's forest sets forth."

Pleasance rose to her feet with extreme caution, struggling to hide her fear. "I am so glad you gentlemen woke me up. I really must be on my way or I shall never make my destination by nightfall."

"You hear that, Sep? She called us gentlemen."

The taller of the pair laughed, revealing blackened teeth. "Pa sure would get a chuckle outta that."

It was clear that being polite was not going to gain her a thing. These men were not even trying to hide their intentions.

"If you will excuse me now, I really must be on my way," she reiterated.

When she tried to take a step toward her horse, they followed her. A voice in her head told her that bolting would be useless. Panic overruled sense, however. She raced for her horse, her only clear thought to get as far out of their reach as possible. Both men laughed as they easily blocked her way. Panting, she stopped and stared at them.

"Now, missy, were you thinking of leaving without even visiting with us?" Sep drawled.

"Someone didn't teach you very good manners, missy."

"I was taught to flee such as you, flee from men who clearly mean me no good."

"Oh, but we do mean to do you some good, missy. Yessir, we mean to do you real good."

"And me and Sep have a lot to do you good with." Dec laughed raucously as he lewdly fondled himself.

"There are people who will worry about me if I am late arriving," she lied. "They will search for me."

"Won't be any need of them troubling themselves. This won't be taking long."

"Don't be too hasty, Sep. She be one fine-looking wench."

"You have a good thought there, Dec. Most folk would never let a little thing like her roam about alone, so I be thinking she is either running away or she ain't got nobody. So mayhaps we oughta take the little missy under our wing like."

Pleasance shuddered with revulsion. Rape by the two muck-encrusted men facing her was terrifying enough to contemplate. Hearing them consider keeping her with them for future abuse eradicated what little calm she had managed to keep hold of. With a soft cry of alarm she turned and ran again.

This time she headed away from her horse, into the depths of the forest. A small, rational part of her mind alerted her to the folly of that decision, but she had no choice. Somehow, she prayed, she might yet be able to circle back to her horse. Her heart pounding so hard and fast she could hear the beat of it in her head, she hiked up her skirts, but the brambles still tore at them. She could do no more than turn her head or duck as she dodged low-lying branches. She stubbed her foot on a large rock and nearly fell, but quickly steadied herself, cursed viciously, and ignoring the pain, kept right on running.

The men whooped and yelled as they gave chase, adding to her horror. She was running for her very life, but they saw it as entertainment, as a game. In her mind that revealed a chilling lack of humanity in her pursuers.

It quickly became clear to her that they had indeed turned the chase into some macabre sport. One or the other kept appearing before her, forcing her to change course, then both would laugh heartily. She soon lost all sense of where she was. Their cruelty stirred her fury.

When yet again one of them appeared abruptly before her she stopped in her tracks. She spied a hefty branch lying on the ground. She picked it up and faced her attacker. At that moment Pleasance hated him more than she had ever hated anything or anybody in her short life.

"Hey, Dec, where is the little missy?" Sep stepped out of the shadows to her right, saw her, and grinned.

Moving so that she could keep both men in sight, Pleasance tensely awaited their next move. She ignored the rational part of her that cruelly pointed out what little chance she had of winning any fight against two hulking assailants. At least she would go down fighting.

"You think you can beat us, little missy?" Dec asked, sarcasm heavy in his voice.

"She sure do look mean." Sep laughed heartily and slapped his guffawing brother on the back.

"Then mayhaps you had best flee while you still can, you bastards!" she cried.

"Now, that ain't no way for a little missy to talk. We don't hold with a woman cussing like some man."

"What you do or do not hold with matters very little to me. I suggest you use what meager wit you have to contemplate the punishment handed down for the crime you plan. I warn you, there are people who will avenge my defilement."

"That they might—if they can find you."

Those ominous words sent a chill of fear racing through her, but again she fought it. Panic would only rob her of what little strategy and skill she might be able to muster.

She tensed as they started to edge toward her. Cautiously she adjusted her stance to keep both men in view. She knew she would probably have only one real chance to strike a telling blow.

"No need to fight us, missy."

"Now, you listen to Dec here. We only mean to have some fun."

"I do not believe I have offered to entertain you."

"You'll change your mind once me and Sep show you how fine a time we can give you."

"I truly doubt that."

They lunged for her. She swung the log at Dec and savored his howling curse as her weapon struck his shoulder, staggering him. As she swung she moved, hoping to elude Sep's grasp. She felt the tug as he grabbed her skirts, heard the material tear, but paid it no heed. Instead, she swung at him with the log and struck him full in the face, sending him sprawling to the ground. Even as she attempted to run, Dec sprang again. He slammed into her back. The breath was knocked from her as she hit the ground, but fear and desperation kept her from being incapacitated by the blow.

When Dec started to turn her onto her back, she saw a brief opening and took it. She slammed her knee into his groin. He howled and, clutching himself, fell off her. Frantically she scrambled to her feet, but she was barely standing when Sep tackled her to the ground. She knew she had just lost her last slim chance to escape, but still she continued to fight.

"Get off of me, you filthy pig." She struggled helplessly against his efforts to pin her to the ground.

"Now, you keep calling us bad names and we might not be so nice to you no more," Sep grumbled.

"Goddamn, Sep, the bitch done ruined me. I know it." Dec knelt next to Sep and Pleasance, still clutching his groin, his face pinched with pain and fury. "She oughta pay good for that."

"Seeing as you be too hurt to take your share, you hold her down for me."

"I will see that you both rot in hell," Pleasance threatened in desperation as Dec relieved his brother of the need to keep her arms pinned down, yanking them ungently over her head and holding them in a painful grip. "I will see you hunted down and gelded, you stinking swine." Sep slapped her face and she cried out in pain.

"I told you to watch them names, missy. Don't want me to be forgetting myself and hurting you bad now, do we?"

The last of Pleasance's bravado was swept away when Sep pulled out a knife. For one brief instant she thought of goading him into killing her before he and his brother could rape her, but the thought was swiftly gone. She did not want to die. Horrifying as what she faced would be, she still wanted to live. She gave a startled screech as he began to cut open her bodice.

Tearlach tensed then cursed when he heard a short screech rise above the normal woodland noises. It was female, and he knew it was Pleasance. The male laughter that followed brought another curse to his lips. It did not surprise him that she had managed to stumble across the most dangerous animal roaming the untamed forest.

He dismounted and secured his horse. His rifle in one hand and his pistol in the other, he cautiously moved toward the sounds. He could hear the men but not the woman, and hoped he was not too late to save her.

When the owners of the voices finally came into view Tearlach felt rage clutch his stomach and disorder his mind. It took a moment before he was able to regain rational thought. He ached to kill the men pinning Pleasance to the ground, but finally he gained the strength to restrain that animalistic urge.

Using their preoccupation with Pleasance to his advantage, Tearlach edged as close to the men as he dared. He did not want to alert them to his presence until he was ready. Total surprise could well serve as his best weapon.

"Let her go," he ordered once he was satisfactorily positioned.

Pleasance heard that familiar icy voice, but dared not

believe her own ears. Rarely had her prayers been answered so directly. Afraid to find that she was only imagining things, she peered warily around Sep, who sat still and taut, his knife still poised to cut open her chemise. When she saw Tearlach standing there, armed and ready to fight, she felt light-headed with relief.

"Now, mister, why don't you just amble on your way. This ain't your concern."

"Ah, but ye are wrong, Septimus Tate."

"Jee-sus and Mary, Sep, it's Tearlach O'Duine."

Pleasance saw Sep pale slightly beneath his dirt. He spread out his arms and let the knife fall from his hand. Clearly the brothers not only knew Tearlach but considered him a force to be reckoned with. She hoped that fear and respect were strong enough to keep them from fighting Tearlach.

"Now, O'Duine, we found this woman first. We got some rights," Dec protested.

"Ye have no rights. She is mine."

"Yours? She was just wandering about the forest on her own. You would never let no woman of yours do that."

"She neglected to ask my permission. Let her up. Now."

The brothers hesitated only a moment before slowly releasing her. Although she trembled badly, she clutched her ruined bodice together and got to her feet. The brothers moved to stand side by side, their hands held out in a gesture of surrender. She prayed they remained acquiescent.

"Well, maybe a little discipline . . ." Dec began, reluctant to give up a prize so easily.

"I believe I am capable of disciplining my own servant." Tearlach finally glanced toward Pleasance, still careful to keep most of his attention and both his weapons fixed on the Tate brothers. "I grow weary of rescuing ye from the consequences of your follies, lassie."

A lot of the pleasure she had felt at his appearance fled at his words. He was furious, more angry than she had ever seen him. Even the Tate brothers sensed it. They attempted to look even more submissive.

"Did they accomplish their task?" Since Pleasance was only partly undressed, Tearlach suspected he had been in time, but he wanted his suspicions confirmed.

"Nay. They had just begun their attack."

"Then ye should be able to get to your mount. The one ye stole from me? I hope ye havenae lost my horse along with your wits."

Pleasance shook her head and hurried to get the horse. Tears welled up in her eyes and her head ached from the effort of fighting them. Overwhelming relief was part of it, but so was Tearlach's fury. She almost wished he had not come to her rescue, then told herself not to be an idiot. Even Tearlach's hatred, for all it could tear her heart to pieces, would be easier to bear than what the Tate brothers had planned for her. She grasped the reins of her mount and tugged the beast along as she hurried back to Tearlach. She found the men exactly as she had left them and breathed a sigh of relief.

"Seems to me, Tearlach," ventured Dec, "that this little missy is a peck of trouble. We could take her off your hands. A woman spends some time with us Tates and she soon learns her place."

The still, cold look on Tearlach's face, almost as if he was contemplating the suggestion, made Pleasance feel ill.

"Tempting as your offer is, Decimus, I will take her back with me."

"Suit yourself."

"I intend to. My horse is directly behind you a few yards, Pleasance. Wait there for me."

Clutching her bodice closed with one hand and leading the horse with the other, she hurried to obey. Briefly she thought of mounting her horse and riding away from them all, but only briefly. She could not make it to Worcester on her own. The attack by the Tates had shown her that. It was hopeless to try. As she stopped to wait by Tearlach's mount, she prayed her rescue would not become a tragedy.

Tearlach stared at the two men and wished he could punish them. He really needed to vent some of his anger, an anger spawned by fear. The Tate clan was a large one, however, and its members were given to seeking vengeance. Even trying to use the law to punish the men could stir up a hornet's nest. He would have to swallow his need to strike at them even though it gagged him.

"Ye had better not follow us."

"Would never think of it, Tearlach."

"I am pleased to hear that, Decimus. Pleasance Dunstan is my woman and, though she is troublesome, I mean to hold on to her."

"Can't say I blame you for that. 'Course, if you get tired of her—"

"I have no plans to. I willnae mention this to your father. But if ye lay one hand on her again . . ."

"Never. We won't never touch her. You have our word as Tates on that," swore Dec. "She be all yours. Take her. We'll just get back to our squirrel hunting."

Tearlach paused a moment. before he nodded and relaxed his stance slightly. "Fine then. Good hunting, lads."

He turned his back on them, though even then he did not fully drop his guard. He had never known the Tates to break their word once it was given, but he did not know Decimus and Septimus Tate well, and he would not relax his vigilance until he was far away from them.

When he saw Pleasance waiting by the horses, he knew a lot of his anger came from the foolish risk she had taken in riding off alone into a dangerous wilderness. He had been deeply afraid for her, he had wanted to kill the men who had dared to touch her, and worst of all, he felt the bite of hurt to know she could walk away from the passion they shared. The fact that she could stir his feelings so effortlessly added to his anger. Until he could get his tumultuous emotions under control, it would be best if he spoke to Pleasance as little as possible. He did not want to spit hurtful words at her, nor did he wish to reveal the turmoil she produced in him.

"Mount, woman. There is no need to linger here."

Pleasance detested being called "woman," especially in that tone of voice, but decided it was a bad time to mention it. "Do you think they will follow us?" she asked as she struggled to get on the horse without Tearlach's aid.

Swinging easily into the saddle, he watched her mount awkwardly, but he made no move to assist her. "Nay."

"You sound very sure."

His cold fury left her feeling intimidated. She waited tensely for a reply as, when she was barely settled in the saddle, he urged his horse into a trot, forcing her to scramble to follow him.

"As sure as I dare be," he said. "They gave their word." Out of the corner of his eye he saw her doubtful frown. "They have never broken it. Also, Jud Tate and his ten sons obey at least one law. None of them will touch a woman who belongs to another man." He nudged his horse into a canter.

Pleasance bit her tongue against a sharp retort. Despite the ordeal she had just been through and her fear of Tearlach's anger, she resented his speaking of her as if she were just another possession. Indentured to him she might be, but she deserved to be considered as more than another cooking pot or broom.

Pleasance sensed Tearlach's anger in every inch of his lean frame as he rode just ahead of her. She could feel it throbbing in the tense silence between them. There was nothing she could think to say that might soothe his temper. She really had no defense. Even his cold treatment of her, which had forced her to flee, did not change the fact that she was indentured to him and had stolen from him. Most everyone would see her as a runaway and a thief, deserving of corporal punishment. She had forced Tearlach to trek through the forest after her and drag her out of danger. When she had fled the cabin she had thought that matters between them could become no worse than they already were.

Staring at Tearlach's stiff back, she had the sinking feeling she would soon be proven wrong.

Chapter Nine

"Put this on your bruise."

Pleasance took the cool cloth from Tearlach's hand and pressed it against her cheek where Sep had struck her. She sat at the table and warily watched Tearlach as he put together a meal for them. His every movement shouted his lingering anger. She wondered when he would turn that anger more directly toward her. She felt sure he would not be able to hold it in much longer.

She was amazed when he managed to remain silent throughout the meal. She found it hard to take even a bite. She was so tense she could hardly swallow.

How she longed for a bath. She was sure she stank of the Tate brothers. Coming into contact with such filthy men had to have left some mark. She ached all over from her brief but violent battle with them.

Tearlach cleared the table. He glared at her briefly when he saw how little she had eaten. Ignoring him, she rose stiffly from her seat.

"Where are you going?" he growled.

"To have a bath. I stink like a Tate."

"A problem ye wouldnae have if ye had stayed where ye belong."

She ignored that goading remark. She had her heart set on a bath. The argument that was already long overdue could wait a little while longer.

Tearlach sipped his ale and watched as Pleasance dragged the tub into her room. Each time she hefted a pot of hot water off the fire he saw her wince and pale slightly. It was obvious she had suffered more injuries from her encounter than were readily visible. Before he could ask her about them, she disappeared into her room, shutting the door with a distinct snap.

For a while he sat drinking and staring at her door. He could hear water splashing. Something was missing and a moment later he realized what it was. She was not singing as was her habit when she bathed. He also knew her own anger was boiling close to the surface. It was hardly surprising. He had been goading her with snide, cutting remarks.

There was going to be a battle royal between them soon. Taking a long drink of ale, he kept his gaze fixed on her door and idly wondered who would start the fight.

Pleasance lingered in her bath until the water became uncomfortably chilled. Chiding herself for being a coward, she reluctantly stepped out to dress and rub her newly washed hair partly dry. She could not avoid the coming confrontation by hiding in the tub until she caught the ague. Straightening her spine, she finally ventured from her room. She headed straight for the fireplace, sat down on a stool, and began to brush her hair dry before the fire's warmth.

Tearlach watched. It annoyed him to feel such desire at the mere sight of her. He glanced down at the note she had left him. While she was taking her bath he had reread it several times. It proved more than enough to restir the anger his desire for her was trying to cool.

"Just what the hell did ye mean by this?" Crushing the note in his fist, he thrust it in Pleasance's direction.

Although startled by the abrupt attack, she glanced at him with relative calm. "Just what it said. I was returning to Worcester."

"Illegal as well as idiotic, but I wasnae speaking of that. What did ye mean by the skills I have taught ye and working all day and night? Did ye mean what I think ye did?"

Turning her back on him again, she returned to brushing her hair. "Although I do not possess the gift to look inside of your thick head, aye, I suspect you interpreted it correctly."

"Ye meant to take up whoring?" he bellowed, her haughty responses to his angry questions only increasing his fury.

"It was but one of three choices. I could get money from Nathan, but if he went the way of the rest of my family, I would need to earn my own coin. I could be a maid or . . ."

"A whore," he snarled. "And ye try to claim I have taught ye that profession?"

She finally turned on the stool to look directly at him. "Aye, you taught me."

Leaping to his feet, Tearlach threw the crumpled note aside and strode toward her. "I told ye that ye were no whore."

"Aye, you did, but you have proven most adept at saying one thing and acting in a way that says something very different indeed."

"What are ye babbling about? I havenae said or done anything that would make any sane person think I was training you to go out and earn your living on your back."

Deciding she had had more than enough of his towering over her in an intimidating manner, Pleasance stood up on the stool. "I beg to differ, Master O'Duine. Your every action has shown me you consider me little better than some ha'penny dockside tart."

He was stunned into silence. Her very real anger showed that she fully believed her words. He was certain she had totally misinterpreted his actions, but he was not sure how to explain himself.

"Oh, you speak very soft and sweet in the dark of night when none can hear," Pleasance continued. "Come the sunrise, however, and I am little more to you than another chamber pot. Not even the most base of courtesies do you offer me." She could feel her hurt welling up inside her and knew she was about to cry. She stepped off the stool. She intended to go to her room, where she could give in to her weakness "I may be fool enough to give in to passion's lure, Master O'Duine, but what little pride you have left me demands that I deny you the right to treat me like some ha'penny whore." She gave a cry of frustration when he grabbed her arm, halting her flight, and forced her to face him.

She bowed her head, hiding her face. He grasped her by the chin and gently but firmly turned her face up to him. Tearlach did not need to see the tears streaking her cheeks to know he had hurt her. It was there to read in her luminous eyes. He was touched in ways he did not fully understand. He did not want to be moved by her pain. Good sense told him to back away quickly, to let her use her hurt and anger to build a strong wall between them. But he knew he could not do that.

"Do ye try to wheedle vows of love and promises of marriage from me?" he growled, shaking her slightly.

She felt strongly inclined to strike him. "Nay, sir, I do not. I have never pressed for such, and well you know it. I but ask for respect."

"I give ye that."

"Nay, you do not. You are warmth at night and ice in the day. You say I am your lover, not your whore, but you do not back your words with actions once the sun comes up."

"Is that why ye fled? Because I dinnae fawn over ye like some lovestruck moonling? Aye, ye are my lover, but ye are still indentured to me."

"Have I once shirked in my duties? Have I once acted as if the use of my body should gain me some easement in the work I must do? Have I even hinted that anything should change concerning my daily chores because of what we share in the night? Nay, I have not.

"You but assumed I would do so, did you not? Assumed then acted upon that groundless suspicion to ensure that this poor witless female knew where the role of lover ended and the one of indentured servant began. Well, if you meant to clearly separate the two, you failed. By your actions you made the role of lover but a slight change from the duties of the servant."

Pleasance shook her head, saddened by his blindness. "By your actions you made the word *lover* but a softer name for *whore*. You dirtied the act. You treated me like a slut, tossing me from your bed each sunrise like some unwanted blanket in August. Unlike the whore, howsomever, I got naught for the warmth I gave."

She yanked free of his hold. "Well, no more. If I must stay, I do so as a servant only. I will not shirk in my duties, but they cease at the bedroom door, Master O'Duine. If you seek a whore, then look elsewhere."

She started to walk away from him, but again he grabbed her by the arm and yanked her into his arms. Despite her struggles and soft curses, he held her firmly. Kicking aside the stool, he tossed her onto the bearskin before the fireplace. She fought him, but he soon had her pinned beneath him. He met and equaled her furious glare.

He had listened to her every word. It was not hard to understand her feelings. What infuriated him was her constant reference to their lovemaking as a duty. Holding her thrashing head still between his hands, he kissed her, and felt a rush of triumph when his deep, lingering kiss weakened her struggles.

"Does that feel like duty?" He watched her closely as he ended the kiss, and felt soothed by the desire she could not fully conceal.

"You will not use your kisses to sway me this time, Master O'Duine." She finally gave up the fruitless and exhausting attempt to break free of his firm hold.

"Can they sway ye, Pleasance?" He almost grinned when she muttered a curse and made one furious effort to buck him off her. "So 'tis duty that brought ye to my bed, is it?" He cupped her breast in his hand and felt the tip harden beneath his touch.

It greatly dismayed Pleasance that, despite all he had done and said, she could still warm to his touch so quickly. "Will you leave me no pride at all?"

"Do I ask for the sacrifice of your pride?"

"Nay, you tear it from me, piece by little piece, until none is left."

"Ye have misread my every action." Feeling her relax beneath him and wondering a little desperately how he could correct her huge misconceptions, he began to slowly undo her bodice.

"Your actions seemed most clear to me," murmured Pleasance.

"Then mayhaps I should have explained myself. I but sought to keep these two halves of our lives separate. One has naught to do with the other. Ye are indentured to me. I cannae and willnae change that. What occurs between us as a mon and a woman mustnae become tangled and confused with that. I acted in a way I thought would make that clear."

She made no attempt to halt his slow undressing of her. He was talking more openly than he ever had before. She did not want to interrupt that. She also admitted with a

touch of selfderision that she wanted to make love with him.
It would steal away the horror of the Tates' attack on her. It
would also soothe her hurts, if only fleetingly.

"You cannot disentangle the two as completely as you
tried to," she said. "The woman who warms your bed at night
is the same one who scrubs your floor by day. Mayhaps you
can play two different men, the lover and the master, but I
cannot cut myself in two so neatly. 'Tis like to drive me mad.
You gave me more courtesy and respect before I shared your
bed. What was I to think when even that was taken away?"

She lay acquiescent now, dressed only in her thin shift. As
he carefully considered what to say next, what he could
safely concede, he stripped down to his breeches.

"Then let it be as ye wish. The lover willnae disappear
come sunrise. Howbeit, neither shall the servant disappear.
I will trust ye to ken the two are separate and distinct."

Although she accepted him willingly when he returned to
her arms, she scowled at him. "Your generosity humbles
me," she said sarcastically.

"Dinnae goad me, Pleasance. Ye acted with the greatest
folly today. Ye put in danger not only yourself but also me.
Had I been a few moments later, or had someone other than
the Tates attacked you, matters could have ended quite differently."

"I know."

"I will play this as ye wish it played. In truth, I found it
difficult to forget ye were the same woman I had just held
in my arms through the night."

She almost smiled. It was comforting to know that he had
had to struggle to maintain his icy demeanor. Feeling more in
charity with him, she trailed her hand across his broad scarred
chest. He might not know it, but he had given her some hope.
Since he would no longer be closing her out each and every

day, she might yet have a chance to touch his heart, to win his love.

"Heed me, though," he warned. "I am willing to go it your way, but play no tricks. If I think ye are trying to use the passion we share against me or to your own advantage, ye will find yourself with far more reason to flee. I have wit enough to see when I am being made a fool."

Yet, even as he spoke the gentle stroking of her hands upon his stomach was stirring a heat within him that threatened to still his tongue and rob his thoughts.

"Aye, and you will suspect you see tricks and ploys even where there are none," she replied.

"Nay, I think I am a fair mon."

He did not trust her an inch, she knew. She ached to continue to defend herself, but forcefully subdued that urge. His distrust could not be broken with pretty speeches no matter how earnest. She had known that from the start and was determined to remember it. She also recalled that on her first day here they had made a pact—she would prove him wrong through her actions. He had agreed to that and she was determined to hold to it. One day she hoped he would shake off that distrust and wake up to the fact that she did not deserve it.

"Fair enough, Tearlach. So"—she trailed her fingers along the waist of his breeches and felt him tremble slightly—"are we to start anew?"

"Aye." He combed his fingers through her thick hair, idly splaying it out over the bearskin and noting how the fire's light drew out the red in her hair.

"The sun has set," she murmured.

"Aye, it has. The Tates handled ye most roughly. If ye have pain, there is no need of ye performing this *duty* tonight."

It was impossible to fully suppress a giggle, which

increased when he scowled at her. "That word *duty* stung, did it?"

Even as he wondered why, he felt a compulsion to be honest. "Aye. I have no great liking for cold duty in my bed."

She slipped her fingers beneath the waistband of his breeches and watched his face tighten with growing desire. "Cold? You claim no great experience in the art of love, but surely you possess enough to know that I was never cold."

"So ye enjoy your duty." He gritted his teeth, fighting to control his rapidly growing passion as she slowly unbuttoned his breeches. "Ye are the one who put the name to it." He flushed, a little embarrassed at the way his voice rose when her small hand curled around his already aroused manhood.

"You are the one who acted as if that was all it was." It was both amusing and exciting to watch him struggle to control his desire as she gently stroked him.

"I have never thought it a duty—yours or mine." He closed his eyes as pleasure swept him with each stroke of her soft hand. "'Tis a dangerous sport ye indulge in, mistress."

"A sport, is it? And by what name is this sport called?"

He laughed hoarsely as he struggled to undo her shift with unsteady fingers. "There is a name or two, but they are far too coarse for your ears, little Pleasance. God above, your touch is enough to crack any man's sanity."

Tugging her tormenting hand away, he eased her shift off her. He wanted to make love to her slowly, savoring every sigh and tremor. As he tossed her shift aside, he suspected that going slowly might be a feat just beyond his grasp. He hoped she never discovered just what she could make him feel. It was too strong, made him too vulnerable. He tossed aside his breeches and slowly lowered himself into her arms.

"This duty," he murmured as he brushed his mouth over hers, "will take a long time to fulfill, little Pleasance."

"A long time?" She made a soft sound of frustration as he continued to hold back the deeper kiss she craved.

"As long as I can make it last." When she began to caress him, he grasped her wandering hands and pinned them to the bearskin. "Nay, none of that. If I allow ye to touch me, I will lose what meager control I have."

"Ah, but I have only just learned to touch you."

"Ye may touch all ye please at another time. Tonight 'tis me who will touch you."

And then he kissed her with a languid hunger that sent her pulse soaring. She mused that there was nothing as intoxicating as Tearlach's kisses, then let desire take full hold of her. She wanted to give herself completely over to the thrill of his touch, the heat of his kiss, and the joy his hoarse love words brought her. His passion at least was real, hot and fierce, and all for her.

She cried out as his warm, slightly fevered kisses reached her breasts. He released his hold on her wrists, and she buried her fingers in his thick hair as he slowly yet greedily suckled. As her passion grew, she tried to rub her body against his, but he held himself apart.

Soon she understood what he had meant. His every kiss, his every touch, was measured. He inched his way from her breasts to her thighs to her toes and back up her legs. When his lips touched the soft curls between her thighs, a brief check occurred in her ever-rising passion. She tried to reach for him, but he caught her hands in his, halting her attempt to push him away. It took but one touch of his tongue to eradicate the cooling effects of her initial shock. When she opened to his intimate kiss, he released her hands. Again she burrowed her fingers in his hair to hold him close as she succumbed to a fever of need, a fever he fed until at last she cried out for him.

On the brink of her climax, she called to him to join with her, but still he ignored her plea and sent her tumbling alone into desire's sweet abyss. She had barely recovered enough to realize what had happened when he began to resurrect her passion. This time he answered her call, driving into her with a force that revealed the strength of his own need. She encouraged his fierce thrusts with hoarse words and the movements of her body. This time his cries blended with hers as their passion crested simultaneously.

As sanity gradually returned, Pleasance neither moved nor opened her eyes. She listened to him secure the cabin and tamp down the fire, hoping he would think she was asleep. Even when he picked her up in his arms she feigned sleep. It was not until he had settled her in his bed and crawled in beside her that she suspected he was not fooled. She could feel him watching her.

"Come, little one, what troubles you?" He eased the blanket below her breasts and watched the tips harden in the cool air.

She refused to open her eyes. "I am shameless."

"I think not. If ye were shameless, ye wouldnae be lying here blushing rose-red with your eyes pinched shut so tightly. Ye are, thank God, a woman of passion. Mayhaps it will ease your embarrassment if I tell ye that what was so new and startling for ye was new to me as well."

She partly opened one eye to look at him, but saw no sign of guile upon his face. "Nay. How could you do what you do not know about?"

"I didnae say I didnae ken what to do, only that I had never done it. A mon doesnae necessarily gain all skill at lovemaking by doing. When men gather to talk, their three favorite topics are politics, money, and the art of love."

Idly swirling his finger around and over the tips of her breasts, he continued. "What women I have been with have all had many men. I found the release I needed with few frills. With ye, I ken that I am the only mon to have touched ye. If ye carry the scent of a mon, 'tis mine." He grinned and kissed the tip of each breast. "Your taste is also most sweet."

She halfheartedly swung her fist at him and he took her into his arms. "So you use me to practice new skills," she accused. It was clear to her that he was contemplating another foray into passion's realm, and she began to wonder if this time she could do the leading.

As she moved her hand caressingly over his stomach, then lower and lower, Tearlach braced himself for that abrupt surge of desire that would come when she finally reached his groin.

"There are a few things I should like to try," he murmured.

"Are there now? Well, mayhaps I have one or two myself," she admitted as she curled her hand around his manhood and felt him tremble.

Easing onto his back and taking her with him, he lay complaisantly beneath her touch, eager to enjoy the pleasure it brought for as long as he could. "Is that so." He began to almost idly caress her, unable to resist touching her.

Settling herself on top of him, she mused that he sounded condescending. It was time to show Tearlach O'Duine that she could be as innovative as he. Besides, she thought as she kissed him and enjoyed his soft growl of appreciation, there was the chance that being the best lover she could be might edge her closer to his heart. The old adage said the best way to a man's heart was through his stomach, but she suspected paying close attention to a place a little lower than that might well prove more effective.

Tearlach murmured his approval as she spread soft kisses over his chest. He placed his hands beneath his head to stop from returning her caresses. If he did, he would drastically shorten the time he could control his passion and simply enjoy her gentle lovemaking. That became harder and harder to do as her kisses moved enticingly lower. The way she was moving her hands over his hips and thighs brought his passion to renewed heights. His control began to slip. He lost it completely when her warm lips brushed his manhood.

Crying out with both pleasure and approval, he reached for her, only to have her grasp him by the wrists to hold his hands away from her. At first, surprise kept him from breaking that light restraint, but then he was glad of it. He wanted to savor the fierce desire she was invoking with every stroke of her tongue. When he felt the warmth of her mouth enclose him, he lost what little willpower he had managed to retain. With a hoarse shout, he dragged her up his body and set her upon him. To his delight, she needed little prompting in the new position and swiftly brought them both to the culmination they craved. So fierce was their passion and its final release that they lay sprawled in each other's arms, recovering for a long while afterward.

"How did ye ken what to do?" he whispered as he held her close to his side, idly smoothing the tangles from her hair.

"Know what?" Pleasance tried and failed to smother a wide yawn.

"How to do that."

There was an odd tone in his voice. She saw no suspicion in his face, just mild wonder. She felt a touch of wonder herself and was a little surprised that pleasuring him had stirred her as deeply as it had.

"You did it to me and said there was naught wrong with such a thing so I felt it must be all right to do the same to you. It was, was it not?"

"Oh, aye, far more than all right."

"That is fine then." She snuggled up against him and closed her eyes. 'I was worried for a moment that I had disgusted you."

"Nay, never that" he murmured, then realized she was already asleep.

Sighing, Tearlach held her close and closed his eyes. Pleasance gave him greater delight than he had ever known. She made him mindless with desire for her. It was going to take a lot of work to keep her from discovering the power she held over him.

Chapter Ten

"Are ye and Tearlach going to be wed?"

Pleasance sighed as she carefully lifted candles out of the dipping kettle. She placed the candle rod across poles carefully laid between two chairs so the candles could cool.

Moira had been home for nearly a week. Several times Pleasance had tried to speak to the girl about what was between her and Tearlach, but she had always balked at the last moment. A part of her had hoped that Moira would either not notice or would simply accept things as they were without question. She knew now it had been a foolish hope.

"Nay, I think not." She felt herself blush and was glad of the need to keep working. It meant she did not have to look directly at the girl.

Moira frowned as she added tallow to one of the two kettles over the fire. "Does he make ye share his bed 'cause ye are his servant?"

"Nay, Moira. There was no force, no coercion. It seems I lack the strength to behave as I ought."

"Or he does."

"Mayhaps we both do, aye. We can begin the bayberry candles soon."

"I like them better than the tallow. 'Tis a pity the berries arenae as plentiful as the animal fat."

"Aye." Pleasance took a deep breath as she prepared to more thoroughly discuss Tearlach and the fact that she shared his bed without the sanction of marriage. "'Tis not right, what Tearlach and I do. I do not wish you to think it is. Not ever. All I said about honor and a woman's good name still hold true."

"Then why do it? Is it because ye love him?"

"Moira . . ."

"I will never tell him. 'Tisnae my place, is it? Ye love him and let him bed ye, but he makes no promises."

"That says it most succinctly. Do not scowl so. There is no law that says he must. I am not sure how to explain this to you."

"Ye dinnae need to mince words with me, Pleasance. We learn the ways of nature early around here. I ken how folk have the urge to rut same as animals. People just dinnae have a special rutting season. They can feel that way each and every day of the year. I ken it can be done without marriage, or in marriage, or for love, or for coin, or," she added softly, "in violence and hate."

Knowing that Moira was remembering what had happened to her mother, Pleasance hugged the child. To her delight Moira returned the gesture. They exchanged soft smiles when they finally parted and returned to candlemaking.

"There is a reluctance within me to talk of this, Moira. It seems as if it is a matter of *do as I say, not as I do.* I tell you how you should act, then act another way myself. Knowing how thoroughly my name is blackened back home certainly weakened my convictions, but I cannot wholly blame that. I am merely weak, and can only stress that when you are grown you should not behave as I have."

"Weel, I cannae see it as all wrong either. There is a lot

here that I must think upon. I saw how Tearlach stalked ye, Pleasance. If ye were home, not here as a servant, ye could have gotten a rest from it. He didnae let ye even try to get strong enough to say nay."

"You must not blame Tearlach, Moira."

"Oh, I dinnae blame him exactly. Still, he hasnae acted weel. Ye are right, Pleasance. 'Tisnae an easy thing to talk on. There are too many twists and turns. I will just say that I see the truth of it all. No need to worry on that. I also see that, even if ye are a good person and want to do what is right and expected, things can go awry. As Tearlach says, people are people. No one is a saint."

"Aye, and he should know that well enough," Pleasance drawled, and grinned when Moira giggled.

As the day wore on, Pleasance realized that Moira not only spoke with a wisdom beyond her years but also meant all she had said. There would be no recriminations from the girl, nor any false expectations. It was a great relief, Pleasance decided as she sent Moira to fetch Tearlach for supper. Either reaction from the girl—placing blame or pushing for marriage—could have made life intolerable for all of them. As Pleasance set the table, she wondered idly if Tearlach had given any thought to Moira's feelings. He had claimed to, but that did not necessarily make it true.

When Tearlach saw Moira walking toward him, he set down the ax he had been using to split logs for the fire. He had subtly avoided his sister since her return, which alternately made him feel guilty and foolish. Although he and Pleasance practiced some discretion when they shared a bed at night, he was sure Moira was fully aware of what was going on. Too often he had caught her watching him and Pleasance with a solemn intensity that made him uncomfortable. He knew he was going to have to get up the courage to talk to Moira, that he would have to stop relying on Pleasance to sort it all out.

"Pleasance is setting the table for supper," Moira announced.

"I will be along shortly," he murmured.

Moira made no move to leave. "Ye should marry Pleasance."

Grabbing up his tools, he shot her a narrow-eyed look and strode toward the barn. "Did Pleasance say that?"

Hurrying to keep up with her brother's long strides, Moira stayed close at his heels. "Nay. She said there is no law that says ye must."

"She is right."

Following him around as he put his things away and secured the barn for the night, Moira continued, "Of course, I have heard it said that a mon ought to wed a woman if he seduces her. Something about it being the honorable thing to do. Of course, if Pleasance is a round-heeled sort of lass . . ."

Tearlach whirled to face his sister, mistrusting her look of sweet innocence. "Round-heeled? 'Tis hardly the sort of talk a young girl should spout."

"Jake said it describes the lass at the tavern, being that she is real easy to tip onto her back."

"Something ye should ken nothing about. And, nay, Pleasance isnae that sort. Not at all."

"She is a good woman then."

"Aye. And I best not catch ye saying otherwise."

"Never. Of course, that still leaves us with the matter of honor."

"Damn honor." Tearlach strode out of the barn, glared at her as she hurried out after him, and shut the barn door. "Give it up, Moira. Ye are too young to play this game."

She shrugged. "If she isnae a tart, then she is a good woman. So-o, ye must marry her."

Sighing, his annoyance leaving him in a rush, Tearlach leaned against the barn. "That is what those in the village would say."

"But ye dinnae mean to do it."

"Nay."

"She says ye dinnae make her sleep with ye."

Tearlach was only faintly surprised to learn that Pleasance had discussed the matter so thoroughly with Moira. He had suffered a flicker of suspicion that Pleasance might use Moira to try to force him into marrying her. Yet again he had anticipated guile on her part and there had been none. His suspicions were often tainted with guilt now. Pleasance was not acting as he had expected. He dared not lower his guard, however. Instinct told him that any rebuff or betrayal by her now would make her earlier rejection of him in Worcester feel like a mere peccadillo, a realization that alternately dismayed and annoyed him.

"'Tis true. Her place as an indentured servant is a thing apart from the rest," he said.

"Ye can do that, can ye? Separate your lives like that?"

"Aye. Can and will."

"Why dinnae ye want to marry her? Cease glaring at me. 'Tis a reasonable question."

"I dinnae think she would be a good choice." But even as he spoke, a voice in his head scorned him as a liar.

"Pshaw. Pleasance is doing all a wife would, and fairly well from what I can see."

"She is still new here. Aye, she is doing well now, but that could change."

"Ye dinnae trust her, do ye? Why?"

"She is like her kin. The spoiled, pampered daughter of rich folk. When I first saw her, I made a dead aim for her. I thought she was different. Weel, she soon showed me the error of my ways and gave me a blunt, cold rebuff. 'Twas clear that she felt herself too good for some poor backwoods farmer." He held up his hand when Moira started to protest. "We both ken that I have a wee bit of wealth of my own. Howbeit, Pleasance didnae know that then, and she doesnae now, and I mean to keep it that way." He started toward the cabin, considering the conversation at an end.

Moira hurried after him. "If Pleasance is so much like her kin, why did they turn her away?"

Tearlach's pace slowed a little, and she knew she had scored a point with her observation. "Ye have e'er told me that people turn from what is different," she went on. "That people turn from me because I am not like they are. Maybe Pleasance's kin set her aside because she isnae like them at all. And mayhaps that cold rebuff ye claim she gave ye had naught to do with who she is and what she thinks, but was forced upon her by circumstances. Ye have e'er told me that there are always two sides to every story. Weel, it seems to me that ye are looking at only one."

"And it seems to me that ye talk entirely too much."

Since they had reached the cabin, and chanced being overheard by Pleasance, Moira made no reply to Tearlach's sullen remark. She simply shrugged and entered the cabin, leaving her brother on the front porch to wash up. In her heart she was firmly decided about Tearlach and Pleasance—they belonged together. She was not, however, certain that her words carried the persuasive weight needed to make her brother reach the same conclusion. She could only hope she had set him to thinking about it.

Tearlach scowled as Moira shut the door behind her. He stood before the washing table, poured water from the heavy earthen ewer into the big washbowl, and rolled up his sleeves. He had made a grave error in treating Moira as an equal, catering to her obvious intelligence and curiosity about people and life. The girl now felt free to lecture her elders, he thought crossly.

As he took a soft cloth from a wall peg and dried his face and hands, he was struck again by Moira's quick mind and unsettling intuition. Although her words occasionally lacked the maturity of her thoughts, her meaning was clear this time. Tearlach sighed. The fact that his young sister's words echoed what Corbin Matthias had said weeks ago added weight to them.

Guilt nibbled at him. He had promised Corbin that he would be fair to Pleasance, that he would not allow his harsh judgment of her earlier behavior toward him to color his opinion of her subsequent actions. Yet as he entered the cabin, he could not be sure he was keeping that promise.

Pleasance grew wary as the meal dragged on. Both Tearlach and Moira were parsimonious with their conversation. If she saw some hint of anger in either of the O'Duines, she would have assumed they had squabbled and dismissed their moods. As it was, their solemnity seemed inappropriate on Moira's birthday. For a brief moment she feared that she had gotten the date wrong.

"You are thirteen today, correct, Moira?" she asked gently when the girl finally finished her meal.

After a quick, nervous look at Tearlach, Moira nodded. "Aye, thirteen."

"Wonderful." Pleasance began to clear the table. "For a moment I had begun to fear that I had misjudged the day. I would have felt very foolish presenting my meager attempts at a celebration."

Tearlach grabbed a couple of dinner plates and followed Pleasance to the sink. "We dinnae celebrate the day," he whispered.

Pleasance took the plates from him and dropping them into the washing tub, stared at him in open surprise. "Why not?"

"Ye need to ask me?" he hissed, struggling to keep his voice low so that Moira would not hear.

"Aye, I believe I do. Why not?"

"I have told ye all about our mother. 'Twas a grievous, painful time. We cannae celebrate that."

"No one asked you to. I mean to celebrate Moira's birth. She had naught to do with that crime or your mother's death. You yourself told me that your mother made no effort to keep on living. Do ye mean to blame Moira for that?"

"Nay. Ye ken verra weel that I dinnae, that I ne'er have."

"Well, it seems to me that by not taking some note of her birthday you are saying to her that you do blame her. In fact, if you will pardon me for offering an opinion on something you may consider none of my business . . ."

"Offer away. Ye will do so anyhow."

She ignored his grumbling. "I think Moira needs to celebrate this day more than many another child. She needs to know that no one blames her for the past, that we are happy she was born no matter how that birth came about or what sadness it brought at the time."

He stared at her, her quiet words pounding in his head. She was right, so right that he was ashamed he had not seen the matter in that light before. Worse, he could almost hear his mother shouting a hearty agreement. He had always felt that the celebration of Moira's birthday was something that could only stir up bad memories, and Moira had seemed to agree with him. Now he wondered if he had ever clearly seen the situation through her eyes.

"I have no gift to give her," he said.

Pleasance took two packages from a cupboard and placed them in his hands. "The top one is from you."

"Is it now? Moira will ken that I didnae get it."

"I think she will see your acceptance of the celebration as gift enough." As he started to walk away, she added, "This time." She met his brief frown with a smile as she picked up the pie and custard she had prepared and took them to the table.

Tearlach plunked the packages down in front of a wide-eyed Moira and took his seat. "Pleasance says that the top one is from me." He returned his sister's quick grin with a wink.

Moira turned to thank Pleasance, only to gasp at the dessert set before her. "Is that rhubarb pie? Oh, and custard?"

"Aye." Pleasance began to slice the pie. "'Tis your favorite, if I remember correctly."

"Ye do indeed. Oh, I dinnae ken which to do first—eat the pie or unwrap my gifts."

"Unwrap the gifts," Tearlach advised. "I wish to ken what I have given ye."

Moira laughed and began to open her gifts. Tearlach was as surprised as his sister when she unwrapped a dress and frilly bonnet. It was hard to figure when Pleasance had had time to make them, yet clearly she had eked out some.

He watched his sister closely. Moira beamed, clearly delighted, as she changed into and showed off her new outfit. Tearlach allowed her to stay up a little longer than usual, and when she did finally head to bed, she practically skipped up to the loft. He entered her room some time later to kiss her good-night, as was his habit, and found her taking a final look at her bonnet. It was yet more proof of how wrong he had been to deny her birthday celebrations.

"I am sorry, Moira," he murmured.

She frowned as she scrambled into bed. "Sorry for what?"

"For not honoring your birthday before." He sat down on the edge of the mattress.

"Oh. There is naught to be sorry for, Tearlach."

"I assumed ye felt the same way I did. Howbeit, I ne'er truly asked ye."

"Weel, I did feel the same, more or less. Yet tonight I thought verra little about Mama and her suffering. Was that wrong of me?"

"Nay. Ye cannae spend your whole life thinking about a sad time ye had naught to do with. Pleasance is right. 'Twas a bad time, but 'twasnae your birth which made it so. That was a good thing. It deserves a happy marking. From now on it shall have one."

"Weel, I did enjoy it. Ye must thank Pleasance again for me. And thank ye for allowing it."

He kissed her cheek. "Ye are most welcome, brat. Now—to sleep." He patted her hand and left after snuffing the candles.

Pleasance looked up briefly from scrubbing the kitchen table when she heard Tearlach return. She had begun to feel uncertain. She had interfered in a standing family tradition. As wrong as that tradition had been, it was not her place to change things. Tearlach had seemed to accept her interference, but maybe only because Moira had been right there. When he sat down in his chair before the huge fireplace without saying anything to her, her heart sank.

She bore up beneath his silence for as long as she could, scrubbing clean everything in the kitchen that needed it and a few things that did not. Finally, it grew too dark to see. Whatever was causing Tearlach to stare into the smoldering fire had to be discussed. If he was furious with her, she meant to face it. She knew she was right about Moira's birthday, but she would concede that she had overstepped her bounds.

After taking a few deep breaths to steady herself, Pleasance walked over to the fireplace and nudged Tearlach's feet off the three-legged stool. She sat down on the stool right in front of him, forcing him to take notice of her. She was a little surprised when he smiled faintly. There did not appear to be even the faintest hint of anger on his face. Pleasance began to feel just a little bit confused.

"Did ye begin to think that I wasnae paying ye enough attention?" he asked as he leaned forward, took her braid in his hand, and began to undo it.

"Well, nay. I thought ye might be angry with me, if you want the truth of it."

"Ah, about Moira's birthday. Nay, ye were right about that. Moira's birth was no crime in and of itself; 'twas a joy and a blessing. My mother's memory still darkens the day for me, however. I sometimes wonder how I can feel that this is my home when 'tis in this land that my mother was killed. Aye, and my father." He idly combed his fingers through her hair, further undoing the braid.

"'Tis hard to leave the land of your birth and sail off to a new place," she said. "Aye, the journey itself often proves more than one can bear. I was fortunate. I was born here, others having already prepared the way for me."

He nodded and sighed. "There is another reason for my moodiness. I have wrestled with it and it leaves me with the bite of guilt. I think it, then feel I shouldnae have e'en let the thought into my mind."

When he fell silent, Pleasance waited before pressing him to explain himself. It was not often that Tearlach spoke about his thoughts, his feelings, or even his past. She did not want one of those rare moments of revelation to slip from her hands.

"What thoughts trouble you so, Tearlach?" she asked, and was relieved when he returned his full attention to her.

"Every so often I feel angry with my mother. I truly believe she simply gave up the will to live. Once Moira was born, she was weak and ill, but not fatally so. She just let herself slip away."

"And so, now and then, you feel as if she deserted you."

Pleasance smiled faintly when he grimaced and nodded. "You are not alone in your thinking. In truth, 'twas the first thought which passed through my mind when you told me the story. The rape must have been more than she could bear. She was not able to forgive herself or to live for the loved ones she would otherwise leave behind."

"She could have tried harder to stay alive."

"Aye, I think she might have. She was your mother, but as long as you do not hate her or curse her, then I do not see any disloyalty on your part. If you simply accept that you have a right to be angry—and I think you do—then you can probably stop this yearly moodiness. You can then forgive her and get on with your life."

"Ye are right. I do need to forgive her. It wasnae easy to raise Moira with no woman about and when there was a problem I had difficulty solving or a decision I couldnae make, I wanted to curse my mother. Aye, and a time or two I did."

"And then you felt very guilty indeed. Ah, poor Tearlach. There is certainly a great deal you should feel guilty about, but being angry because your mother gave up on life is not one of them."

Tearlach saw the teasing glint in her wide eyes. He stood up, gently toppled her off the stool, and pinned her to the bearskin rug. The moment his body touched hers, his desire for her stirred to life.

"And is this something I should feel guilty about?" he asked as he brushed a kiss over her lips.

"Most definitely, you rogue."

"Weel, 'tis a guilt I can live with," he murmured, and gave her a slow, hungry kiss.

At last he ended the kiss and looked down at her. She was such a source of confusion for him! She worked hard and knew how to do many domestic chores he had not expected her to know about. More important, there was a quality of understanding and compassion to her that surprised him. And that Pleasance had become so close to Moira puzzled him. Even his desire for her was unexpected, for she was slim, shy, and occasionally a little prudish—not his usual type at all. In fact, Pleasance Dunstan aroused in him a bundle of contradictory feelings that he was not sure he could ever untangle even if he wanted to. He shook his head as he began to undo the bodice of her gown.

"Would it not be better to go to your room?" she asked, curling her arms about his neck and making no attempt to halt his deceptively idle removal of her clothes.

"Aye, it might, but 'twould take more time than I care to spend."

She slid her hands down to his trim hips and slipped one hand between them to unbutton his breeches. "You are feeling an urge to hurry, are you?" She eased her hand inside to slowly stroke him.

Tearlach closed his eyes and gave himself over to the enjoyment of her touch. Each time they made love she grew a little more daring, a little more sure of what he liked. There was a large part of him that readily acknowledged it was going to be hard to let her go when her year of indenture ended. Most of the time he was able to wrestle that voice into silence, push that concern aside, but when his passion ran hot, the voice grew very loud indeed.

"Oh, aye, I am in a hurry." he finally replied, and began to tug off her clothes with more haste. "Ye have the skill to make me eager, lassie. Aye, verra eager indeed."

He tossed aside the last of her clothes and sat up to quickly shed his own. Watching him, Pleasance felt her desire grow. Tearlach O'Duine was a powerful, beautiful figure of a man, from his broad, smoothly muscled chest to his well-shaped calves. Whenever she saw him naked, a hint of doubt and uncertainty would briefly dim her passion before his touch would start it climbing rapidly again. How could she, thin small Pleasance, win the heart of such a man?

When he returned to her arms, she swiftly wrapped her limbs around him. Their relationship would be loudly, repeatedly condemned by anyone who chanced to discover it, but she could not bring herself to worry about that. For a little while she could call Tearlach O'Duine hers, and she intended to savor that possession to its fullest.

Chapter Eleven

Pleasance gaped at Tearlach and wondered if a few hard slaps to his head would knock some sense into the man. He could not be in his right mind. She had sensed a growing tension in him in the fortnight since Moira's birthday, but she would never have guessed his plans.

"We had a frost last night," she said. She glanced at Moira, who was dutifully eating her honey-sweetened oatmeal and watching her brother closely.

"Aye, it did get cold." Tearlach sipped his coffee, cradling the heavy earthenware cup in his hands.

"And you yourself said that snow is definitely in the offing," Pleasance added.

"Aye, 'tis. I swear I can smell it in the air."

"Then why are you going hunting, you thickheaded Scot?" Pleasance lightly but firmly banged both fists on the table. "The last time we discussed your hunting, you specifically said that this was a bad time of the year to hunt and trap. Now you say you plan to trudge off at first light."

Tearlach nodded and, pushing his plate aside, rested his forearms on the table. Pleasance had abruptly stopped eating the moment he made his announcement, and he wondered if he should have waited until after they had finished breakfast. She worked too hard to miss even one meal, he mused, then turned his full attention to the matter at hand. Everything Pleasance said was right—it *was* a poor time to go hunting. He had to try to make her understand why he was going to do it anyway.

"Aye, going hunting now could prove risky because of the uncertain weather," he said. "Howbeit, this year I must take that risk."

"But why? It seems unnecessarily reckless."

"It may be, lassie, but all that time I was laid up in bed recovering from my wounds, I should have been out in the forest. There was good hunting then, hunting I couldnae afford to lose. I have made a bargain for a certain number of pelts with a man back in Worcester. He and I will lose money if I cannae make the quota. Weel, now I plan to try and make up for lost time."

"By getting yourself killed?"

"Truth is, I hadnae planned on doing that." He almost smiled at the look of disgust she sent his way, but knew that would be a mistake considering her present temper. "As ye say, I ken the risks, and I mean to keep them in mind. Aye, I do," he said when she just frowned. "And I will keep myself near home so that I can hurry back if the weather turns dangerous."

"It seems mad to go out at all."

"I have to try and recoup the time I lost. There is no arguing it."

"Nay, but that will not stop me from trying."

Not many hours passed before Tearlach realized that Pleasance was serious about trying to stop him. No matter where he went—in the cabin, outside, or in the stable—she would soon follow. Most often she did not even make an excuse for her sudden appearance. She told him he was an idiot for wanting to go out hunting when he knew it was dangerous, then she left. Occasionally Moira was right behind Pleasance to echo her sentiments. Tearlach was torn between laughter and anger, touched by their obvious concern for his well-being, but annoyed at being told what to do.

Late in the afternoon, he went out to the stable on the excuse of rechecking his saddle. Sure that Pleasance would soon follow, he hid by the side of the stable door. Just as he began to think she was going to miss the opportunity to badger him, the soft sound of skirts rustling against hard-packed earth reached his ears. His smile turned wicked.

Pleasance stepped inside, placed her hands on her hips, and frowned as she looked around. She was certain Tearlach had said he was going to the stable for one last check on his mount and saddle before supper, yet there was no sign of him. All the way from the cabin she had rehearsed what she would say, and it annoyed her that he was not there to hear her say it. Then again, maybe, having caught on to her ploy, he was hiding to escape the nagging that had been coming at him in an unrelenting stream since breakfast.

A soft sound from behind her drew Pleasance's attention. She was just turning toward the noise when two strong hands grasped her waist. Her screech of surprise was choked off when she was pressed up against a stack of hay bales. Her momentary fear was swept away when she saw that her captor was a grinning Tearlach. She scowled at him.

"You have just taken ten years off my life," she grumbled.

"May I say that ye age beautifully, Mistress Dunstan." He chuckled.

"You were lurking here, just waiting for me to walk into your trap." Pleasance could not keep the scolding note from her voice even when he began to kiss and nuzzle her throat. "I do not appreciate being the victim of such childish trickery."

"'Tis strange, but I find your attempts to be prim and

haughty verra alluring." He began to undo her bodice, placing a lingering kiss upon each newly bared inch of skin. "I am inspired to kiss and stroke your bad mood away, to change it from cool and aloof to hot and welcoming."

When he tugged her bodice down, freeing her breasts, and cupped them in his hands, Pleasance lost her power of speech. The way he stroked her nipples into hard inviting buds with his lightly calloused thumbs left her struggling to breathe. She tried to recall where they were and what she had wanted to say to him.

"I did not come here for this," she murmured, only to thread her fingers into his thick dark hair as he began to kiss and suckle her. "I came here to give you a scolding."

"I ken it." He undid her skirt, tugged it over her slim hips, and let it drop to the ground around her ankles. He did the same with her two petticoats—one by one. "Ye came to tell me that I am a great fool to go out hunting."

"Aye. I did." When she realized he had stripped her to her chemise and hose, she grasped him by the arms. She knew she had no strength to push him away, however, and as he tongued the small hollow of her throat, she was not sure she wanted him to stop. "'Tis the middle of the day," she protested, her voice a husky whisper.

"Nay, 'tis nearly time for supper." He chuckled again as he finished tugging off her chemise and paused to pleasure her taut stomach with several kisses. "'Twas good of ye to bring the feast to me." His desire intensified when Pleasance responded with a husky giggle.

It was almost impossible to talk when he was kissing the inside of her thighs, but she struggled to remind him of a few pertinent facts. "Tearlach, I am standing here in broad daylight in naught but my hose and garters . . ."

"And a bonnie sight it is too." He stepped back from her only enough to undo his breeches. He grinned faintly when he realized she had already unfastened his shirt without his even noticing it. "I really dinnae think I have ever seen a prettier one."

"Thank you very kindly, but do you really wish others to see me?"

"Nay. Why would ye e'en ask such a fool question?"

"Because you have left the stable door wide open. 'Tis hardly private here. Anyone could look right in at us."

Tearlach saw the sense of that and quickly moved to shut and bar the door. When he turned back to her, he had to pause for a moment to catch his breath. She stood watching him, a faint blush on her face. Her long chestnut hair hung down to her waist in thick waves, providing a faint concealment of her charms. The way she looked with her hair loose and wearing only her hose and blue ribbons for garters made it difficult for him to think clearly. He did not believe he had ever seen a fairer, more tempting sight. When she frowned a little and glanced down at her clothes, pooled around her feet, he finally found the strength to move.

"Nay," he said as he reached her and took her into his arms. "Dinnae even think of getting dressed yet. I shut the stable door. We are private now."

"Are we now. And what about Moira?"

"She willnae intrude upon us, and weel ye ken it. Aye, and she is busy working that old butter churn anyway. Nay, we will be left alone for quite a while."

He turned so that his back was against the bales of hay and lifted her into his arms. The moment she put her arms around his neck, he grasped her hips and silently prompted her to wrap her slender legs around his waist. Tearlach eased her body onto his at the same moment he began to kiss her.

Pleasance shuddered with delight as their bodies were joined. She knew Tearlach was just trying to divert her from her campaign to get him to cancel his hunting trip. Such trickery deserved a stern rebuff, but she had no intention of giving him one—not yet. His lovemaking she could not refuse. She suspected she would pay dearly for her weakness later, but for now she intended to partake of it with lusty greed.

"Lean back, loving," Tearlach whispered.

She obeyed and gave a soft cry of pleasure when he drew the tip of one breast deep into his mouth. With his hands on her hips, he moved her in a slow rhythm that left her gasping. Pleasance closed her eyes and gave herself completely over to his lovemaking. When she felt the culmination of her need burst within her, she pulled herself closer to him. He kissed her, plunging his tongue into her mouth with the same ferocity that he moved her body on his. He groaned and held her tightly as he sank to his knees and pressed his sweat-dampened face against her breasts. Pleasance gave a moan of deep satisfaction as he released his seed deep within her.

Tearlach held Pleasance closely, moving only enough to cradle her face against his throat and smooth his hands over her hair. He could feel the straw poking through his breeches, but ignored it. He did not want anything to ruin the pleasure of the moment. Tearlach knew the warmth, the tenderness he felt for Pleasance were dangerous, but for a little while he gave them free rein.

After a few more minutes, he reluctantly eased their bodies apart. He continued to hold her on his lap as he settled himself more comfortably, resting his back against the hay bales. Pleasance felt good curled up in his arms. He could not stop from thinking that that was where she belonged . . . for far more than one year. It was a thought he was entertaining more often than he wished. He still suffered the sting of her abrupt rebuff when he had tried to court her as a gentleman should. That was something she had yet to explain satisfactorily.

"Such a dark frown," she murmured, and lightly ran her finger over his lips. "Mayhaps I succumb to the sin of vanity, but I thought I had just made you happy."

"Oh, aye, ye did that, lassie." He tucked her hair behind her ears and gave her a faint smile. "Ye made me verra happy indeed. So happy, I clean forgot until just now how straw can impale a mon." He grinned when she laughed, then tightened his light hold on her when she started to move away. "And where are ye going?"

"Back to the cabin." She made no further effort to break his grasp. "I should not neglect my duties for so long."

"They will be waiting for ye on the morrow, but I will be gone."

"Aye, so ye shall—out into the December cold to hunt beasts who are no doubt already sensibly curled up in their warm burrows. I believe I came to tell you how foolish you are." She frowned when he made no reply, but continued to idly spread her clothes out on the hay. "Now what are you doing?"

"Making a wee bed for us."

He laughed when she gave a soft squeal of surprise as he tumbled her down onto her clothes. Before she could say anything he kissed her and kept on kissing her until she lay still beneath him. He sat up and began to shed the rest of his own clothes.

Pleasance only briefly considered protesting his actions. She much preferred making love with him to returning to her never-ending chores. As he had reminded her, he would be gone by morning, but her chores would still be there. When he was finally as naked as she was, she readily welcomed him back into her arms.

"Moira is going to begin to wonder what has happened to us," she said, softly humming her delight when he began to cover her breasts with kisses.

"Nay, she will ken what is about."

"Mayhaps that is not such a good thing."

"Hush, lassie. Ye worry too much. Enjoy. There is so little in our short, accursed lives that can truly pleasure us. Why not grasp what does?"

There was a flaw in that simple, somewhat selfish view of life, but Pleasance decided not to argue with him. "Some of us can get a bit greedy."

"Ah, now, with ye, Pleasance, I can get verra greedy indeed."

She found Tearlach's greed for her a heady thing. Each time they made love she grew a little more wanton. She suspected that once she was alone and back in Worcester, she would occasionally have good reason to regret that wantonness, but for now she found it exciting.

When Tearlach rolled onto his back, pulling her on top of him, she knew what he wanted. She took control of their lovemaking without further urging. That he made no secret of his pleasure increased her own. They both gave soft groans of desire when she eased their bodies together. For a while Pleasance teased Tearlach, holding back the ferocity he so clearly wanted from her. But soon her own needs broke her control and she took them both to the heights before she collapsed into his welcoming arms. It was a long time before she found the strength to sit up.

"Now, I really must return to my work," she said as she idly smoothed her hand over his broad chest. "If I do not, there will be no supper for you, Master O'Duine."

"Am I going to have to hear another scold as I dine?"

"Quite possibly. I suspect I shall recall the one I meant to give you when I first stepped in here and you managed to distract me."

"Ye willnae change my mind."

"Oh, I realized that quite early on."

"Then why have ye—and Moira—continued to torment me all day long?"

"I want to be very sure that I have said all that needs saying before you actually embark on your foolish journey."

As he reached to grab her, Pleasance leapt to her feet. He just laughed and rolled to a sitting position. He reached for his clothes, and she turned her attention to getting dressed. She rested her foot on one of the bales and straightened out her stocking, retying her garter. When she moved to do the same with her other stocking, her attention was drawn to the small cracks and knotholes in the back wall which let in slivers of light. She grew very still, narrowing her eyes at one particular spot as she struggled to understand what was wrong with it. And then she realized—someone was peering at her through the small opening! She froze in place, then gasped out Tearlach's name as she snatched up a petticoat and held it in front of her.

"What is it?" Tearlach asked as he yanked on his boots.

"Someone has been watching us . . . *is* watching us." She pointed a shaking finger toward the knothole where she had seen an eye.

"I dinnae see a thing."

"He probably heard me and has run away, but I swear to you, I saw someone peering at us."

"Stay here," Tearlach ordered, and he grabbed his knife before slipping out of the stable.

Pleasance scrambled to finish dressing. Only briefly did she wonder how long the person she had seen might have been watching her and Tearlach. She did not want to know how many of their intimate moments together had been witnessed by some stranger. While she was still doing up her bodice she went to find Tearlach.

* * *

Tearlach moved swiftly but cautiously. He saw no one around the side of the stable, but he searched the whole area, even going a short distance into the wood. There was no sign of anyone.

He knew Pleasance was not the sort of woman to imagine things. He also *felt* that someone had been there, *felt* that some presence had come and gone. No matter how often he told himself it was utter nonsense, he could not shake the feeling. Worse, he had the strongest sense that the presence had not been a kind one. He hurried back to the stable only to find Pleasance rounding the corner looking for him.

"I thought I told ye to stay inside." He searched the ground in front of the knothole Pleasance had pointed out to him from the inside, crouching down to study it closely. "Nothing," he grumbled as he stood up. "No sign at all."

Pleasance wrapped her arms around herself, feeling suddenly chilled to the bone. "I really did see someone, Tearlach. I swear I did."

"Aye, and I believe ye." He stepped closer and gave her a quick kiss on the cheek. "Go on back into the house, lassie. I will have another good look around the place."

"But you do not think that you will find a thing do you?"

"Weel, nay. There is no sign or trail to follow."

"Shall I bring you your musket?"

"Nay. If whoever it was had meant us any harm, he wouldnae have disappeared."

Although Pleasance did not wholeheartedly agree, she did not argue. She quickly returned to the cabin. It did not surprise her when Tearlach returned a half hour later and just shrugged.

"Are you sure whoever it was is not a danger to us?" she asked as she began to set the table for the evening meal.

"If he was, he would have stayed to stir up trouble instead of fleeing like a frightened hare."

Tearlach sat down at the table and smiled when Moira hurried inside from the back garden. In reply to his question, she said that she had not seen anyone around the cabin all day. Tearlach reassured Pleasance, wishing he actually felt the calm confidence he affected.

Briefly he considered delaying his hunting trip and staying to guard the women, but he dismissed the thought. He needed to make up for the weeks he had lost after being mauled by the bear. The only person he suspected was Moira's father, Lucien, and he doubted the man would simply peek at him and Pleasance, then run away. By the time the meal was over, he had almost convinced himself that their Peeping Tom had been the young son of one of his closest neighbors. He would just remind Pleasance and Moira to be careful, and they would be as safe as always.

Pleasance kept her back toward Tearlach as she slipped out of her shift and reached for a long, warm nightdress. A startled laugh erupted from her when Tearlach abruptly grabbed her around the waist and tugged her down onto the bed. He easily pulled her beneath the covers with him. Pleasance gave him a light slap on the arm when he grinned at her.

"I was putting that on because it gets very cold at night now," she said, snuggling into his arms.

"I intend to make this a very warm night," he said as he playfully nuzzled her neck, causing her to laugh.

"If you intend to get up and go hunting at first light, should you not get some sleep?" She idly smoothed her foot up and down his muscled calf.

"Aye, some. A few hours' less sleep is a small price to pay for enjoying your sweet warmth."

"How you do flatter me, Master O'Duine." She giggled

when he blew in her ear, but she quickly grew serious again. "Nothing I have said has changed your mind about this hunting trip, has it?"

"Nay, lassie. I lost nearly a full half of the hunting season lying about in bed because of that bastard Lucien. I have a chance to make up for some of that lost revenue by hunting now. In truth, I have always wondered in the past if I have cost myself some profits by quitting the field before the other hunters do. Now I will learn the answer to that question. Hunting and trapping are why I am out here, Pleasance."

But even as he spoke, Tearlach realized that his enthusiasm for the hunt had waned in the last few months. He was reluctant to leave the cabin, wander through the forest, and spend the nights alone. To his chagrin, he strongly suspected that Pleasance was the reason for his lack of interest, something he had no intention of admitting. "I am not here just to farm the land. Furs still pay weel too. I cannae ignore that."

"Of course not." She traced the shape of his jaw with one finger, hating the need to trouble him with her fears, but driven to do so by the added worry over Moira's safety. "And what about the man who was spying on us today?"

"If it was a mon."

"Some instinct tells me that it was."

"Aye, I have the same feeling. Still, he ran away." When she started to protest, he gave her a quick kiss. "I cannae give up a chance to earn my livelihood just because we saw a ghostie."

"Nay, I understand. And, aye, before you say any more, I will be most careful. 'Tis not only myself that I must watch out for but Moira as well. Such responsibility will keep me very alert."

"And I shall be sure to leave ye with a loaded musket and a pistol." He held her a little more tightly. "Now, lassie, there is the wee matter of a proper fareweel for your hunter."

"I do not believe you have anything proper in mind, sir," she murmured.

Pleasance muttered sleepily and stretched out in the bed. She moved her hand over the sheet and frowned as she came fully awake. She turned to stare at the empty place next to her and sighed. Tearlach had slipped away without a word.

As she got out of bed she shivered and scrambled to get dressed. There was the definite bite of winter in the air. She hurried over to the window, opened the inside shutters, and cautiously opened the leaded paned window itself. The blast of cold air that slapped her in the face caused her to gasp and hastily relatch the window. After a moment's consideration, she secured the shutters and closed the heavy draperies as well.

"This time even *I* could smell the snow in the air," she grumbled as she lit the lamps in the room and began to make the bed. "And that great big idiot Scotsman has gone hunting in it."

"He will be all right, willnae he, Pleasance?"

Moira's voice caught Pleasance by surprise. One glance at Moira's worried expression and unsteady bottom lip caused Pleasance to hurry over and hug the girl.

"Aye," she assured Moira. "Your brother is far too pig-headed to be beaten by winter."

Pleasance prayed that she would not be proven a liar.

Chapter Twelve

Tearlach studied the pile of pelts and muttered a curse. They were good pelts, but there were not many of them. It had not been a successful hunting trip after all. He had been roaming the woods for a fortnight and was no richer, just colder, more exhausted, and increasingly eager to return home.

After he had been out hunting for only a few days, there had been one small snowstorm to add to his misery. It had not been serious enough to drive him back to the cabin, but he was keeping a closer eye on the dull skies. What really bothered him was that the snow, little though it was, had not melted, which meant that he left a clear trail wherever he went. He did not like that at all.

He poked at the small campfire he had allowed himself. It provided barely enough warmth to stay alive, although it had served to cook the rabbit he had caught for his supper. Tearlach swore that he would never go hunting in the winter again unless faced with starvation. It was the act of a madman, especially when it meant leaving behind a warm bed and a willing lass. He shook his head. He had been a fool.

Spreading his blanket on a patch of ground he had cleared of snow, Tearlach curled up on it and covered himself with two more thick blankets. Near at hand was more wood to feed the fire. This was the last night, he promised himself. At first light he would begin the trek home—back to Pleasance, back to Moira. He smiled faintly as he closed his eyes. Just thinking of Pleasance brought him a little more warmth.

As he crept through the leafless underbrush, Lucien Dubois slipped his knife free of the sheath strapped to his thigh. He made no sound as he approached the sleeping man. He could not believe he had found his enemy alone and so vulnerable. He scratched his thick beard with his mittened hand, then tugged his knit cap down over his ears. Leading the enraged bear to Tearlach had been a brilliant plan, and Lucien had been furious to hear that it had failed. He had been waiting a long time for a second chance.

He grinned and tightened his grip on his knife as he studied his prey through the dim gray light of a near dawn. Tearlach O'Duine was getting soft, he thought as he edged closer to his enemy's sleeping form. The man had spent too much time enslaved by women and locked up in a cabin. He would pay for that weakness now. Lucien almost laughed as he scented victory.

When he was only one step away from Tearlach, Lucien prepared to strike. It would be a real coup to take Tearlach O'Duine's scalp. The man had an admirable reputation amongst friend and foe alike. Lucien savored the thought of proving those tales all wrong.

As he raised his knife, ready to bury it deep into Tearlach, a hand lashed out and grabbed him by the wrist, halting his strike. Lucien found himself staring into Tearlach's fury-hardened features. A scream of pure rage escaped him even as Tearlach punched him full in the face, sending him sprawling backward onto the frosty ground.

Flinging aside his blankets, Tearlach leapt to his feet, his knife in one hand and his pistol in the other. As Lucien slowly rose, Tearlach took aim. He fired, only to curse viciously when the inhumanly lucky Lucien flung himself to the side and escaped wounding. There would be no time to reload.

"So, *mon ami,*" drawled Lucien as he faced Tearlach, a knife in his hand, "we meet face to face, man to man." He skillfully tossed his knife from hand to hand.

"Ye mean mon to beast, dinnae ye?" Tearlach matched every step Lucien made until he and his enemy began to steadily circle each other. "'Tis only the lowest of beasts, a belly-crawling cur, who rapes a woman and beats her near to death. Your payment for that crime is long overdue, Lucien."

"Crime? What crime?" Lucien laughed, a high, nearly girlish giggle. "Your mother begged to be taken. She was a hungry white bitch. Her cries of pleasure nearly deafened me as I drove into her again and again."

Tearlach gritted his teeth and struggled to hold back his rage. He knew Lucien was goading him, trying to make him lash out without thought or strategy. It was an old trick. But Tearlach would not allow the man to use his mother's rape to bring him to his death.

He studied his old opponent as they circled each other, looking for an opening, an opportunity to strike. Beneath his heavy woolen and homespun outer clothes, Lucien wore filthy torn buckskins and moccasins covered with buckskin leggings which laced up the calves of his slightly bowed legs. The man's blanket coat was thick, filthy and worn through at the elbows.

The sad state of Lucien's clothing came as a shock to Tearlach, for the renegade had always provided well for himself, through theft if not hard work. That he had no money to obtain new clothes, and no woman to repair the old ones, suggested to Tearlach a level of obsession in Lucien that made him far more dangerous now than he had ever been in the past.

The bottom half of Lucien's narrow face was almost completely hidden by a thick, gray-streaked black beard. His black hair, visibly dirty, was done in two thin braids and he wore a stained knit cap. Lucien looked as wild and evil as he was, no longer able to hide his twisted soul beneath good looks and fine clothes.

Tearlach finally looked directly into Lucien's eyes, eyes whose similarity to Moira's had often made him painfully aware of her patrimony. This time that likeness was not present. Lucien's eyes were black with hate, fury, and madness. In losing his tenuous grip on sanity, Lucien had lost all resemblance to his bastard daughter.

"Ye willnae spur me with your lies this time," Tearlach said.

"Lies? I think not Scotsman. Ah, *mon ami,* your mama was nearly as wild a lover as the pretty girl you have now. What is her name? Pleasance? *Oui,* that is it. That is the name I heard you call her in the barn."

"'Twas ye peering in at us."

"Oui, and a pretty sight it was too. I peek in and there you are getting up out of the hay. I am sorry I missed what went before. I got a good look at her soft skin and pretty curves, and I will enjoy having the little lady under me."

"Ye will ne'er get your filthy, murdering hands on her!"

"And who will be there to stop me, eh? You will be rotting out here in the snow, and it will be easy enough to rid myself of my bastard daughter. Ah, *oui, mon ami,* I *will* have your 'lassie.' She has very fine legs, and I look forward to having them wrapped around me. I will have her many, many times before I cut her pretty white throat. Now, shall we cease circling each other like buzzards o'er a corpse and finally prove which one of us is the better man?"

Tearlach fought to keep his head as Lucien began the battle in earnest. When it was Lucien's knife which drew first blood, cutting a deep slash in Tearlach's left forearm, he almost lost control. For a brief moment the wound weakened him, but he quickly regained his balance. He knew this would be his last battle with Lucien, for only one of them would survive this fight.

A nearly successful lunge by Lucien, his knife slashing through the front of Tearlach's thick blanket coat, warned Tearlach that he had dangerously let his concentration lag. Lucien was mad, but he was still skilled with a knife. Tearlach would be hard-pressed to hold his own. He suspected that even the gray light of early dawn was helping Lucien. The man was more wild beast than human.

"Come, O'Duine, why do you fight so hard? It makes no sense to struggle so much, only to lose." Lucien thrust his knife at Tearlach and giggled when he jumped out of the blade's reach. "You can never beat me at the knife fighting, eh? *Non,* you are but a babe in arms in such a battle, a suckling child. And you have not the stomach to kill a man."

"I will kill ye, Lucien. 'Twill be no more to me than putting down a mad dog."

"You are very slow to put down this dog, *mon ami.* Twelve years? I am thinking that my little bastard could do a better job." He feigned a lunge and laughed again. "Maybe I should take the time to train my little bastard."

"Dinnae go near Moira. Ye have done her enough harm."

"I have never touched her. *Merde,* you have ever kept her from me. Is that fair? True, she is only a worthless girl child, not the son a man needs, but she is still my own flesh and blood. Now that I am thinking on it, the brat could prove to be of some use. She must be nearing an age to begin her flux and become a childbearer. She could bring me a good sum in Canada. *Oui,* some lusty and lonely trapper will pay plenty for her. Maybe that is what I should do with your woman too, eh?"

The very thought that his sister and Pleasance could be sold off to any of the brutal scum Lucien knew enraged Tearlach. He hurled himself at Lucien, tackling his tormentor. Luck was with him. He caught Lucien completely by surprise and, grabbing the man around the knees, knocked him to the ground. For a little while, Tearlach felt victory within his grasp.

But Lucien proved to be a lot stronger than Tearlach had anticipated. As they wrestled across the campsite, smothering the low campfire with their bodies, he began to lose his hope of victory. He was strong and skilled, but so was Lucien. Lucien also had one thing Tearlach lacked—a savage love of killing. Although Tearlach fought desperately, knowing that he was fighting for his very life, he hated every moment of it, while in Lucien's face was a look of pure delight. The man was eager to make a kill and Tearlach found that chilling.

"Now, Scotsman, this game will end," Lucien said, breathing heavily as he finally pinned Tearlach to the ground.

His teeth clenched from the strain, Tearlach knew he was in a desperate position. Lucien had a tight grip on his right wrist, preventing him from pushing his knife into Lucien's chest. He also had a firm grip on Lucien's right wrist, thus halting him from cutting him. It was a standoff Tearlach knew he would be hard-pressed to maintain.

"You will die here, Scotsman, far from those pretties you wish to protect."

Before Tearlach could challenge Lucien's grim claim, Lucien slammed his forehead into Tearlach's. The move stunned him so that Lucien was able to disarm him. Tearlach twisted to roll out from under his enemy. That move kept

Lucien's knife from piercing his heart, but Tearlach bellowed out his pain when the blade cut into his chest.

Pain gave Tearlach the strength to knock Lucien off him. He lunged for his knife, but Lucien was quicker. The man stabbed him in the lower back. Tearlach screamed and tried to grasp his knife, but Lucien got to it first. His wounds rapidly sapping his strength, Tearlach stumbled to his feet, only to have Lucien punch him in the face. The blow sent Tearlach back down onto the cold, hard ground. Before he could attempt to rise, Lucien launched a furious attack, kicking and punching him until Tearlach was unable to discern one pain from another. Finally it took him a moment to realize that Lucien had stopped beating him. He forced his swelling eyes open and saw a grinning Lucien standing over him.

"Finish it, ye mad bastard," Tearlach said, his voice an unsteady rasp.

"Why should I trouble myself?" Lucien giggled and bent down to clean his knife on Tearlach's coat. "You are bleeding like a stuck pig, probably have a few broken bones, and you are miles from help. I will leave you here to slowly rot."

"I might survive and come after you."

"Oui, you might, but you will be too late to save your two pretties. *Oui,* maybe leaving you alive is a good plan. If you die, it will be slow and painful. If you live, you will learn that I have killed or stolen everything you possess."

Tearlach cursed. He mustered enough strength to grab at Lucien's ankles, but his enemy danced out of his reach. The man's giggle made Tearlach want to scream, but he would not give Lucien the pleasure of seeing the terror that was eating away at him; he would not let the man hear him beg. If he had the smallest hope that begging for Pleasance's and Moira's lives might sway Lucien, Tearlach would have groveled as much as the madman wanted. But Lucien was a coldhearted murderer, and Tearlach knew that nothing short of killing the man would save his sister and his lover.

"They arenae alone," he said, unable to move as Lucien picked over his belongings.

"You are a poor liar, Scotsman. You leave your woman alone a lot. I have been watching you since you brought home the pretty woman with the long white legs. Tsk, tsk. Is that any way for you to act before my innocent bastard, Moira? I think I must take my child away from you and your bad example. *Oui,* that is what I must do." Lucien finished taking what he wanted from Tearlach's things and stood up with a smile.

"Only a coward would hurt a woman and a child," Tearlach bit out.

"Such nobility. I do not mean to hurt those pretties, *mon ami. Mais non.* Your death will leave them without a man's protection. I merely intend to provide for them. Now, I cannot do it myself, for I am a busy, busy man, but I am sure I can find someone willing to take them. For a fee, of course. But if they anger me, I may be forced to kill them. And you? You must lie here, bleeding and dying, and think about it."

Tearlach tried to move, but only succeeded in flopping over onto his stomach, one arm outstretched in a useless attempt to grab hold of the departing Lucien. He cursed when Lucien slapped his horse on the rump, sending the animal trotting off, then nimbly mounted his own horse after securing his sack of stolen goods to the saddle. Lucien nudged his mount toward Tearlach, who briefly thought he was about to be trampled, and reined in the animal mere inches from Tearlach's head.

"Ah, 'tis a shame." Lucien shook his head. "I have enjoyed our games over the years, *mon ami.* I am almost sorry. Good dying, Tearlach O'Duine. May it be long and tormented."

Tearlach watched Lucien ride away. A harsh cry of pain escaped him at his own inability to pursue his enemy. Soon Pleasance and Moira would pay dearly for his failure. Tearlach was not sure which hurt more—his injuries or knowing he was unable to protect them.

For a long time, Tearlach lay on the icy ground. The bleeding of his wounds slowed and his first thought was that now he would die of the cold. Weak and dizzy, he could only lie still and imagine the worst. Distressful visions of Lucien abusing Moira and Pleasance sapped even more of his strength. It only added to his pain to realize now how much Pleasance meant to him. He was still not sure what sort of woman she was—a hardworking, honest woman or one of the idle, disdainful gentry—but he both wanted and needed her. The thought of Lucien touching her was pure torment to him.

A soft whinny yanked Tearlach out of his black mood. He looked up and saw his horse amble back into the campsite. Tearlach cursed himself. He had given up, accepted defeat like some weak-kneed dandy. It had taken a dumb animal to shake him back to his senses.

Fighting waves of dizziness, Tearlach sat up and inched backward until he could rest against a tree trunk. It required a few minutes for him to regain the strength to take the next step. He leaned forward and grasped one of the shirts Lucien had tossed from his saddlebag. It took several attempts before he was able to tear the shirt into strips, and then he began the awkward task of bandaging himself. By the time he was done, he was trembling and soaked in sweat.

Tearlach struggled to his feet, using the tree for support. He called to his horse and whispered a prayer of thanks when the animal meandered over. Unsaddled, the horse proved difficult to mount. When Tearlach finally got on the animal's back, he had to lie there for a while. By the time he was able to grab the reins and nudge the horse on its way, the sun was already climbing in the sky.

"I will ne'er catch Lucien," he grumbled. "The mon must be miles ahead of me by now."

A few deep breaths and Tearlach successfully subdued yet another urge to give up. He might not stop Lucien right away, but that did not mean the renegade would win. There were people he could turn to for help. He had friends, and Pleasance's brother Nathan.

Tearlach hoped Nathan was as loyal as Pleasance thought he was, and not just for the sake of Pleasance's emotional well-being. If Lucien did take Moira and Pleasance away and sell them to some Canadian trapper, Tearlach was going to need all the help he could get to find them.

Nathan Dunstan rubbed his hands together and held them before the fire as he waited impatiently for his family to join him in the parlor. He promised himself that from now on he would cease his wanderings earlier in the year. Midwinter was too cold to be far from the comforts of home.

The subdued greeting he had received upon his arrival, the housekeeper's nervous look, made him uneasy now. Not even Pleasance had appeared to greet him, and he found that especially troubling. Out of all of his family he had always felt the closest to Pleasance. He wanted to see her in particular because he had been unable to shake the feeling that she was in some sort of trouble. It had been nagging at him for days, and he was anxious for someone to dispel it— either Pleasance herself or one of their irritating family.

The sound of the door opening made him turn. He was puzzled when only his father stepped in. He briefly wondered if his father had discovered his illegal customs-running schemes, then shrugged the concern aside. Thomas Dunstan was too much of a businessman to be bothered by how his son made his money. Nathan also suspected that his father often sold smuggled goods. Nevertheless, his father's solemn, evasive expression only strengthened Nathan's conviction that something was wrong.

"Hello, son," Thomas murmured, and moved to a decanter of wine on a small table. "A drink?" he asked even as he poured himself a glass.

"Mayhaps later. Where is everyone?"

"At tea at Mistress Delaney's home."

"Pleasance too? She loathes Mistress Delaney and those two shrewish nieces of hers."

"Pleasance was, perhaps, more choosy in her selection of acquaintances than she had any right to be." Thomas sipped his wine and went to the window. "Your sister Pleasance no longer lives here."

For a moment Nathan was too stunned to speak. "What? What are you saying?" he finally rasped.

Thomas looked at his son. "Pleasance is not here. She is indentured to one Tearlach O'Duine and has gone to live with him in the Berkshires. I should not trouble myself about her any longer."

"Oh, I think I will, thank you. And so will you. You cannot tell me that my sister has become a servant and leave it at that. There has to be an explanation and I want it now." He met his father's look of irritation squarely. "She is my sister. I cannot dismiss such shocking news as easily as you apparently have."

"Fine then. You will have your explanation, but you will not like it. Your precious sister has not emerged from this scandal smelling of roses. Now, perhaps you will finally see that your devotion is misplaced and you will put your loyalties where they belong."

"They are where they belong," Nathan said, his voice so

cold it was like a slap. Thomas flushed a dull red. "What has happened to Pleasance?"

As Thomas related the story, Nathan became rooted to the spot by shock. He could not believe that Pleasance could have been so stupid as to become involved in a scandalous scheme that was obviously of Letitia's making. His father's efforts to keep Letitia's name out of the story was an old ploy that Nathan easily recognized. The harder Thomas tried to make her sound no more than an innocent bystander, the more sure Nathan became that Letitia was the true culprit. Clearly, Pleasance had been misused, then utterly betrayed by her family.

"After all we have done for that child, it pains me that she could turn against us so completely," Thomas said.

"You bastard," Nathan whispered.

"I beg your pardon?" Thomas grew red in the face as he glared at his son.

"As always, the precious Letitia creates a scandal and Pleasance is made to take the blame." He held up a hand to silence his father's protests. "Do not insult me by telling me any more of your lies. Accept that I have the wit to know the truth. And, God help me, I have too often accepted the way Pleasance takes the blame for Letitia. But this time? Why did you not speak up, talk to this Master O'Duine, or even to Corbin? How could you have let Pleasance be convicted and taken off into the wilderness by a stranger?"

"To do or say anything would have been to bring scandal upon Letitia and thus ruin her chance to wed John Martin."

"And so you destroyed Pleasance's good name and allowed her to be dragged off to spend one long year with that man? Besides, John Martin would never give up his chance to wed Letitia. You simply abandoned Pleasance. Nay, worse than that—you saw it as an opportunity to be rid of her. God help us all, you tossed your own daughter aside, protected the guilty, and allowed the innocent to suffer."

"You forget who you are speaking to," snapped Thomas.

"Nay, I do not forget. Not for one moment. However, I think you forget who I am. Aye, and who Pleasance is. 'Tis you who forget your place. When I return, I think we had better discuss that more fully."

"Where are you going?" Thomas demanded as Nathan started out of the parlor.

"To see Corbin Matthias. If naught else, I will get the full truth from him—the full truth about what happened to Pleasance and about the man into whose hands you so cavalierly tossed her."

Corbin Matthias grimaced as Nathan Dunstan paced his office. "I tried to send you word."

Nathan sat down in the chair facing Corbin's desk. "I am not easy to reach when I am away from home. I . . ."

"I prefer not to hear where you were or what you were up to. For the moment, I am still the magistrate here." Corbin smiled when Nathan gave a brief laugh.

"What do you mean by 'still'? Is there a chance you will lose your post?"

"I have already asked to be relieved. 'Twill soon be time to take sides, either with the angry Colonists or with the ruling English. I do not wish to be in the position of having to send people I know to the gallows as traitors. Your sister's trial showed me that the law can force one to act in a way one knows is neither fair nor just."

"Did you really have to send her off with that man?"

"I swear to you that, since your family had cast her aside, it was my only choice. 'Twas that or prison."

"And you were so certain that a year spent with Tearlach O'Duine would be better than prison?"

"Your sister will return from his home alive and as healthy as God will allow." Corbin grimaced faintly when Nathan looked at him sardonically. "I can promise no more, but 'tis still far better than prison."

"I must assume that you know this man then."

"Fairly well—aye."

"Then tell me about him—all about him."

The hard, angry look in Nathan's blue-green eyes made Corbin a little nervous. Nathan was not a man he wanted as an enemy. Since Tearlach was Corbin's friend as well, he felt caught in a bind. He wanted to soothe Nathan's anger and turn it away from Tearlach, but that looked to be a Herculean task. Tearlach had erred and, although Corbin could forgive and understand, it was Nathan's sister whom Tearlach had wronged.

"Why do you wish to know all about Tearlach?"

"Besides the fact that he holds my sister?" Nathan drawled. "I want to know the man because I mean to get my sister back and I need to know how best to do that."

Corbin looked out of the window at the falling snow. "You will not be getting her back soon, I think."

Nathan cursed when he saw the snow. "It might stop."

"Aye, it might, and you might even get to the Berkshires before the truly dangerous weather starts. But you would be a fool to chance it. Your sister's life is not in danger. I promise you that. Howbeit, *your* life would be put at risk if you tried such a journey at this time of year."

"Then I shall head out at the first sign of spring," vowed Nathan. "And God help Tearlach O'Duine if Pleasance is harmed in any way."

Chapter Thirteen

"Are you certain that child is not a witch?" Mary Peterson asked as she watched Moira leave the house.

Pleasance almost laughed. She found Mary Peterson a little silly at times, but the woman had a good heart. And after two weeks of being alone with only Moira for company, she was glad Mary had come to visit. The woman still found Moira difficult to understand, however.

Moira knew Mary was trying to overcome her superstitions about Moira's gift of insight and to ignore the gossip that still labeled the girl a witch. But Moira could not resist playing on Mary's fears by acting a little oddly around her. Pleasance vowed to chastise Moira later, but now she smiled across the table at her guest.

"Moira is merely teasing you, Mary," Pleasance explained. "Would you like some more coffee?"

"Nay, I should go home. It grows dark so early these days and I always fear that I will be caught out in the snow."

"Aye, I can well understand that fear." She frowned, staring toward the front window. "I wish Master O'Duine would return. I truly feel there is a major storm brewing."

"We often have some harsh weather, that is for certain."

Mary idly tucked a silver curl back under her mobcap. "It has caused a few deaths in the past."

"I think I should prefer not to discuss who has died because of winter weather."

"Oh, dear, of course not." Mary reached across the table to pat Pleasance's hand. "Forgive this old woman."

"You are not so old."

"Older than some and more foolish than many." Mary smiled when Pleasance laughed faintly. "Your young man has lost his wits in going hunting at this time of year, if you ask me, but then men are often stupid."

"True. But Master O'Duine needed to make up for time lost while he was recovering from the bear mauling. A man must earn a living."

"That is the truth, dear, but does he need to earn it in such a dangerous way?"

"'Tis not my place to criticize what Master O'Duine does." Pleasance inwardly grimaced, hating to mouth such sentiments, but knowing such things were expected of her.

"Nonsense. 'Tis also a man's place to protect the women in his household. Master O'Duine cannot do either if he is traipsing about the forest. My Henry says that trapping and hunting are no longer good ways to make a living. Not unless one wishes to keep moving deeper into the wilderness. I have never heard Master O'Duine talk of leaving here. I have always considered him one of the permanent residents."

Pleasance smiled and nodded. "I believe he is. He talks of this cabin as his home."

"Then he should stay in it more." Mary stood up. "He certainly should not leave you and young Moira alone."

As Pleasance fetched Mary's cloak, she said, "Jake comes to stay with us when he can."

"That old goat. He is not much protection and he has his

own home to tend to." Mary slipped into her cloak and tugged on her gloves. "Well, my dear, I hope you will make use of those cranberries. They are the first of the season."

"Oh, I will, and I thank you very much for the gift."

"If my cousin sends me more, I will be sure to share them with you."

Pleasance followed Mary out to the veranda and stood watching as Mary mounted her dappled gray mare. "Thank you kindly."

Mary took up the reins, adjusted her skirts and cloak, and looked down at Pleasance. "If you find living here alone too much to bear, you and that witch child are welcome to come and stay with us."

"That is very kind and generous, Mary, but I believe we will be all right here."

"Child, you need not fear that the gossips will start on me. I am too old and my Henry is too dull and cantankerous. 'Tis true that that child still troubles me from time to time, and I will confess that I wonder how proper it is for you to be here at all."

"'Tis not proper, but I have no choice, I am indentured. I cannot believe you did not know."

"Oh, I know. Old Jake and my Henry are close friends. Henry went to pay a brief call on Jake the day after you arrived and got the full tale. My Henry told me your story. And my cousin is from Worcester. She sent me a letter with those cranberries. Do not look so alarmed, child. I would believe Old Jake over those Worcester gossips any day, and my own cousin was scornful of the tale heard from your neighbors. You should be more free with the truth. It cannot hurt your family out here, and it could make a few people treat you more kindly."

"Perhaps." Pleasance shrugged and smiled. "Those who would condemn me for my place here would probably remain unconvinced. And my stay will be a short one. Why struggle to change closed minds when I will soon leave them behind? Not many people are as kindhearted as you, Mary."

"You do not know me, child," Mary replied, but blushed with pleasure. "And your stay may not be as short as you think. Now, do not forget. If you cannot abide it here any longer, pack up yourself and Moira, leave that young man a note, and come stay with us. Take care of yourself." Mary nudged her horse into a slow walk. "Lazy beast," she muttered.

Pleasance waved and watched until Mary was out of sight. She sighed. She had enjoyed the visit, but it had been difficult not to voice her concerns for Tearlach. Yet, to speak openly of her fears and worries about the man to whom she was indentured was a sure way to inspire speculation, and none of it good. Mary Peterson had proven to be a warm-hearted woman, but she did like to talk.

"Maybe we should go to the old crone's cabin."

Pleasance turned sharply to frown crossly at Moira, who stood slouched against the cabin wall. It was past time to teach Moira a few lessons in manners. The girl moved far more like a limber young boy than a girl about to become a young woman.

"If you keep creeping up behind me like that, you will have to go to her by yourself, for I shall have keeled over dead. A person's heart can withstand only so many shocks."

Moira ignored Pleasance's grumbling. "It could well be safer at the Petersons'."

"Safer from what?" Pleasance leaned against the veranda railing and crossed her arms beneath her breasts. "Are you aware of some danger? Have you noticed some warning sign that I have missed?"

"Nay." Moira shrugged. "I dinnae ken what I am feeling or thinking."

"Mayhaps 'tis just the effect of this oppressive grayness. We get no sun yet we get no storm. Just day after day of dull gray skies. It would make anyone fearful, overwrought, and imaginative."

"Waiting for the cursed snow promised by those heavy skies does sorely try my nerves. Pay me no heed. We should be safe enough right here."

"I wish you would put a little more confidence behind your words." Pleasance smiled when Moira laughed. "I confess that I do not like staying here, just you and me alone. 'Tis not like Worcester, where you dare not have too loud a quarrel for fear your neighbors will catch every word. Here, even if there were an alarm one could sound that some of the people might hear, they would ne'er reach you in time to be of help. At first I liked that solitude, but now I can see its drawbacks. I could almost wish for a few of my prying neighbors from Worcester. Well, only for the winter, then I would probably want them gone again."

As Pleasance shook her head, Moira giggled. "At times ye can be nearly as silly as I am, Pleasance." She grew more serious as she stared out toward the woods. "I dinnae like it. I have never felt so restless, so unsettled, yet I cannae determine why."

"Try not to let it prey upon your mind. Sometimes when one tries too hard, things become more muddled."

"Do ye think my problem could be as simple as that?"

"Why not?" Pleasance shuddered and rubbed her arms. "I think I had better get back inside. There is a cruel sharpness to the wind today." She moved toward the door, pausing to give Moira a comforting pat on the shoulder. "You have a great gift, Moira, yet I think it is at its best when you don't force it."

"Ye are right. The clearest, most successful warnings I have ever gotten have come as a complete surprise to me. If my instincts wish to tell me something, they will do so in their own sweet time and in their own sweet way."

"Good. And now I think we should do our best to finish up any outside chores and perhaps do a little extra," Pleasance said as she stepped into the cabin with Moira following. "I really believe it is past time for us to prepare for a very heavy snow."

"Aye," agreed Moira. "We may soon be knee-deep in it."

Pleasance set the bread aside to rise and washed off her hands. As she dried them she walked over to the window to the right of the front door and stared out toward the surrounding forest. She was not surprised to see the first snowflake drift down from the sky. With a sigh she bundled herself up in her warm outer clothes and stepped outside.

"Moira," she called from the veranda, and rolled her eyes when the girl appeared before the sound of her voice had faded away. "You do that just to make me feel stupid," she said.

"Nay." Moira giggled as she stepped up onto the porch. "'Tis snowing."

"My, you are a smart child." She laughed when Moira lightly swatted her arm.

Moira said, "I reckon there are a few added chores to do, arenae there?"

"Aye. We must be sure we have enough wood, food, and water for several days and that the livestock are equally well supplied. I would rather be overprepared and wake up to a sunny morning than find ourselves buried in drifts of snow."

"Weel, which chore do ye choose—making sure the animals are ready for a hard storm or lugging more wood inside?"

"Since I have not had very much to do with the farm

beasts, I shall leave that to you. I will see to the wood and maybe retrieve an extra piece of meat from the smokehouse."

As soon as Moira had skipped off, Pleasance fetched a bit of ham and some venison from the small smokehouse behind the cabin. Next she began to restock the sheltered woodbox at the rear door. Her arms were aching before she was finished.

Then she baked the bread. She turned to wash up a few of her baking utensils only to realize she would need a goodly supply of water. She collected her buckets and went out to the pump.

She was filling her buckets for the second time when, suddenly, Moira was at her side. She started to ask her to help carry a bucket when she noticed the still, pale look on the girl's pretty face. Pleasance forced her fear aside and waited patiently until Moira spoke.

"We had best get back inside," she finally whispered. "Aye, and we had best stay there."

"Because of the approaching storm?" Pleasance asked, following when Moira picked up one of the buckets and hurried toward the cabin. "I was right then? This will be a very big storm?"

"Oh, aye, it will be." Moira held the cabin door open for Pleasance. "'Tis good to be ready, although I dinnae think it will be so very dangerous."

"So that is not what has you looking so troubled." She set the buckets on the kitchen table and frowned as Moira did the same.

"Nay." Moira sat down at the table. "'Tisnae the storm. There is something verra bad out there, Pleasance."

Pleasance could not restrain a quick, nervous glance toward the closed door. "What do you mean?"

"I cannae say. I just feel it. 'Tis bad. Aye, and as evil as the devil himself. I think we are going to have a lot of trouble and it will be coming verra soon." She stared at Pleasance. "Do ye ken how to shoot the musket or the pistol?"

"Aye, I am not such a bad hand with either."

Moira regarded her with slight surprise. "Truly? Then why do ye always have Tearlach load them for ye?"

"He never gives me the choice." She exchanged a brief grin with Moira, a look resonant with a female's understanding of men. But then she grew serious again. "You are very sure about what you are feeling now?"

"Verra sure, curse it," Moira told her. "Though I really dinnae want this bit of intuition to be true." She slammed her fist down on the table. "And why cannae it tell me more? Why cannae it tell me who, when, and where?"

The fear in Moira's tawny eyes was clear to read. Pleasance quickly sat down next to the girl and put an arm about her slim shoulders. Clearly, Moira found her strange gift as much a curse as a blessing. Pleasance could only imagine how painful it must be for her to know something was wrong yet not know exactly what it was. It was as if someone were yelling "Watch out" but not staying around long enough to answer "Watch out for what?"

"Come, we will securely bar the doors and shutters. Perhaps your anxious feelings will fade when you feel safer." Pleasance stood up and tugged Moira to her feet.

"About all these cursed feelings are good for is to scare us both to death."

"But if that makes us wary, we will be ready for the danger when it comes. We can only be grateful for that." She closed the shutters on the window next to the front door, and Moira dropped the bar across the door. Once the front of the house was locked, they moved to secure the rear door and window.

"Nay, why cannae I see more? All I can do is say that

something bad is out there. I sound like some bairn who doesnae ken how to explain what she means."

"I can only imagine how frustrating that must be. It must be very much like having someone tell you only a tiny piece of some very tantalizing secret." She was a little relieved when a brief smile crossed Moira's face.

"'Tis a bit like that. But at times I cannae stop from wondering if I really am a witch," Moira whispered.

"Nay," Pleasance said sharply, then sighed and rubbed her temple as she struggled to think of something to say. She desperately wanted to say the right words, words that would ease Moira's fears about her gift and where it had come from. "You are no witch, Moira O'Duine."

"Ye dinnae believe in witches, do ye?"

"I could not say that I do, but I am also not sure that I do not." Pleasance met Moira's earnest gaze. "But, I am sure you know, those feelings and warnings you get often make me very nervous indeed."

"Because they mean I could be a witch." Moira jerkily wiped away several tears.

"Nay, because I do not understand them. Most people think of witches as evil and hurtful. You could never be either of those things. A witch supports the devil's work, and you could never do that." Pleasance handed Moira her lacy handkerchief.

"Nay? But what if these feelings and visions are from the devil?" Moira dabbed at her eyes with the crisp white handkerchief and began to twist it in her hands.

"If they were the devil's work, then you would be causing people untold trouble and grief, not helping them."

"That sounds so verra reasonable. But wouldnae the devil try to trick us all? Tricking me about my feelings and tricking ye about what I am?"

Pleasance rubbed a hand over her chin. Moira was young and impressionable. She must choose her words carefully.

"Come along, we had best latch the shutters upstairs," she finally said, and started toward the steps.

"Ye didnae answer my question," Moira pressed as she hurried after Pleasance. "Is it the devil playing tricks on us?"

"'Tis true that the devil does trick people." Pleasance agreed. "He does not trick people by having them consistently do helpful things, however. If everything our church fathers say is even remotely the truth, then they would have to agree with me."

"But, Pleasance, some verra righteous people have said that I am a witch."

"If they said such a thing about you, then they were not very righteous. They were simply people who went to church."

"There is a difference, is there?" Moira smiled faintly over the sardonic look Pleasance gave her.

"A great deal of difference, and if your heathen brother took you to church more often, you would soon see that particular truth for yourself. People can be mighty hypocrites, spouting Bible verses even as they ignore their teachings. As for calling you a witch, they should be thoroughly ashamed of themselves. Pay such people no heed, Moira. No heed at all."

"That is what Tearlach always says."

"For once the man is right, although it galls me beyond speaking to admit it." She shared a quick grin with Moira, then, as they reached the top of the stairs, pointed to Moira's bedroom door. "You take care of your window and I shall secure Tearlach's room."

Pleasance took a quick peek out of the small window in Tearlach's room, but she could see nothing. Shivering a little from the cold, she quickly closed the shutters and dropped the latching bar into place. She gave the thick wooden bar a pat, feeling sure that it would hold up against most any attack. As she stepped from the room she met Moira. The girl did not look as pale and fretful as before, and Pleasance was glad.

"Come help me put all that water we brought into the tub." She started down the stairs.

Moira followed. As they worked, Pleasance could tell that Moira was still worried and confused. Pleasance partly blamed Tearlach. Apparently he had taken few pains to assure the girl she was not a witch. Pleasance promised herself she would give him a piece of her mind when he finally got home.

Working together, the two females emptied the buckets of water into the tub and began to prepare the evening meal. Pleasance hoped Moira's morose mood would begin to lift, but one tense hour later, it was clear to Pleasance that the girl was growing increasingly restless and worried. As Pleasance scrubbed down the table, Moira stood motionless by the front window, having opened one shutter to look outside. She stood almost too still, too straight. As the minutes ticked by and still she did not move, but simply continued to stare out at the gently falling snow, Pleasance grew increasingly nervous.

She draped her washing rag over a hook to dry and cleaned her hands, then went over to Moira and put her arm around her shoulders as she stole a quick peek outside.

"The snow is still falling lightly," she murmured. "'Tis still a pretty snowfall, not at all threatening."

"'Twill turn threatening soon enough. But 'tisnae the snow we must fear."

There was such an ominous tone to Moira's voice that Pleasance could not suppress a shudder. She had never liked being left alone in the cabin while Tearlach was away, but until now she had never really been afraid.

She silently cursed Tearlach for his absence. "I do not suppose you have any clearer picture of who or what is out there," she said.

"I already told ye that I have no sense of who, what, how, or when."

"I was just hoping," Pleasance murmured, ignoring Moira's testiness. "Oh well, at least we are locked up nice and safe."

"Aye, and we would be wise to keep ourselves locked up." Moira crossed her arms and scowled. "We must keep the doors barred no matter what happens. I begin to think it would be a good idea if we each kept a pistol at hand and took turns keeping watch. Aye, and I'd best cease courting danger by leaving this shutter open."

"Is so much precaution really necessary? We are already locked up so tight it feels like a tomb in here."

"Aye. I would rather it merely felt like a tomb than actually became one." Moira closed the shutter on the window she had been staring out of. "If we are lucky, the storm will drive away that evil I feel."

Pleasance moved to help Moira light the lamps as the house grew increasingly dark. Only briefly did she consider questioning what she was doing. It might be only a child's dire prediction, but Moira's intuition had often proved accurate. Pleasance would be a fool to ignore the girl's warnings. The question now was—could they withstand whatever evil was out to get them?

Pleasance chastised herself for not having demanded that Tearlach teach her everything he knew about self-defense. It was probably not enough that she knew how to use a gun.

"I suppose it is too late to run to Jake's cabin or even to the Petersons'," she said. "If we were with one or the other, we would not face this threat all alone."

"The threat is already out there, Pleasance," Moira said as she sat down at the table.

Pleasance retrieved the rifle from over the fireplace and joined Moira at the table.

"Are you sure?"

"Aye. If we tried to flee anywhere now, he would get us for sure." Moira's hand shook as she poured herself a glass of cider.

"He? You said he?"

"Did I?"

"Aye, you did. Do you now know it is a man?"

"Aye, 'tis a he. 'Tis a two-legged devil."

"You now know what danger we face? You are now clear on that?"

"'Tis a mon."

"Are you certain you are not allowing your fears to twist your perceptions? Perhaps you just sense Tearlach returning home."

"My brother is not evil, and I do feel that evil is near."

"Well, mayhaps Tearlach was hurt by something evil and that is what you are sensing." Pleasance knew she was grasping at straws, but she could not seem to stop herself.

Moira shook her head. "I would ne'er wish Tearlach any harm, but in this case I wish ye were right."

"But I am not."

"Nay, I fear not."

Pleasance swore softly and muttered an apology. When Moira took no notice, though she usually liked to catch Pleasance acting less than a perfect lady, her disregard underscored for Pleasance the seriousness of their situation. She took several deep breaths as she fought to control her terror.

"I wish I could tell ye what ye want to hear, Pleasance," Moira whispered.

"I dearly wish you could as well. But the truth is always best."

"Weel, I ken the truth now. The evil is as clear as creekwater in my mind. 'Tis a mon."

Pleasance took a long, close look at Moira's face. "You know which man too, don't you?"

"Aye."

"Who?"

"'Tis the mòn who defiled my mother."

"Lucien?"

"Aye—Lucien, the rabid cur."

"When will he be here?"

"Now. He is here now."

Chapter Fourteen

"Hallo? Hallo in the cabin there," called out a deep voice with a heavy French accent.

Pleasance continued to stare at Moira, the girl's words still spinning in her head. The man who had defiled Moira's mother was Moira's father—Lucien. A chill flowed through her as she realized what lurked outside the cabin door— a man Tearlach had called demented, a man Moira had just labeled a rabid cur. For whatever reason, Lucien had turned from his murderous pursuit of Tearlach and come after his daughter.

An agonizing terror gripped Pleasance's heart as a chilling thought entered her head—maybe Lucien had finally beaten Tearlach. Maybe that was why he now sought out Moira.

Pleasance prayed that she was wrong.

"Mayhaps 'tis just some trapper who seeks shelter until the storm has passed," Pleasance said in a very quiet voice, not taking her eyes from the door the man kept pounding on.

"Nay." Moira clenched her hands into tight, white-knuckled fists. "'Tis him. 'Tis the mon who raped my mother and stole away her wish to stay alive. 'Tis the mon who has been trying to kill my brother."

"So, you know all about that, do you?" Pleasance glanced toward Moira and grimaced at the girl's mildly disgusted look. "Tearlach had hoped to keep it a secret."

"Tearlach cannae keep protecting me from the truth just because 'tis ugly."

"Would you leave a poor man to freeze to death on your steps?" Lucien yelled.

"He cannot get in," Pleasance reassured Moira when the girl's face paled a little.

"I hope ye are right."

"Come, my pretties, I know you are in there," Lucien yelled in a singsong voice.

"That yelling and banging is tedious, but at least it lets us know where he is." Pleasance rubbed at her temples as she struggled to come up with a plan.

"Hallooo? I know you are in there." Lucien rattled the door latch. "Would you leave a man out in this terrible storm?"

"Aye—when that man is a low scurrying cur like ye," yelled Moira.

Even as she reached across the table to put her hand on Moira's mouth, Pleasance knew it was too late. She got up and hurried over to take the extra powder and shot from the chest next to the fireplace. As she returned to the table she gave some thought to whom she was planning to shoot.

"Dinnae look so horrified, Pleasance." Moira got up and fetched the pistol and extra shot from the small pantry near the rear door.

"I have never shot a man before and this one is your father."

"He is my mother's rapist, my mother's killer, and my only brother's tormentor. Ye need not fear I shall fault ye if ye have to shoot him."

Pleasance picked up the rifle, went to the front window,

and cracked it open a little so that she could look out at the man still pounding on the door. He did not look particularly impressive or frightening as he thumped away, just hairy and filthy. A light dusting of fresh white snow on his head and shoulders accentuated his filthy state. Pleasance wondered how he could make any kind of a living as a hunter. She was sure every animal for miles around would smell him coming. She also began to sense the danger he represented and wondered if she could successfully fight it.

Lucien suddenly turned, sensing that he was being watched. He saw the face in the window and drew in a deep breath. It was not his child's face so it had to be the face of Tearlach's lover. It was more clearly lit now than it had been when he had spied her and Tearlach getting dressed in the stable. Lucien felt immediately drawn to her. He started to reach out for her, only to curse when she leapt back and slammed the shutter closed.

"You will not be able to keep old Lucien away," he muttered, staring thoughtfully at the front door.

Banging on the door and yelling was not going to work, he decided. He could torment them with it, but it would not get him inside. He was going to have to devise some plan that would trick them into letting him in, or maybe he could find a crack in the well-sealed walls and get inside unseen. As he stood there scratching himself, Lucien tried to figure out how to do both without allowing his intended victims to guess what he was up to.

"What is he doing?" asked Moira.

"Staring at me. At first look, I did not think he was very impressive, but then he looked at me. There is a feral look in his eyes. He will not give up. I seriously considered shooting him right then and there."

"Why didnae ye?"

"I told you—I have never shot a man. He was just standing there. It would be too coldblooded."

Moira took a plug of wood out of a knothole and peeped out. "Do ye think he has hurt Tearlach?"

"I feared that myself, but we cannot know that. What is he doing now?"

"Just staring at the window. I suspect he kens I am having a wee peek or two."

"That does not sound particularly promising. It means that he is thinking, planning something."

"Such as what?"

"Making us deaf so that we cannot hear him creeping up on us," Pleasance muttered when Lucien started pounding on the door again. "Cease that," she yelled, "or I shall shoot you where you stand."

"Shoot me?" Lucien called back. "Why would you shoot me? You do not have a grievance with me."

"Ye killed my mother," Moira said.

"Oh, my child, who has told you these lies, eh? I am your papa. Come, let me in out of the cold."

"You can freeze where you stand," Pleasance replied. "You will never get in this cabin." She frowned as she looked around at all the closed shutters and barred doors. "Moira, if all the shutters are pulled closed, how can we shoot him if we are forced to battle it out?"

"There are musket slots." Moira showed Pleasance the openings in the front shutters where a person could sight a target.

"Of course. I should have known."

"Heard of these, eh? Is it so civilized where ye live that they are just a memory?"

"We are too isolated here. Lucien has come here for some reason. I wish I could guess what it is." She set the rifle aside and moved to stoke up the fire.

"Maybe the storm will grow so fierce it will force him to flee."

"That would only buy us some time, which is not such a bad thing. But after the storm he would come back."

"He is here to kill us, isnae he?"

Pleasance sighed. "We cannot be sure, but I know he is not here to make friends. Does your gift tell you anything?"

Moira shook her head. "Nothing. Why are ye building the fire up so high? We will roast."

"I want to make sure that the chimney cannot be used as a way to get in here. A small fire might not be enough of a deterrent." She tensed, then quickly grabbed her rifle.

"What is it?"

"He has stopped banging on the door. Quick, we have to find him."

As she and Moira moved from peephole to peephole, Pleasance prayed that the man was gone. Then she saw his poor horse still fully burdened and secured to the paddock gate. She cursed and moved to peek out of the window by the rear door. Lucien was standing next to the smokehouse, his back to her.

"I found him," she called to Moira. "He is by the smokehouse."

"What is that devil doing?" Moira asked as she hurried over and peered out. "He is relieving himself on our smokehouse."

"Disgusting but the least of our troubles. Somehow we are going to have to keep one step ahead of the man, try to anticipate his every move."

"But for how long?"

"I have no idea. We can only hope that if we keep him outside long enough, the snow will drive him away." Pleasance cursed when Lucien began to bang on the back door. "I hope he breaks his hand." She suddenly put her rifle down and moved to get the kettle by the fire.

"What are ye going to do?" asked Moira as Pleasance poured the steaming water into a heavy pewter jug.

"A little ancient battle technique. Your bedroom window looks out over this back door, right?"

"Aye." Moira's eyes widened. "Are ye going to pour that on him?"

"I am going to try. You stay here and keep your pistol in hand."

Pleasance went up to Moira's room. She could hear Lucien banging and banging and banging against the door. The sound began to echo painfully in her head. She set the pitcher on the floor and eased open the shutters that overlooked the back door. A long silent breath of relief escaped her when she accomplished it without drawing Lucien's attention.

As Pleasance picked up the pitcher of hot water, she prayed it had not lost any of its scalding power. Careful not to make a sound, she leaned out of the window and took aim. To her dismay something warned Lucien and he suddenly looked up. She hurled the water at him, but in that instant of awareness he had enough time to escape the worst of her attack. His bellows and curses told her she had inflicted some damage, but not the crippling blow she had intended. She quickly resecured the shutters and ran back downstairs.

"I missed him," she told Moira.

"Not completely," Moira replied as she watched Lucien. "He is rubbing snow on his face, neck, and hand."

"Then I did better than I thought." She took a small bucket of tallow from the pantry and began to spoon some of it into a pot.

"Now what are ye doing?"

"I am going to melt some of this and, if Lucien is fool

enough to get beneath another window, I shall pour it on him. He will not be so easily able to rub this away with snow. It will cling to him as it burns."

"Now you have angered Lucien," he bellowed as he returned to pounding on the door. "When I get ahold of you, you will be sorry. Very sorry."

Moira gave a shriek of fright and shut the peephole when he banged on her window. Pleasance put her arm around Moira and they stood silently as Lucien went from window to window, door to door, pounding on each and screaming curses at them. She wondered how the man could keep it up.

"You have one last chance to stay alive, my pretties. Give yourselves up to Lucien and he will forgive you for hurting him."

"Go to the devil," Pleasance yelled, then cursed as he started pounding on the cabin again. "Does he think he can beat the walls down with his bare fists?" she muttered as she rubbed her temples.

"Nay, he just means to make us as mad as he is."

"It could work." She put the pot of fat on the hearth, near enough to the fire so that it would melt evenly. "I am still thinking we ought to just shoot him. He means us no good, so it would still be self-defense. And yet, a part of me is appalled that I would even think such a thing. Another part tells me it would not work anyway, because the man is undoubtedly keeping a close watch on any window or door he is near. The moment we open a musket hole, he will run." She scowled at the window he was pounding on. "I wish I could guess what he is going to do next, but 'tis not easy to outguess a madman."

"Perhaps if we each try to shoot him at the same time it would work."

"I would prefer it if you did not have to act against him."

"I told ye—I dinnae think of him as my father."

"And I believe you, but you are only thirteen. You should not be getting the blood of a man on your hands." She stood up and brushed off her skirts. "I am going to see just how close a watch he is keeping on us." She took the rifle and went over to the front window as Lucien pounded on the back door again. When she opened the musket slot, she cursed. "Your brother has put glass-paned windows over the musket slots."

Moira grimaced. "He put them in before he went to Worcester. Ye will have to break the glass."

"And Lucien will hear that."

"Mayhaps not with all the banging."

Pleasance doubted they would be so lucky. She slammed the musket butt against the glass, but it only cracked and she had to hit it again. She smashed out an opening the size of the musket slot. To her ears, it sounded dangerously loud but there did not seem to be any change in Lucien's persistent pounding. She readied her rifle and waited for him to enter her sights, using the time to convince herself that what she was planning to do was right and necessary.

The moment Lucien came into view, Pleasance fired. He went down, out of her gun sights, but she was not sure she had hit him. She pulled the rifle back in and peered out, but there was no sight of him.

Then, suddenly, he was there, his blood-smeared face inches from hers. Pleasance screamed and tried to leap back, but he reached through the musket slot and grabbed her by the throat. She scratched at his hand but could not loosen his choking grip. Moira rushed over but she could not loosen the man's hold either. He was impervious to the pain as Pleasance and Moira scratched, punched, and even bit his arm. His heavy clothes gave him protection from their assault. Whenever she or Moira tried to reach out toward him, he backed up and slammed Pleasance against the window.

"I cannae get his hand off of ye," cried Moira.

"Get the pistol," Pleasance tried to say, but the words came out as a strangled whine.

Moira raced to get the pistol from the table where she had left it in her panicked rush to help Pleasance. When she returned to the window, however, she was unable to use it. Each time she tried to aim, Lucien used Pleasance as his shield.

Pleasance was close to fainting and she suddenly sagged in Lucien's hold. Before Lucien could drag her back up, Moira got in the way. He immediately released Pleasance and ducked as Moira fired her pistol. She started to step back, but was not fast enough. Lucien was back on his feet, thrust his arm inside, and grabbed Moira by the throat. Pleasance picked up her gun and staggered to her feet. With no time to reload, all she could do was use the butt of the musket as a club.

Again and again she brought it down hard on Lucien's arm, each strike bringing a howl of curses from him. When he finally released Moira, who slumped to the floor, Pleasance had one chance to strike again and she took it. Using all of the strength she could muster, she slammed the musket butt into Lucien's face. He howled with pain as he covered his face with his hands and staggered backward. Pleasance shut the musket slot, latched it, and then sank down to sit next to a still gasping Moira.

"You are dead," screamed Lucien. "Dead! Do you hear me?"

"Aye, I hear you," Pleasance said, her voice little more than a whisper, "and I am sick to death of you." She rubbed her bruised throat and looked at Moira. "Well, it appears that simply shooting him where he stands will not work."

Moira laughed, a hoarse, painful sound tinged with fear. "He almost killed you."

"Almost. How is your throat?"

"Sore, but I dinnae think 'tis as sore as yours. Unless ye are whispering on purpose."

"Nay, this is all the sound I can make. I hope he has not damaged anything." Pleasance coughed and rubbed her eyes. "Now we must come up with another plan." She tensed. "Do you hear anything?"

"Nay, 'tis quiet again." Moira coughed and winced, rubbing her throat.

"He has ceased to scream his fury at us, which means he is doing something else."

Pleasance scrambled to her feet. She picked up the musket and handed the pistol back to Moira. "Reload them." She started to cough again, her eyes watering, and then she tensed. "'Tis smoke."

Pleasance stared at the fireplace. At first it was hard to see because her eyes were so awash with tears. She hastily wiped them away and finally saw what she had begun to suspect. Smoke was billowing out of the fireplace. At the same time she heard the muffled sound of someone walking on the roof.

"Oh, sweet Mary, he is on the roof and he has plugged up the chimney. Help me put out the fire," she cried as she ran toward the fireplace.

Together they hurriedly carried over buckets of water and, coughing and sputtering, doused the fire. Their efforts produced more smoke, and when they were done, they both had to bathe their faces in cold water. Pleasance pressed a cool damp cloth to her eyes. She cursed the time it was taking to clear her vision, for she could still hear Lucien stomping around on the roof.

"I can see, Pleasance. I will reload the guns," said Moira, pausing briefly to pat Pleasance on the arm.

As she continued to bathe her eyes, Pleasance could hear

Moira reloading the guns. "Curse it, why is it taking so long for my eyes to stop stinging? I can hear that bastard doing something up there."

"So can I. Mayhaps I should go upstairs."

"Nay!" Pleasance snapped. "You cannot face him alone." She put the cloth down, dried her eyes, and looked around. "Still a little blurred, but at least I can see where I am going," she said as she moved to the table and picked up the musket Moira had just finished reloading. "We shall go upstairs together and see what that madman is doing. Ready?"

"Aye." Moira took the pistol and followed Pleasance up the stairs. "I dinnae like the sounds he is making."

"Neither do I. It sounds as if he is trying to get in. The question is—how and where?"

Pleasance stepped into Tearlach's room, Moira close behind her. They both stood and listened for a moment before Pleasance shook her head and moved toward Moira's room. Once inside, she knew exactly what Lucien was doing. Somehow he was trying to break in through the roof. Pleasance located the spot he was banging away at from above. A small pile of debris already littered the floor, but she could see no sign that he had actually broken through yet.

"Get the powder and ball, Moira."

"What are ye going to do?"

"Try to shoot him. Hurry."

As Moira raced back down the stairs, Pleasance tried to see exactly where Lucien would come through. The pounding echoed so loudly in the room that it was difficult to hear anything else. Worse, the man was no longer stomping around, so she was going to have to guess his position in relation to the hole he was so vigorously trying to make.

Moira returned with the powder and ball to reload the guns. "Now we start shooting?"

"Aye, but one at a time," Pleasance replied as she tried to

decide where to take her first shot. "I will take a shot, and once I have reloaded, you can take a shot."

"Why wait?"

"Because he could get in here if we do not stop him from making that hole, and I do not want to be caught with two empty guns." She aimed at a place where she thought he might be. "The musket ball will go through this wood, will it not?"

"At this distance? Aye, I believe so."

Carefully she took aim. Gently she squeezed the trigger. There was a deafening roar, and immediately the pounding stopped.

"Merde!" Lucien bellowed. "You will pay for that, you white bitch!"

"Your threats grow tedious," Pleasance yelled back as she hurried to reload the musket. "I suggest you get out of here while you still can."

"Non. You will not drive Lucien away, and you will regret not being more welcoming."

The pounding started again and Pleasance cursed. "I cannot believe he could think we would be so stupid as to just open the door to him. There, my musket is ready. Now you can take a shot, Moira." When the girl hesitated for a moment, Pleasance recalled the fact that Moira was only thirteen. "Do you want me to do it? You could just reload the guns and I will do all the shooting."

"Nay, I was just trying to decide where to shoot."

"You have no feeling about where he is?"

"Not a twinge." Moira shot her pistol, but this time there was only a brief hesitation in the pounding. "Missed him."

"Do you think I hit him then?" Pleasance asked as she pondered where she would shoot next and Moira reloaded her pistol. "He stopped for a moment and did all that swearing."

"He could have just been startled."

"I could almost hope I did not hit him."

"Why?"

"Because I grazed his head when I shot him just before he attacked us. There was blood on his face. Then I am sure I broke his nose when I hit him in the face with the musket butt. If I wounded him again when I shot through the ceiling, it has not slowed him down at all. That is very worrisome. It means he is a strong man, and he is very, very determined to get his hands on us."

"Maybe we should take this chance to run. He is on the roof." Moira finished reloading. "We could run to the stable, get a horse, and ride away."

"It sounds tempting." Pleasance stared up at the ceiling, trying to decide where to shoot. "But I do not think it will work. He could be off that roof and after us before we could get the horses out of their stalls. Besides, 'tis growing dark and the storm is worsening. We would be out in the open where Lucien can manage a lot better than we can. In here we have a slight advantage."

Pleasance aimed the musket and fired. She gaped as Lucien screamed out something in French. That was followed by the sound of him sliding down the roof. She held her breath, waiting tensely for some sound indicating he had hit the ground, but there was none.

She handed Moira her musket to reload and grabbed the pistol. As quickly as she could she opened the window. Cautiously she peered out, but there was nothing on the ground below. She saw the ladder he had used to get up on the roof, but there was no sign of him. A faint sound caught her attention and she looked up just in time to see his feet disappear over the eaves. She cursed and quickly resecured the window.

"He is still alive, isnae he?" asked Moira.

Her question was answered by the resumption of the pounding on the roof. Pleasance took aim and fired, cursing when there was no change in the pounding. She handed Moira the pistol and took the musket. It was frustrating beyond words that they were having no real success in stopping Lucien. She could almost believe that the fates had taken his side. When she shot again and the pounding continued uninterrupted, she met her failure with an odd sense of resignation.

"'Tis as if he can see us," she muttered. When she started to hand Moira the musket, she realized the girl had not yet finished reloading the pistol because she was trembling so badly. "Moira, I know this is terrifying, but we have to try and put aside our fear."

"I am trying."

"I know, Moira. I know. But you must try harder."

Pleasance was just about to take over the reloading when she felt something cold and wet on her face. Its chill went straight through her as she slowly looked up, and was not at all surprised to see that Lucien had finally broken through. For one brief moment she watched in horror as the hole grew bigger, pieces of wood falling to the floor. When she caught a glimpse of Lucien himself she finally broke free of fear's tight grip. She turned to Moira only to find the girl staring up at the ceiling, the still unloaded pistol in her hand.

"Moira," Pleasance cried. "He is almost inside. We need the pistol."

Although Moira immediately returned to reloading the pistol, Pleasance knew it would not be ready before Lucien was inside the cabin. Neither did she have time to load the musket. She held the musket like a club and waited for him.

She had barely gotten into position to fight when Lucien dropped through the ragged hole he had made and swung his body at her. Pleasance struck him with the musket, but it did nothing to stop him. His feet hit her square in the chest and she fell to the floor hard. He landed on top of her before she could get out of his way. Winded and in pain, she fought him.

As she and Lucien wrestled across the floor, Pleasance got a glimpse of Moira. She was trying to get a fixed aim on Lucien. Pleasance tried to keep Lucien in one place long enough, but it was impossible. Even when she stopped fighting him for a moment, he made sure she was between him and Moira.

The man was too strong and Pleasance soon lost the battle. He dragged her to her feet and imprisoned her in front of him, painfully holding her wrists behind her back and wrapping one arm around her neck so tightly that she found it hard to breathe. Even the smallest movement she made added to her pain. Moira stood, the pistol aimed at them, but Pleasance could see that she was terrified. She was not sure how much help Moira would be.

"Shoot him," she ordered Moira, but her voice was little more than a hoarse whisper, not enough to pull Moira out of her shock.

"Non, my little bastard will not shoot me," Lucien said. "So, my child, do you have a kiss for your papa?" He puckered his lips and made a lewd smacking noise. "Ah, me, maybe not. You do not look so very good, my baby. You are too white, eh?"

"Let her go," Moira demanded in a high, tremulous voice. "I will shoot ye."

"The only way you can shoot me is to make a big hole in this whore first."

"I can shoot ye in your ugly face. I can still see that."

Lucien laughed. His amusement was cut short when Moira pulled the trigger.

Chapter Fifteen

The shot missed. Lucien screamed and pushed Pleasance aside. She hit the wall so hard it left her groggy, and she sagged to the floor. Moira's cries gave her the strength to stand. Even as she moved to help Moira, Lucien wrenched the pistol from the girl's hand and hit her over the head with it. Pleasance gasped as Moira crumpled to the floor, a trickle of blood running down her face. As Lucien turned to face her, Pleasance lunged for the musket. She got it in time to halt Lucien's advance, swinging it at him each time he tried to move toward her.

"If you have hurt Moira, Tearlach will kill you," she warned Lucien. "He will hunt you down like the mad dog you are."

"Tearlach?" Lucien laughed. "If he hunts me down, I will be very amazed. *Oui,* and *hunting* is maybe not the right word, I am thinking. *Non,* it should be *haunting.*"

The way Lucien giggled after his own words made Pleasance feel nauseous. She did not want to believe the dark implication of his words. Yet, it all made sense. It explained why Lucien was there at all. It also explained why Tearlach had not returned from his hunting trip despite the bad storm.

Pleasance shook her head, trying to shake away the meaning of Lucien's words.

"Ah, such confusion on your pretty little face," Lucien said. "Do you maybe not understand what I say to you? My accent—*oui?*"

"I understand that you are trying to tell us a whopping great lie, that you want us to believe that you have finally beaten Tearlach." Pleasance felt such anger it made her voice very hard and sarcastic, and she could see that that infuriated Lucien.

"I did beat him. I left him bleeding his life away in the woods."

"Nay," cried Pleasance and she swung the musket at his head, but he easily danced out of her reach. "You are lying, you twice-cursed coward."

"Lying? You are a very stupid woman." Lucien shook his head and spoke very carefully, as if he was trying to explain something to a witless child. "I have beaten Tearlach. He no longer matters. He will no more be fighting or hunting me, and he will never be coming here to help you. He is dead."

"Nay. You did not say that you actually killed him. You just said you had left him bleeding in the woods. Tearlach might still be alive." Pleasance desperately wanted to believe her own words. "Unless you actually watched him take his last breath, you cannot be sure he is dead."

"You know that is not the truth, my pretty whore. I can see in your face that you do not believe your own words. *Non,* you do not. I left Tearlach O'Duine so weak that he could not have evaded a death stroke if I had decided to give him one. I could have cut his throat with ease. Even if he found the strength to try and save himself, he would have had to crawl here, for I sent his horse racing off into the forest. He has no food and no water and no way to get back here. Nay, the fool is a dead man even if he has not yet breathed his last. I made sure he knew what I planned to do, that I was coming here, for I wished him to think about it as he died."

It was nearly impossible to push aside the horror of his cold words, but Pleasance knew she had to. Their lives were at stake. She could do nothing to help Tearlach, but she could at least attempt to save herself and Moira.

"So, since you have beaten Tearlach, you should have no need of us. As you have so delicately said, Tearlach is sure to die where he is. You told him what you meant to do to his sister and me, so he will be tormented by that. There really is no need to actually do the deed. Just let us go."

"Non. I have told Tearlach what I would do and I will do it. And you have made me very angry. You have hurt me, and now I will hurt you."

Lucien lunged at Pleasance. She swung the musket as hard as she could, hitting the side of his head. He howled and staggered backward. As he slumped up against the wall, Pleasance raced over to Moira, who was stumbling to her feet. She grabbed the girl's arm and pushed her out of the room, pausing only to pick up the pistol. Once outside, she shut the door and handed Moira the guns.

"Get downstairs and load these." She saw how pale the girl was. "Can you do it?"

"Aye. He didnae hit me that hard."

"I will give you as much time as I can. Hurry!"

Moira ran downstairs. To Pleasance's dismay only a few moments passed before she heard Lucien start to curse. His bellow of rage filled the cabin. Pleasance wished there was something she could use to bar the door, but there was only herself. When Lucien slammed into the door she knew her weight would not be enough to hold him, but she pressed her back against the door, determined to keep Lucien a prisoner for at least long enough for Moira to load both guns.

On Lucien's fourth try, Pleasance knew she could restrain him no longer. In truth, she was surprised she had done as well as she had. The blow to his head had clearly weakened him, but he had his full strength back now. She waited until she heard him start to run at the door, then she scrambled down the stairs. She heard him hit the door and curse as he burst out of the room and ran into the wall opposite the door. She took one quick look over her shoulder. He was already after her.

Moira was at the kitchen table frantically trying to finish loading the pistol. Pleasance turned to face Lucien, only to find he was just feet away and still running hard.

She cried out in surprise and pain as his bulky frame slammed into her and she was catapulted to the wooden floor with Lucien landing on top of her.

She wriggled and squirmed as she struggled desperately to get out from under him. His rank smell made her cough. She gritted her teeth as she fought to keep from being completely pinned down. The only thought in her head was to stop Lucien from harming her.

But even as she struggled, she prayed that Lucien had been lying, that Tearlach was not dead or dying, that he was on his way back to the cabin. She and Moira had never needed him more.

Tearlach jerked awake, forcing himself not to give in to the unconsciousness that beckoned him so strongly. Despite the increasingly heavy snowfall and the bitterly cold winds, he did not feel any real discomfort. It was a dangerous sign. He was at serious risk of suffering from frostbite and slipping into a fatal cold-induced slumber. He also knew that he was growing too weak from loss of blood to fight such threats for long.

He looked around to try to determine where he was. The grogginess and blurred vision caused by his wounds robbed him of his usual tracking skills. He was dependent upon his mount to take him home. At least the cold had slowed the bleeding, which helped him cling to what little strength he had.

"What good will I be to them?" he grumbled as he tried to maintain his hold on his mount's neck. "I cannae even push this accursed horse into a faster pace." He tried to kick the animal into something more than a frustratingly slow amble, but he simply lacked the strength to get the animal to heed his commands. "I cannae fight with Lucien like this. He will laugh right in my face before killing me."

He muttered a curse as his eyes began to burn and tears ran down his face, to turn to ice on his beard stubble. When he lifted a hand to wipe at his eyes, he nearly slid off of his horse. He spat out another curse and clung even more tightly. Tearlach closed his eyes in an attempt to soothe them, only to feel the strong pull of sleep. He fought it as he clung to his mount and tried to soak up some of the animal's warmth.

Just as he decided he would have to open his eyes or fall into unconsciousness, a tangy scent came to him on the cold, clean air. The smell was easy enough to recognize, and a swift surge of hope gave him a little strength. He stared ahead but still saw nothing. Anther deep breath confirmed that the scent was growing stronger.

"Chimney smoke, laddie," he said to his horse. "There is a cabin near at hand. Let us pray that ye have led me to my own."

In anticipation of a confrontation with his deadliest enemy, Tearlach straightened up, but renewed pain tore through him and he fell forward again, clutching the animal's neck tightly as he fought the engulfing black of unconsciousness. As he lay there panting and trembling, sweat chilling on his back, he released a bitter laugh. The only way he could defeat Lucien was if he fell on the man.

"Nay, ye great fool," he scolded himself. "Dinnae let your own mind defeat ye. Be strong. Or as strong as any mon can be when he is bleeding like a stuck pig," he added in a grumble of disgust.

Tearlach began to doubt that he would be able to see a cabin even if he rode through the front door, but a moment later his dismal evaluation was proven wrong. The snow-covered trees began to thin and he recognized the square shape of a cabin. After blinking away some of the blurriness affecting his sight he realized that his steadfast mount had indeed brought him home.

But the horse callously left outside in the snow also told him that he might be too late. Lucien had already arrived.

Tearlach eased himself off the horse, but the moment he tried to stand on his own he collapsed. As he lay helplessly on his back in the snow, unable to summon any strength in his limbs, he wondered if he was fated to die within sight of his home, within yards of the two people who needed him most.

Pleasance felt her dress tear and bit back a scream. She tried to bite Lucien's arm, and he slapped her so hard that her ears throbbed.

"Tearlach will kill you," she threatened when Lucien finally pinned her down.

He laughed. "You did not listen to me, woman. Tearlach is dead. The carrion are picking at his bones in the forest." Lucien trailed the point of his knife blade down the bodice of her gown. "He will not help you and he will not avenge anything I now do to you."

"Then God himself will see that you pay for this." She sucked in her chest as he pressed the knife point closer.

"God will have a difficult time sorting through all of my crimes to find you, my pretty. *Oui,* and when he does find you, he will have to think on all the sins you have committed. Sins like the one you committed in the barn with your Scottish lover—*non?*"

"It was you who was peering at us that day," Pleasance whispered, shock and revulsion stealing her voice.

"Oui, my lusty pretty," Lucien replied as he began to cut open her bodice inch by inch. "I watched you and your Scotsman putting your clothes back on. And I had a good look at these pretty legs, *oui?* I will be looking more closely soon."

"You are a pig." Pleasance tried to buck him off her as he eased open her cut bodice. All she got for her effort was a sharp scratch as the knife he held against her cotton chemise slipped against her.

"Is that the way a woman should talk to the man who is about to become her lover?" Lucien clucked his tongue in an exaggerated manner as he slowly shook his head.

"You could never be my lover." Pleasance spoke in a firm, cold voice despite her swiftly rising fears. "You are taking what you want, stealing it. You are no better than the lowest, most evil rapist."

"You will give me what you gave the Scotsman."

"Never."

"Oui, I am thinking that you will. You are a hungry little pretty and you will be hungry for me."

"You want me to entertain your lust before you kill me? You must be mad." She could not fully restrain a cry of pain when he slapped her across the face. "Beating me will certainly not change my opinion."

"Such a foolish woman you are. You should think about

the pain I could cause you and try to keep from making me angry with you."

"You tell me again and again that you have murdered Tearlach. How much more pain can you cause me?" she asked in a soft voice, the fear that Lucien spoke the truth briefly pushing aside any terror for herself.

And then Moira's voice cut through their argument. "Get off her," she demanded.

Pleasance joined Lucien in looking up at the girl. She was aiming the pistol directly at Lucien. Although she was white and trembling, she held the pistol firmly in both hands.

Lucien sat up a little. "Come now, my pretty little bastard, you cannot kill your own father."

"Ye are no father to me. Ye are a murdering pig. Ye killed my mother and ye have killed my brother."

With a speed that was startling, Lucien leapt up and ran straight toward her. She shot him, winging him on the shoulder, but he barely missed a step. He grabbed Moira by the wrist, ripped the pistol from her hand, and tossed it aside.

Pleasance did not wait to see what would happen next. She scrambled to her feet. Her heart beating hard and fast, she ran to the kitchen table, where the musket lay.

She turned around, the musket in her hands, and aimed it at Lucien. He punched Moira again and again, then shoved the unconscious girl aside. The look on his face when he turned to find Pleasance armed and ready gave her a brief moment of satisfaction.

He took a step toward her and she pulled the trigger. The musket went off and she stumbled backward, caught off balance by the weapon's violent recoil. As she regained her feet the sudden stillness filled the cabin with an ominous tension.

She hardly dared look at the gruesome results of her action. One peek showed her Lucien sprawled on the floor— silent and unmoving. Beyond that, she did not want to know.

She covered her eyes with a shaky hand and collapsed in a chair at the table.

The crack of a musket shot pulled Tearlach from his stupor. He cried out as he forced his cold, stiff, pain-riddled body into a kneeling position and grabbed his nervous mount to pull himself to his feet. Although he knew he would be of little help, he staggered toward the cabin. He had to know what had happened.

"Pleasance," Moira said as she moved to the older woman's side. "The danger has passed. We are safe now."

Without looking, Pleasance put her arm around Moira. "Have I killed him?" she asked in a small whisper.

"Aye. Shot him clean through the heart, ye did."

Pleasance opened her eyes to see Moira callously prod Lucien's limp body with her foot. "Do not touch him."

"I was just making sure he is really dead." Moira gingerly touched her split bottom lip, then cautiously wriggled her jaw. "I dinnae want him popping up to punch me in the face again."

Gently cupping Moira's chin in her hand, Pleasance inspected the girl's bruised face. There would be an increasingly dramatic array of bruises, but no other damage. The fear was already leaving Moira's eyes, a hint of color returning to her face. After taking a deep breath to steady herself, Pleasance finally took a good look at Lucien. He lay sprawled on his back staring sightlessly up at the ceiling. There was a hole in his clothes surrounded by powder burns, for he had been close when she had fired the musket. Only a small trickle of blood seeped out from beneath him. Pleasance experienced a somewhat ghoulish sense of surprise, for she felt there ought to be a great deal more blood when a man was shot to death. She knew she had done the killing, yet her mind was having a difficult time accepting that fact.

In an attempt to come to terms with what she had done, she looked into Lucien's face. The gray pallor of death was already settling on his dirty skin. She looked into his blindly staring eyes and shuddered. Again she could not ignore how much his eyes resembled Moira's. Pleasance found it chilling to see those eyes cold and drained of life. Muttering a curse, she quickly bent down and closed his eyes, hating to touch him but desperate to close those eyes.

"He doesnae deserve such tender treatment," Moira said, her hands planted firmly on her hips as she frowned at Pleasance. "I would leave the man to stare up at his maker. Aye, and up to heaven where he will ne'er go."

As she went to the kitchen sink to scrub her hands, Pleasance glanced over her shoulder at Moira. "I could not bear to see those empty eyes. I closed them for my own peace of mind." She grimaced. "'Tis foolishness, but I could not endure seeing them—looking so much like yours—drained of all life."

"I dinnae see it as foolishness," Moira said in a quiet voice. "'Tis a comfort to ken that someone felt the same way I did." She gave a small, self-conscious smile when Pleasance returned to her side and hugged her. "I feared I was being weak and silly when I felt afraid looking into his dead eyes."

"Nay. Never weak and silly."

"I wasnae much help."

"You were scared."

"So were you."

"Moira, you did fine. We are alive."

"Aye, but is Tearlach?"

"I do not know. I can only pray that Lucien was lying about killing Tearlach."

She felt such uncertainty and pending grief that she hugged Moira again. Just as Moira was returning the hug a banging sounded at the front door. Pleasance echoed Moira's soft screech of surprise and fright. She started to push Moira behind her even as they both turned to stare wide-eyed at the door.

"Sweet Mary, what is it now?" whispered Pleasance as she glanced around to try to locate a weapon.

A weight fell against the door just before the pounding resumed.

"Curse ye, Lucien," a voice yelled. "Open this door."

Pleasance and Moira exchanged a look of total disbelief, and Pleasance took a tentative step forward. "Tearlach?" She tried and failed to stop Moira from racing to the window to peer through the peephole in the shutters. "Be careful, child."

"I will, dinnae worry o'er that." She peeked out and gasped. "Oh, sweet Mary, Pleasance, I daren't believe my eyes. 'Tis him. 'Tis Tearlach, and he looks gravely hurt." She rushed to the door only to find Pleasance right at her side. "Lucien lied to us. He didnae kill my brother."

"It would appear that your brother has as many lives as a cat."

But the moment Pleasance flung open the door and took a good look at Tearlach, sagging against the wall, she began to doubt her own words. The man looked so close to death that she wondered how he had made it back to them. It was hard to tell whether he suffered more from his wounds or from the cold. His skin was gray with an alarming touch of blue, his eyes were glazed, and he swayed so badly that she instinctively held out her arms to catch him when he started to fall.

"I heard a shot," he said, his voice a hoarse whisper.

"I shot Lucien." She edged closer to him, wondering how

to give him the support he so badly needed yet not add to whatever pain he might be suffering. The swirling snow and storm-darkened skies made it impossible to see exactly where or how badly he was wounded.

It was difficult to see very much inside the cabin either, but Tearlach finally caught sight of the body stretched out on the floor. He looked from a pale, worried Moira lurking on his right to an equally pale and worried Pleasance edging up on his left. It was a little galling to think that two such dainty females had accomplished what he had been striving to do for eleven years.

"That ye have managed to save yourselves is a sore blow to a man's pride, ye ken," he muttered, then cursed as he lost his final tenuous grip on consciousness.

Pleasance cried out as Tearlach collapsed. With Moira's help, she barely kept him from hitting the floor.

"We had better take him to your room," Moira said as she moved to help Pleasance lift him.

"He will never fit in my tiny bed."

"Ye mean we will have to take him upstairs?"

"I fear so. 'Tis either that or lug his huge bed down here."

"I think Tearlach isnae as heavy as that cursed bed. So, he goes upstairs. I just hope we dinnae drop him."

The two of them were finally able to lift Tearlach and heft him up the stairs to his room. Once they got him up on the bed, Pleasance struggled to get his cold, wet clothes off him while Moira hurriedly collected the materials needed to treat his many wounds. Once he was stripped the brutality of the attack he had endured at Lucien's vicious hands was clearly revealed.

Aside from the knife wounds, many of them deep, there was some serious bruising. Pleasance feared he might have suffered internal injuries. Although she was concerned about the cold he had endured, she had to close his wounds first. Any further loss of blood would only hinder her chances of getting him warm.

Moira began to cry, and Pleasance almost joined the girl, but she gritted her teeth and fought the urge. "He needs our help now, Moira, not our tears," she said in a cool voice as she started to clean Tearlach's wounds.

It took a moment before Moira was able to control herself enough to help. They cleaned the blood from his body until they could see the knife cuts more clearly. While Moira helped to hold him still, Pleasance stitched the deeper wounds. Then they carefully bandaged each injury with clean strips of linen.

As soon as she could, Pleasance sent Moira to find Tearlach's and Lucien's horses and see to the poor animals' comfort. Moira reluctantly obeyed, and Pleasance finished tucking blankets around Tearlach, washed up, then sat by his side to watch and wait.

Now that he was in a warm bed and his wounds had been seen to, he looked much better. His coloring had improved and his breathing was quiet and even. Pleasance relaxed in her chair, feeling a little more confident. She knew that, as had happened when he had been mauled by the bear, a fever might set in and steal what little strength he had, but at least for now he was alive.

A faint sad smile curved her mouth. Tearlach's swoon had been very well timed. When she had seen him standing there—alive despite all of Lucien's efforts to kill him—she had been so relieved, so filled with joy, that she had almost blurted out her love for him. She was relieved that she had been saved the painful embarrassment of declaring feelings that Tearlach had no wish to be burdened with. As far as he knew, she had remained strong and levelheaded during the crisis. Maybe the proof that she could take care of herself and Moira would convince him that she was indispensable to him. Pleasance sighed as she accepted the fact that it would take longer than a year to win Tearlach O'Duine's elusive heart.

"Is he all right?" Moira demanded as she entered the room. She stood by Pleasance's chair and watched her brother. "Ye were looking at him with a deep frown on your face, and I feared that he had already taken a turn for the worst."

"Nay. My expression was prompted by my own thoughts, not Tearlach's condition. In truth, he looks and breathes very well. I make no promises, for I have no power to shape fate, but I think he may recover from these injuries. There is still no sign of fever and the chill is leaving his body. It appears that getting him warm and tending his injuries might be all that was really needed."

"Do ye think he can be left alone for a wee bit then?"

"Well, aye, I suppose he can be, but why? Is there something we must do that requires both of us and cannot wait?"

"Depends upon your point of view," said Moira. "I dinnae really have the stomach for being snowed into the cabin with a dead Lucien. I rather thought we might try to bury the man before the storm grows too fierce."

"Oh, sweet heaven, I completely forgot about him." Pleasance got to her feet and after a final thorough check of the sleeping Tearlach, started out the door. "I just hope that the two of us can manage such a chore alone."

"I hope so too, because we also have to put something over that hole in the roof."

It was four hours before Pleasance was able to return to Tearlach's side. They dragged pieces of wood onto the roof and nailed them into place, then turned to burying Lucien. She and Moira finally gave up trying to dig out a traditionally sized grave for him in the frozen ground. They wrapped Lucien's body in a blanket and placed it in a shallow grave near, but not too near, the family plot. By the time they had piled enough rocks on top to thwart any carrion eaters, the storm had reached its full glory, the icy winds blowing the snow into blinding clouds. Pleasance was heartily glad that she would not have to venture outside again until the storm was over.

Once inside, she and Moira did a little more work on the roof from Moira's room. It was not a skilled job, but it was enough to keep the weather out. She finally left Moira to finish cleaning up and returned to Tearlach's side.

Rubbing her hands together in a vain attempt to warm them up, Pleasance entered his chamber. A cry of surprise and alarm escaped her. He was struggling to get out of bed. She rushed to his side and forced him to lie back down.

"What do you think you are doing?" she demanded even as she gently wiped the sweat from his face.

"I should be asking ye the same question," he declared, his voice unsteady.

"It seems that I am fated to take care of fools. 'Tis bad enough that you go running off hunting when any other man with a shred of wit would have remained home," she continued as she helped him drink some herbal tea. "Then you go and get yourself cut up into little pieces by that mad beast Lucien, drag your bleeding carcass home, and collapse at my feet. Now that I have been forced to patch you up— again—you could at least have the good sense to stay in bed and allow your injuries to heal." Realizing that she was scolding him as if he were some small child, she sat down in the chair by his bed, clasped her hands together tightly in her lap, and struggled to stay quiet.

Tearlach stared at Pleasance for a moment in utter, speechless surprise, then smiled at her obvious struggle to regain her poise. When he had woken up to find her gone, when no one had answered his calls, all his fears had returned. Common sense had told him that Lucien could not have come back to life and harmed Pleasance and Moira, but he had not been inclined to be sensible. He knew now that he would not have made it even to the door of his room. That was not something he was ready to admit to Pleasance, however. Nor did he intend to acknowledge the truth and good sense of her scolding.

"I woke to find you and Moira gone. No one answered my bellowings. Considering all that has happened, I was naturally worried."

Pleasance nodded and relaxed a little. "Moira and I had to bury Lucien. We felt we ought to be about it before the storm grew too fierce and it became impossible. As it was, we were not able to dig out a full-sized grave in the frozen ground. Finally we just put him in the ground and covered the grave with stones. We also had to fix the hole Lucien made in the roof. That was how he got in. We did not do a very pretty job, but 'twill keep the cold and snow out."

He reached out to take her hand in his. "I am verra sorry that ye were forced to deal with such ugliness. Lucien didnae hurt ye or Moira, did he?"

"Well, he did punch poor Moira in the face a few times, but she appears to have suffered only some bruising. As for me—he tore my clothes but never managed to do more than that. We both will have a lot of colorful bruises, but neither of us was seriously hurt."

"Are ye sure?"

"Quite sure." She frowned when his grip on her hand tightened. "I am fine—truly I am."

"Well, how do you feel about having to actually kill the man?" he asked in a soft voice, keeping a close eye on her as she replied.

"Ah, that. I think it may take me some time to recover from the horror of that." She sighed. "I took a man's life, Tearlach. I still find that almost impossible to believe."

"Nay, he planned to kill you both, and would have felt no remorse."

Pleasance nodded. "I know that. 'Tis the truth I cling to, and I feel sure it will eventually ease my remaining qualms."

"Is Moira all right then?"

"I told you—she was not seriously hurt."

"Nay, I meant about Lucien being killed, and by you."

"She has told me that she accepts it. I believe she feels no regret."

"She kenned all about the mon, didnae she?" murmured Tearlach.

"Aye. There is no use trying to keep secrets from her. Now, you should get some rest, Tearlach. I believe you will heal without too much difficulty, but only if you take care to rest."

"Aye, I do feel the need to sleep." He closed his eyes. "Ye did weel, lass. Verra weel indeed," he whispered.

When he said no more, Pleasance realized he was already asleep. She smiled crookedly, eased her hand free of his, and sat back in the chair. His praise left a warm glow in her heart, yet her feelings were mixed. She felt proud, flattered, hopeful, and irritated.

Yet she would hold fast to the grain of hope his compliment had given her. She had proven her strength to him, clearly shown him that she could take care of herself and Moira. There was even a chance that he would want her to stay on with him now that he recognized that strength. And now that she no longer needed to prove her fortitude and ability, she mused, she could set her sights on winning his love.

What made her sad was the aching conviction that winning Tearlach O'Duine's love could prove an even more difficult task than defeating the hated Lucien.

Chapter Sixteen

"Now there is a pretty sight to greet a mon on a fine spring day." Tearlach crossed his arms over his chest and grinned down at Pleasance, who was bent over her kitchen garden.

She briefly glanced his way before deciding to ignore him. If she gave in to her own high spirits, she would only encourage Tearlach's impudence. She yanked out the last few weeds from the area she had been clearing, then straightened up and absently rubbed the small of her back. Since it was only the first week in April it was still too soon to plant anything, but now she would be ready when the time came.

She looked at Tearlach as she wiped her hands on her apron. He was still a little thin, but otherwise he had healed completely. A little hard work outside in the clear warm air, and she was sure he would soon look his old self. He would regain that robust swarthiness stolen by his injuries and three long months spent inside the cabin.

"Do you have nothing else to do except trouble women at their work?" she asked him.

"Nay. Not today." He grasped her arm and started to lead her into the woods.

"Tearlach," she cried in protest, stumbling after him as she fruitlessly tried to wrest her hand free. "What game is this? We cannot leave Moira alone. She will worry about us."

"I am taking you away for a while."

A carefree giggle escaped her as she fell into step beside him. It would be nice to leave her chores behind for a little while. It would be even nicer to do so with Tearlach. There was an intriguing playful air about him, a mood she had rarely glimpsed, and she badly wanted to get to know this Tearlach much better.

Pleasance knew it was dangerous to hope he would one day return her love for him. Still, they had grown close over the winter. During the long confinement they had begun to talk more openly to each other. He had told her something about his life, and even revealed a few of his more private thoughts and feelings concerning his past and his plans for the future. For the first time since he had dragged her out to the Berkshires, she had felt truly accepted in his life.

When they were curled up together beneath the covers, talking in soft contented whispers, it was hard to remember that he had yet to offer her any words of love. The man could speak beautifully about his passion, about how she fired his blood and about how much she delighted him. That was all very well, but those sweet words were not the words of love and commitment she craved. There were times when she felt compelled to demand some firm expression of his feelings for her, but she knew that would be a big mistake. Pushing Tearlach to give her more than he was ready to give could easily lose her what few gains she had made in their tenuous relationship. She just wished that the road to his well-armored heart was not such a long one. She did not have an endless wellspring of patience.

She was so caught up in her moody thoughts that she was not aware that Tearlach had halted, and she walked into his back. Gently rubbing away the itchiness caused by bumping her nose against his red blanket coat, she ignored his soft laughter and looked around her. The clearing by the brook was familiar to her, yet it looked different. The new grass and budding leaves were a soft brilliant green. Early-blooming wildflowers in white and purple dotted the area.

"'Tis such a sight that makes one love spring," she murmured. Then she noticed the blanket spread out beside the brook, a basket set in the middle of it. "And what is this? An offering for the squirrels?"

"'Tis for m'lady." Tearlach gave an exaggerated bow and gestured toward the blanket. "'Twould please me greatly if you would take a seat. I have prepared a fine luncheon for us."

"You have prepared?" She smiled at him as she moved to sit down.

"Aye." He took a seat next to her. "I told Moira what I wanted, helped her put it in the basket, then carried it out here."

"Ah, aye, that is an extraordinary amount of preparation for a man."

"Now, there will be no impertinence from ye." He began to unpack the basket. "Bread, cheese, cider, sweet butter, cold ham, and some cranberry jam. Ah, and best of all—gingerbread."

"Somehow it does not seem right to leave Moira to eat lunch all by herself," Pleasance said even as she cut herself a thick piece of bread. "I am sure she would enjoy eating here by the brook, surrounded by all these uplifting sounds of spring."

"I am sure she would too. Howbeit, the three of us have closely shared each other's company for several long months. 'Tis past time that ye and I had a moment or two of privacy."

Pleasance smiled a little shyly as he filled a cup with

cider and handed it to her. "We did have some privacy over the winter. Each night we were alone in your bedchamber."

"True—with Moira just across the hall. As dear as my sister is to my heart, 'twill be pleasant to just sit for a while—ye and I—without her being but feet away."

"Mmmm. Now she is at least several yards away."

"The spring air makes ye a verra impertinent lassie, doesnae it? And Moira is more than a few yards away. Jake took her into the village. She will be gone for most of the afternoon. So, my bonny wee lassie, we can be as idle as the gentry."

Pleasance laughed and sipped the cider, savoring the tartness of beginning fermentation. It would not be much longer before the drink carried a real kick with it. Even now she knew it would be foolish to drink too much too quickly. Only once had she overimbibed. It had been during a celebration with Nathan and his friends over a particularly successful customs run. Afterward she had not been able to recall much of the evening, and that, combined with a lot of teasing from Nathan, had taught her to be a great deal more careful. Since the very last thing she wished to do was to embarrass herself before Tearlach, Pleasance knew to be cautious.

As she quietly shared the light repast with him, she savored the beauty of their surroundings. The brook was running high and fast due to the melting snows. It looked cold and dangerous yet beautiful. It made a pretty, restful sound despite its turbulence, and helped make Tearlach's land rich and fruitful.

When Tearlach edged closer and draped his arm around her shoulders, she just smiled and rested against him. He had grown more affectionate over the winter and she thoroughly enjoyed it. She just wished that a few words would accompany all the hugs, handholding, and kisses. It required more courage than she could muster to wager her heart's future on how he acted without a few spoken pledges to back it up. After all, she thought with a hint of sourness, Tearlach was also very affectionate toward Moira. And he did not hesitate to tell Moira how he felt about her, she grumbled silently, her pleasant mood fading with chilling alacrity.

Then Pleasance scolded herself. It was a beautiful day. Tearlach was acting charming, affectionate, and seductive. She had a pleasing meal to enjoy, a lovely landscape to view, and no work to do. It was foolish to ruin it all by dwelling on unhappy thoughts. Only a fool lied to herself, but there was no real harm in ignoring the distasteful truth for a little while.

"There is something else spring brings besides a young lass's impertinence," Tearlach murmured, idly stroking the thick braid that hung down her slim back.

Glancing up at a pair of noisy, frisky squirrels, Pleasance could not fully restrain a grin as she drawled, "I do not think you need to tell me that."

He looked toward the squirrels, who were loudly indulging in their mating ritual, and laughed. "Ah, aye, there is a lot of that in the air." Ignoring her scolding look, he began to undo her braid. "'Tis the season to begin hunting again."

"Hunting?" She felt a shiver of alarm. "Is there no time when you let the poor animals rest from your pursuit?"

"I did—over the winter." He chuckled when she made a soft noise of disgust. "Hunting isnae always as treacherous for me as it has been since ye arrived here. In truth, if I were the superstitious sort, I could begin to think that ye have been cursing my luck."

"That is not amusing." Especially since I have occasionally wondered about that myself, she thought. "I thought that hunting as a livelihood was losing its viability. Would not spring be a good time to start something new rather than to continue what has been called a dying trade?"

She tensed, not able to read the expression on his face and growing afraid that she had angered him. The last thing she wanted was to prompt some tart reminder of her place as an indentured servant, thus souring this pleasant interlude. There had been no such reminders during the winter, but Pleasance did not feel confident that such stinging remarks were now a thing of the past.

"Ye are right," Tearlach said after a long moment of thought. "Fur trading in this area is a dying business and I have no wish to plunge even deeper into unexplored lands. That is what I would have to do if I intend to go on."

"Yet you still plan to go hunting again?"

"Aye. I made a deal with a mon back in Worcester for a set number of furs. I willnae lose if I cannae get all he required, for he will pay the going rate for each fur I am able to bring him. Howbeit, he promised me a handsome bonus if I meet his quota. I shall make one more attempt to fulfill the order and then I shall direct all my efforts at farming."

Pleasance recalled all the talk she had heard about trappers and hunters being a restless breed of men. "Are you certain that is what you want to do? Is that what will make you happy?"

"Do ye fret much o'er what can make me happy, sweet Pleasance?" He brushed a light kiss over her cheek.

A shiver of delight rippled through Pleasance as his soft, rich voice stroked her senses. She stiffened her spine, refusing to allow that alluring voice to make her say something she did not want to say. His question was a dangerous one. No matter how she responded, it could easily tell him something about her emotions, something that she would prefer to keep private. Pleasance decided to shrug off his query as if it were unimportant banter.

"If you intend to become a farmer, you will need to clear a bigger field than you have now."

Tearlach frowned, sensing her evasion. Pleasance had become adept at shying away from making even the lightest reference to what she might or might not feel. He knew he carried the blame for that, but he was not sure how to fix the problem. There was only one thing he was sure of—as the time to take her back to Worcester drew nearer, the more he wanted her to stay with him.

He laughed silently as he admitted to himself that he had no real idea of what was in his own heart. Cowardice kept him from looking too closely . . . in case she rejected him again.

There were a few truths he really ought to tell her. If she discovered them on her own, there could be a rift between them that he might never be able to mend. Yet, he hesitated. In the beginning he had felt no need to tell her anything, for he was still hurt, angry, and did not trust her. That had all faded as he had come to know her. She was not the spoiled, heartless, useless female he had bitterly called her. But now that he wanted her to stay, he wanted her to do so because she had some affection for him and not because he was wealthy.

There were also a few truths she had yet to tell him. Why she had rejected him back in Worcester, for one thing. He knew that the real Pleasance did not resemble the haughty lady who had spurned his courtship. There were times when he ached to grab her by the shoulders, stare her right in the eye, and demand to know why she had rebuffed him as she had. But always cowardice kept him silent. No matter how hard he tried, he could not convince himself that having Pleasance as his lover now made up for her callous rejection of his earlier and far more honorable overtures.

"Tearlach?" Pleasance smiled when he gave a faint start

of surprise. "You were lost in your thoughts. Were you thinking of what work to do next?"

It took a moment for Tearlach to recall what they had originally been discussing. The voice of reason told him that now was his chance to tell Pleasance the truth about his financial situation—that he could sit on his front porch and whittle for the rest of his life and still have enough to support himself and a sizable family. He ignored the voice. After all, who was there to tell her the truth if he did not? Only Moira and old Jake knew, and they had been sworn to silence. Tearlach decided to wait until he was more sure Pleasance cared for him. Then he would tell her that the pockets she thought nearly empty were actually very full indeed.

"Aye, I will become a farmer. 'Twas always the plan. 'Tis why I planted those apple trees a few years back. And 'tis one of the reasons I have decided to build a new home this spring."

"A new home?" Pleasance was intrigued yet alarmed. To build a new home indicated an urge to settle down, which sounded very promising. But what if she was not the woman he intended to settle down with? "Do you really need one?"

"The cabin is sturdy, but, aye, I need a larger place to live." He idly nibbled her ear, smiling faintly when he caught the heavy-lidded look growing on her face.

"There is only you and Moira." Pleasance knew that, if she wanted to have a reasonable conversation with the man, she ought to put an end to his sweet seductive kisses. But the warmth of his lips on her ear and neck felt too good to refuse.

"There is also ye, Pleasance Dunstan." Tearlach nudged her until she lay on her back, then gently pinned her unresisting body beneath his. "That makes three people."

"But I shall be here for only a few more months. Then my year of servitude will be over and I will return to Worcester."

"Plans can be changed, lass."

Before she could ask what he meant, he kissed her. The slow hunger of his mouth on hers stole all thought from her mind. She curled her arms around his neck and eagerly returned the stroke of his tongue. Pleasance thoroughly enjoyed his caresses until a cool breeze lightly brushed the newly bared skin of her shoulders. She was startled to find that Tearlach had undone and removed her bodice. It was not until that breeze had alerted her to how far their lovemaking had progressed that she became painfully aware of where he intended to make love to her.

"Tearlach," she whispered as she fruitlessly attempted to halt his removal of her skirt and petticoats, "we are out in the open. Someone could see us."

"Then they would be trespassing on my land." He sat up, still straddling her, and began to take off his shirt. He studied her as she lay there blushing, her hair splayed out beneath her and wearing only her thin lace-trimmed chemise. Her thick chestnut hair shone with color, catching every ray of sunlight and rippling with red and gold. Tearlach did not think he had ever seen her look more beautiful. Then he laughed. He thought that a lot. Yesterday he had thought it when he had caught her taking bread out of the oven and she had smiled at him over her shoulder, her cheeks flushed and a dusting of flour on her chin. He wondered if he was suffering from some sort of lovesickness, then shook the thought away.

Love was not an emotion he wished to be tangled up in, for it stole a man's wits, made him addled and foolish. It could even make him weak, force him to subjugate his honor in order to please the subject of his heart's desire. His earlier attempts at romance had taught him that. Recalling how he had felt as he struggled to get home a few months before, knowing that the murderous Lucien was probably already at the cabin, he inwardly grimaced. Despite his reluctance to admit it, he strongly suspected he was in love. This troubled him, for he still felt the sting of Pleasance's rejection those many months ago. He did not like to think of what she could do to him now.

He moved off her just long enough to finish shedding his clothes. As he eased himself back into her arms, he found it easy to push his concerns aside. The passion they shared was strong and real. He had no doubts about that, or that Pleasance felt it as strongly and as deeply as he did. Their passion was what would keep her with him once her indenture was over.

"You are staring at me very hard," Pleasance murmured, slipping her arms around him. She had some lingering concerns about making love out in the open, but his big, warm body felt too good to push away. "You are staring so hard that I fear you can see right through me."

"I was enjoying the sight of ye with your hair spread out and lit by the sun." He began to carefully unlace her chemise.

Pleasance felt the heat of a blush touch her cheeks. She thought it a little amusing that lying naked in the woods did not bring the color to her cheeks, but Tearlach's gentle compliment did. It also struck her as a little sad that she was so used to being seen naked by him yet so unaccustomed to hearing any flattery from him. She sighed with pleasure when he tossed aside her chemise and they were finally skin to skin, but there was a lingering sadness in her. Yet again she was painfully aware of a distance between them.

"Ye dinnae look to be taking my flattery very kindly, lass," he said, and kissed her lips.

"Nay, 'tis not that. I still fear someone might find us here." She slowly ran her hands down his sides to his hips.

"'Twould be somewhat embarrassing. 'Twould also be years ere the resultant gossip would fade."

"Aye, that it would, but no one will wander by here. As I said, 'tis my land. 'Tis also not a place anyone crosses going from one place to another." He kissed the hollow of her throat. "We will be left quite alone."

She drew idle designs on his trim hips with her fingers, watching his eyes darken. "Are you sure 'tis wise for a man in your weakened condition to be left so completely alone with me?" She had to bite back a grin, for they both knew that he had regained the strength to make love weeks ago and had proved it many times, much to her delight.

"Weakened condition? Is that a challenge?" He closed his eyes when she eased one slim hand between their bellies to stroke him. "Ye ought to be able to judge my strength weel enough now, pretty Pleasance."

She laughed softly, her laughter increasing briefly when he growled. The heated ferocity of his kiss fired her passion and quelled her urge to be playful. She wrapped her body around his, meeting him stroke for stroke, kiss for kiss. When he joined their bodies, she cried out in welcome. Tearlach raised himself up slightly and Pleasance held his gaze as he took them to the heights they sought. She caught a fleeting glimpse of the way his release altered his features before she was swept away by her own. He slumped in her arms and she held him close as they regained their senses. When he finally eased their intimate embrace, she protested faintly, then murmured her pleasure when he rolled onto his side and pulled her securely into his hold.

"Well, I guess you might not be as weakened as I thought," she drawled, and laughed with him.

"Ah, lass, this is the way to live." Tearlach flopped onto his back and tucked her up against him. "Ye couldnae enjoy this sort of play back in Worcester." Out of the corner of his eye, he closely watched her face.

"I suspect there are a few secluded spots that lovers take advantage of even in Worcester. But so close to one's own home? Nay, probably not. And 'tis probably a good thing too. 'Tis shameless." She started to sit up, intending to get dressed, but Tearlach held her firmly in place.

"Weel, I am not done behaving shamelessly." He grinned as he dragged her on top of him.

It still made Pleasance a little nervous to be cavorting in such an open place, but she subdued her twinges of modesty and fear of exposure. He was going on another hunting trip and she suspected it would be a long one. After such a long winter he had a lot of lost time to make up for. She also suspected that he would be leaving soon, perhaps even in the morning. That was undoubtedly one of the reasons for this private time away from Moira.

She cupped his face in her hands and came to a decision— she would do her best to make their remaining hours together unforgettable. She wanted him to keep thinking about her the whole time he was out in the wilderness. As she brushed a kiss over his mouth, she hoped she had sufficient skill to create an unshakable memory in his mind. It would have to be a strong one in order to, in some small way, make up for being apart.

Tearlach stretched out under the blankets, his arms behind his head, and watched Pleasance prepare for bed. Although they had spent most of the afternoon making love by the brook, he was still eager for her. He would be leaving in the morning and faced several months without her. But more important was the memory of how she had made love to him—seductively, boldly. It aroused him just to think about it. She had revealed an uncanny knowledge of how and where he liked to be touched, and he wanted her to display that expertise again. He hoped her skill had not been randomly inspired by the freedom of making love outdoors. If it was, he knew he would be turning himself inside out trying to inspire her again, he mused with a silent chuckle.

When she kept standing before the mirror in her thin chemise, brushing out her hair, he decided she was taking too much time.

"Ye will brush yourself bald," he said, frowning at her.

Pleasance set the brush down on the table and turned to look at him. He was lying on the bed with the covers pulled up just high enough to maintain his modesty. Despite his scars he was breath-stealingly handsome in her eyes. He also looked impatient for her to join him. She felt a warm surge of confidence, for she knew instinctively that he was recalling their afternoon romp when she had been so bold and accommodating. As she stepped over to the bed, she decided to stick with the plan she had adopted that afternoon. It was apparently working and—she glanced toward his pack in the corner of the room—she clearly had only a few hours left.

"You intend to leave in the morning," she said as she toyed with the lace on her chemise.

"Aye. Sooner out, sooner back."

"And how long will you be gone?"

"Several months."

He reached for her, but she stepped back. "Arenae ye coming to bed?"

"Oh, aye." She smiled, feeling an exhilarating boldness. She began to slowly unfasten her chemise. "Would I be so unkind as to make you spend your last night home all alone?"

"'Tis hard to say, for ye have been acting a wee bit

odd today, lassie." Tearlach found her slow disrobing intensely erotic.

"Odd?" Her chemise undone, she eased it off her shoulders, holding it against her breasts so that it did not immediately fall to the floor. "I am not sure that sounds flattering."

Tearlach sat up a little straighter, his gaze fixed upon the swell of her breasts above the lace-trimmed neck of her chemise. "Ye are also being a wee bit slow."

"Patience, sir." She smiled at him, the passion that darkened his eyes urging her on. "I wager that you are one who unwraps his gifts with unbecoming haste."

"There are certain gifts a mon wishes to get to swiftly."

She laughed, and even she recognized it as a seductive sound. Tearlach was right—she was acting oddly, but it was highly enjoyable. Still smiling, she released the chemise, letting it tumble to her feet. The hungry look on Tearlach's face stirred her own desire. He immediately curled one strong arm around her waist, but she resisted his attempt to tug her onto the bed. This time she intended to lead the dance.

"I see," he murmured, eager for her yet curious about what she was planning, "Ye mean to torment me."

"I would never be so cruel. 'Twas my thought that you need your rest since you intend to set out so early in the morning. 'Twould be inconsiderate of me to insist that you do all the work tonight."

He tugged her close enough to kiss her smooth stomach, savoring the light tremor that passed through her, then he leaned back against the plumped-up pillows. "'Tis most considerate of ye, lass, although I should ne'er call it work to make love to ye."

"How kind of you." She pulled the covers off him, smiling faintly when she discovered that he was already fully aroused.

Pleasance climbed into bed and lightly straddled his taut

body. She had only tested her wings that afternoon, sharing the lovemaking with Tearlach, participating but not leading. That experience had given her confidence, however, and she intended to be the aggressor tonight. She intended to make him as mindless with arousal as he so often made her. A brief fear of failure rippled through her, but she easily shook it off. One thing she was certain of was that Tearlach desired her, and she knew that would make even a less than expert performance on her part still good enough.

She smoothed her hands over his broad chest as she bent down to kiss him. There was no submission in his kiss, but he did not take control either. She was a little short of breath when the deep, sensuous kiss ended, and she could not resist returning his cocky smile. Using her hands and body to caress him, she began at his strong throat and kissed her way down his body—slowly, lovingly. She lingered a little over each of his scars, silently assuring him that they did not dilute her desire for him.

Tearlach found it harder and harder to remain passive. He wanted to grab her slim body and take over the lovemaking, hurrying to the union his body achingly craved. He fought that blind, instinctive urge, for he wanted to savor the sweet, heady delight of her kisses, her touches, her hesitant yet nearly perfect seductive skills. As her kisses reached his lower abdomen, he groaned and closed his eyes. He knew what he craved from her, but he dared not ask for it. He just lay still, taut and trembling with hopeful anticipation.

A cry of delight burst from his lips when her soft, warm mouth touched his erection. He shifted with increasing restlessness beneath her intimate caresses, his teeth gritted as he fought for the control he needed to enjoy the pleasure for as long as possible. That control was irretrievably lost when she slowly engulfed him in the hot moistness of her mouth. He muttered incoherently, desperately trying to encourage and compliment her, yet not sure that he was making any sense. When he knew his release was heartbeats away, he grabbed her beneath the arms and pulled her up his body.

Her soft, husky laugh increased the fire in his veins tenfold. She neatly eluded his attempts to take the lead and he groaned. He took several deep breaths as he fought to clear his head of the blinding passion she had let loose inside him. Then she slowly lowered herself onto him, uniting their bodies with a seductive leisure that had him shuddering from the rich, intense pleasure of it. He grasped her slender hips, but Pleasance proved to need no direction as she took them both to desire's final destination. Tearlach heard her hoarse cry of release blend perfectly with his own, felt her small body press close to his even as he tried to bury himself more deeply within her. When she collapsed in his arms, limp and breathing heavily, he barely had the strength to hold her.

It was a long while before Pleasance had the energy or the inclination to end the deep intimacy of their embrace. She slid off his body and curled up at his side. Beneath the hand she rested on his chest she could feel his heartbeat. It was still a little fast, but it was slowing down. She smiled with proud contentment and kissed his neck.

"I thought ye intended to help me preserve my strength, not steal it completely away," Tearlach murmured, then smiled when she chuckled. "I havenae felt so exhausted in many a year."

"I wished to give you something to remember me by while you are gone."

"Oh, I believe that performance will do that admirably. Such loving tends to linger in a mon's mind. 'Twill make those long nights out in the forest seem even longer and a great deal colder."

"To my way of thinking, that is not such a bad thing. You may make an effort to return to the cabin a little sooner."

"Oh? Is that important to ye? Will ye miss me then, Pleasance Dunstan?"

She avoided his gaze. "Well, I guess I am curious to see this house you say you plan to build," she finally answered. "Surely that cannot be done if you are not even here."

Tearlach was sorely tempted to curse, but he bit back the words. It would accomplish nothing to push her. He did not intend to let her think she had won the little game of evasion, however. It was past time to start being more honest with each other.

"The house will'be begun and worked on while I am gone," he replied. "I have already set my plans before the carpenter and we have agreed on the building of it. I have also made sure that Jake knows all of my preferences, and he will come by on a regular basis to assure that everything is going smoothly. The carpenter knows to talk to him."

"Will that not be expensive?"

"My furs have brought me enough income."

He grasped her by the chin and gently but firmly forced her to look at him. "When I return I will take over the building. And there is one other thing I mean to do when I get back home."

"And what might that be?" She sighed with open pleasure when he slid his hand over her body and cupped her breast.

"Ye and I must have ourselves a long talk." He kissed her throat, lingering on her pulse point, as he brushed his thumb back and forth over her hardening nipple.

"Talk?" When he circled her nipple with soft, teasing kisses, she murmured her frustration and, threading her fingers through his thick hair, urged his mouth toward that aching tip. "You do not wish to talk to me now?" She arched toward him when he finally answered her silent plea and began to gently suckle.

"Nay, there isnae time and I have much better things to do with the few hours we have left. Howbeit, when I return, 'twill be the second thing I will do."

"Talk about what?" She looked up at him when he nudged her onto her back and straddled her.

"About how well I have taught ye to be evasive."

"Evasive?"

"Aye, lass. And I think we had best discuss our future."

"Our future?" Since he was paying intense attention to her breasts, heightening her desire with each kiss, each stroke of his tongue, she found it hard to concentrate on what he was saying, even though it sounded like something she would very much like to hear.

"Mmmm. Our future. But now—ah, aye, now—I can think of only one thing—enjoying as much of your sweetness as I can ere the sun rises."

Pleasance closed her eyes and let her passion run free.

Chapter Seventeen

Taking a deep breath, Pleasance savored the rich scent of the spring breeze with its heady promise of new life. She cast another handful of flax seed across the ground, confident it would flourish in the rich earth. She had arrived too late last year to fully appreciate the goodness of the land Tearlach had chosen for his own, but that richness was evident now. Even in a poor year, the land would provide more than enough for their survival.

A brief glance toward the cabin made her smile. She had considered it a prison at first. Now, even though she was not yet sure what lay ahead for her and Tearlach, she felt good when she looked at the sturdy cabin. So too could she look at the framing for the new house only a few yards away and feel hopeful, hopeful that she might be able to share it all with Tearlach. After what he had said before leaving, she could look at that new house going up and feel that she might be the one to help him fill those extra rooms. He had been gone for only a fortnight, but she was already eager for his return so that they could talk about their future. She just hoped she was not foolishly letting her heart place too much weight on his subtle remarks or seeing what was not really there.

"Pleasance."

She gave a start and realized that Moira was standing in the cabin doorway. She pointed to the east, where a lone horseman approached. Pleasance tossed out the last of the flax seed and moved to greet their visitor. She was nearly to the veranda when she recognized the rider.

"Nathan!"

Even as she raced toward him, he dismounted and held out his arms. Pleasance laughed as her brother caught her up in his embrace and swung her around a few times. The last of her fears that he too would reject her like her family had were hugged right out of her.

As she introduced her brother to Moira, Pleasance had to smile. Nathan gallantly kissed the girl's hand, and Pleasance could see the beginnings of infatuation in her huge dark eyes. Like many an older maid, Moira was smitten by Nathan's fair-haired handsomeness. Pleasance had no fear that Nathan would do anything to hurt Moira's tender feelings, so she saw no real harm in allowing matters to take their natural course.

Pleasance urged both Nathan and Moira into the cabin. She invited her brother to sit down at the table and fetched him food and drink. Although Nathan conversed pleasantly with Moira, Pleasance sensed a tension in him that began to worry her. Was some new trouble about to be set at her feet? After serving Nathan, she poured herself and Moira some cool cider and joined the couple at the table, then waited impatiently for her brother to finish eating.

"What is wrong, Nathan?" she demanded when he finally pushed his plate aside.

He smiled faintly and took a drink of cider before answering. "Mayhaps Moira should leave us alone for a little while."

"Nay. There is nothing Moira cannot be allowed to hear. We are as close as sisters."

"I am pleased that you were able to find at least that here." Nathan set a small leather pouch on the table. "You are free."

Pleasance stared at the pouch and felt her heart skip alarmingly. "What?"

"You are free. This is the amount of the fine Tearlach O'Duine paid out for you. There is also a letter from Corbin." He lay the missive next to the pouch. "In it Corbin agrees to let me pay off the rest of your indenture to Master O'Duine, thus gaining your release from the man's service."

"Father—"

"I paid it. Father holds as tight to his coin as he ever did."

"Then what good is my being free? I have no home to go to. He cast me out."

"He overstepped." Nathan reached across the table to take her hands in his. "There is something I must tell you, a secret I have held close for too long." He glanced at Moira. "Are you certain, Pleasance, that you wish her to hear everything I say?"

"Ye are going to tell Pleasance that she is a bastard," murmured Moira.

Nathan stared at the child. "And what makes you say such a thing?"

"I just feel it."

"Is that true, Nathan?" Pleasance whispered the question, shock briefly stealing her voice.

"Yes, Pleasance." Nathan grimaced as he nodded. "You and I are bastards. Our father had a woman to keep him company before he sent for Mother—his legal wife, Sarah Cordell—to join him in Worcester. Well, Sarah is not our mother, just his wife. We are the products of that previous illicit liaison with one Elizabeth Thurston."

"Then why have we always lived with Father? Why did

he keep us with his legitimate family? 'Tis not as if he loves us dearly."

"Thomas Dunstan kept us for the same reason he does most anything—money. The woman he took up with to fill the days until his wife arrived was not some poor wench. The money our father used to build his business, to set up his fine life, all came from Elizabeth Thurston."

"Where is she now? What happened to her?" Pleasance was amazed at how easily she was able to accept the shocking news.

"Dead. I fear my birth, so soon after yours, weakened her beyond any chance of recovery. I have sometimes wondered how much our father did to help her—or how little. After all, her death solved a great many of his problems. The woman we now call our mother was the daughter of a powerful and wealthy man. Father needed him to maintain his business. Old Rupert Cordell could have ruined Father with ease. Father needed our natural mother's money and he needed Sarah Cordell's father's power. Our mother died before he was forced to choose between the two. We would have been cast out save for one reason."

"Which is?"

"He could not cast us out of a house that we owned."

Pleasance gaped at him. "We own that house?" she finally managed to ask.

"Aye. It was Elizabeth Thurston's. If she knew what sort of man Father was, 'tis hard to see why she would have become involved with him. I think she must have discovered his greediness later, when it was too late to protect herself, but not too late to protect us. She left us the house and a fair sum of money handled by lawyers in Boston."

Shaking his head, Nathan continued. "Knowing all of this, I was doubly enraged to discover how Father had betrayed you. I could easily have seen that your fine was paid. In truth,

Father should have paid it himself, for 'twas our coin jingling in his pocket. This past year our loving family has lived off of *our* funds. I approved that funding, for, poorly done or not they did raise us. You see, Father recently made some poor investments. He has done so before and our money always freed him from debt. Our mother's will allowed for such payments. She wanted the family to stay together, not be pulled apart by such troubles as paying the bills. She may also have realized how vengeful Father can be."

"And you think that their betrayal of me was some sort of revenge against me for owning the things he wanted—the house and the money?"

"Oh, aye. 'Tis certain. Father deeply resents what we have. He feels it should have been his. He has never ceased trying to make it all his in one way or another."

"How did you learn the truth?"

"The lawyer told me everything the day I turned sixteen."

"I am the oldest. Why was I never told?"

"Our lawyer felt that you should not yet be told, at least that is what he explained to me. I agreed, for I felt that there was no real need to tell you. But I can see now that I was wrong. You need to understand the reasons for the deplorable way you have been treated. Now you know that you need not depend on Father for your livelihood. You need not even reside with the man, if you do not wish to."

Pleasance laughed aloud at the irony of her situation. In the past there had been many times when she had desperately wished to escape from her cold parents and spoiled sister. Now, however, the very last thing she wanted was to live alone somewhere. Suddenly nothing was as she had believed it to be.

"We shall return to Worcester now," continued Nathan, "but if you find you cannot bear living with them, I shall find you your own place. Despite what they did to you, I

cannot toss them into the street. However, I have informed
Father that, as soon as his fortunes improve, he is to find
himself another residence. In truth, I have reached an age
where I wish to have my own home."

So, Nathan had come to take her away from Tearlach.
"Would it not be just as well if I stayed right here?" she
asked.

"Nay." Anger toughened Nathan's voice. "No sister of
mine shall work as some man's unpaid drudge. You will
come home."

"Go," Moira said.

The argument Pleasance had been about to put forward
died in her throat. Moira had that still, concentrated look on
her pretty face, the one that indicated she was having a
"feeling." It never failed to send a faint chill up Pleasance's
spine. This time, however, she also felt hurt. Moira seemed
eager to have her gone.

"Moira? You want me to leave?"

"Ye have to. I love ye, Pleasance. I have ne'er loved
anyone but Tearlach. Weel, Jake too. But now I love ye as
weel. Go. 'Tis best. I feel it. I feel it strongly. 'Tis better if
ye are free. Go home with your brother Nathan."

Moira was right and Pleasance knew it, but that realization did little to ease her pain. It would indeed be better if
she and Tearlach settled what was between them as equals—
as free man to free woman. If he had no hold over her, save
for that of love, they might come to some understanding.

Or he might simply let her go.

"It will take me a little while to pack my things, Nathan."

"Fine." He stood up, smiling at Pleasance and Moira. "I
need to fetch the other horses. I left them hidden in a sheltered copse down the road a ways since I could not be certain of my reception here. It seemed wise to come unfettered.
I will not be gone long."

The moment Nathan left, Pleasance started packing her few belongings. Moira did the same, for they decided that she would go to stay with old Jake until Tearlach returned. They would pasture the animals on Jake's land. It was the note she must leave Tearlach that caused Pleasance the most difficulty. She wanted to beg him to come after her, yet she dared not do so. Finally, she wrote a simple message saying where she had gone and where Moira could be found. The words sounded cool, distant, yet she could think of no better ones.

"You leaving?" Old Jake gaped at Pleasance, unable to believe his ears.

"Aye. My brother Nathan paid off my indenture so I am a free woman now."

"'Tis best, Jake." Moira took the old man by the hand as she joined him on the rickety front porch of his cabin. "'Tis best."

"Well, I will be damned three ways to Sunday if I can understand it. No matter. Hope you have yourselves an easy journey. It was a real pleasure having you about for a while."

"I feel the same, Jake. Thank you for everything. Good-bye." She kissed him on the cheek. "Good-bye, Moira," Pleasance briefly but firmly hugged the girl. "I hate to leave you. Are you sure—"

"This must be done," Moira said. "'Tisnae forever. Trust me. I feel it strongly."

After staring into Moira's eyes for a moment, Pleasance felt some of her grief and fear at leaving fade. "You feel it strongly, you say?"

"Aye, verra strongly. Take care, Pleasance," Moira urged as she kissed her cheek.

"Tearlach ain't going to like this one cursed bit," Jake muttered as he watched Pleasance and Nathan ride away.

"Nay, he certainly willnae." Moira smiled slowly when Jake stared at her. Understanding began to glow in his aging eyes. "He willnae like it at all."

The two of them laughed heartily.

Pleasance sighed. She and Nathan had stopped to spend the first night of their journey at a pleasant inn. The existence of the place had surprised her, but then maybe Tearlach had simply avoided such places on their original trip because of his lack of money. The food she was idly rearranging on her plate looked healthy and tasty. She knew she should savor all the comforts while she could. They would come with increasing rarity until they drew nearer to Worcester. It would be a while before the road to the western wilderness would become as well used and as settled as the road to Boston. And all the while, she wanted to rush out to the stables, saddle her horse, and hie back to Tearlach's cabin. She wanted to be there waiting for him when he returned.

"You love the man, don't you?"

Startled, Pleasance looked at Nathan. It was on the tip of her tongue to deny what he had said. But there was such sympathy in Nathan's blue-green eyes, she was driven to confess.

"Aye, I do."

"A man who laid false accusations and forced you into indenture?"

"It was not quite like that. Tearlach expected the family to extricate me from Letitia's brangle. All he intended was to frighten me a little. We had badly stung his pride by rejecting his courtship of me. He but sought to pay that back in kind. Not very laudable of him, but no great sin either. Many of us might have acted much the same."

"Mayhaps. Or we should wish to."

She nodded. "Still, he is but a poor, struggling farmer who traps and hunts to supplement his livelihood."

Nathan choked on his cider and stared at her as if she had completely lost her wits. She frowned. "What is wrong, Nathan?"

"Tearlach O'Duine? Poor? Struggling?"

"You saw where and how he lives. He does show great promise though, Nathan."

"Oh, aye, he still does show promise, though he has surpassed most people's expectations many times already."

"What do you mean?"

"The man is rich. Name the industry, what little Mother England allows us, and Tearlach O'Duine has had a hand in it. He is spread so wide and has invested so well that he could buy me out ten times over."

"Nay." A chill crept over her. "You saw where he lives. Why would he live like that if he is all that you claim he is?"

"'Tis his family's lands. When Moira was left alone, he decided to stay too, but he has a brigade of lawyers handling most of his business. 'Twas probably for her sake that he stayed, for she has a better chance of being accepted out there. He said nothing of all this to you?"

"Not a word. Are you certain?" She did not want to believe that Tearlach had lied to her.

"Very certain. I arrived in Worcester too late in the year to come right after you. Winter was setting in. Hoping to ease my worries about you, I looked into the matter of what sort of man had taken you. Our lawyer in Boston was most helpful, as was Corbin Matthias. Knowing who Tearlach O'Duine was eased my fears that you had been taken to some wattle-and-daub hut with a skin-clad trapper of little wit and fewer manners, but I was enraged that a man who could afford twenty servants with ease should bind you to him in base servitude."

She stared at her hands, hands roughened by months of backbreaking work. Not once had she minded, not after she had lost her heart to the man. Now her calloused hands seemed to represent all the lies he had told her—or, rather, the truth he had denied her.

Thinking Tearlach was poor, she had worked hard to prove to him that she was able and willing to help him build a good life. Now she discovered that he already had the means to achieve that good life. She felt like a complete fool.

"Father was also unaware of his wealth?" she asked.

"Aye."

"I thought so. Otherwise, he would have urged the man on Letitia. She chose John because she thought he was the wealthier one, you know."

"Tearlach O'Duine could buy John Martin a hundred times over. He and Letitia were married a few weeks ago, by the way."

"Poor John probably hoped to get her married and out of trouble as fast as possible. So, you did not tell Papa about Tearlach's wealth?"

"Nay. There was no point. It would only have caused another brangle." He frowned as she continued to stare at her hands. "Are you all right? I do not mean to distress you, but I feel you should know the truth. 'Tis always best."

"Aye, the truth is best. I wish Tearlach had told it. I've made a complete ass out of myself."

"Nay, Pleasance."

"Aye, Nathan, I have. I have spent these past months turning myself inside out in an effort to show Tearlach that I could be the hardy pioneer woman I thought he needed and wanted. I wanted him to see that despite my privileged upbringing, I would not be a burden. I have labored from dawn to dusk. I have never worked so hard in all my life.

"Do not mistake me. 'Tis not the work I mind," she went

on. "I feel a sense of accomplishment and pride in a job well done. 'Tis that I did it all to prove myself to him when there was no need. To think of the grief I suffered when I made mistakes, for I believed Tearlach could little afford the waste that resulted. He allowed me to think that. I was left to believe I had little time to learn so much, to believe that such a poor man could not afford a mate who could not do everything— from scrubbing floors to spinning flax. And yet, the truth was that my candles did not have to be perfect every time. He could have bought more. I fretted, worried, struggled, and worked so hard at times that there seemed to be no part of me that was free of aches. 'Twas all a game he played. 'Twas all a waste."

Reaching across the table, Nathan took her hands in his and watched her closely when she finally looked at him. "God alone knows why I should defend the man, but mayhaps you judge him too harshly. He may have intended no slight. It may just be his way. He worked hard too, did he not?"

"He did. Dawn to dusk. I told you, 'tis not the work I resent. 'Tis that everything I did, every move I made, was based upon a lie. For all those months he lied to me. He led me to believe that he was something he was not." She shook her head. "During all that time, even in the moments of darkest uncertainty, there was one thing I felt certain of— that Tearlach O'Duine was an honest man. Now it seems I was wrong."

Nathan opened his mouth to argue, to try to ease her hurt, but maybe it was for the best that she suffer now. Pleasance loved Tearlach O'Duine, but Nathan had heard little about the man to suggest that he returned those feelings. Let her heart break now, when she was feeling anger and outrage over her misuse. It would give her the strength to heal.

He also sensed that Pleasance had done a great deal more for Tearlach O'Duine than scrub the man's floors. Although

Nathan ached to press his sister for answers to the question pounding in his head, he chose to remain silent on that as well. As she excused herself to seek her bed, leaving behind an untouched meal, Nathan felt that Pleasance would tell him what he needed to know in her own good time.

Pleasance lay in bed and stared up at the ceiling. She felt sure she would get little sleep despite the comfortable accommodations. There was simply too much preying on her mind, too much gnawing at her heart. So many questions clamored for answers that her head ached. Everything she had believed as fact was a lie. Truth, she thought sadly, was not necessarily a pleasant thing.

The truth about her parentage was something she had little difficulty in accepting. It brought her no real pain. Her only sorrow was that she had never had a chance to know her real mother. Knowing that she was a bastard explained a lot of what had hurt her in the past.

Her illegitimacy would not become public knowledge, if only because Thomas Dunstan would do everything he could to avoid such a scandalous disclosure. That also helped her accept the truth with relative calm. She knew she would suffer little rejection or embarrassment over the matter.

It was what Nathan had told her about Tearlach that really troubled her. It cut her deeply. His lie tainted everything they had shared. Never before had she felt such a complete and utter fool. As far as she could see, there had been no good reason for him to keep the truth of his status from her. How could she have fallen in love with such a callous man?

She brushed away a tear. She would not weep over Tearlach O'Duine, not yet. For the sake of her belief in her own good judgment, she would wait to decide about Tearlach and his lies. If he did not come after her, she would know the truth, know that he had simply toyed with her. If he did follow her, she would give him a chance to explain himself. She owed it to herself.

She just hoped that if he did appear on her doorstep, she could refrain from slamming the door in his handsome face!

Tearlach abruptly stopped whistling a jaunty tune as his cabin came into view. It looked curiously empty. As he drew nearer, the pace of his steps and his heartbeat increased. He could think of no reason to be afraid, yet fear gripped him. The nearly four months he had been gone suddenly weighed heavily on him. With Lucien dead and the danger of winter passed, he had thought Moira and Pleasance would be safe. Suddenly he was not so sure.

He flung open the heavy door and stood in the doorway, looking frantically around. No one was there. Even more alarming, no one had been there for a long time. Then his gaze fell upon a piece of paper on the kitchen table.

He snatched up the message and read it quickly, then reread it: *Dear Tearlach: My brother Nathan came for me barely a fortnight after you left. He has paid the fine and I am no longer indentured to you. Nathan has taken me back to Worcester. Moira is safe. She and your livestock are at Jake's. Pleasance.*

Damn! He crushed the note into a ball and threw it across the room.

How could she have done it? How could she walk away from him and all they had shared? Her abandonment hurt him far more than he cared to think about. He snatched up the sack of coins left on the table and threw it against the wall.

Then he put his belongings away, washed up, and donned

clean clothes. Soon he was back on his horse and galloping toward old Jake's cabin.

Moira laughed softly as, from the front window of Jake's cabin, she watched her brother gallop into view. "Here he comes."

"Riding fast and furious?" Jake joined her at the window.

"Aye, until he saw your cabin. Now he is just ambling over here as nonchalant as ye please." Moira shook her head as she moved to the cabin door. "Men and their pride. He doesnae want us to see that he is fretting o'er his woman."

"Don't you go teasing him, girl."

"I willnae, Jake. But that doesnae mean I cannae shake my head in disgust now and then." She stepped out of the cabin to greet her brother, a chortling Jake right behind her.

Tearlach sat sprawled in a chair at Jake's battered table and scowled into the tankard of cider he had been served. Moira had been able to tell him little more than he already knew. Pleasance's message might have been cool and terse, but it had apparently said it all. She left shortly after he had, which meant that she had been back in Worcester for three months, perhaps even a little longer. Moira was being irritatingly vague. The thought of Pleasance back amongst her own kind, a Pleasance more confident and sensual, further darkened his mood. Men could sense a woman of passion, a woman who knew about desire, and Tearlach was sure that she was being assiduously courted.

"So, she just up and went home, broke her bond," he grumbled.

"Nay." Moira set her bag of belongings next to Tearlach's chair. "Nathan paid the fine and there was a letter from

Corbin saying that the arrangement was legal. Ye had her because she couldnae pay the fine levied against her. 'Tis paid now so ye dinnae get to have her anymore. Her brother left the money. Didnae ye see it?"

"I saw it." He drained his mug and stood up. "Let's go home, Moira. Thank ye kindly for keeping her, Jake. I will collect my livestock tomorrow."

"No trouble." Jake hurried after them as they strode out to their waiting horses. "You ain't going after Pleasance?"

After tossing Moira up on her horse, Tearlach turned to scowl at his old friend. "Go after her? What for?"

"Well, I could think of one or two reasons," mumbled Jake. "She was a help."

"Aye, she was a help. I can get just as much help from any boat arriving from the mother country." He mounted, his expression increasingly dark. "She could have stayed and weel she kenned it, but instead she chose to go back to Worcester. I have far more important things to do than chase after some petticoat." He spurred his horse into a quick start, wanting to get back to his own cabin, where he could think in some privacy.

That evening Tearlach sat by the fire, scowling into the flames. He had spent his whole hunting trip carefully planning out all he wished to say to Pleasance, only to find that she was not around to hear it. He sternly told himself he was better off without a woman who could so skillfully twist his feelings. He resolved to put her out of his mind and get on with his life. He and Moira had managed well enough before Pleasance Dunstan had burst into their lives. They would go along well enough now that she had deserted them.

Tearlach fought to keep that vow for two long weeks. It took every ounce of willpower he possessed. Pleasance's spirit seemed to haunt him at every turn. While sitting before the fire after Moira had gone to bed, he would find himself staring at the empty rocker Pleasance had favored and recalling their quiet—and sometimes not so quiet—discussions. He missed seeing her slim figure in the doorway of the cabin. He missed hearing her sing softly to herself as she mended his shirts, spun, or baked. Mostly he missed her curled up by his side in bed. He missed the passionate moments as well as the quiet ones. Even working night and day on his new home did not banish her from his thoughts because he kept wondering what she would think of it.

"Tomorrow I will take you to Jake's," he announced to Moira as they ate supper on the night that marked exactly two weeks since he had returned from hunting. "I have to go away for a while."

"I am going with ye." Moira pushed aside her bowl, rested her arms on the table, and watched her brother closely.

"Ye never go hunting with me." He was a little surprised at this sudden spark of rebellion in his young sister.

"But ye arenae going hunting for squirrel or deer this time. Nay, ye are hunting Pleasance Dunstan."

There were times when Moira's insight could be extremely annoying. "I havenae said so."

"Didnae have to. Could see it coming. Every time ye stared at her chair by the fire or at the table or at the churn or at the spinning wheel or—"

"That is quite enough. Ye make me sound like some moonstruck laddie. I am too old for that."

"No one is too old to feel lonely, Tearlach. I am lonely for her too. I miss her bad."

"Then ye will be pleased to ken that I intend to get her back for ye."

"Nay, I willnae."

"What?"

"I said nay, I willnae be glad if ye get her back for me. Ye have to go and bring her back for *you.* I ken that she loves me and all, but ye have to tote her back here 'cause ye want her for yerself. And ye have to tell her so. Ye have to do it proper too. Marriage and all of that. I dinnae want ye shaming her anymore."

To have a thirteen-year-old point out things he should have seen for himself did not make him feel very kindly toward Moira. He was tempted to tell her he had changed his mind and would not be going after Pleasance after all. But he could not say the words. He had to bring Pleasance back.

"Oh, go to hell," he mumbled.

"Weel, if ye insist, but if ye dinnae mind, Tearlach, I think I will go to Worcester first."

Chapter Eighteen

"Are you finally going to tell me or shall I continue to pretend that I do not notice?" Nathan demanded as he stopped pacing the small parlor and stared at Pleasance, who sat on a small padded settee making lace.

She glanced up from her tatting, saw Nathan's significant glance toward her middle, and blushed deeply. No doubt he had known about the child she carried for some time. It explained his easy, quick agreement to find them a small cottage outside of town, away from prying eyes, barely a month after they had returned to Worcester. She was a little surprised that he had remained silent for another two months after that.

Scandal was not the only thing she feared if it became widely known that she was with child. There were still laws on the books which punished fornication, and occasionally they were enforced. To flaunt those regulations could easily bring the weight of the law down on her and thus down on the innocent child she carried.

Heaving a sigh, for she had lived in dread of this confrontation, Pleasance set aside her tatting, folded her hands in her lap, and watched Nathan closely. "Aye, I am with child."

"Did you mean to hide it from me until he gave his first cry?"

"Nay. I was but reluctant to deliver such shocking news. Each time I thought about telling you I wavered. Cowardice silenced my tongue."

"Why were you afraid of telling me?"

"I was afraid of disappointing you."

He quickly moved to sit beside her and gave her a brief hug. "You could never disappoint me. Never." He frowned as he sat back a little. "Such a slight upon your honor demands payment, however." He stood up and began to pace the room.

As Pleasance saw the anger Nathan could not hide, she sighed. "And here is another reason I was loathe to tell you. I could not bear the thought of you and Tearlach coming to blows over me or, worse, facing each other over swords or pistols. That would surely tear the heart right out of me. I had some very upsetting nightmares about it, believe me."

He sighed and ran a hand through his thick fair hair. "I know, Pleasance. I know. 'Tis why I have fought so hard these past few months to bury my anger at the man."

"I am sorry to bring this trouble down on your head, Nathan."

"'Tis not me I am worried about. 'Tis you. Shunning is the very least you will face when your pregnancy is discovered. And it will be. 'Tis not something you can hide forever."

"I know it."

"I was only fourteen when I saw a woman flogged at the stake for the crime of fornication," he whispered, then grimaced when he saw how pale she had gone. "The punishment was not much approved of," he added, trying to reassure her. "It caused a bit of a scandal in and of itself. I did not mean to frighten you."

"Do not worry." She stood up slowly. "Do you think we

could walk in the garden? I find that I need to move about from time to time."

"Of course."

Nathan linked his arm through hers, and they stepped through the parlor doors out onto a brick courtyard. For a few moments he just walked with her, saying nothing. He smiled faintly as he looked over the garden she had put together in their early days at the cottage.

Out of the corner of his eyes he studied his sister. She was looking more rounded, more curvaceous, but he had to admit that he did not yet see much of the physical signs of her pregnancy. She was either carrying very small or she dressed very cleverly.

There was something else, something he would have been hard-pressed to describe, which had alerted him. It was why he had already been planning to move out of the house they had been sharing with their father and his family before Pleasance had even asked. The days spent in their old home upon their return from the Berkshires had been filled with tension. The scandal of her arrest had not yet faded and Pleasance had changed. She was no longer so compliant, so eager to please.

The instant he had suspected that Pleasance was carrying Tearlach O'Duine's child he had been determined to get her as far away from the Dunstans as possible. He would have thrown his family out of the house in Worcester except that he knew it would be better if Pleasance was kept out of the public eye until she had the child.

As he had waited for her to tell him about the baby, he had plotted and planned what he would say and do. What should be done, what really needed to be done, was not something Pleasance was going to accept with grace. He was going to have to try to convince her to accept it, however.

"Pleasance," he murmured, clasping his hands behind his

back and watching her as she stopped to pick a few dead blossoms off a rosebush, "there is, of course, one solution to this dilemma."

She waited for the words she knew were going to open up the very argument she had tried so hard to avoid. "I suppose you are going to tell me about this perfect solution even if I do not particularly wish to hear it."

"Aye, I am. The answer is Tearlach O'Duine—he must marry you."

"Must he now? You have discussed the matter with him, of course."

Nathan swore softly under his breath and regarded her with annoyance. "I can see that you mean to be difficult about it. Ere we begin an argument that could easily continue for days, would you tell me how much time we have."

"What do you mean?"

"Just when is this child due to enter the world?"

"Oh." Pleasance was annoyed to feel a blush tint her cheeks. She shrugged. "I am not sure."

"By that you mean you have no idea at all, am I right?"

"There is no need to be so sarcastic." She felt very defensive, for her lack of knowledge about what was happening to her own body annoyed and embarrassed her.

"How can you not know? 'Tis a woman's province to know such things."

Pleasance put her hands on her hips and glared at her brother. "Then it would be very kind if someone told us women more about it. I saw a colt born once, or as much as one can see with only an occasional peek. Even that was considered far too much of real life for me to know about. I know nothing, Nathan."

Since he did not know very much either, Nathan did not like to hear her confession of ignorance. "Nothing?"

"Absolutely nothing." She picked a daisy and idly plucked

the petals off one by one, reciting the age-old rhyme in her head. "I could be six months along. I simply cannot be sure. I was working so hard and so constantly, that could have been the cause of the, er, delay in my monthly flow. That I carried a child never occurred to me until the quickening reached such a strength within me, it told me very clearly what was ailing me."

Nathan softly but viciously cursed and kicked the head off of a dandelion. "Six months. Little time was wasted in conceiving this child."

"Aye, I must admit the truth of that—to my shame."

"To *his* shame, Pleasance. That rogue seduced you."

"I cannot say in full honesty that he did. Tearlach O'Duine stirred some very strong feelings in me from the moment I first set eyes on the man. Aye, mayhaps he did seduce me, but it took very little effort on his part. I was drawn as a moth to a flame. The time I did spend in resisting the man's overtures was a miserable, annoying time. Despite the travails that face me now, I do not regret giving myself to Tearlach O'Duine. I remember and savor our moments together."

"You are always so cursed fair." Nathan's voice held a hint of complaint. "Can you also be fair and admit he has put you aside?"

She turned very pale, and he cursed his insensitivity. A stone bench was near at hand and he led her to it. He sat down with her, took one of her hands in his, and gently rubbed it.

"That was cruel," he murmured. "Forgive me."

"There is nothing to forgive. It is the truth."

"I still should not have said it. I do not like to see the pain in your eyes. In truth, 'tis that which makes me ache to help you. At least let me demand that he give his name to the child you carry, Pleasance. You know how a bastard can suffer for the lack of a father's name. Why do you think our own illegitimacy was kept such a dark secret for so many years? Aye, and is still kept very quiet? Surely, when you were with Moira, you got a very good look at how it could be."

"Aye, I did."

"Then let me demand the man's name for your child. He owes you at least that much."

Pleasance stared down at her hands and struggled to think straight. She must seriously consider Nathan's warnings. Her child was going to be a bastard, a breed that was openly scorned. She had seen how Moira suffered for her bastardy and she lived in an area where people were less condemning than in the more settled parts of the colonies. Pleasance knew that, unless she moved far away, into a more remote and dangerous area, the baby she was carrying would suffer dearly for the lack of a father.

She smoothed her hands over the front of her light brown day dress and let them rest over her womb. Soon she would need larger dresses. Soon even hiding in a tiny cottage outside of Worcester would not be enough to keep her condition a secret. Then, if she still had no husband, she would have to lie. If she concocted lies to save the child from scorn, the child would be forced to live out those lies. Pleasance did not think she could openly ask her child to speak and live lies.

Inwardly she cursed. She cursed Tearlach most of all, but she also cursed herself. She had been a blind fool, caught up in her own plans for a future with Tearlach. Here was her future, she mused as she stared at her rounding stomach. One child without a father. She sat in a tiny garden outside of Worcester and Tearlach stayed blissfully in the Berkshires. Time was running out for her. She would have to decide something. She was just not sure she had the strength to make the decision that would be best for her child.

"Pleasance," Nathan said when she had been sitting quietly for several minutes.

"Can we make a bargain, Nathan?" she asked.

"Of course we can, sweeting. Just do not make me promise things you know I cannot do. Not even for you."

"I would never do that to you, Nathan. I want to ask one thing. When you came for me, Tearlach had just set out on a long hunt. Even now, he may have only just arrived back, may have been at the cabin for only a few days. Please, give the man another month to appear. I am well hidden away here. It will not hurt to wait just a little while longer. If he does not show up on his own volition at the end of one month, then you will be free to set out after him and do whatever you feel you must."

"Just one month?"

"Aye, just one more month. And if he does not come and you must confront him, all I ask is that you carefully judge his reactions to your demands. If his reluctance is too strong, then you will not be doing me a kindness by forcing him to wed me, even for the sake of the child."

"So you do not want me to force him to marry you. You cannot expect me to agree to that."

"Think about it, Nathan. If Tearlach is absolutely furious about being forced to marry me, do you think such a reluctant husband will help my child?"

"Nay, but no father at all will not help your child either." Nathan held up his hand when Pleasance started to protest. "I must think about it. All I can agree to for now is that I will wait one month before I act. No more than one month though." He stood up and brushed off his breeches. "The rest I will consider."

"I wish I could make you understand how much I dread having an unwilling husband. Aye, and how much I believe that, if he is too angry about it, he will only hurt the child we are trying to help."

"I said I will consider it. But I think you are wrong even to consider *not* marrying the man, no matter what the circumstances. You will quickly regret not having a husband, no matter how reluctant."

"Mayhaps you have a point. We each have a month to think about it."

Nathan nodded. "Fair enough. You are sure it will be at least a month before you give birth?"

"At least that. Do not worry." Pleasance found his concern both touching and irritating.

"There is one other thing. Since I cannot be here with you all the time, we need a housekeeper or maid to help you."

"You do not mean to tell her that I am with child, do you?" Pleasance was well acquainted with how such servants could gossip, and she wanted to judge the woman's trustworthiness for herself before sharing her secret.

"Nay, not at first. You can decide when to tell her." He held out his hand. "Shall we go back inside?"

Pleasance shook her head. "If you do not mind, Nathan, I will stay right here for a little while. The weather is fine and the fresh air will do me good."

"As you wish. I need to talk some business with Corbin anyway. I will be back in time to share the evening meal with you."

"There is one last small favor I would like to ask of you."

"And what is that?" Nathan eyed his sister a little warily, knowing that she could easily play upon his sympathy and get him to agree to things he would later regret.

She laughed softly. "Do not look so wary. All I wish to ask is that, if Tearlach does come here, please, allow me free rein at first. I fear that if he is confronted with the news of my pregnancy right away, I shall never know what truly lies in his heart."

"All right. I can agree to that. I just hope that I have the strength to keep from knocking him down," Nathan grumbled as he walked away.

Another muted laugh escaped Pleasance as she watched her brother return to the house. He had been so good to her. Nathan's goodness made up for all the hurt and callousness she had suffered at the hands of her father's family. There were times, however, when Nathan was too protective of her.

As she idly smoothed down the wrinkles in her full skirt, Pleasance thought of her many experiences since she had been dragged out from under Tearlach O'Duine's bed and caught with his possessions in her hand. Her life had been turned upside down from that day onward, and it did not look to be any different in the long days ahead.

Tearlach—she said the name in her head and then cursed it. The man still haunted her when she was awake and when she was asleep. There did not seem to be any escape from him. No doubt he would leave his distinctive physical stamp on their child and thus she would be reminded of him for many years to come. That seemed an especially cruel punishment for giving in to her passion.

"And in return the man will suffer nothing for also having appeased his passion," she grumbled as she stood up to return to the house. "Tearlach is as guilty as I am."

More so, she decided, for he had had some experience with desire. He had known both how to control his passions and how to stir them up in a woman. She had let herself be seduced, but he had knowingly led her astray. It did not seem fair that she should be paying the highest, perhaps the only, penalty for their lovemaking. But then, she decided, a woman always paid the highest price for succumbing to passion.

A soft, vile curse escaped her when she realized that all the things she had hoped for in her brief liaison with Tearlach O'Duine had never come about. Their love affair was now reduced to who was at fault and who would pay the most for that folly. She found it easy to resent him for that.

Pleasance caught a glimpse of herself in the glass in the parlor door. When she was dressed there was little sign of the child yet. Her figure had filled out but the changes were easily hidden beneath her long full skirts. Soon, however, not even the fullest of skirts would hide her condition.

For one brief moment, Pleasance wondered if she had even the month she had asked Nathan for, but she shook away her sudden panic at the thought. If her calculations were wrong, the child could be born any day now, and she was simply carrying small. But the very thought of a completely unwilling Tearlach as a husband was chilling. If risking exposure by waiting a month meant that she might have Tearlach actually come after her, then it was well worth it.

As Pleasance sat down on the settee and resumed her tatting, she muttered. "A month, Tearlach O'Duine. That is all I can grant you. I just pray that you do not choose to make this much more difficult than it needs to be. Just come after me," she whispered. "Just come for me. You need not make any promises or murmur words of love. Just come for me and show me that you miss me." She sighed and wondered if even that modest wish would end up becoming another source of pain for her.

"Pleasance, I would like you to meet Martha." Nathan watched his sister carefully as he introduced the woman he had just hired.

Although she felt weighted down and awkward, Pleasance sat up on the settee where she had been resting and shook Martha's hand. It was a strong steady handshake, and Pleasance began to feel better about the woman. It would be good to have someone around to help with the housework, which Pleasance was beginning to find a little too much to handle.

"I am pleased to meet you, Martha. I hope you will find service with us acceptable."

Martha nodded. "Mayhaps you can describe my chores, ma'am. Master Dunstan was not clear."

It was hard not to laugh at the look on Nathan's face. He obviously felt he had told the woman all she needed to know. Pleasance got to her feet and took Martha by one plump arm. "I will be glad to show you what must be done and answer all your questions."

Grumbling under his breath, Nathan watched his sister and the new maid leave the parlor. He then poured himself some of the brandy he had slipped through customs just before winter. Martha was a necessity, he decided, and took a sip of the brandy as he prayed that he could manage with two women in the small house. Pleasance returned a lot sooner than he had expected her to and he frowned as she sat down.

"That was a short visit."

"Aye, it was. Martha may speak a little bluntly, but she also speaks very little."

"Well, do you think she will do?"

"She will do just fine. You found and hired a woman a lot sooner than I had anticipated. It is only a week since you mentioned it."

"I saw no reason to wait and many reasons to proceed. You need the help. Mayhaps you will cease doing so much work and will rest a little more."

"I agree wholeheartedly." Pleasance did not add that she felt she would need all the rest she could get to face what would happen in three weeks' time. Rest would give her the strength to accept what little Tearlach might offer if he did show up, and it would help her endure the hurt if he offered her nothing and had to be forced to share responsibility for their child.

Chapter Nineteen

Two weeks later, Nathan found his self-control sorely tested when he answered a brisk rap at the door and found Tearlach O'Duine standing before him. He ached to hit the man. He was torn between disappointment that Tearlach had come, thus taking matters out of his hands, and hope that Pleasance might get a little of what she needed to be happy.

Nathan managed a brief smile for young Moira, who stood beside her brother, before he turned to greet Tearlach with cold formality. "What has brought you to my door, Master O'Duine?"

Tearlach found Nathan Dunstan an uncomfortable person to face and not just because he was Pleasance's brother. Despite Nathan's fair hair, the resemblance between brother and sister was strong. It was Pleasance's lovely eyes that stared at him with cold hard fury. He found himself sweating and knew it was not from the September heat. Quickly removing his tricorne, Tearlach swore to himself that he would be courteous and calm no matter what the provocation.

"I seek to pay a visit to Pleasance. We were told that she has moved here and now resides with you."

"That she does. Step inside. Pleasance is resting in the

parlor. 'Tis the coolest place in this oppressive heat." He turned to look at Martha, who lurked at the rear of the small hallway. "Something cool to drink, Martha, if you please. Mayhaps something light to eat as well." The plump, wide-eyed Martha curtsied and hurried off to the kitchen while Nathan led his guests into the parlor.

Pleasance could hear more than one person approaching the parlor door, and she hastily sat up from where she was sprawled somewhat gracelessly on the settee. The heat and her increasing girth made almost any position uncomfortable. She quickly arranged her skirts and crisp white apron to hide the size of her stomach. She then spread the shirt she had been mending across her lap for added protection. When she saw who stepped into the parlor with her brother Nathan, she was heartily glad she had taken such precautions.

"Tearlach." Pleasance felt a flicker of annoyance that he could still look so good to her.

"Pleasance." Tearlach gave her a stiff bow of greeting. "Ye look weel."

Moira hurried over to hug and kiss her. Pleasance could tell by the girl's quick glance at her middle that she had guessed her condition. As a visibly curious Martha brought in food and drink, Pleasance sent Moira a sharp look that begged her to keep silent. Moira gave a quick nod of agreement and Pleasance breathed a sigh of relief as the girl sat down next to her.

As cider and cakes were passed around, Pleasance studied Tearlach. He looked tense and uncomfortable in his finery, the lace of his shirt looking starkly white against his sun-burnished skin. He was perched stiffly on the edge of a chair facing her. She realized that, for all of his wealth, he was more at ease in a worker's shirt and buckskins. It was dangerously flattering to think that he had gone to such trouble as to dress well for her.

Tearlach attempted to make small talk. Pleasance decided that polite but frivolous conversation was not something he was very good at. She tried to remain calm as she waited for him to announce the reason for his visit.

Finally Martha curtsied and left the room. The door had barely finished shutting behind her when Tearlach leapt to his feet. "I have come to take Pleasance back to the Berkshires with me."

Nathan also leapt to his feet. "Mayhaps she wishes to stay here with me."

Startled by how quickly the confrontation had begun in earnest, Pleasance twisted the shirt in her lap. She wondered if she should swiftly interrupt what looked to be the beginning of a rousing argument between the two men, then decided to wait a little while. Sometimes, in the middle of such confrontations, the truth came out. Notwithstanding that, she was certain she would learn why Tearlach had come for her, and rather loudly at that. A brief flicker of amusement went through her as she watched Tearlach and Nathan face each other with open belligerence. Tearlach was going to find a worthy adversary in Nathan.

Tearlach glanced briefly toward Pleasance before facing her brother squarely. He had no patience. One long look at Pleasance after spending so many weeks without her had him in turmoil. The urge to rip off her prim mobcap, grab a hank of her thick hair, and drag her away with him was a very strong one. All the persuasive arguments he had planned to use, all the gentle words and flatteries he had practiced, were completely forgotten.

"She owes me work," he said, glaring at Nathan.

Moira muttered what sounded to Pleasance like a vile curse, but she did not bother to reprimand the girl. All of her attention was on Tearlach. He had said the very words she had hoped and prayed he would not say. She fought to hide her pain.

"She owes you nothing," snapped Nathan. "I paid her fine."

"A bond was made. She should honor that bond."

"Honor a bond based upon lies? No, Master O'Duine. You have had months of my sister's hard work. I have paid her fine. You will get no more."

"If you need a slave, I suggest you meet the next ship sailing into Boston Harbor," Pleasance said, and watched as Tearlach tensed before turning slowly to look at her. "You could buy the lot of whatever wretched souls sail in her hold."

"Ye know." Tearlach felt what little hope he had nurtured for Pleasance's return begin to waver.

"I told her," Nathan said, the hint of a challenge in his voice.

Glaring at Nathan again, Tearlach demanded, "What right did ye have to pry into my affairs?"

"Every right. You had my sister in your home. The moment you took Pleasance away, anything I could discover about you became my business. You have the money that you paid to gain her indenture. Take it and find the servant you seek elsewhere. My sister is no longer available."

"Ye cannae break an indenture by simply tossing the money down on a table and taking the person away. The law requires my agreement to the deal, and I gave none."

"Oh, get out, Tearlach." Pleasance could not tolerate hearing any more and still maintain some dignity. "Just leave. I cannot bear the sight of you."

He jerked as if she had shot him. He stared at her for one long moment, but she did not say another word. Not even when he slapped his tricorne on his head and strode out of the room. Pleasance sighed and slumped in her seat. She finally looked at Moira, who lightly kissed her cheek.

"Take heart, Pleasance." Moira winked and hurried after her brother.

Pleasance groaned softly and laid down on the settee. "Pleasance?" Nathan frowned and moved to her side. "Are you unwell?"

"My head roars and my stomach churns like a whirlpool. Aye, Nathan, I believe I am unwell."

"Would you like a cool cloth soaked in lavender water to place on your forehead?"

"I would be eternally grateful."

It was several moments after Nathan had gently placed the cloth upon her forehead and helped her take a few bracing sips of wine that Pleasance finally felt an easing of the throbbing pain in her head. She was almost glad to be feeling so poorly. Tearlach had cut her heart into ribbons, but at the moment she was simply too sick to think about it.

Her only clear thought was that, if whatever ailed her could be contracted by others, she hoped Tearlach O'Duine had just gotten a double dose.

With a soft sigh, Tearlach pushed his plate aside and sipped at his ale. His sister stared at him unrelentingly. They had not spoken a word since they had returned to Cobb's Inn from Pleasance's cottage. Tearlach had the sinking feeling that the silence was about to be broken. He fought down the urge to bolt from the table and flee to his room. If he gave in to his weakness, he would feel very foolish later at his failure to confront a girl who was young enough to be his own daughter. He just wished Moira did not have such adult insights or such a cutting tongue.

"Not hungry?" Moira looked at his half-eaten meal, then pushed aside her own empty plate and smacked her lips in an exaggerated expression of appreciation. "I suspect that the taste of boot leather could work to steal a mon's appetite."

"If ye are trying to tell me that I put my foot in my mouth, that wasnae a verra subtle way of doing so."

"Subtle? Ye scold me for a lack of subtlety? Ye werenae verra subtle when ye talked to Pleasance today. Ye didnae really talk to her at all. Ye had a loud, stupid argument with her brother. I ne'er kenned that my own brother could be such a woodenheaded noddy."

Tearlach did not see why he should sit quietly and tolerate such insubordination. "I think ye forget who ye are talking to, young lady."

"Nay, I dinnae forget. I love ye and respect ye, Tearlach, but when it comes to women, ye are thickheaded. Purely thickheaded. This meeting with Pleasance was real important. And what did ye do? Ye walked in there, opened your big mouth, and didnae say one right thing."

It was true, but Tearlach did not like having it pointed out to him. He knew he had done everything wrong. There had been no need to look at Pleasance's pale face to know that. He sighed again, stretched out in the chair, and stared down at the toes of his boots.

"It helped verra little that ye lied to her," continued Moira.

"I never lied to Pleasance," snapped Tearlach, glaring at his sister.

"Never? How can ye say that? Ye ne'er told her the truth about your money, and ye kenned verra weel that she thought ye were a poor mon. Ye even told me not to tell her anything, for ye said it was your place to tell her. Weel, it appears that ye never told her. Not saying something is the same as lying."

"Aye, 'tis true. Weel, we had best get some rest. We shall get an early start."

"For what?"

"To go back home." Tearlach nearly winced beneath his sister's contemptuous look.

"So, ye mean to simply give up and crawl home."

"Pleasance said she could not bear the sight of me." He was a little surprised at how deeply those words had hurt him, deeper than any knife ever had.

"That doesnae mean that she willnae want to look at ye on the morrow or the next day, especially if ye gain the wit to say what ye should have said today," Moira said. "Those were just angry words, Tearlach. If Pleasance really could-nae stand the sight of ye, ye wouldnae ever have gotten inside her door."

Tearlach sat up a little straighter. There was some truth to what Moira was saying. He now recalled thinking that the Dunstans had been carefully instructed to tell him exactly how he could find Pleasance. She would never have left such a clear trail if she had not wished to be found. The ap-palling way he had handled matters could easily have made her so furious that she had wished him out of her sight.

"Why did ye have to make it so difficult?" Moira grum-bled. "I ken that ye dinnae want her back just to scrub your floors and mend your shirts. I ken ye dinnae want her just to help me either."

"She did a lot of good for you," Tearlach murmured, re-alizing how much more calm and mature Moira was since she had known Pleasance.

"Aye, she did. But 'tisnae the reason ye want her back. Why couldnae ye have said something pretty and flattering, or even just up and asked her to wed ye? Now ye are going to have to court her."

"Court her?"

"Aye, court her. Even Tom Purdy, who is as rough a mon as I ken, courted his woman some, bringing her posies and the like."

"Posies." Tearlach grimaced. "I have no time for such nonsense."

"If ye want Pleasance, then ye had best find the time. Ye have to soothe the hurt ye just gave her. Why do ye look so surprised? Ye could see that ye had hurt her."

"I am not sure Pleasance has the sort of feelings for me that would allow me to hurt her."

"What foolishness. She was warming your bed."

"Moira!"

She ignored his admonishment. "Weel, she was. Ye did nothing to hide it from me. That proves that she has feelings for ye. Pleasance is no round-heeled wench like Liza at Purdy's tavern. Pleasance is a good woman who would only give herself to a mon because she had some strong feelings for him."

"How do ye ken about Liza at the tavern?"

"Jake told me."

"Jake tells ye far too much."

"That isnae the problem just now. The problem is how do ye get Pleasance and ye back together? Now, as I see it, if ye could get such a good woman to sin with ye, then ye ought to be able to get her to believe that ye want her for far more than mending your shirts. Ye must have used some pretty words then. Find some now."

Tearlach frowned for a moment, then smiled crookedly at her. "Weel, we had best seek our beds. We will need to make an early start in the morning."

Moira gaped at her brother. "Ye are still going home?"

"Nay, my dear, interfering baby sister. I but acknowledge that the road to Pleasance Dunstan's hand in marriage might be long and bumpy, and 'twould be best for all concerned if I am weel rested when I start out on it."

* * *

Pleasance sighed as a grinning Nathan handed her another small bunch of violets. She was going to be utterly buried in flowers, followed by sweets and baubles. She had not set eyes on Tearlach in nearly a fortnight, but he was smothering her in gifts. Only the first gift, a silver spoon, had carried any message for her. A note wrapped around the handle had said "Apologies, Tearlach." She wondered if he ever intended to say anything else.

"This is getting to be very silly." She set the flowers on the settee at her side.

"I believe the man is courting you." In the last few days, Nathan's concerns for Pleasance's future had begun to ease.

"'Tis a most silent courtship. Just one note with two words? I know not if this is all still just part of the apology or if he is really trying to court me."

"Oh, I believe 'tis courting our Master O'Duine engages in." Nathan glanced at her rounded stomach. "I but hope he is not too slow at it. You are certain you are only seven and a half months along?"

She grimaced. 'I am not sure. I do not believe that I am due yet, however. That would mean that only a few weeks was needed to create the child and 'tis rare that that happens."

"Rare but not impossible." Nathan studied her, thinking that it might be time to interfere. "Mayhaps, I should—"

"Nay, please, Nathan. Wait just a little longer. Give me but a few more days. I so need to know that he wants me and not just my babe. Please?"

"A few more days then." When Pleasance started to rise from the settee, Nathan moved to assist her.

"I believe I shall go for a little walk. There is a cool breeze and I am feeling restless."

"Do not wander far afield. Mayhaps I should join you."

"Nay, you have your own work to do, Nathan. I will stay close by."

Once outside, Pleasance took a deep breath of the flower-scented air and smiled. Flowers were one thing she was not short on. Shaking her head, she ambled toward the woods that surrounded the cottage.

She had wandered through the cool forest for several minutes when she heard her name being called. She glanced over her shoulder and gasped. Tearlach was vaulting the low split rail fence to hurry after her. Now was not the time to confront him. Due to the oppressive heat, she wore only her lace-trimmed chemise, a loosely tied bodice, and her pale blue petticoat. She had no layers of petticoats and skirts nor her apron to hide her condition. One look at her and he would know all about the child. All she could think of was the need to hide, and so she bolted deeper into the woods.

A harsh curse followed by the sound of jackboots pounding the ground told her that Tearlach was pursuing her. She could never outrun the man. Just as she considered stopping, hastily sitting down, and bunching up her clothes in an attempt to hide her stomach, she tripped over an exposed root. Pain exploded in her ankle. She put her hands out to cushion her fall, barely stopping herself from sprawling on the ground face first. An instant later, Tearlach was at her side. Quickly, Pleasance bunched up her petticoat as she sat up, but Tearlach's attention was all on her ankle.

"Did ye twist it?" He took her slim ankle in his hand and gently turned it back and forth.

"Only a bit. Already the pain is easing. I am sure it will be fine if I but rest it for a minute or two."

He sat down beside her. "Why did ye run? What have I ever done to ye that would make ye want to run away from me as if I am your enemy?"

"I was reluctant to speak to you here—alone."

Pain abruptly gripped Pleasance's middle and she nearly gasped. For a brief instant she was terrified that she had harmed her child or had started her labor dangerously early, but instinct quickly soothed her fears. She suddenly knew that it was simply her time. That was what the discomfort and restlessness she had suffered from all day long had been trying to tell her. The time she had wanted to smooth matters with Tearlach had just run out.

"Are ye sure ye are all right? Ye have grown rather pale."

She wondered what he would do if she told him she was in labor with his child. With his gaze fixed upon her face he had not seen what her bunched-up skirts could not fully hide. She also knew that she was carrying small and thus showing less than many another woman would. Just another minute or two, she told herself. She really needed to know why he had come.

"Aye, I am fine," she answered. "Why are you here, Tearlach?" She stared at her hands in her lap as she fought to conceal the pain of another contraction.

"Ye didnae like the flowers?" He had to clench his hands to keep from pulling her into his arms.

"They were very pretty." Pleasance wished he would hurry up and say something of substance, for she did not think she could remain silent much longer. "Your apologies are accepted."

"I wasnae apologizing with every gift I sent ye. Weel, mayhaps some. I was trying to court ye. If ye didnae see that, then I was doing a verra poor job of it. Poorer than I thought. Gifts, pretty words, and flatteries. That is how they tell ye to court a woman."

"You forgot the pretty words and the flatteries."

"I was coming to see ye today to try my hand at them. I cannae promise much. I am no gallant courtier."

She managed one long look at him before another contraction forced her to turn her face away. "Why are ye doing it at all?"

"Why else does a mon court a lass? I wish to marry ye."

Her heart skipped with hope. "To keep your house?"

"Nay, I can hire people to do the work if ye have no stomach for it."

"For Moira."

"Nay. For me. I wish ye back for me."

"And can I now be sure I know exactly whom I would go back to? Tearlach the poor farmer and trapper? Or mayhaps Tearlach the wealthy trader? Or is there yet another?"

"I am sorry I hid the truth from ye. Soon after I had some coin to jingle in my pockets, I learned how that sound could draw the women. Suddenly, I was a mon of wealth, a mon worthy enough to marry. I didnae wish to buy a wife. The vows say 'for richer or poorer.' I had to ken that the woman I wed would mean the words when she spoke them. Is that so wrong of me?"

"Nay. It hurts to have been tested, but I can understand what drove you to it. I have seen the difficulty you speak of with the women who pursue Nathan."

"Then marry me." When she made no reply, he pressed her, "What more do ye want of me?"

There were several things, but she knew she did not have the time to press him for them now. He had explained the lie, tried to court her, and said that he wanted her for himself. It would be enough. The child twisting her womb into a knot of pain would claim the name of bastard only if she did not act quickly.

"There are three things I wish of you right now, Tearlach O'Duine."

"Aye?"

"Aye. Help me to the house." She looked directly at him. "Then you may fetch the justice of the peace."

"So quickly? Ye have no wish for some celebration?"

"I fear I have no time for one." She gritted her teeth as a

fresh pain rolled through her, and she tugged her skirt taut over her rounded belly, finding some amusement in the way he gaped at her. "The third thing I want from you is for you to fetch the midwife or the doctor."

Pleasance marveled at how swiftly Tearlach recovered from his shock. He scooped her up in his arms and loped toward the cottage. All the while he cursed the foolishness of women in language that was both colorful and profane.

He burst into the cottage and, with one huge bellow, brought Nathan and Martha rushing to her side. He snapped out orders even as he cursed Nathan for allowing Pleasance to keep her pregnancy a secret from him, thus risking their child's being born illegitimate. Pleasance observed that Nathan took as little notice of the maligning of his character as she did. Tearlach had her upstairs, in her room, and turned over to a flustered Martha's care in a remarkably short time. Then he raced off.

An hour later Pleasance was beginning to fear Tearlach would not return when he strode into her room tugging a tousled Corbin behind him. She barely managed to gasp out a polite greeting before the wedding ceremony began. Tearlach held her hand in his and waved aside Corbin's gentle questions about possible irregularities. Although she noticed that both men grew paler as her contractions continued, the ceremony did not falter once in deference to her increasing pain. Despite her concerns about what did and did not exist between herself and Tearlach, Pleasance felt relieved when Tearlach finally brushed a kiss over her lips. The child that was pressing so hard to enter the world would not be a bastard.

At that moment a disheveled Nathan burst into the room to announce that he could not find the midwife or the doctor. All three men stared at Pleasance with such helplessness and horror that she almost laughed. The usually quiet Martha then took over. Whatever Pleasance's concern that

Martha might not be skilled in midwifery was swiftly dispelled by the woman's efficiency. With Martha's competent, soothing assistance Pleasance soon gave birth to a squalling, healthy boy.

When Tearlach stepped into the room nearly twenty minutes later, Pleasance had to smile despite her exhaustion. He looked hesitant and uncertain. It was the first time she had ever seen him so and, oddly enough, it endeared him to her all the more.

"We have a son, Tearlach."

"Aye," he whispered. "Martha says that ye are fine?" He felt so full of emotion as he stared down at her and their child in her arms that he could think of nothing to say.

"Aye. Weary but hale."

There was a lot Tearlach wished to say, but the words were locked up in his throat. He bent to gently kiss her. "Thank ye, wife."

Such simple words, Pleasance mused, and yet something in the way he said them made her smile, with hope for their future swelling her heart.

Chapter Twenty

"The villagers will all guess we shared intimacies ere I left here." Pleasance spoke quietly, shyly returning Tom Purdy's wave as they drove their wagon past his tavern. "No announcement could be louder than this babe." She rubbed her son's tiny back in a vain attempt to quiet him and wrapped him more securely in his blanket to protect him from the chill in the early November air.

"Aye, Thaddeus has a good voice on him." Tearlach glanced over his shoulder at Moira, who sat in the back, and winked when she giggled.

"That is not what I meant and you both know it," Pleasance retorted. "How can I face these people?"

"Squarely. These arenae your stiff-rumped Puritans of Worcester. They have more important things to do than worry about what their neighbors are up to. They are also more forgiving." When Richard Treeman hailed him he halted the wagon, carefully took his two-month-old son from Pleasance's arms, and proceeded to show off the child.

Pleasance was torn between amusement and embarrassment, but as a small group of people gathered around the wagon, her anxiety began to fade. A few sly winks told her

that they were all all fully aware that the child had been con-
ceived before the marriage, but it appeared that the marriage
changed that sin to a mere peccadillo. She thought of how
the people at home, her family and acquaintances, would act
and was able to meet Hope Treeman's smile with ease. Face
them squarely, Tearlach had said, and she would.

By the time they had passed through town, Pleasance
knew that most people in the area would not trouble her
about Thaddeus's birth. There were a few who would never
accept it, but she had the strength to ignore them. Most of
them were the same people who treated Moira as if she were
an affront and believed her claims of being a witch. Pleasance decided her life would be far more comfortable if she
never had the companionship of such people.

As soon as they were out of sight of the others, Pleasance
undid her bodice, bared one breast, and began to suckle her
child. From the corner of her eye she saw Tearlach staring
at her and she blushed. It was going to take time to adjust to
his ogling, but she knew she would never get him to stop it.
He truly enjoyed watching her feed their son. She found that
touching and just a little bit puzzling.

In fact, there was a great deal that puzzled her about Tearlach O'Duine. When she gave birth to Thaddeus, Tearlach
had been so tender she had been inspired to hope again that
she could win her husband's love. For a little while, she had
even thought that she had already captured his heart. It had
been a short-lived dream. Tearlach had quickly gone back to
being Tearlach—endearing, irritating, and elusive. Occasionally she had even felt a tickle of fear, fear that his passion had waned. He had grown very sparing with his kisses.

Several times she had tried to prompt some discussion of
the future, of their feelings and expectations, but Tearlach had
proven adroit at eluding such talk. That hurt and confused her.

She sighed as she rubbed Thaddeus's back to push out

any air he might have swallowed. Their arrival at the cabin abruptly captured her thoughts and Pleasance hurried to fasten her bodice. There was nothing changed about the cabin, but the house next to it made her gape. It had been no more than a frame when she left with Nathan. Now it was complete, right down to the lovely railed veranda that curved around the front. She realized that Tearlach had halted the wagon and she turned to him.

"You never said a word," she said, her voice little more than a whisper.

"I wished to surprise ye and I couldnae be certain that the house would be finished in time. It seems old Jake continued to supervise the work. When I left to go after ye, I told him to keep up the good work. Aye, and to push the men a wee bit harder. When we stopped in town, Tom Purdy whispered that it had been finished. There are still a few touches that need doing, but it is livable."

"'Tis lovely, Tearlach. I must make a point of thanking Jake."

"Here he comes now. He has moved into the old cabin." Tearlach's voice dropped to a whisper. "He really shouldnae be out at his rickety cabin all on his own, not at his age."

"Nay, he should be right where he is, near us."

The next few hours were exhausting for Pleasance. Tearlach took her on a tour of the new house. She remained speechless with delight, especially over the big fireplaces in the bedrooms. The house needed decorating, Tearlach's furnishings being neither enough nor really suitable in every case. She had to blush when he showed her their bedroom, for he had already bought one new piece of furniture—a huge four-poster bed.

What with unpacking, preparing a meal, and tending to the baby, she had little time to relax until bedtime. When she found a hot bath waiting for her in her bedchamber, she was taken aback but did not hesitate to make use of it. By the time she had soaked away her aches and donned her night-gown, she felt a great deal better.

She sat on the bearskin rug before the fireplace and brushed out her hair, letting it dry from the heat of the low fire. Such comfort, she mused. Before she had left in the spring, if Tearlach had drawn a bath for her she would have immediately expected a seduction. Now she was not so sure.

When the door opened and he walked in, she caught her breath. His hair was damp and hung in thick waves around his shoulders. He was barechested and wore only a plaid wrapped loosely around his waist so that it hung to his knees like a skirt, with one long strip pulled across his chest and draped over his shoulder. There was something decidedly bar-baric about it that she found very attractive. Since he had never dressed himself as a Scotsman before, she wondered what he was up to as he walked over and sat down next to her.

"Ye are staring at me rather fiercely, lassie," he murmured as he took the hairbrush from her hand and began to brush her hair.

"I was just wondering why you have dressed yourself up like that when you have never done so before." She would not mention that she was tempted to discover how the plaid was secured so that she could take it off him.

"When we spoke in the wood on the day of Thaddeus's birth ye asked me which mon ye would be going to the Berkshires with."

"I was referring to what you had kept secret from me, but we settled that."

"Aye, but I have decided I will show ye who Tearlach O'Duine really is, what ye would have if I had no home, no money, no livelihood. If I was back in my Scottish homeland."

"You do look very impressive," she whispered, and

smiled faintly. "I suppose I am to thank you for the bath and the warm fire."

"Aye. 'Tis a special occasion."

"What?" Pleasance worried she had forgotten some important date.

"Wee Thaddeus is two months old. We need not tiptoe around each other anymore." He frowned when she just stared at him. "Unless ye dinnae feel ready. I can wait a while longer." He scowled when she suddenly giggled. "What is funny?"

"I am sorry. 'Tis just that I had not realized you were merely being careful with me. And, I must say, your offer to wait was said like a true martyr."

He laughed and, tossing aside the hairbrush, tumbled her onto the bearskin. After giving her a kiss that left them both breathless and eager for more, he frowned at her. "What did ye mean—ye hadnae realized I was just being careful?"

Pleasance blushed and kept her gaze fixed upon his chest. "Well, I was a little concerned that you had lost your . . . well, your passion for me." She heard a soft choking noise and looked up at him. "Are you laughing?"

"I was trying verra hard not to, but I cannae help it." He buried his face in her neck and laughed heartily.

She punched him on the arm. "I am so glad I have given you such entertainment."

"Oh, lassie, ye can be so endearingly dumb." He lifted his head and gave her a brief kiss on the lips.

"You will understand if I do not thank you for that compliment."

"Ye really did think that I had lost my hunger for ye?" Tearlach shook his head. "Ah, lass, that hunger has been there from the start. I think it was the cause of all of our troubles."

"Really? I thought the start of our troubles was when I rejected you." She saw a dark frown come and go on his face and gave him a gentle smile. "You have never asked why I did that."

"Ye had the right to change your mind about me. I shouldnae had gotten so angry about it."

"On the contrary, you had every right to be angry. I allowed you to believe that I was pleased to be courted by you. And I was."

"Then why did ye turn me away? 'Twas a fickle thing to do and I havenae discerned that characteristic in you at any other time."

"My parents ordered me to give you to Letitia." She was not surprised when Tearlach stared at her in total astonishment and slowly sat up.

"Ye were told to give me to Letitia?"

"Aye. She had decided she wanted you. My father had promised her that she could choose her own husband and she said you were her choice. So, I was told to make it clear that I was no longer interested in you."

Tearlach shook his head, but it did not make what she was telling him sound any more sensible. "And ye actually did it. That is what I cannae understand."

Pleasance sat up slowly, wrapping her arms around her knees. "Perhaps it is time for you to know what sort of a coward you have married."

"Now, lass, after all ye have been through, I cannae call ye a coward."

"I used to be. I did anything my family told me to. I was desperate to please them. When they told me to step aside, I protested, but not for long. I simply did not have the courage to tell them no. I found it easier to give up the man I wanted than to upset my father or mother or even that spoiled brat Letitia."

Tearlach grinned and took her into his arms. "So ye did want me then."

"Did you listen to anything else I said?"

"Aye, I think it a little strange, but I can understand what drove ye. And ye dinnae have that problem any longer."

"But I stung your pride just because I could not stand up to my family."

"Ye stung a great deal more than that, dearling. Did ye think I would grow so furious just because ye bruised my pride? I have more pride than I should have, but it can take more than a pinch now and then without turning me so bitter."

Pleasance tensed, watching him closely. He was speaking so openly about things he had thought and felt in the beginning. She hardly dared to move for fear of breaking the mood that was compelling him to be so forthcoming.

"You felt that I was a fickle, spoiled aristocrat," she said.

"And that was unfair. Aye, ye had turned me away with less tact than I deserved, but I shouldnae have lashed out at ye as I did again and again. It hurt, lass. I didnae want to admit it then, but I couldnae ignore it either and that made me angrier."

"I am sorry, Tearlach. I never wanted to hurt you."

"I apologize for turning so mean. While 'tis true that I never meant the charges to lead to a trial, I need not have had ye arrested at all. I was just striking out the only way I knew how."

Pleasance gave him a soft kiss. "In a way, I think you did me a service. You took me away from my family and, out here, I learned the strength to stand on my own. When I returned to Worcester, I found that they no longer intimidated me. Of course, learning that I am not their legitimate daughter, as I explained to you, also helped me to see our relationship with them in a new light. So, it seems that those who say some good can come out of bad are right after all."

He cupped her face in his hands and kissed her as he eased her back down onto the bearskin. With an enticing slowness he undressed her, praising each newly exposed inch of skin with a lingering kiss. Tearlach knew they still had a lot to talk about, but he could no longer wait to make love to her.

"Lord above," he whispered after he had stripped off his plaid and their flesh met for the first time in months. "I have sorely missed this, lass."

Pleasance curled her arms around his neck and pulled his mouth down to hers. "So have I, Scotsman. So have I."

Their lovemaking grew fierce. Pleasance held nothing back, returning his every caress in equal measure and giving her own sensuality free rein. She tried to tell him how she felt with her body since she had not yet gained the courage to tell him in words. Her release was swift and fierce and kept pace with his. For a long time she held his sated body close to hers and told herself that she was happy with what she had.

"Pleasance," he whispered, "I think we had best learn to be a little more sparing with this passion that we share or I shall be old before my time."

She laughed and swatted him on the arm, smiling when he propped himself up on his elbows to look down at her. "That did rather sap my energy," she agreed.

"Ye are a rare find for any mon, lass. I am blessed to have found ye for myself. 'Tisnae verra often that a mon can find a woman who can be such a good wife, such a loving mother. Ye are a fair-faced lass who can give me strong sons and a lover who can leave me as weak as a bairn."

"Well, thank you." She knew she was blushing if only because he was grinning so widely. "I feel I have gotten the best of the lot too. I may complain from time to time and call you thickheaded, but I do feel fortunate to be with you."

She was suddenly very annoyed with her own cowardice, but his kiss briefly diverted her.

"We will do well enough then." Tearlach knew it was wrong not to have told her how he felt, but he was still disappointed that she did not speak of love. He wanted her love.

There was a sudden restraint between them which puzzled Pleasance. She knew exactly what was troubling her, but it was not easy to see what, if anything, was troubling him. After a few minutes of lying in his arms while they almost absentmindedly caressed each other, she decided she had had enough.

"I think it is past time for us to speak a few cold hard truths and hope for the best," she muttered as she gently pushed him off her and sat up. "I do not want what has just happened to keep on happening all through our marriage."

Tearlach watched her as she tugged on her nightdress. "What just happened?" He wondered if she was referring to the lovemaking, then decided that made no sense at all. That left his sudden change of mood and he was not sure he liked how easily she could read his moods. "Is something wrong?"

"Is something wrong? Did you feel no change at all? We just made love with a fire that left us both gasping, yet a moment later we were distant and patting each other like pet dogs."

"Pet dogs?"

Pleasance sat up very straight, clasped her hands tightly in her lap, and forced herself to look him straight in the eye. "I have decided to stop being a coward, to stop hiding what I feel."

He tensed. "Why does that sound dangerous to me?"

"It should not. I have one little thing to say," she told him a soft voice. "I love you." She felt herself grow very tense, all too aware that she had bared her soul.

Tearlach could hardly believe his ears. She had said it in a tense, soft whisper, as if she expected him to admonish her for the confession. He began to doubt he had heard it at all. "What did you just say?"

"I said, I love you."

When he began to laugh she thought she would die. He saw the wounded look on her face and quickly pulled her into his arms. "Nay, lassie, nay. Dinnae look like that. Ah, dearling, no mon has ever heard more welcome words."

"Welcome? You are laughing at me."

He peppered her face with kisses, and was mortified when he felt the slight damp of tears beneath his lips. "Dinnae be hurt. That is the verra last thing I want. Sweet wee Pleasance, I love ye. I have loved ye for longer than I have wanted to admit."

She froze in his hold and stole a cautious glance at his face. There was an expression in his eyes that made her heart clench with joy, yet a still-skeptical voice warned her to be careful. She was terrified of making an even greater fool of herself.

"You love me?"

"Aye. Do ye need me to repeat the words while I am looking ye right in the eye?"

"That might help me believe—aye."

"I . . . love . . . ye . . . Pleasance . . . O'Duine." He kissed her quickly on the mouth after each word, then gaped when she buried her face in her hands and began to weep. "Lassie, that was supposed to make ye feel better." He frowned when she reached out one damp hand and patted him on the cheek.

"It does," she choked out, then fought to control herself, but it was several minutes before she was successful. "I am sorry."

Tearlach felt confused and he did not like the feeling at all. "Ye can set a mon on his ear, lass. I will give ye that."

"I had braced myself to be a brave little soldier and tell you exactly what I felt, but I had not prepared myself for the possibility that you felt the same way."

"So ye burst into tears?"

Pleasance smiled and put her arms around him, resting her cheek against his chest. "Do not try and understand, Tearlach. I am not at all sure why I reacted that way myself."

He kissed the top of her head. "I am glad I am not alone in my confusion." He smiled when she giggled softly. "Ah, lass, I do love ye, even when ye act like a madwoman. I am still not sure I like the feeling, for it often makes me act like a fool, but I ken that I will be feeling it for the rest of our days. Ye are stuck with me, Pleasance."

"I can think of no place I would rather be than right here, and no man I would rather be with." She sighed with enjoyment when he tightened his arms around her. "There is only one last puzzle I need to have solved."

Tearlach pushed her down onto the bearskin. "And what is that?" He idly undid the front of her nightgown.

"It really is not any of my business and I will understand if you tell me just that, but I really have to know—about those letters from Letitia . . ."

"Your sister can pen some very wicked sentiments."

"Were any of them justified? I mean, did you and Letitia . . ."

"Roll about between the sheets? Nay. I gave it some serious thought, for I was so angry with ye, but nay, I didnae want her." He chuckled when she breathed a sigh of relief, then he kissed the tip of her nose. "Ye already had my body captured, even if I was too stupid to let my heart follow. The world saw ye as indentured to me, but the truth is far different. There was no coin paid out, but the bond still holds me as firmly as any bond ever can or ever will."

"I know exactly what you mean, my braw Scot. I feel the bonds myself, but I will never shake them off. They are too much a part of me."

"Then we should march along quite contentedly." He touched his mouth to hers. "The links between us can never be broken."

When he kissed her, Pleasance knew that he spoke the truth for both of them. They were linked together in a way that would endure for the rest of their lives.

Secrecy and intrigue ignite dangerous passions in
New York Times *bestselling author Hannah Howell's*
seductive new novel . . .

It is whispered throughout London that the members
of the Wherlocke family are possessed of certain
unexplainable *gifts*. But Lord Ashton Radmoor is
skeptical—until he finds an innocent beauty lying
drugged and helpless in the bedroom of a brothel.

The mystery woman is Penelope Wherlocke, and her
special gift of sight is leading her deep into a dangerous
world of treachery and betrayal. Ashton knows he should
forget her, yet he's drawn deeper into the vortex of her life,
determined to keep her safe. But Penelope is no ordinary
woman, and she's never met the man strong enough to
contend with her unusual abilities.

Until now . . .

Please turn the page for an exciting sneak peek of
Hannah Howell's
IF HE'S SINFUL,
coming in December 2009!

London—fall, 1788

There was something about having a knife to one's throat that tended to bring a certain clarity to one's opinion of one's life, Penelope decided. She stood very still as the burly, somewhat odiferous, man holding her clumsily adjusted his grip. Suddenly, all of her anger and resentment over being treated as no more than a lowly maid by her step-sister seemed petty, the problem insignificant.

Of course, this could be some form of cosmic retribution for all those times she had wished ill upon her step-sister, she thought as the man hefted her up enough so that her feet were off the ground. One of his two companions bound her ankles in a manner quite similar to the way her wrists had been bound. Her captor began to carry her down a dark alley that smelled about as bad as he did. It had been only a few hours ago that she had watched Clarissa leave for a carriage ride with her soon-to-be-fiancé, Lord Radmoor. Peering out of the cracked window in her tiny attic room she had, indisputably, cherished the spiteful wish that Clarissa would stumble and fall into the foul muck near the carriage wheels.

Penelope did think that being dragged away by a knife-wielding ruffian and his two hulking companions was a rather harsh penalty for such a childish wish born of jealousy, however. She had, after all, never wished that Clarissa would die, which Penelope very much feared was going to be her fate.

Penelope sighed, ruefully admitting that she was partially at fault for her current predicament. She had stayed too long with her boys. Even little Paul had urged her not to walk home in the dark. It was embarrassing to think that a little boy of five had more common sense than she did.

A soft cry of pain escaped her, muted by the filthy gag in her mouth, when her captor stumbled and the cold, sharp edge of his knife scored her skin. For a brief moment, the fear she had been fighting to control swelled up inside her so strongly she feared she would be ill. The warmth of her own blood seeping into the neckline of her bodice only added to the fear. It took several moments before she could grasp any shred of calm or courage. The realization that her blood was flowing too slowly for her throat to have been cut helped her push aside her burgeoning panic.

"Ye sure we ain't allowed to have us a taste of this, Jud," asked the largest and most hirsute of her captor's assistants.

"Orders is orders," replied Jud as he steadied his knife against her skin. "A toss with this one will cost ye more'n she be worth."

"None of us'd be telling and the wench ain't going to be able to tell, neither."

"I ain't letting ye risk it. Wench like this'd be fighting ye and that leaves bruises. They'll tell the tale and that bitch Mrs. Cratchitt will tell. She would think it a right fine thing if we lost our pay for this night's work."

"Aye, that old bawd would be thinking she could gain something from it right enough. Still, it be a sad shame I can't be having me a taste afore it be sold off to anyone with a coin or two."

"Get your coin first and then go buy a little if'n ye want it so bad."

"Won't be so clean and new, will it?"

"This one won't be neither if'n that old besom uses her as she uses them others, not by the time ye could afford a toss with her."

She was being taken to a brothel, Penelope realized. Yet again she had to struggle fiercely against becoming blinded by her own fears. She was still alive, she told herself repeatedly, and it looked as if she would stay that way for a while. Penelope fought to find her strength in that knowledge. It did not do any good to think too much on the horrors she might be forced to endure before she could escape or be found. She needed to concentrate on one thing and one thing only—getting free.

It was not easy but Penelope forced herself to keep a close eye on the route they traveled. Darkness and all the twists and turns her captors took made it nearly impossible to make note of any and every possible sign to mark the way out of this dangerous warren she was being taken into. She had to force herself to hold fast to the hope that she could ever truly escape, and the need to get back to her boys who had no one else to care for them.

She was carried into the kitchen of a house. Two women and a man were there, but they spared her only the briefest of glances before returning all of their attention to their work. It was not encouraging that they seemed so accustomed to such a sight, so unmoved and uninterested.

As her captor carried her up a dark, narrow stairway, Penelope became aware of the voices and music coming from below, from the front of the building which appeared to be as great a warren as the alleys leading to it. When they reached the hallway and started to walk down it, she could hear the murmur of voices coming from behind all the closed doors. Other sounds drifted out from behind those doors but she tried very hard not to think about what might be causing them.

"There it be, room 22," muttered Jud. "Open the door, Tom."

The large, hirsute man opened the door and Jud carried Penelope into the room. She had just enough time to notice how small the room was before Jud tossed her down onto the bed in the middle of the room. It was a surprisingly clean and comfortable bed. Penelope suspected that, despite its seedy location, she had probably been brought to one of the better bordellos, one that catered to gentlemen of refinement and wealth. She knew, however, that that did not mean she could count on any help.

"Get that old bawd in here, Tom," said Jud. "I wants to be done with this night's work." The moment Tom left, Jud scowled down at Penelope. "Don't suspect you'd be aknowing why that high-and-mighty lady be wanting ye outta the way, would ye?"

Penelope slowly shook her head as a cold suspicion settled in her stomach.

"Don't make no sense to me. Can't be jealousy or the like. Can't be that she thinks you be taking her man or the like, can it. Ye ain't got her fine looks, ain't dressed so fine, neither, and ye ain't got her fine curves. Scrawny, brown mite like ye should be no threat at all to such a fulsome wench. So, why does she want ye gone so bad, eh?"

Scrawny brown mite? Penelope thought, deeply insulted even as she shrugged in reply.

"Why you frettin' o'er it, Jud?" asked the tall, extremely muscular man by his side.

Jud shrugged. "Curious, Mac. Just curious, is all. This don't make no sense to me."

"Don't need to. Money be good. All that matters."

"Aye, mayhap. As I said, just curious. Don't like puzzles."

"Didn't know that."

"Well, it be true. Don't want to be part of something I don't understand. Could mean trouble."

If she was not gagged, Penelope suspected she would be gaping at her captor. He had kidnapped the daughter of a marquis, brought her bound and gagged to a brothel, and was going to leave her to the untender care of a madam, a woman he plainly did not trust or like. Exactly what did the idiot think *trouble* was? If he was caught, he would be tried, convicted, and hanged in a heartbeat. And that would be merciful compared to what her relatives would do to the fool if they found out. How much more *trouble* could he be in?

A hoarse gasp escaped her when he removed her gag. "Water," she whispered, desperate to wash away the foul taste of the rag.

What the man gave her was a tankard of weak ale, but Penelope decided it was probably for the best. If there was any water in this place it was undoubtedly dangerous to drink. She tried not to breathe too deeply as he held her upright and helped her to take a drink. Penelope drank the ale as quickly as she could, however, for she wanted the man to move away from her. Anyone as foul smelling as he was surely had a vast horde of creatures sharing his filth that she would just as soon did not come to visit her.

When the tankard was empty he let her fall back down onto the bed and said, "Now, don't ye go thinking of making no noise, screaming for help or the like. No one here will be heeding it."

Penelope opened her mouth to give him a tart reply and

then frowned. The bed might be clean and comfortable but it was not new. A familiar chill swept over her. Even as she thought it a very poor time for her *gift* to display itself, her mind was briefly filled with violent memories that were not her own.

"Someone died in this bed," she said, her voice a little unsteady from the effect of those chilling glimpses into the past.

"What the bleeding hell are ye babbling about?" snapped Jud.

"Someone died in this bed and she did not do so peacefully." Penelope got some small satisfaction from how uneasy her words made her burly captors.

"You be talking nonsense, woman."

"No. I have a gift, you see."

"You can see spirits?" asked Mac, glancing nervously around the room.

"Sometimes. When they wish to reveal themselves to me. This time it was just the memories of what happened here," she lied.

Both men were staring at her with a mixture of fear, curiosity, and suspicion. They thought she was trying to trick them in some way so that they would set her free. Penelope suspected that a part of them probably wondered if she would conjure up a few spirits to help her. Even if she could, she doubted they would be much help or that these men would even see them. They certainly had not noticed the rather gruesome one standing near the bed. It would have sent them fleeing from the room. Despite all she had seen and experienced over the years the sight of the lovely young woman, her white gown soaked in blood, sent a chill down her spine. Penelope wondered why the more gruesome apparitions were almost always the clearest.

The door opened and, before Penelope turned to look, she

saw an expression upon the ghost's face that nearly made *her* want to flee the room. Fury and utter loathing twisted the spirit's lovely face until it looked almost demonic. Penelope looked at the ones now entering the room. Tom had returned with a middle-aged woman and two young, scantily clad females. Penelope looked right at the ghost and noticed that all that rage and hate was aimed straight at the middle-aged woman.

Beware.

Penelope almost cursed as the word echoed in her mind. Why did the spirits always whisper such ominous words to her without adding any pertinent information, such as what she should *beware* of, or whom? It was also a very poor time for this sort of distraction. She was a prisoner trapped in a house of ill-repute and was facing either death or what many euphemistically called a fate worse than death. She had no time to deal with blood-soaked specters whispering dire but unspecified warnings. If nothing else, she needed all her wits and strength to keep the hysteria writhing deep inside her tightly caged.

"This is going to cause you a great deal of trouble," Penelope told the older woman, not really surprised when everyone ignored her.

"There she be," said Jud. "Now, give us our money."

"The lady has your money," said the older woman.

"It ain't wise to try and cheat me, Cratchitt. The lady told us you would have it. Now, if the lady ain't paid you that be your problem, not mine. I did as I was ordered and did it quick and right. Get the wench, bring her here, and then collect my pay from you. Done and done. So, hand it over."

Cratchitt did so with an ill grace. Penelope watched Jud carefully count his money. The man had obviously taught himself enough to make sure that he was not cheated. After one long, puzzled look at her, he pocketed his money and then frowned at the woman he called Cratchitt.

"She be all yours now," Jud said, "though I ain't sure what ye be wanting her for. T'ain't much to her."

Penelope was growing very weary of being disparaged by this lice-ridden ruffian. "So speaks the great beau of the walk," she muttered and met his glare with a faint smile.

"She is clean and fresh," said Cratchitt, ignoring that byplay and fixing her cold stare on Penelope. "I have many a gent willing to pay a goodly fee for that alone. There be one man waiting especially for this one, but he will not arrive until the morrow. I have other plans for her tonight. Some very rich gentlemen have arrived and are looking for something special. Unique, they said. They have a friend about to step into the parson's mousetrap and wish to give him a final bachelor treat. She will do nicely for that."

"But don't that other feller want her untouched?"

"As far as he will ever know, she will be. Now, get out. Me and the girls need to wrap this little gift."

The moment Jud and his men were gone, Penelope said, "Do you have any idea of who I am?" She was very proud of the haughty tone she had achieved but it did not impress Mrs. Cratchitt at all.

"Someone who made a rich lady very angry," replied Cratchitt.

"I am Lady Penelope—"

She never finished for Mrs. Cratchitt grasped her by the jaw in a painfully tight hold, forced her mouth open, and started to pour something from a remarkably fine silver flask down her throat. The two younger women held her head steady so that Penelope could not turn away or thrash her head. She knew she did not want this drink inside her but was unable to do anything but helplessly swallow as it was forced into her.

While she was still coughing and gagging from that abuse, the women untied her. Penelope struggled as best she could but the women were strong and alarmingly skilled at undressing someone who did not wish to be undressed. As if she did not have trouble enough to deal with, the ghost was drowning her in feelings of fear, despair, and helpless fury. Penelope knew she was swiftly becoming hysterical but could not grasp one single, thin thread of control. That only added to her terror.

Then, slowly, that suffocating panic began to ease. Despite the fact that the women continued their work, stripping her naked, giving her a quick wash with scented water, and dressing her in a lacey, diaphanous gown that should have shocked her right down to her toes, Penelope felt calmer with every breath she took. The potion they had forced her to drink had been some sort of drug. That was the only rational explanation for why she was now lying there actually smiling as these three harpies prepared her for the sacrifice of her virginity.

"There, all sweets and honey now, ain't you, dearie," muttered Cratchitt as she began to let down Penelope's hair.

"You are such an evil bitch," Penelope said pleasantly and smiled. One of the younger women giggled and Cratchitt slapped her hard. "Bully. When my family discovers what you have done to me, you will pay more dearly than even your tiny, nasty mind could ever comprehend."

"Hah! It was your own family what sold you to me, you stupid girl."

"Not that family, you cow. My true parents' family. In fact, I would not be at all surprised if they are already suspicious, sensing my troubles upon the wind."

"You are talking utter nonsense."

Why does everyone say that? Penelope wondered. Enough wit and sense of self-preservation remained in her clouded mind to make her realize that it might not be wise to start talking about all the blood there was on the woman's hands. Even if the woman did not believe Penelope could know anything for a fact, she suspected Mrs. Cratchitt would permanently silence her simply to be on the safe side of the matter. With the drug holding her captive as well as any chain could, Penelope knew she was in no condition to even try to save herself.

When Cratchitt and her minions were finished, she stood back and looked Penelope over very carefully. "Well, well, well. I begin to understand."

"Understand what, you bride of Beelzebub?" asked Penelope and could tell by the way the woman clenched and unclenched her hands that Mrs. Cratchitt desperately wanted to beat her.

"Why the fine lady wants you gone. And, you will pay dearly for your insults, my girl. Very soon." Mrs. Cratchitt collected four bright silk scarves from the large carpetbag she had brought in with her and handed them to the younger women. "Tie her to the bed," she ordered them.

"Your customer may find that a little suspicious," said Penelope as she fruitlessly tried to stop the women from binding her limbs to the four posts of the bed.

"You *are* an innocent, aren't you." Mrs. Cratchitt shook her head and laughed. "No, my customer will only see this as a very special delight indeed. Come along, girls. You have work to do and we best get that man up here to enjoy his gift before that potion begins to wear off."

Penelope stared at the closed door for several moments after everyone had left. Everyone except the ghost, she mused, and finally turned her attention back to the specter now shimmering at the foot of the bed. The young woman looked so sad, so utterly defeated, that Penelope decided the poor ghost had probably just realized the full limitations of being a spirit. Although the memories locked into the bed had told Penelope how the woman had died, it did not tell her when. However, she began to suspect it had been not all that long ago.

"I would like to help you," she said, "but I cannot, not right now. You must see that. If I can get free, I swear I will work hard to give you some peace. Who are you?" she asked, although she knew it was often impossible to get proper, sensible answers from a spirit. "I know how you died. The bed still holds those dark memories and I saw it."

I am Faith and my life was stolen.

The voice was clear and sweet, but weighted with an intense grief, and Penelope was not completely certain if she was hearing it in her head or if the ghost was actually speaking to her. "What is your full name, Faith?"

My name is Faith and I was taken, as you have been. My life was stolen. My love is lost. I was torn from heaven and plunged into hell. Now I lie below.

"Below? Below what? Where?"

Below. I am covered in sin. But, I am not alone.

Penelope cursed when Faith disappeared. She could not help the spirit now but dealing with Faith's spirit had provided her with a much needed diversion. It had helped her concentrate and fight the power of the drug she had been given. Now she was alone with her thoughts and they were becoming increasingly strange. Worse, all of her protections were slowly crumbling away. If she did not find something to fix her mind on soon she would be wide open to every thought, every feeling, and every spirit lurking within the house. Considering what went on in this house that could easily prove a torture beyond bearing.

She did not know whether to laugh or to cry. She was strapped to a bed awaiting some stranger who would use her helpless body to satisfy his manly needs. The potion Mrs.

Cratchitt had forced down her throat was rapidly depleting her strength and all her ability to shut out the cacophony of the world, the world of the living as well as that of the dead. Even now she could feel the growing weight of unwelcome emotions, the increasing whispers so few others could hear. The spirits in the house were stirring, sensing the presence of one who could help them touch the world of the living. It was probably not worth worrying about, she decided. Penelope did not know if anything could be worse than what she was already suffering and what was yet to come.

Suddenly the door opened and one of Mrs. Cratchitt's earlier companions led a man into the room. He was blindfolded and dressed as an ancient Roman. Penelope stared at him in shock as he was led up to her bedside, and then she inwardly groaned. She had no trouble recognizing the man despite the blindfold and the costume. Penelope was not at all pleased to discover that things could quite definitely get worse—a great deal worse.

More by Bestselling Author
Hannah Howell

Romantic Suspense from
Lisa Jackson

See How She Dies	0-8217-7605-3	$6.99US/$9.99CAN
Final Scream	0-8217-7712-2	$7.99US/$10.99CAN
Wishes	0-8217-6309-1	$5.99US/$7.99CAN
Whispers	0-8217-7603-7	$6.99US/$9.99CAN
Twice Kissed	0-8217-6038-6	$5.99US/$7.99CAN
Unspoken	0-8217-6402-0	$6.50US/$8.50CAN
If She Only Knew	0-8217-6708-9	$6.50US/$8.50CAN
Hot Blooded	0-8217-6841-7	$6.99US/$9.99CAN
Cold Blooded	0-8217-6934-0	$6.99US/$9.99CAN
The Night Before	0-8217-6936-7	$6.99US/$9.99CAN
The Morning After	0-8217-7295-3	$6.99US/$9.99CAN
Deep Freeze	0-8217-7296-1	$7.99US/$10.99CAN
Fatal Burn	0-8217-7577-4	$7.99US/$10.99CAN
Shiver	0-8217-7578-2	$7.99US/$10.99CAN
Most Likely to Die	0-8217-7576-6	$7.99US/$10.99CAN
Absolute Fear	0-8217-7936-2	$7.99US/$9.49CAN
Almost Dead	0-8217-7579-0	$7.99US/$10.99CAN
Lost Souls	0-8217-7938-9	$7.99US/$10.99CAN
Left to Die	1-4201-0276-1	$7.99US/$10.99CAN
Wicked Game	1-4201-0338-5	$7.99US/$9.99CAN
Malice	0-8217-7940-0	$7.99US/$9.49CAN

Available Wherever Books Are Sold!
Visit our website at **www.kensingtonbooks.com**

Thrilling Suspense from
Beverly Barton

Available Wherever Books Are Sold!

Visit our website at **www.kensingtonbooks.com**